THE HEAD OF THE SNAKE

Lucy Hooft

Book Two in the Sarah Black Series

Burning Chair Limited, Trading As Burning Chair Publishing
61 Bridge Street, Kington HR5 3DJ

www.burningchairpublishing.com

By Lucy Hooft
Edited by Simon Finnie and Peter Oxley
Cover by Burning Chair Publishing

First published by Burning Chair Publishing, 2023

ISBN: 978-1-912946-31-0

Also by Lucy Hooft

The King's Pawn – Book 1 in the Sarah Black Series

For Salone

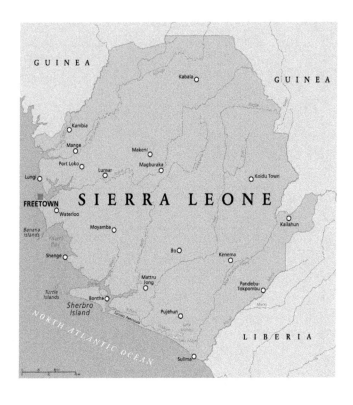

Map of Sierra Leone

PROLOGUE

Skarparov watches the fog creep across the Captain's gold tinted sunglasses. He can surely no longer see. But if the Captain is bothered by the blinding mist, he doesn't let on.

"Papa wants to know when you can get him a chopper?" The Captain cocks his head. He wears heavy chains, camouflage fatigues and a salt-licked vest in faded black. An oversized hat— gold braid with stars and a pompom—dangles over one eye to complete the look, consciously styled to intimidate. Power, ruthlessness, and a trace of madness spoken by the slip of a hat.

"I am happy to talk to Foday Sankoh directly, anytime he wishes," Skarparov replies, refusing to use an affectionate nickname for a rebel warlord.

"Papa sent me. I am him. You talk to me." The Captain thumps his sinewy chest, rattling his chains, and cracks the butt of an AK-47 against the floor. But his posturing flounders on the white leather of the sofa. It was the right decision to bring him here. In the jungle camps, Skarparov always feels on edge: the constant itch of the unknown, the unpredictability of animals in the wild. But his home imposes a layer of civility on the rebels. Their mud-stained threats are muffled by white leather and glass.

"I'm talking to you now," Skarparov says, "and I'm telling you that the helicopter will have to wait."

The Captain leaps to his feet, shoving the nose of his gun into Skarparov's face. He can smell the sweat rising from the Captain's racehorse-lean muscles and for the first time registers the sour tang of fear. These animals need him, he'd made sure of it. But you never know when one of them might forget themselves.

"What if we no want to wait?" the Captain jeers, his voice echoing around the cavernous glass cylinder of Skarparov's living room. He jerks his powerful shoulders forward, giving another push to the gun into Skarparov's nose.

Skarparov curls his palm over the tip of the barrel and pushes it away. "Let's not forget who got you those," he nods at the weapon. "You know I can deliver, and now I expect you to keep up your end of the deal. You protect my diamond operations in Koidu, I make sure you get what you need."

A security guard appears from behind the tall metal panel of the front door. "Mr Skarparov, Sah, the next visitors are here. You want them to wait outside?"

"No, no, bring them in now. We're finished here." He touches his fingertips together and turns to the Captain with a serene smile. Perfect timing. He had taken every step to ensure that the Libyans would arrive to witness this carefully orchestrated scene. They could have been late, or worse, arrived while he had the back foot. But, as planned, they enter the room to be met by a disgruntled rebel commander licking his wounds and retreating. In the simple puppet-show of power, Skarparov is the winner of the bout.

"Tell Mr Sankoh to call me with anything he needs," Skarparov says, a hand placed firmly on the Captain's sweat-flecked bicep to guide him out the door.

The Captain takes in the new arrivals with a shrug, slinging the AK-47 across his shoulder.

"Do come in, so sorry to keep you waiting." Skarparov ushers his next guests towards the white leather sofas.

Two men in dark suits, two red ties loosened against the tropical heat. They look like an image and its negative placed side by side: the same careful step, the same air of deeply held suspicion. One with grey hair and a black moustache, the other black hair with a grey moustache. Two more perfect puppets for Skarparov's show.

"Sorry about that." He waves towards the door, now firmly closed behind the Captain. "I'm sure you can understand how it is. You have to have them on side if you want anything done."

His guests nod cautiously, the grey moustache stealing a glance at his colleague, waiting for a lead.

"And there is so much here to do!" Skarparov claps his hands together with the enthusiasm of an estate agent selling flats in a flood plain. "So, I think I can guess why you're here."

Another pair of greedy scavengers come to sniff out what everyone wants a piece of. And for once, the vultures circling in Freetown have nothing to do with diamonds.

CHAPTER 1

Sarah buzzes the unmarked bell and waits. Despite her short tenure working for MI6, or at least for Michael, she has never set foot in their imposing headquarters at Vauxhall Cross. Michael operates in anonymous spaces: soulless restaurants, tourist attractions busy with transient observers, unmemorable corners of a public gallery. Today it is a private address on a quiet street behind Saville Row.

Sarah is ushered into a room lined floor to ceiling with ghosts. Phantom figures in curls of brown rustle against the walls. The bodies of suit jackets and waistcoats cut from tracing paper pack the triple-stacked rails in a strangely insubstantial crowd, the cloakroom of a ghostly ball. Undisturbed amidst the ethereal host stands Michael, wearing the beginnings of a beautiful suit: a classic three-piece in grey glen check. Waistcoat cut high up the chest, trousers with a double pleat—roomy enough to use the pockets. And to conceal a weapon.

The cutter quickly sets to works tidying away his tools: swatches of fabric, oversized scissors, tape measures and long sharp rulers litter the large table. "I do apologise for the mess; we don't usually serve our clients in here. But we make exceptions for Michael."

Michael greets Sarah with a broad smile—welcoming if not quite warm. "Well? What do you think?" He makes a slow turn to show the perfectly sculpted waist of the half-finished jacket.

"It suits you," Sarah says. "The grey sets off your hair."

"I'll take that as a compliment, although I'm not sure that was quite your intent. I'm glad you came."

"I need to talk to you." She watches the cutter still fussing around the main desk. "In private, preferably."

"Of course. Matthew, could you give us a moment?"

The cutter gives a discreet nod and bows out the room through a heavy green curtain.

"Can we really talk here?" Sarah circles the table, slipping a glance towards all the exits, looking for ears lurking behind the elegant fabrics and rustling paper crowd.

"Of course. You could talk in the middle of the shop floor if you liked. These men are the most discreet in London. They've made their name on having ears as dull as their scissors are sharp. But they also know when to get lost. Now, what was it you wanted to talk about?"

"Skarparov."

"You're not still on him, are you?"

"Of course I am. But my contact at the CIA has gone cold and won't take my calls. They have the wrong guy locked up for a plot to assassinate the presidents of the US and Georgia, and Skarparov has got away with everything."

"So?"

Is he doing this on purpose? Michael's disinterest is infuriating. "So we need to stop him. He must be made to pay for what he did in the Caucasus."

"Which, thanks to you, was very little."

"That's not the point. He was willing to do it, and kill hundreds in the process. And he took payment in advance. A full jungle warlord's worth of weaponry and ammunition has been delivered to Sierra Leone. We have to stop him before he has a chance to use it."

Michael brushes a trail of chalk from his shoulder. "Why bother? If anything, he could be more useful to us now that he's compromised."

"And what about his uncle? Ibragimov may be no angel, but

5

he's being held in solitary confinement by the Americans under false charges."

"Sadly, Ibragimov is no longer able to benefit from your concern." Michael speaks with a practised indifference, the hint of a smile turning up the weaker side of his mouth. "He died of a heart-attack while resisting arrest."

"He did not," Sarah insists, trying to read Michael's enigmatic expression—is he trying to wind her up, or put her off? "I saw him being held by the Americans. I spoke to him." The memory of Ibragimov's hot foul breath as he pleaded with her to help him is still appallingly fresh in her mind.

"Perhaps you did? Either way it doesn't help him now. He's dead. But luckily, I have something much more interesting in mind for you. What are your thoughts on Hong Kong?"

Typical Michael—nonchalant to the point of brutality, nothing ever taken too seriously, inconveniences swept away by the promise of something more exciting. Sarah's throat constricts, remembering how often she let him get away with these tricks. She was fascinated by his air of experience, his allure and the thrill of the world he represented—enough to accept everything on his terms. But not anymore. He sent her to the Caucasus, untrained and ill-prepared, on a mission that she suspects was as much about personal revenge as it was to disarm a threat. And now Ibragimov, the target of Michael's revenge, is dead. She will not make the same mistakes again.

"What are you talking about?" She perches on the edge of the cutting table, forcing him to turn to face her. "I don't work for you anymore. Why would I want to throw myself into another of your messes?"

"Oh? If you don't work for me anymore, why are you here?" His blue-eyed stare is so penetrating it feels like an assault. "I knew you wouldn't be able to let it rest; it's one of the reasons you're made for this." He pauses, his gaze softening. "But we can put that tenacity to better use than chasing down Skarparov. Leave him to me." He turns his attention to the sleeves of his jacket, making minor adjustments to ensure the fall just above the shirt cuff.

"No. Skarparov must be brought to justice. He needs to face the International Criminal Court for what he's done. We just need the right evidence to indict him."

Michael remains silent, picking pins out of his sleeve and stabbing them into a small red pincushion.

"I know him," Sarah insists. "I know how he operates."

Michael glances at his watch but does not respond.

"I'm going, whether you agree to help me or not."

"Sarah, I have to warn you." Michael's voice drops. "If you do decide to go chasing Skarparov in Sierra Leone, you do so without my blessing and without my cover. I will consider your engagement terminated."

"Fine." Sarah says, undeterred. As far as she is concerned their arrangement was already over, although she had hoped he might agree to some support. His help would be invaluable in bringing evidence against Skarparov to the right people to make a swift arrest. To say nothing of the risks of going after a man with a warlord's arsenal on her own. But Michael's intransigence, if disappointing, is not surprising. She should have known he'd never be persuaded by doing what is obviously the right thing.

She leaves Michael standing in the tailor's shop, his confident bearing exaggerated by the lines of the unfinished cloth, his red-blooded obstinacy thrumming amongst the lifeless paper crowd.

"Please think about this again before you do anything rash," he says.

"Goodbye, Michael."

CHAPTER 2

"You were serious then. You're really going?" Sarah's father perches on the end of her childhood bed, legs neatly crossed, fingers tightly clasped.

"Yes, I'm really going." Sarah contemplates the collection of items spread across the floral duvet, brushing half of it onto the floor before fitting what remains into a small duffel bag. She focuses on her packing, hoping a look of concentration will be enough to ward off her father's offensive.

"And you think it's a good idea?" He tries to relax, leaning back against the wall, but the height of the bed and the bounce of the mattress only make him look more uncomfortable.

"No, not really."

"But you're going anyway?"

"Of course I am." To Sarah's relief, her father only looks half cross.

"You do know it's a war zone?"

"The war's been going on for ten years. It doesn't mean I'm going to get killed. Life does go on."

"It does, but yours could go on perfectly happily here, and with a considerably higher degree of certainty. If you had seen some of the telex reports coming out of there."

"He got away once. He can't be allowed to get away again." Sarah rolls a t-shirt into a neat tube and wedges it between two books. Her father is the only person in the world that she can talk to about her plans. He is the only one she told about what really happened in Tbilisi, and after a lifelong career in the civil service, her father is the only person who understands that world well enough to believe her. But just because she can talk to him doesn't mean she wants to.

"So it really is about your Skarparov chap? Can't you just let him go? I thought you beat him in the end," her father says.

"I blocked an attack, but he got away. I didn't win."

"Stalemate not enough?" Her father picks up a photo frame from her desk, rubbing the glass against the soft cotton of his shirt. "I hope you realise," he says, addressing the photo, "what you've created. Your daughter, holder of the world record for shortest time employed by MI6, is proposing to fly to Sierra Leone to track down some crackpot oligarch."

"Don't do that." Sarah chucks in a pair of hiking boots without looking up.

"What?"

"Don't talk to Mum as if she's here." Before her mother died, her father had always shied away from sentiments as if they might be catching. It is, strangely, one of the things that Sarah finds most difficult to accept in the new existence of the last two years. That her father's grief has opened up a side of him so unfamiliar from what she thought she knew.

"Why not? I used to talk to her when she was here."

"It's weird."

"I find it helps."

"Well, don't bring her into this. It's unfair: she can't answer and tell you not to be so unreasonable."

"You're the one trotting off into the Heart of Darkness on your own."

"I won't be on my own. Elias is there." Sarah rummages through the obscenely large medicine bag her brother deposited with her when he heard she was going to the tropics. Hypodermic syringes, five different forms of compression bandage, sterile eye pads—come on, Jack, does anyone ever really use any of this stuff? It must be exhausting going through life as a doctor, endlessly aware of all the things that might go wrong. Sarah pulls out some mosquito repellent, a tube of sun cream and some paracetamol, just in case.

"Oh dear, there's a man." Her father's eyes roll heavenward. "I might have known. There's always a man. Well, out with it, who is he?"

"He's a friend."

"What is the sound of his voice? Does he collect butterflies?"

Sarah laughs, happy to be back with her father's more familiar eccentricities. "His voice is deep and disarmingly monotone. And I wouldn't put it past him to be a secret lepidopterist."

"Is he any good at chess?"

"I don't know; we've never played."

"Good. Then it can't be that serious."

Her father does have a point, even if he draws the wrong conclusion. It is odd for her not to have challenged Elias to a game by this stage in their relationship. It is normally her favourite way to get to understand the way a person thinks, to watch how their mind approaches complex problems, how they behave when under attack. She is confident she can take the measure of most people after a hard-fought game or two. And it gives her the chance to show off. But with Elias the right moment has never presented itself. Or she never looked for it.

She grabs a handful of underwear, a little too racy to be stringing up in front of her father, and stuffs the bundle into the top of a hiking boot while he isn't watching. A few cotton tops for the tropics, a black linen dress—you never know when you might need to impress. Finally, she lifts the duvet and tips everything that remains into the top of the bag.

Her father laughs. "That's one way to do it."

"What? I can see it's going to fit now. What's the point in having everything carefully folded just to stick it in a duffel bag?"

"You have a point." He opens his mouth as if about to speak, but nothing comes. His gaze rests fixed on Sarah, eyes magnified by the thick lenses of his glasses, topped by a pair of wildly unkempt eyebrows. "I didn't really want to show you this, but

I think you ought to see it." He hands Sarah a folded piece of paper, fished from his back pocket.

The paper shakes in her hand as she reads.

British link to grenade attack in Tbilisi
By Associated Press
TBILISI, Georgia (AP)

A new suspect has come to light in the investigation into the grenade thrown at visiting US President in Tbilisi earlier this year. A suspect, identified only as Levon, has confessed to throwing the grenade but named an Azeri national, Mikhail Ibragimov, as the mastermind behind the attack. Mr Ibragimov died while resisting arrest last week.

New pictures have emerged of a British woman receiving a suspicious briefcase from Mr Ibragimov in the weeks leading up to the attack in Freedom Square. The woman, named locally as Sarah White, claimed to be an embassy employee working for the Department for International Development. But witnesses have reported seeing a woman who matches Ms White's description being refused entry to the British Embassy on Freedom Square on the day of the attack.

Ms White's current whereabouts are unknown and investigations are continuing.

The article is accompanied by a photo of Sarah getting into Ibragimov's car in Baku, with a briefcase on her lap.

"They've got the name wrong—but you can't pretend that's not you in the photo," her father says gently.

Sarah is too stunned to speak. Her stomach writhes like a bag of eels. "But this is nonsense; it's an old photo set alongside a completely fabricated story. Where could this have come from?"

"I had a journalist on the phone this morning asking to speak to Sarah White. God knows where they got the number from.

11

I called a contact in the press office at work, and they sent me this. Apparently, it came in on the wires from the AP stringer in Tbilisi. Luckily it hasn't been picked up by the major papers yet. No sources are named, and it doesn't say anything about police involvement, which means it is probably just something the journo was slipped late last night in a bar. But what were you doing taking that briefcase?"

"It's a long story. I was in Baku. I was set up. The briefcase was a plant to make the pictures look better. The embassy team managed to kill the story at the time—a case of mistaken identity. God knows where these photos came from now."

A growing coldness spreads through Sarah's core, but her face flushes uncomfortably warm. Who would want to do this to her? Could this be Skarparov tying up loose ends? Or is this Michael's way of decisively ending their arrangement? There is no possibility of a return to MI6 now that her face and half of her name are linked to a terrorist attack. And Ibragimov, the only other person who could clear her name, is dead. Who would vouch for her if the police came asking questions? Michael is the only one who knows the whole truth, but she has never felt less confident of his support.

"Come here," her father pulls her into a one-armed hug, her head nestled into the crook of his neck. "Don't you think this might be MI6's mess to clean up?" he asks, his voice faltering.

"Yes." Sarah bows out of his embrace. "But as far as I can see they're not planning to do anything about it."

"And you can't just let this one go?" Her father's body sags into the mattress. His extravagant eyebrows draw together with a concern that Sarah finds difficult to counter.

"After this?" She holds up the news article. "No, Dad. I can't."

"No." His hands reach for each other before pressing against the rough wool of his trousers. "No, you never could."

CHAPTER 3

The humidity hits like a brick wall.

Stepping out of the plane onto the rickety staircase, Sarah flinches at the face-on affront. Air thick enough for gills. And the smell—a clamorous cooking pot of sap, hot tarmac and blossoming mould. Blood rushes to her skin and her sweat pores crank into overdrive to match the atmospheric dampness.

A giggling red-faced stewardess pushes her through the door. "Welcome to Freetown," she sings. "Is it your first-time love?"

"Um, yes." Sarah answers between deep gulps of air.

"Whatcha here for? Diamonds or do-gooding?"

"Neither."

"Really? Well, see you on your way out."

The crew of the charter airline looked dishevelled in Gatwick five hours earlier. As the plane soared over the Sahara sands, their cheeks began to glisten, their gait grew unsteady, and their mumbled announcements into the microphone were choked out through stifled giggles. Dutch courage must be a pre-requisite for landing in a war zone.

Sarah tightens her grip on the metal handrail before following the stream of men in crumpled suits down to the tarmac below. Even the ground feels spongy: cement and tar at saturation point from the tropical air. A strong hand clamps around her bicep and a young man, perhaps boy, grins at her with a smile that is all cheekbones. He wears loose camouflage-print trousers, a faded t-shirt advertising a summer camp in Colorado, and bare feet.

"Miss Sarah?" The vowels are long and soft, the two syllables of her name made equal length, "Welcome to Salone." The boy fishes a piece of crumpled paper from his back pocket and smooths it against his chest—a large, roughly-cut heart in pinky red. "Mr Elias said to give you this," he says, proudly handing her the drooping valentine.

"Tell Mr Elias thank you," she says, stifling a giggle. She reads the message written on the paper. *'Follow your heart'.* Typical Elias. Nothing with him ever comes close to conventional. He had promised to meet her at the airport and help her across to Freetown—none of the ways to cross the wide estuary that separate Lungi airport from the capital city inspire confidence, and she is glad not to be doing it alone. A board with her name would have been too obvious.

Outside, the sky is treacle black. The heart-bearer hoists Sarah's bag onto his back, motioning for her to follow him into the darkness. She hesitates. The other passengers have disappeared, shambling off towards a cracked patch of concrete where a helicopter waits with drooping rotors. Soon, all that remains visible of the porter is the pale soles of his feet as he treks into the bush.

"Elias, where the hell are we going? You'd better appear soon." Sarah tries to stay optimistic. As she follows the porter out of the airport perimeter, the springy tarmac gives way to soft sand that pushes her back with every step. At least the oddness of the arrival covers her nerves. The thought of seeing Elias again makes her heart sing, but her stomach clench.

It is only two months since their delicious weekend together in Istanbul, but it could just as well be a lifetime. They had escaped to celebrate their victory in Tbilisi, away from the world and everything in it: posing as tourists at the top of the Galata Tower, spotting Gorgons in the Cisterns and searching for long-forgotten maps in the Topkapi Palace. But then she returned to London, he went back to wherever it was that he went, and the blissful forgetfulness of being with him was replaced by the stubborn solidity of the real world. As soon as she was back in her familiar environment, he became more difficult to believe. The reassuring inefficiency of Heathrow, the quiet drizzle of the weather, the echoing announcements on the train out of London—all seemed to strip him of flesh and blood. He became a figment of her imagination—a swaggering mountain man who had helped her foil a plot to assassinate the leader of the free world. Pull the other one. Nothing of the kind could possibly exist in the home counties.

She sank back into life at home—spending time at her father's house playing chess, solidifying the weave of lies she put together about her time in Georgia, taking refuge in her empty London flat when her mother's absence in her family home became too much to bear.

She met friends in the pub—once again rolling out the magic carpet of made-up stories to explain her sudden absence from London. She went to watch obscure French films with her brother—to share each other's company without the need to talk. The lie felt enormous, but only to Sarah. She covered well enough for those around her. She probably could have come to convince herself that she really had just been an impulsive tourist, soaking up the oddity of the post-Soviet world. But then there was Elias. A text message while she was on the bus home, a midnight phone call as she lay in bed listening to the chimes of Big Ben—momentary reminders of another world where he existed: a vigorous, forceful, brilliant being and not just a thread of vibrant colour on her carpet.

Across the distance, their plan had taken shape. What started as a joke grew into a plan and suddenly it was real. Sarah could hardly believe that Elias agreed to follow Skarparov to Sierra Leone, to pick up where they had left off in the Caucasus, to be the one to get close to him when she could not. She has scarcely heard from him since he left—fuzzy phone calls from far away, messages answered days late. But now, finally, she is here to join him.

Her guide has disappeared into the darkness, leaving Sarah only his footprints in the sand. The noises are distinctly tropical—birds calling, insects throbbing and something else like a low murmur ahead, growing stronger as they approach. Sarah steels herself. This is not as crazy as it feels. Walking alone through the dark of a country in brutal conflict. She has Elias's guide—well, she has a boy with a pink paper heart.

The rumbling grows louder until the vegetation on either side of the path opens up and Sarah recognises the noise—the sea, just visible as a moving surface of darkness beyond the edge of the sand. The hum of an engine approaches from the inky swell and a tiny speed boat with a single twin-stroke motor banks on the soft sand several metres from the shore. The porter wades out with Sarah's bag balanced on his head, before gesturing for her to climb onto his shoulders to be deposited with the luggage.

"Thank you, Sam, I think I can manage from here," a deep voice cuts in. He is impossibly tall, even barefoot in the sand, red hair sticking up in all directions and skin the shade of burnished pink only found on fair Dutch skin in the tropics.

"Elias." The knot of tension in Sarah's neck dissolves. "You're here."

"So are you." His blue eyes flash in freckled cheeks. "I wasn't sure if you were going to make it. Welcome to Salone. Here, climb aboard." He bends down to pick her up.

"I'm fine." Sarah ducks out of his grasp. "I think I can manage climbing into a boat by myself."

"Of course you can. But you're also tiny, so rather than have you sink in up to your chest, you might as well hitch a ride." He hoists her over his shoulder and wades into the surf.

The smell of his head, like chocolate and forest floor rich with tropical sweat, weakens Sarah's resistance.

The boat swings to one side as Elias hoists himself aboard. "Sarah, this is Iain."

The captain in a dark baseball cap nods to Sarah, his slight figure hunched over the steering wheel, his features a curious mix of African and European.

"Iain agreed to bring us across. I didn't think you'd fancy the flying death trap so soon after arrival. And the view is much better from the water."

Sarah can see nothing across the indistinct horizon.

"Sorry we're late." Iain speaks in the deep throated accent impossible to place. "A spot of engine trouble on the way out. Are you ready?"

She grabs the metal rail and squats on top of her duffel bag. "Yup!"

*

With only the moon for light, the sea is blank but for the spray thrown up around the prow. Slowly the shape of the peninsula solidifies in the view—the lion mountain that gave Sierra Leone its name looks to Sarah more like a woman lying on her side, shoulders and hips rolling off beyond the city as densely-knitted forest.

For a city of over half a million people, it is amazingly dark. Ten years into civil war and little remains of municipal infrastructure. The city is illuminated only by private points of light—a generator growling in an individual dwelling, a car snaking down the slopes of the hillside or cruising along the beachfront. The effect is strangely peaceful—lights on a Christmas tree dotted at random through thick branches. It is difficult to reconcile the horrors she has been led to expect with the tranquil scene as the city comes into full view beyond the lighthouse at the tip of the peninsula.

Iain pulls the boat in as close to the beach as the berth allows and Elias bounds over the edge preparing to help, but Sarah is quicker this time, springing over the side of the boat into waist-deep water, steadying her bag on her head with both hands as she walks confidently up the sand.

Iain laughs at her stubborn determination. "You tried your

best, eh?" he says to Elias.

A battered car with an incongruous set of ski racks waits by the beach. The driver introduces himself as Ibrahim—short but solidly built, his physical presence and obvious strength made less intimidating by eyelashes that curl tightly up like a child's. Soon they are flying over the bumpy gravel of the peninsula road.

"The road," Ibrahim says as he launches the car over an unexpectedly high bump. "*Bad tumohs, plehnti galohp.*"

"I think I can hear my bones rattling," Sarah says.

"It's good for you, Miss Sarah. Top quality massage, thrown in for free." Ibrahim grins at her through the rear-view mirror over his collection of trinkets—a large wooden cross, a laminated page of Arabic script and a pine tree air freshener that has long lost its scent.

As they leave the city, the darkness of the forest on either side of the road seems to swallow all noises. "Is it always this quiet?" Sarah asks, watching the moths dance in the tunnel of the car's headlights.

"What were you expecting?"

"I don't know. Guns and rebels? Machetes?"

"Since the rebels were last beaten back from Freetown, it's been mostly quiet. They're back up-country. It's a lot easier to reign terror over a village of a few hundred than a capital city. But don't be fooled by the calm. Word is they're moving in. More brazen, gaining in power. There've been a few incidents not far from the city." Elias's voice trails off.

"Incidents?"

He takes hold of her hand. "I didn't think you'd come."

Sarah squeezes his hand, her skin thrilling at his touch. The small skin-to-skin contact of fingers entwined rebuilds a lost connection, restores life to something she had doubted. "Neither did I. I very nearly lost my nerve. But I couldn't let Skarparov get away with it."

"With what? There was nothing to get away with, thanks to you."

"But he would have done it. He would have killed countless innocent people, dragged a country on the brink of democracy back into instability and violence. And for what? A dodgy business deal? Some smuggled weapons? He has to be stopped."

"It may not be as clear cut as it seems." Elias keeps hold of her hand, but turns away.

*

They pull up in front of a low set of buildings under the palm trees. A small white sign announces 'Pietro's Resort'.

"Thank you, Ibrahim." Elias reaches forward to pass over a handful of slippery notes. "Will you join us for a drink?"

"Not today, Boss. You know how it is, I've always got two other places I need to be." Ibrahim waves out of the window as he rolls off, windscreen collection swinging wildly.

"Where are we?" Sarah asks. "I thought you were going to fill me in on Skarparov's operations?"

"Tomorrow. But first we need to sleep. This is Pietro's: the finest, freshest lobster Salone has to offer and one of the most beautiful spots in the world. Look at that, it seems they may be expecting us." He nods towards the ground of the entrance, strewn with paper hearts.

A man in a faded Hawaiian shirt bursts through a swing-door, his hands extended as if to sweep them both up in a bear hug. His thick bush of black hair is shot through with grey and his skin is the colour of leather after many years of unapologetic tropical sun. A scruffy grey dog follows adoringly behind. "Elias!" the man says in a heavy Italian accent. "Everything is ready. And this must be Sarah." He kisses her on both cheeks. "But she is even more beautiful than you told me? It must be love. Not many girlfriends visit us out here, but it is their loss! Ah, it's a hard life in Africa," he says with an exaggerated twinkle.

Elias smiles. "Pietro's been here—how long is it? Twenty-five years?"

"Thirty years next February," Pietro says, squeezing out his vowels as if he has just left Naples. "I came here as a young geologist working on the Bumbuna dam and gave the best years of my life to those hills." His gaze drifts over Sarah's shoulder towards the door. "Did you know," he says with a conspiratorial air, "that I was the one who—"

"Who found the diamond deposits?" Elias interrupts. "You're going to need a new story. They have been mining diamonds in Sierra Leone since the twenties. Surely even you aren't that old?"

"Small fry, small fry," Pietro dismisses Elias with an elaborate hand gesture and turns again to Sarah. "I was the one who found the biggest reserves, or at least I worked out where they were most likely to be."

"And were you right?" Sarah asks.

"Of course! And the iron ore, one of the biggest deposits in all of Africa. I was telling people about it for years before anyone bothered to go looking for it. But do they listen? Who ever listens to the lowly geologist with his muddy boots and dirty hands?"

Sarah finds it difficult to turn Pietro—with his brightly coloured shirt, his deep permanent tan, gold chain at his neck and bare feet—into the lowly geologist he is describing. But she is willing to humour him; everyone is entitled to their foundation myth, and thirty years seclusion in the jungle would no doubt ripen the imagination.

"I believe our room is this way." Elias lifts the corner of another paper heart with his toe, the first in a growing trail of pink snaking away from the lobby. The hearts grow denser until they bunch up at the door of a white concrete hut as a full puddle of pink; Hansel and Gretel's valentine basket upturned on the doormat.

"How on earth did you persuade them to do this?" she asks Elias, who carefully maintains his deadpan expression, tucking a paper heart behind his ear and another in his breast pocket.

"What makes you think it was my idea? Perhaps they do this for all the girls?"

Inside the room, a mosquito net is tied up to make a lumpen heart shape above two single beds pushed together in the centre of the room. The floor is covered with the same red bathroom tiles as the path outside and greying net curtains hang limply from the windows. The astringent perfume of mosquito coils almost covers the overwhelming background of damp.

"What do you think of our palace?" Elias asks with a sweep of his arm.

"It's perfect." Sarah steps inside, giggling at Elias over the top of her armful of pink hearts. "What am I going to do with all of these?"

"Anything you like. But for now," he takes her hand and drags her down on top of him on the sagging mattress. "I think we need to spend a little time getting to know each other again." He kisses the top of her knuckles. "I have missed you more than you can imagine."

It is ridiculous. Arriving in a warzone, drenched with sea water and sweat, following a trail of paper hearts. But it is exactly Sarah's kind of ridiculous.

"What did you mean, it may not seem that clear cut with Skarparov?" she asks. "Was he happy to have you back or do you think he might be suspicious?" She hates being in the dark and can't help but envy Elias's position. This is supposed to be her mission, but he has a two-month head start on her and seems to know more than he is willing to share.

"I'll tell you in the morning," Elias says. "He has no place in our bedroom."

Sarah relents, allowing herself to be swept into his inviting arms.

CHAPTER 4

"Yes, of course, *Agha-ye mohandis*, we can have all the information ready for you. No, I prefer to meet face-to-face. Can you arrange to have a representative come to Freetown? We will be sure to look after him."

Skarparov's cheeks ache from his artificial smile. Even on the phone his face moulds into its most eager to please when talking to potential customers. It is exhausting. He scribbles a few notes in his agenda and sits back to contemplate the morning's work. He needs at least three serious buyers to all throw in lines at once, to start any sort of useful bidding war. And they each need to know that the other is interested. It is a hell of a lot of legwork to pull off from Freetown.

But who could be trusted to take his message to the customers? It is a question he has pondered many times but, as always, he draws a blank. He doesn't trust anyone.

Sadiqi knocks and sidles in without waiting for a response. He hovers in the doorway, head tilted to one side, tongue protruding slightly from his lips.

Skarparov recognises the pose—his sidekick is trying to read his mood. He works his aching cheeks into another smile while returning Sadiqi's contemplative stare. Could he be sent to help tout for business in Tehran? Having been rescued from a rebel attack, he is certainly loyal. But could he pull it off? Sadiqi sits down in the chair opposite, faded baseball cap in hand, spreads his legs and places a comforting hand on his testicles. Not a hope.

"Boss, I just spoke to my friend at the airport."

"And?"

"And he says the rumours are true. It's definitely her."

"Sarah? Sarah Black?"

"Yes, Boss. She's here in Salone."

"Huh." Skarparov pinches his lips shut with his thumb and forefinger. He is flattered, of course. Which man in his position wouldn't enjoy having a young blonde trotting around the world after him? She'd caused quite a headache in Tbilisi, but she had certainly caught his attention. He had very rarely been outplayed, and never before by someone he had taken for a rookie. Besides, even with her meddling, he'd still been paid. Perhaps he should thank her? He was glad to get away without too much blood on his hands.

She has great potential. But he's been in the game long enough to know when vanity might cloud his judgement.

"Sadiqi, I want you to find out where she is, and organise a bit of a scare."

"A scare, boss?"

"Yes, a scare. Make sure she gets the fright of her life."

CHAPTER 5

"That was a waste of time." Chris trots down the stairs of the Foreign Office building on King Charles' Street, closing the top button of his royal blue suit jacket. "It's like they are on another planet sometimes."

"I don't know," Michael says. "Some progress was made. Just because they don't roll over and pant every time you open your mouth, doesn't mean they aren't listening." He winds a black cashmere scarf around his neck against the London spring-time chill.

"I just don't get how they can spend so much time talking without making any decisions, it's like they are paid to pontificate."

"Perhaps they are. That's why they need us to do the dirty work. What did you make of the new Africa Director?"

"Beverley Moreton? Weak. Clearly pleased with her exalted position, but she didn't say anything interesting."

"Really? I found her most refreshing. I look forward to seeing what she makes of the role." Michael trails off, walking briskly down Whitehall towards Westminster. "Up or down today?"

Chris casts his eye over the crowd of tourists bunched up at the traffic lights ahead. "Down, it's always quicker."

"So you say. How about you take down and I'll take up and we'll see who gets to the bridge first?"

"You're on." Chris skips towards the entrance to the underground station, trying to keep his pace relaxed but unable to hide his determination to win. He walks too fast down the stairs, his gaze focused too pointedly ahead to look convincing as a commuter.

Michael has a natural harmony, moving with the control of a hunter as he joins the crush of tourists trooping their way through the pedestrian pens at the traffic lights. Viewed up close, his appearance is striking—perfectly parted silver hair, eyes an arresting shade of blue, his face displays a hardness born of a life lived under tension and control. Yet he is able to shrink his presence in a crowd, to be unremarkable among the sightseers and civil servants waiting for the green man.

Chris ducks into the underground station, taking the racing line towards the Westminster Bridge exit. His bearing ruler-straight, shoulders pinned back with an unquestioning level of self-confidence. He bounds up the stairs, feeling a twinge of guilt as he hurries past a lady with a pushchair, but he has a point to prove. He shoots out the exit just in time to catch the lights to the embankment.

Michael is waiting for him at a crowded stall selling London memorabilia, casually inspecting a selection of novelty t-shirts.

"How the hell did you manage that?" Chris asks, his heavy breathing sealing his defeat in the face of Michael's effortless calm. "You must have sprinted through that crush in front of the station?"

"I told you, up was quicker. Come on, I have something for you I'd like to discuss before we get back to the office."

They walk over Westminster Bridge, Chris's confidence only momentarily dampened by Michael's victory.

"You remember Sarah?" Michael asks.

"Your Skarparov bait in the Caucasus. I thought she slipped the hook?"

"If you mean she isn't working for us anymore, yes. Her. I thought we parted reasonably amicably—I congratulated her on a job well done and we agreed to go our separate ways."

"You make it sound like a breakup."

"Well, you know how it is. I invest a lot in people. Especially

25

at first. But it was clear this wasn't for her. I thought she would settle back into her old life, and we wouldn't need to trouble ourselves about her too much further."

"So why are we troubled now?"

"I just heard from the border agency that she's in Sierra Leone."

"Odd place for a holiday?"

"It's not a holiday. I imagine she's on a one-woman revenge mission to track down Skarparov. I want you to go and get her. She has no idea what she's doing out there, and besides," he pauses, "things are complicated on the Skarparov front."

"Why don't you just leave her to her own devices? Surely she won't last long somewhere like that. Isn't it in full civil war?"

"I wouldn't write her off too quickly. She may seem weak, but she has an uncanny ability to survive."

Chris's response is lost in the insistent moan of the bagpipes played by a stoical Scotsman at the centre of the bridge, tartan cap at his feet. Even competing with four lanes of traffic, the trembling notes drown out all other noise.

"Why not bring her back onside? She might be just the person we need there now," Chris says as they approach the Southbank end of the bridge.

"Sarah? I doubt it. She's too unpredictable. Besides, I don't think she fundamentally wants the same things we do. She's certainly got sheer bloody-mindedness, but I don't think she has the loyalty we need."

A pair of policeman trot by on wide-bellied horses wrapped in fluorescent jackets. Michael darts to the railing, staring down into the murky waters of the Thames. Chris peers over his shoulder to see what has suddenly caught his eye. "What is it?"

"Nothing. Just letting the horses pass."

"Have you got a thing about horses?" Chris asks, forever on the lookout for chinks in his boss's apparently impenetrable armour.

"No. But they often have a thing about me. I seem to spook

them by my presence if they pass too closely."

Chris laughs. "Really? You could cause a pileup at Trooping of the Colour? Could you have a more inflated view of your own self-importance?"

"Only by taking tips from you." Michael leads Chris as the crowds separate—tourists cleaving off towards the South Bank and the London Eye, civilians carrying on towards the back side of Waterloo or up the river to Vauxhall Cross, the Secret Intelligence Service's imposing headquarters that looms on its haunches at the next bend of the river.

"What do you want me to do?" Chris asks.

"Just bring her back. We need things there to stay as they are for now, and we certainly don't need her meddling."

"And Skarparov?"

"Leave him. I almost have him where I want him—I have a feeling he is going to prove a rather useful friend. Last thing I need is Sarah charging in and upsetting the balance. Just get her back."

CHAPTER 6

Sarah braces against the headrest and tightens her grip on the shoulder straps as the helicopter comes down to land in Koidu, the biggest town in the diamond-mining heartland of Sierra Leone. Gaining control of these cursed stones is what brought Skarparov here. The temptation of riches hidden within this red earth had led him to take on the KGB's mad assassination plot in Tbilisi. To fully understand her opponent, Sarah has to see it with her own eyes.

Elias, his broad shoulders spilling out of the fold-down seat opposite her, flashes his easy grin. He spent most of the flight crouched behind the cock-pit—snatching shouted conversation with George, their pilot, and enjoying the best view. Sarah was paralysed at take-off—the deafening noise sent vibrations through every soft tissue in her body. But the view from the front is too good to stay stuck to the wall in the cargo section. The dotted roofs of Freetown give way to forest in ever denser green, plumes of smoke rising from folds in the hillside, irregular patches of burnt scrub, flashes of red earth breaking through the sea of green.

George is barrel-broad, heavy-set, but exudes a gentle grace. His big hands reach regularly to his forehead to push the curly mop of hair away from his tan-tinted sunglasses. He handles the chopper with the confidence of one who has been often tested, and always escaped.

But still Sarah is nervous. The hovering and swaying required to steady the Soviet-era beast enough to bring it down feels no less precarious than the unlikely thrust that took them up in the first place. Solid ground is announced with a reassuring thud.

"So this is diamond country." Sarah wipes the laterite dust from around her eyes, taking in the landscape—grassland, low hills, clusters of palms and mango trees. "Can you really just find them in the rivers?"

"Apparently."

"I'd love to have a go—playing the lottery with a big metal sieve."

"You'd be mad to even try around here. Any find would be ripped out of your hand as soon as you'd looked at it. Every inch of river that has turned up anything interesting is now being watched by a guy with a gun. It's not the poor sods with wet feet who win the lottery."

"Are we going straight to Skarparov's operations?" Sarah asks as Elias helps her into the passenger seat of a battered pickup truck.

"Eventually. I've got a job to do first."

*

They drive through the main street in Koidu—two-storey concrete buildings, shop fronts open to the red laterite road, overhanging roofs and gridded shutters protecting the upper floors from the grinding sun.

"So, how did Skarparov respond to you coming back?" Sarah asks. "Do you think he was suspicious?"

Sarah sent Elias to Sierra Leone to work his way back into Skarparov's trust. Elias had worked for Skarparov in Georgia, but only in a casual way—arranging a few connections, setting up meetings. Sarah may have the instinctive understanding of how Skarparov operates, but Elias has the access and a way in that she could never match. She persuaded him to try. If he can work his way back into Skarparov's operations, and his trust, he could gather the evidence she needs to bring Skarparov to justice.

"I think someone like Skarparov is professionally suspicious of everyone. But for now he seems to think I'm worth the risk. I've managed to make myself pretty indispensable to him, so even if he doesn't trust me, he has to protect me." He flashes her a grin.

"What does he have you doing?"

"I'm fast becoming his right-hand man in Koidu, allowing him to stay out of the dirtier sides of his business. I've been working on the local mine owners to convince them of the benefits of his services."

"Services?"

"Diamond export. For a mere sixty percent of the value, he gets the stones out of the country and straight to his own cutting and polishing business in Amsterdam."

"Sixty percent? People agree to that?"

"They don't really have much choice."

"And the Russian weapons? Any idea what he plans for them."

"They've already been handed over."

"To who?"

"Foday Sankoh, the leader of the rebel movement—the Revolutionary United Front or RUF, although in truth I don't think they're united in much. How else do you think Skarparov secured the mineral rights?"

Sarah's heart sinks. She had known it was a false hope that she could stop Skarparov before his weapons fell into the wrong hands, but she had clung to it all the same. The weapons were given as payment for a failed job; they are as good as stolen goods. Of course Skarparov would want to have them off his hands as soon as possible, he is too shrewd a player to linger in a position of risk.

"So you go around peddling Skarparov's dodgy services?"

"And I'm very good at it."

The low-rise buildings of the town sink into the distance. The road leaving Koidu is golden red—Saharan sands churned through the continent's iron core—framed on either side by tall dust-covered grasses.

Sarah finds Elias's enthusiasm for his new role difficult to stomach. She had told him to go back to gain Skarparov's trust. But she hadn't thought through what he might be asked to do to gain that trust. She should be pleased at the ease with which he has slipped into the role of Skarparov's fix-it man. But he isn't supposed to be enjoying it.

"Just make sure you don't get too close. We don't want you to look complicit when we get him indicted."

"That's the plan, is it?" He takes his eyes off the road to look at her, sending the car flying over an unexpected bump.

"Of course." Sarah braces herself against the sagging upholstery. "If he's already handed over the weapons, it should be easy. Surely he can be indicted for arming the RUF?"

"Except that Foday Sankoh, the leader of the RUF and Skarparov's patron, is now the Vice-President and immune from all prosecution." Elias's deep monotone, with just a trace of Dutch in his accent, is unreadable.

"I don't understand why the President agreed to sign a deal that made the rebel leader his Vice President with control over the diamond mines. Surely that's madness?"

"Most people would agree. It was a deal that could only ever have looked appealing to the most war-weary of politicians. But it certainly suits Skarparov. Foday Sankoh is now in his debt and happens to be in charge of the country's mineral resources."

"But how did Sankoh ever negotiate that?"

"American lawyers, pushed to achieve any outcome other than stalemate, drafted most of the text while their presidential envoy, the Reverend Jesse Jackson, spent his time pleading with Foday Sankoh to leave the luxuries of his hotel suite. The Freetown gossip mill thinks that Skarparov was lobbying the Americans on behalf of Sankoh."

"That's something already in the case against him, isn't it? Can we use it?"

"Skarparov, Man of Peace? The only one who could bring both sides to the table? The architect behind the longest lasting peace of the war? There are many different ways to spin the story. Nothing here is ever entirely as it seems."

Golden clouds of dust rise through the floor of the car, covering them both in a layer of grit. Is Elias defending Skarparov's position or just playing Devil's advocate to test hers?

"But surely if we can prove that the Vice President is receiving weapons from the Russians," she insists, "then peace agreement or not, we can discredit him and remove the RUF from the power share?"

"And then?"

"And then we can indict Skarparov for arranging the transfer and have him hauled up in front of the International Criminal Court."

"And then?"

"What do you mean, and then? Then we've won. Then he will have to pay for what he's done." Surely this is obvious. Is he deliberately trying to wind her up?

"Look around you, Sarah. Skarparov is not the problem here. Yes, he's profiting from the chaos, and yes he's about as morally corrupt as they come. But he's just one snake in this knot of vipers. The problem is not him, it's the war. This endless war that brings decent politicians to their knees and allows the most base and corrupt to flourish. Defang Skarparov, and the snake will grow another head. There's always another who will rise to take his place."

Sarah is silenced. She has spoken to Elias very little about her plans for coming to Sierra Leone. Their conversations were always playful, teasing, the intimate language of lovers. She had assumed that he would not be here if he didn't agree with her. She can contradict nothing he said, and yet she is deeply unsettled by his arguments. Is he seriously suggesting they should try to end the war? Or is he coming up with excuses to protect Skarparov?

"How does Skarparov get the diamonds out?" Sarah asks.

"Scrap metal exports. All kinds of junk gets gathered up and sold by the kilo. But there are no facilities in the country to process it, so it all gets shipped out, mostly to China. No one goes through that stuff with a fine toothcomb."

Towering clouds gather overhead, white at the top with a purple edge like a blossoming bruise. The road surface continues to deteriorate, and Elias is forced to take ever wilder paths to avoid the biggest potholes, straddling deep ruts where whole sections of the road have been washed away.

"Where are we going?" Sarah tries not to show her niggle of resentment at being forced to follow his lead. She had sent him here to help her, but now she feels like a tag-along on his mission. Her body is weakened by the journey, a headache pushes at her eyes and a tightness takes hold of her throat.

"To see the local Chief, keep him sweet." Elias gives a reassuring smile. "He needs to give his seal of approval if you want to operate in his Chiefdom. I want to ask him about the rumours of the rebels moving in. His network should know whether it's just stories or something we need to act on."

"How do you keep the Chief on Skarparov's side?" Sarah asks, troubled by the complicity of the question.

"Regular visits to show respect, plenty of presents."

"Sounds like you're courting a difficult mother-in-law. What does one bring a Paramount Chief?"

Elias nods to the assortment of boxes in the footwell under her feet. "A bucket of kola nuts, a family pack of soap, and a box of AK-47 cartridges." He grins. "Just call me Jungle Father Christmas."

CHAPTER 7

They pull up in front of the largest house in the village. A concrete porch with widely spaced steps sets it apart from its neighbours. Their car, the only vehicle in the village, is quickly swarmed by children staring open-mouthed. Elias throws a kola nut to the littlest boy, who catches it with a high-pitched squeal and runs off to announce their arrival.

In the front room, the Chief sits with stooped shoulders in a short-sleeved suit, sunk into a dirty peach armchair. He acknowledges them with a raise of his chin. The room is dark, the windows boarded shut, and only a dim glow comes from a soot-stained hurricane lamp on the central table. Elias and Sarah are swallowed by a sofa positioned opposite the Chief—the foam cushions collapse into a deep crease in the frame leaving Sarah hanging by the inside of her knees on the wooden crossbar.

After a moment of silence, the Chief indicates with a brief nod that Elias should begin.

"*Aw di bohdi?*" Elias asks in convincing-sounding Krio.

"*Di bohdi fayn. A tel God tenki.*"

"*Aw di fambul?*"

"*Di fambul fayn.*"

The list of questions is lengthy—family, business, health, the day—but without a change in intonation, the Chief declares all to be fine. Considering the stories he would have to tell, Sarah realises there is mercy in his manners.

Elias presents the gifts. The Chief touches his right hand to the bucket of nuts and nods to a girl watching from a darkened doorway to take them. The girl approaches, her face caught between shyness and curiosity. She looks about Sarah's age, early twenties, although she could be much younger, her angular figure still more child than woman. She takes the gifts, staring at the strange visitors with undisguised fascination. Sarah smiles back.

"My daughter," the Chief says, sending her back with a dismissive nod. He maintains his expression of dignified disinterest, but Sarah notices a softness in his eye as his gaze follows her out of the room.

"We thank you for your gifts, Mr Elias," the Chief begins, labouring each word. "But what can Mr Skarparov do for us to help us feel safe? Last week, the house of the Chief of the next village was attacked. The week before, the village to the other side was attacked and several of the houses burnt. They are coming closer, Mr Elias, and they are hungry."

"Perhaps we can extend our security network to pass your village."

The chief heaves a sigh that seems to shrink his entire body. "Fattmatu? Bring tea."

His daughter appears again and nods, with a quick ogle at the towering redhead and the blonde girl sweating on the sofa.

She returns with a plastic tea tray and white china cups. As she kneels to serve her father, a noise erupts outside: a whooping shout, like a singsong call of a drunk. Fattmatu dives to her father's feet, dropping the tray where she stands. Shards of shattered china skip across the floor.

"Quick. Out." The Chief jumps to his feet with a speed Sarah would not have thought possible. He pushes Sarah and Elias towards the door.

"Eh-oh?" Another call from outside, but louder this time, accompanied by a rhythmic thud that shakes the floor.

Five men appear in army uniform, AK-47s swung loosely across their chests. Their leader, hardly more than a boy, reels into the room, swaying like an uninvited drunk at a dance.

The whites of his eyes swell unnaturally as he takes them in. A grubby piece of adhesive tape hangs limply from his sweat-soaked forehead. Four more boys in green vests and camouflage combats stand behind him. One of them is wrapped in belts of ammunition, another casually swings a machete.

The rebel grins with misplaced delight. "I know you," he says, dancing back and forth in front of Elias, undaunted by Elias' superior height and size. He leers at Sarah, showing the gums of his back teeth. "He is Mr Skarparov's man. And who are you?" He swings his gun like a toy and prods the muzzle into Sarah's chest.

Sarah is too scared to speak. She looks to Elias, who keeps grim silence, jaw clenched, his breathing visible in the heave of his shoulder. He does not meet her eye.

"What's the matter? You shy?" The protruding eyeballs press up to Sarah's face, the overwhelming smell of body bathed in jungle makes her gag.

The ammo-clad sidekick takes hold of Elias's arm. "Shall I take the white man outside?"

"Take Mr Skarparov's man," the leader replies, his gibbous eyes fixed on Sarah. "The girl can stay with me." His teeth erupt from ruby red lips as he laughs at Sarah, bouncing on his tiptoes like a tethered pony, a thick vein rising at his neck.

Sarah watches as Elias is led away. The door closes behind them. A second sidekick who wears a drooping feather tucked behind his ear takes hold of her arms, one in each hand, clasping her in front of him like a shield, his grip too tight for her to move. She feels feverish under his touch, his heavy breath cool against the flushed skin of her throat.

"What you got for me?" the lead rebel calls, swinging his gun towards the Chief.

The Chief plants his feet wide, standing completely motionless as the rebel leader struts and sways around him. "How much do you want?"

"We no want your money, Chief." He tips his head to one

side, his tongue lolling pinkly out of his mouth. "Gimme your generator."

"My generator is broken." The Chief's voice shakes.

"Why you think we want a broken generator? You give us one that works, or we burn your house." The remaining sidekick laughs in a high-pitched giggle. He picks up the hurricane lamp from the middle of the table and swings it over his head, smashing the glass against the door. He continues to wave the lamp, spraying the kerosene across the room like a perfume censer. The air stings with fumes.

"Please, the generator has not worked for months. I cannot fix it. I have no other for you." The Chief clasps his hands together in front of his chest. "I have money. I can pay you if you leave."

"We no want your money, Chief. We want power. Fix it for us, and we go. Otherwise, we stay." He roams the room like a failed firework, caustic and unpredictable, tapping the furniture with the end of his gun. His shifting gaze falls on Fattmatu cowering on the floor next to her father's armchair.

"Eh-oh?" He pulls her up by one arm. With one hand clamped around her wrist, he circles her, swaying from the knees and whistling. "This one sweet titi. She yours, Chief?"

"Get away from my daughter," the Chief roars. He lurches towards the rebel leader, but the sidekick with the machete springs forward, pressing the shining blade against his throat.

Fattmatu's whole body shakes. Her chest heaves as she tries to stand, tears streaming down her face. "Don't hurt me," she whispers between clattering teeth.

The boy runs the tip of his gun along her throat, thrusting his hips into hers and grinding against her abdomen. "Dance for me, titi," he commands, swaying her jerkily from side to side.

"Papa," she cries, but her father remains rooted to the spot, hands clenched in prayer, the blade of the machete digging into the crease of his chin.

The rebel grabs her shirt, pulling the fabric tight in his fist before snatching his hand away. It tears at the neck, exposing her naked chest, breasts and prominent ribs. He pulls harder, removing the rest of the shirt, hissing in her ear, "Here puss, puss, puss."

Sarah wants to scream, to divert attention, anything to pull the crazed rebel away from Fattmatu. But she can not move. She has no strength against the hands that hold her, even to turn away. She is powerless, a useless observer. Ill-equipped, weak and frozen. Even her attempts to scream falter in her throat.

Fattmatu has no trouble screaming, her wails frantic and growing in intensity, like a dying animal. The rebel stuffs her ripped t-shirt into her mouth to dampen the noise. She gags on the fabric, nostrils flaring. He prods at her flesh with the nose of his gun—fondling her breasts with the metal, drawing a line from her sternum to the soft tautness of her belly. Flicking out a knife, he continues his journey across her body with the tip of the blade. Suddenly he turns her around, bends her forwards and shouts to his sidekick to hold her in place. The boy flings the hurricane lamp across the room and licks his lips as he tightens his grip around her neck.

Sarah is burning up, fear and disgust boil her blood, her ears pound, a metallic taste ripens in her mouth. If only Elias was here, perhaps he could help. Why was he taken, and she forced to stay? She refuses to think about what might be happening to him outside.

The lead rebel raises his hand and slashes at the skin on Fattmatu's back, piercing the soft flesh across the small of her back, where two dimples sit above her buttocks. Fattmatu's muffled screams grow weaker as he continues his work. Sarah flinches with each slash, her body convulsing with every tear of the blade. Gradually his slashing becomes more controlled. He pushes the knife harder, carving deeper into the skin until with a final flourish she falls to the floor. In crudely made letters, Sarah can read the initials RUF dripping in blood across her back.

"Next time, we take her," the rebel shouts at the Chief. "And you," he fixes Sarah with his swollen eyes. "Don't mess with things where you don't belong."

The Chief falls upon the body of his daughter, shoulders heaving with sobs, as if trying to cover her modesty, to heal the wounds in her violated body and to cover her with his strength. "Forgive me," he whispers. "Fattmattu, please God forgive me."

Sarah closes her eyes to the horror and weeps.

CHAPTER 8

Beverley Moreton taps the polished surface of the table. Her nails, square cut with rounded edges and painted the perfect shade of pink, give a pleasing clack against the wood. The High Commissioner is late. He would no doubt come with a volley of excuses about previous meetings running over and so much to fit in during a brief trip. But she is his boss' boss, and it irks her that he thinks it acceptable to keep her waiting. *Clack. Clack.*

At last, he enters, wearing a shabby mackintosh still dripping with rain. He lurches at her for a handshake, but she directs him to sit. He steps back awkwardly, struggles with his wet coat and takes a seat, smoothing his mess of grey hair against his forehead. *Clack. Clack.*

"So, Benjamin. Thank you for finding the time to fit me in," Beverley begins. "And how are things in Freetown?"

"Sorry to be late. There's always so much to cover in these quick visits."

Beverley nods. So far, so predictable.

"To be honest, I'd say we're in for another rough patch pretty soon. The rebels are getting bolder by the minute. Just last week they targeted a group of UNAMSIL peacekeepers, Pakistani troops, who were carrying out a regular patrol around Freetown. The soldiers were mostly unharmed, but the rebels took their vehicles and all their weapons. They've been seen driving them around Freetown, shamelessly flaunting their spoils."

"A UN vehicle? But why doesn't someone stop them?" Beverley is appalled. "Can't the police arrest them?"

"No one can. The police are pretty much non-existent. The army themselves are under-supplied and who knows when they were last paid. UNAMSIL, the UN mission, is toothless and chaotically organised, and ECOMOG—"

"Who?"

"The Economic Community of West African States Monitoring Group—it's a group of—"

"Oh yes, the Nigerian army, isn't it? I can't imagine they're much use."

"Well..." he hesitates. Beverley wishes he would get to the point. "Well, they were the ones who pushed the rebels back last time they made it to Freetown. They're pretty much the only effective force left now that Executive Outcomes have been chucked out."

"So, you were saying?" *Clack.*

"That things are getting worse. There is certainly scope for continuing to work to sharpen up UNAMSIL's mandate, but I also think the time is ripe to consider a UK-led military intervention."

"But there's a peace agreement in place? The RUF has committed to disarming? Why on earth would we want to send in troops?"

"Because the peace agreement isn't worth the paper it's written on." Benjamin stops, as if surprised by the force of his own statement. Beverley hopes this isn't the way he speaks to everyone. "It has given Foday Sankoh the immunity he craved, but he has shown no intention to stick by his side of the agreement."

"I see."

"What do you think?"

"Of what?"

"Of the military intervention? Do you think it's something you could push within Whitehall?"

"I think it's important that we don't get too emotional in response to a few isolated incidents. I'm sure it feels quite jittery

41

where you are on the ground, but we need to keep our eyes on the bigger picture."

"With respect, Beverley, this is a culmination of events that have been characteristic of the rebel movement for the last ten years."

"Yes indeed. But there is an awful lot that would need to be factored into the equation if we were to change the status of our support." *Clack.*

He fiddles with his raincoat, top lip pulled tight across his teeth. Her message is received.

"I tell you what," she offers, sugaring the pill. "I'll get it on the agenda of the weekly cross-Whitehall crisis meeting. I'll be sure to put forward your views to the rest of the team." She smiles broadly, her head tilted slightly downwards to indicate that the meeting was over.

"And if the situation should deteriorate before—"

"We'll discuss it in the meeting."

CHAPTER 9

It is Elias who wrenches Sarah out of the arms of the rebel, crushing his feather underfoot when it falls in the scuffle. Elias who picks up her crumpled body and holds her tightly in his arms, rushing them out of the house and into the car. Elias who drives them back to the Koidu airstrip, a journey made in silence but for the growling of the engine and the occasional crack as loose gravel strikes the wheel hubs. He negotiates a place for them on the next chopper back to Freetown and holds her hand in his for the duration of the flight. But nothing Elias can do can stop her from shaking.

Everywhere, Sarah sees Fattmatu's exposed body cowering at her father's feet. When she closes her eyes, the image remains locked in place by cold, rough hands forcing her to watch.

Elias brings her back to Pietro's, where they stayed on the night of her arrival—no paper hearts to follow this time, no romantic set-up. He lies next to her on the slumped pair of beds, bringing comfort with his physical presence, although no more able than Sarah to find words to address what they had seen. He warps his arms around her shuddering shoulders until, finally, she gives in to her exhaustion. When she awakes, he is gone.

A weak light peels through the curtains. Sarah throws off the thin blanket, drenched in sweat. She needs water. Is it worth risking the tap water? Surely nothing can make her feel worse than she does now.

Her body wages a full rebellion against all that she has witnessed. A fever rises to sear out the image of what she has seen, a sweat to wash away the culpability and a pounding in the ears to drown out the sound of Fattmatu's cries. Her limbs feel matchstick brittle. As she tries to stand, her knees give way and she slides to the floor. The red-striped tiles now look like bloody smears, roiling and stirring. She summons the strength to half-crawl, half-slide across the slithering tiles to retrieve a bottle of water from her bag. Only a few mouthfuls remain, tepid and foul smelling. She sinks back against the wooden bedpost, watching the room sway in and out of focus.

A crashing sound draws her gaze towards the door, the room following drunkenly behind. Elias stands in the doorway, looking pale and exhausted, carrying a paper bag and a large bottle of water. Her saviour.

"What are you doing on the floor?"

"I was looking for water." Sarah struggles to control her slurring tongue.

"On the floor? Come on, let's get you back onto the bed." He scoops her up and lies the damp sheets like an icy shroud across her feverish skin.

"Shit, you're really burning up. Here, take these." He opens a box bearing the crude outline of a mosquito, and pops a pair of white tablets out of the foil.

"What is it?" Sarah murmurs. "You can't just shove tablets in my mouth. I don't want them." She tries to spit them out, but her tongue is dry and tacky.

"It's chloroquine. And you're going to take them. It doesn't always work, but it's better than nothing. Here, swallow." The tablets stick in her throat, leaving a bitter taste and powdery trail snaking down the back of her tongue.

"How do you know I have malaria?" Sarah asks.

"I don't. But it's better to be safe than sorry." He throws himself backwards on the bed, striking his head on the wooden post. "Listen, Sarah, I'm so sorry... I don't... I'm sorry I brought you into that. I had no idea the Chief would be targeted. I thought they would be left alone out of some vestige of respect.

But those animals—"

"You couldn't have known."

"But I should have been more careful. You've just arrived. You haven't even had time to get used to this god-awful climate. I spent my first week here doing little more than sweating in bed and feeling feverish."

"I seem to have got the hang of that," Sarah smiles weakly.

"Never one to do things in half-measures, are you? You need to rest, to regain your strength. I can't stay—if the rebels are growing in boldness Skarparov needs me back in Koidu—but I'll come back to Freetown next week to find you. And then we can—"

"What am I doing here?" Sarah interrupts.

Elias takes her hand. "You're here to stop Skarparov."

"But this country is in full civil war. It is madness. What we saw yesterday… I can't stop that. No one can. Or it's the UN. Or a properly trained army. There's nothing I can do."

"But it's people like Skarparov who are keeping it going. Without his money, weapons, and influence, the rebels would be severely weakened. Now's not really the time to discuss this, but I have a plan of how I can use my access from working for Skarparov to gather information on the rebels' positions—"

"You said yourself, Skarparov is just one snake. Someone else will rise up to take his place. And if I get killed in the process, who wins then?" She tries to swallow, but her tongue feels thick and swollen in her mouth. "I can't, I just can't. This is not my fight."

"Sarah, you're ill. Your fever must be at forty degrees. This isn't the time to make this kind of decision. Come on, come outside, get some sunshine on your skin. You'll feel better in no time."

Sarah shakes her head weakly.

"Look, I won't go," Elias says, taking her hand. "It's crazy to leave you alone in this state. We'll stay here as long as you need. Pietro can get you whatever drugs you want and after a few days of eating lobster, fresh sea breezes and bracing swims and my personal care and attention, you'll be ready for anything."

"I'm sorry I brought you here, Elias. I'm sorry I dragged you into this hell."

"I knew what I was letting myself into."

Sarah squeezes her eyes tight, but she still can not escape the image of Fattmatu's spoiled skin cowering on the floor. "What was I thinking? How did I think I stood any chance against Skarparov? I can't even defend myself."

"Sarah, you're rambling, you're feverish."

"Do you know what I felt in the Chief's house, watching that animal attack Fattmatu?"

"Terrified?"

"I felt powerless. Powerless to act, powerless to prevent what was happening. Even if I'd been strong enough to struggle free, what could I have done against a crowd of rebels with guns? I don't even know how to shoot."

Elias covers a smile. "I thought they taught you that sort of thing as part of your training?"

"Michael forgot to give me any. I'm totally under-qualified for what I need to do."

"I can help you."

"I need to get out of here until I can breathe again."

"You're leaving?"

"There's someone I want to see."

"But what about—"

"Wait for me. I'll be back."

CHAPTER 10

Michael unwinds his scarf and hands it to the waiter who is hovering behind his chair. Outside, the spring Amsterdam air still holds a bite, but the best riverside table of the Amstel Hotel is bathed in warm sunshine, filtered through the giant elms in bright new leaf towering over the riverbank.

He gazes out of high windows across the river at a scene that could not be more Dutch: a broad thoroughfare of water, a messy crowd of bikes, narrow houses standing shoulder-to-shoulder with vast open-facing windows. Michael itches for some curtains to close—how could anyone bear to have their inner lives so prominently on display? He turns back to the door in time to see Skarparov enter. His blue overcoat looks brand new, his deep walnut tan clashes with the muted colours of the dining room. He is close to Michael in age, but the purple-tinged blackness of his hair makes him look older. More to hide.

"Ah Amsterdam, is there anywhere like this in the world?" Skarparov says, opal-eyes fixed on Michael. "There is something in the light, don't you think? It makes me want to paint."

"You're an artist?" Michael asks with a slight raise of one brow. He does not like to feel underprepared.

"No, I never held a brush!" Skarparov gives a deep laugh from his sizeable paunch. "But every time I'm here I wish I was."

Michael unfolds a starched white napkin from a silver ring and smooths it across his lap. "You must spend quite a bit of time here. How is the casino business, Mr Skarparov?"

Skarparov accepts the water poured by the waiter and downs

the glass in one gulp. "It's never that good. But never that bad. I used to have a few more, but this one is the only one I kept. I have a fondness for the city. It gives me an excuse to come back."

The waiter takes their orders and asks if he might help them select a wine. "What sort of character are you looking for today, gentlemen?"

"You'd better ask my friend." Skarparov smiles at Michael, his eyebrows dancing like the supporting act. "He's in charge."

"We'll have the Sancerre." Michael snaps the wine card shut.

"Very good." The waiter stoops a little lower and retreats.

"And how about the diamond polishing?" Michael asks with a wry smile.

"You don't like to beat about the bush. I thought at least we might be able to enjoy our meal before we got into the dirty talk of business. Tell me, Mr Smith," Skarparov lingers on the name as if tugging at a fake beard, "what did you actually come here for?"

"To make you an offer." Michael butters a bread roll with a heavy-handled knife. "We know what you did in the Caucasus. You did a nice job of setting it up to look like it was your uncle behind the attack on the US President. And now he's dead and you are free to swan around in Amsterdam enjoying the light. But I know it was you. It only takes a phone call to the CIA, and you would be blinded by the shitstorm that descends."

Skarparov keeps up his smile, but the dancing eyebrows droop. "Come now, no one actually got hurt."

"Indeed," Michael nods.

The waiter sets down two oversized plates with miniature portions of food. Skarparov chose the salmon with black rice. Michael, the scallops. He sweeps aside the black shavings that have been artfully arranged over the dish with a clinical flick of his knife. When did good food become this fussy?

"Monsieur doesn't care for the dehydrated balsamic vinegar?" the waiter asks, his accent hovering between French and Dutch. "Can I get you something else?"

"Just saving it for later." Michael smiles and holds his eye until the waiter is forced to look away. He stabs a scallop with his fork.

"Okay, now you have my attention," Skarparov says. "What is it you had to offer?"

"It's lovely to meet you here in Amsterdam, but it's your activities in Sierra Leone that really interest me."

"Most of my work in Sierra Leone is development-based. I'm implementing a project for the European Union that is helping to build—"

"You don't need to string your stories for me. I'm talking diamonds, as you well know." Michael finds Skarparov's response surprisingly hard to read. Is he irritated to be called out so bluntly or pleased to be brought round to his favourite subject? His warm, convivial face with its quick smile is disappointingly opaque. Michael expected easier cues. He presses on. "And as you may have guessed, I'm actually interested in uranium."

"Uranium? What makes you think there is uranium in Sierra Leone?" Skarparov dabs at his purplish lips with a napkin.

"The fact that you've been putting out feelers for a buyer."

Skarparov studies his opponent. "Who have you been talking to?"

"That doesn't matter. What I'm interested in is what we can do on this together." Michael raises his glass in a half toast.

"The British government want to work with me on an untested uranium discovery in war-torn Africa?" Skarparov asks.

Michael breaks out his most charming smile. Both now have their cards on the table, this is the moment to bring him onside. "Who said anything about the British government?"

"Oh?" Skarparov pauses and hurries another couple of mouthfuls of fish into his mouth. "Mr Smith, you see I was under the impression that you worked for Her Majesty's government," he fingers the solitary tulip in the centre of the table. "On the shadier side, of course."

"Who I work for is not all that important to you. What you

49

need to know is that I have the ability to protect you at the very highest level."

"Why would I need protection?"

"From the Russians. They paid you for the job in Tbilisi, but as you just acknowledged, no one actually got hurt. So unless you were planning on sending back the weapons I believe you've already handed over to Foday Sankoh, I thought perhaps you might seek a little patronage elsewhere." He leans back into his dark wooden carver chair and takes a mouthful of wine.

To Michael's irritation, Skarparov laughs. A laugh loud enough to draw the eyes of the neighbouring table, a nervous-looking couple with matching round glasses. "What makes you think you have that sort of control over the KGB? If they want me dead, I'll die."

That should put off the nervous eavesdroppers.

"Your KGB handler is Nikolay Kuznetsov." Michael does not pose it as a question. "I have known Nikolay for many years. We've been through a great deal together. I'm sure I could suggest a deal that would allow you to play both sides. At least for now."

Skarparov digs at another chunk of fish, scraping his cutlery across his plate. "And in return for this 'arrangement', what assistance did you want from me?"

"I think we might be able to make our interests align."

"You want a piece of the uranium deal?" Skarparov asks.

"I want you to tell me everything you know about the find, and then I want you to sell it to my buyer."

"Which is who?"

"Which is who I tell you it will be. I assume that the fact that you are already testing the market means you are convinced the find is viable?"

"The guys who came to me are good guys. I believe them. They know the country, they know their stuff. Samples have all been sent to the laboratory at the Rössing mine in Namibia and the test results look pretty conclusive."

"But the government has not contacted Areva or any of the

big players?"

"Have you been to Sierra Leone? You think any of the serious mining companies want to talk to the government of a country like that? You think they take the calls of a snake like Foday Sankoh?"

"Rumour has it that your lobbying helped put a man with the blood of thousands on his hands, into that position."

"Rumour can be very flattering." Skarparov tears a bread roll in two and uses it to mop up the juices on his plate. "Rumour has it, Michael, that you received some handsome kickbacks for your own role in the negotiations." He looks at Michael, cunning playing in his opal eyes.

"I'm not the only one who's been doing my homework." Michael takes a sip of wine. It is no surprise that Skarparov would work out who he was, but he always preferred to work with at least the pretence of anonymity. Who could possibly have told him about Michael's involvement in the peace negotiations? He isn't ashamed of the fundraising—running an off-the-books unit comes with its own budget demands. His operations need funding, as does his lifestyle. And it helps win him credibility amongst the most corrupt of his targets. But he still has to be careful about who knows.

"There are plenty of people who won't do business in Sierra Leone," Skarparov says, pressing his advantage. "I'm more interested in those who do."

Michael recharges his smile. If their relationship is going to work, Skarparov needs to feel like the victor. "It sounds like we can work together."

"Of course, I'm just the middleman in this deal," Skarparov continues, his unnaturally tanned face oozing confidence. "I only agreed to find a buyer on the promise of a serious commission. You need to promise me my cut, otherwise it's not worth my while."

"So you'd take the risk with Nikolay Kuznetsov?"

"It wouldn't be the first time," Skarparov says with a shrug.

"One more thing… My position in Sierra Leone is secured by my connections to Foday Sankoh, by my excellent 'export services' and by my dazzling reputation among the Freetown elite." He grins. "All of these things rely on the unique set of circumstances that we currently find in Sierra Leone."

"Of course."

"I've heard rumours that the British government is considering a change of tactics, bringing out the big guns instead of relying on the UN to do their ineffectual job."

"I have no insight into government policy."

"Of course, Mr Smith. Why would you? But supposing you knew someone who did? Supposing you knew someone who could use their influence to make sure no one jumps to hasty decisions?"

"Supposing I did?" Michael prompts, surprised by Skarparov's boldness. The ability to pull on secret strings is often tacitly understood to be part of the services he could offer. But he's never dealt with someone before who has been so bold as to come out and ask him to keep feeding a civil war.

"Then the chance of this uranium," Skarparov says, "ending up in the hands of your buyer, what did you say his name was again?"

"I didn't."

"Well, the chance of me being able to secure the deal for your mystery man would be that much higher. I do hope he can pay. There are plenty of others interested with very deep pockets."

"Don't worry," Michael says. "Money is no object. So long as I come out of this a happy man, so will you."

"Ah Michael, you know as well as I do, money is always the object."

CHAPTER 11

Sarah waits for Dilara on a suburban street on Istanbul's Asian side. After two days of sweating and shivering through budget flights and empty airport terminals, she basks in the sunshine, enjoying the warmth in her bones and the feeling of strength returning.

Colourful apartment buildings line the street in brick red, pistachio green, and hazelnut yellow. Twisted metal balconies cling to the ice-cream facades, shadowed by clusters of satellite dishes. A man leaves the grocer's shop on the corner, his gaze falling heavily on Sarah, uncomfortably direct. She holds his eye, refusing to be intimidated by his sticky stare, until he jumps on his scooter and speeds off.

She checks her watch. Another scooter approaches and for a moment it looks like the same starer back for another gawp. But both the bike and its rider are too slick. Dilara pulls off her helmet and shakes out her mane of dark chestnut hair. She smiles at Sarah with impossibly shiny lips, painted dark red to match her Vespa, her skin like evening light on a hot stone terrace.

Sarah had been surprised that Dilara had taken her call, let alone agreed to meet her so soon. It had felt strange to make her request out loud, but Dilara sounded reassuringly nonchalant. "Of course I can help, my dear. Come see me."

She is not even sure if Dilara was the right person to call. She is, after all, Michael's friend and Sarah has to assume that anything she tells Dilara will go straight back to him. She has only met her once before in the flesh—when she flew Michael into a disused landing strip in Tbilisi. But she helped her then, so Sarah is counting on her doing the same again. There is something about Dilara that speaks to Sarah—beyond the outlandish glamour and high-maintenance grooming. She is clearly a woman who knows what she wants and how to get it. She knows how to handle herself in Michael's world. She has exactly what Sarah needs.

Dilara kisses her on both cheeks. Her skin brushes against Sarah's like freshly powdered velvet. Her hair wafts a rich cloud of jasmine and animal musk. "This is your first time, darling?" she purrs, taking Sarah by the hand and leading her down a small alley between the condominiums. Her gleaming boots clack smartly against the concrete.

"I've never even held one before," Sarah says.

"I'm sure you're a natural." Dilara winks a heavily mascaraed eyelash. "First you must choose your favourite." She opens an unmarked door into a blue-lit foyer thick with cigarette smoke. "Ata!" Dilara calls. Her voice is deep for a woman with a rich harshness that makes each syllable sound like an invitation.

A man with thinning hair and a bushy brown moustache greets Dilara with a weak-kneed smile. How strange it must be to go through life having this effect on people. Ata's face, a witness to many dark hours in a windowless room, shines when he sees Dilara. "We are ready for you. Would you like tea first?"

Dilara guides Sarah with a gentle hand on the small of her back. "No, I think my friend wants to get down to business."

"Be my guest." He ushers them through the entrance foyer and closes the door behind them, locking heavy bolts at top and bottom. Inside, the walls are lined with guns—from pocket-sized pistols to a massive assault rifle longer than Sarah is tall. "Pistols first." Dilara points to a display of handguns hooked to the wall through their trigger guards. "Go ahead, pick," she instructs.

Sarah has no clue how to select from the lethal array. She points to a classic-looking revolver—black grip, silver metal cylinder.

"Go on, take it," Dilara says, watching her. "You have to hold the thing and see how it feels."

Sarah unhooks the revolver and is surprised by the weight in her hand. She holds it up, points towards the door and lines up her eye with the sight.

"Well?" Dilara asks, clearly struggling to keep a straight face.

"I like it," Sarah says.

"Girls always choose that one first. It's the prettiest, no? But here, try this one too." She reaches a perfectly manicured hand for a grey semi-automatic pistol. With its thick, mean lines it looks like a tank next to the one Sarah chose. Stamped down the side is the manufacturing mark: *'Steyr Mannlicher, Austria'*.

"This is the one the boys choose, but you should try it." Dilara tosses it to Sarah. "Let's go."

The firing range is a narrow corridor. Two targets hang on parallel tracks at one end facing two desks, separated by a wall of black chequer plate.

Dilara sweeps up her waist-length hair into a coiled bun and holds it in place with a black baseball cap with scarlet panels. Her powerful-looking neck is so long it might have an extra vertebra. She wears tightly fitting combat trousers in camouflage print that cling to her suggestive hips, a top with a stiff black collar and red epaulets to match the hat. "So, given that you have plenty of shooting ranges in London, I'm guessing you're not just here for the guns."

Sarah laughs. "I felt out of my depth. Something told me you would be able to help."

Dilara studies Sarah's profile. "Why would you not go to Michael if you need help? Isn't that supposed to be his job?"

"I don't work for Michael anymore."

"Oh? You broke up?"

"It wasn't really like that. And besides, I don't know that I trust him."

Dilara laughs, laying out the weapons and the ammunition

on a metal table. "Does anyone really trust a man like Michael?"

"Do you?"

"I have known Michael for a very long time. I know I could ask him anything and he would do it for me. But would he sell me out, if he had to? Probably." She laughs again, but something in her smile looks forced.

"How did you and Michael first meet?" Sarah asks, hoping to open up Dilara's carefully cultivated mystery.

"I forget," Dilara waves away the question. "Too long ago. Okay, we start with your favourite. You know how to load it?"

"No idea," Sarah smiles. She might as well embrace being a novice. There is no use pretending knowledge that she clearly doesn't have.

"Your girly gun is a little trickier to load. But you get the hang of it. You take it in your right hand like this."

"And if I'm left-handed?"

Dilara tuts with her tongue. "Then you use your left, and do it all back-to-front, but I guess you're used to that. Release the cylinder by pushing here and rotate it towards you out of the frame." A flash of diamonds catches Sarah's eye as Dilara's hands move with practised ease. "You load each cartridge into the holes, then click it back into place. You try." She empties the cylinder and hands the six red cartridges to Sarah.

Sarah repeats Dilara's actions clumsily. She fumbles one of the cartridges, sending it clattering to the floor.

"Start again," Dilara instructs.

The second time is smoother, the actions feel less strange.

"I'd love to hear the story," Sarah says.

"Which story?"

"How you and Michael met."

Dilara gives a theatrical sigh. "I was young and foolish. Michael helped me. He made my mistakes disappear. But that's a conversation for another day." Her voice trails off. "Now you shoot." Dilara loads a new black and white bullseye and sends it down the range.

"We don't get to aim at a gangster?" Sarah asks.

"Not yet; you need to start with accuracy."

Sarah approaches the desk, her hands tightly wrapped around the grip, hips angled towards the partition wall.

"No, not like that." Dilara places her hands on Sarah's hips and gently rotates them to face the target. "Like this is better."

Her muscles still taut from Dilara's touch, Sarah lines up the sight with the centre of the bullseye and squeezes the trigger. The noise is amazing. Her arms fly up and her body shoots backwards. The target does not twitch. "Where did it go?"

"Up, of course, try again. Stand stronger this time."

Sarah takes aim, broadening her stance and steadying her feet. She shoots, and once more her hands fly up as the gun recoils.

"Harder than it looks, huh?" Dilara slams a magazine into the well of the semi-automatic and hands it to Sarah. The gun, fully loaded, is significantly heavier than the revolver, and her arms feel weak without even raising it to aim. Once more her hands fly up, but this time she leaves a mark on the target sheet.

"You know," Dilara says, with a mischievous look. "Your Michael met Skarparov in Amsterdam last week—he was your man in Tbilisi, no?"

"Michael met Skarparov?" Sarah drops the gun. "How do you know?"

"I helped him set up the meeting."

"What did they talk about?"

"I don't know. I wasn't there. And I never ask too many questions." She twists an escaped tendril of hair around her finger before tucking it back into the cap. "I thought it was strange he didn't ask you to set it up. Now I know why."

Sarah's mind races. Why the hell is Michael meeting Skarparov in Amsterdam? What could they possibly have to discuss? And why did he tell Sarah to drop Skarparov if he was intending to make contact? Could there be a reason why Michael hadn't simply handed Skarparov over to the CIA? The very idea of Michael helping Skarparov turns her stomach. Her former puppet master, hand in glove with the man who planned carnage and devastation in the Caucasus and escaped to profit from another country's misery.

"What about professionally?" Sarah asks, eyeing up the target, imagining how it would feel to send the bullet straight into the bullseye. "Would you trust Michael to do the right thing?"

Dilara throws back her head, exposing her long throat. "Michael is a longstanding British spy." She emphasises the *'British'* as if that sews up her point. "You'd be mad to trust him on anything to do with his work. But he's committed. And he has a lot to prove."

"In Tbilisi, I heard rumours of a disgrace, a suggestion of impropriety that halted Michael's stellar career rise? Was he really caught accepting a bribe?"

"It's easy to make things look the way they are not. Especially in a world where no one is telling the truth."

Sarah remembers the photos from Baku—Michael may have been caught in a similar sting.

She raises her arms again, but a head full of Michael and Skarparov plays havoc with her stance, hunching her shoulders, pulling her arms forward.

"It's here," Dilara traces her fingers along the muscles of Sarah's spine, just between her shoulder blades. "This is where you get your strength. Lock here." She places a firm hand on Sarah's neck. "And relax here, and the rest will follow."

"Do you think Michael could be cooperating with Skarparov?"

Dilara shrugs. "I don't pretend to understand Michael's world. Skarparov seemed happy afterwards. But Michael can make anyone believe whatever he wants them to believe. My guess is that Michael was fishing for information about the uranium."

"What uranium?"

"The uranium in Sierra Leone? You didn't hear about it?"

"That's the last thing the country needs. The diamonds are enough of a curse."

"Maybe it's nothing. And you can't smuggle uranium between

your toes." She flashes Sarah her obscenely large diamond ring. "But Michael will definitely want to know if the rumours are true."

Sarah takes aim, feeling her shoulder blades separating again. Dilara places a dark red glossy nail on Sarah's spine. "Here," she whispers.

Sarah's muscles jump to attention, squeezing in around Dilara's finger. She pulls the trigger.

"Again! Finish the magazine."

Sarah shoots four more times, her feet rooting through the floor and her shoulders locked around Dilara's magic spot.

"I knew it," Dilara brings the target back in for Sarah to inspect. One hole through the top right of the paper, and five holes centred around the bullseye. "You're a natural. Now we get to try the fun one." She loads a new target sheet—a gruff-looking thug holding a woman in a neck lock. "Kill the bastard," she purrs as she sends it back down the range.

Sarah takes aim and fires six quick shots, aiming tight between the man's sour eyes. Dilara fires six shots with the revolver at an identical target from the next-door booth. She brings in the targets. Sarah has five shots on the man's head and one that went through the woman's ear. "You got him, but you killed the woman." Her own has only two holes in the paper, one in the centre of each of the man's eyes. "You're good, but you can still be better."

"You even used the girly-gun," Sarah says with a grin. She knew from the moment she first saw Dilara land her bright red Beechcraft on a broken strip of runway in Georgia that this was a woman who would be useful to know. "How about that tea now?" Sarah asks.

"We'll drink tea. And then you practise. Ata!"

Dilara leads Sarah to a waiting room—two tulip-shaped tea glasses wait on a low table.

"Why did you agree to meet me here?" Sarah asks. "You're supposed to be Michael's friend, why help me? Why tell me about him and Skarparov?"

"I thought you would want to know. And I like you. But why all the Michael questions if you're not working for him anymore?"

Sarah bites her lip. "Some unfinished business."

"You know, once you set foot in his world, you don't ever really leave?"

"I did already," Sarah says with overdone defiance.

"So you're learning to shoot for your new career in cake design?" Dilara raises an eyebrow, shaped like a freshly sharpened arrow. "It's okay, Sarah, you don't need to tell me everything. I understand. Some things are too big to easily let go. I think perhaps you are a bit like me. When you've started something, you have to finish it, am I right?"

Sarah nods. That is exactly her bind. The mad urge that brought her here and would send her back to Sierra Leone against all her better judgement.

"And what's next? How are you with martial arts? You won't always have a gun with you when you need it."

"The move you used when you trussed up that guy in Georgia who was sent to follow me?"

"The one we fed to the pigs?" Dilara fans her face in mock horror.

"I want to learn that."

Dilara shakes her head. "Maybe we start with the basics. Find what you're good at. Play to your strengths."

*

Sarah spends the next week in Dilara's private boot camp. She shoots until her trigger finger aches, punches, kicks, boxes, and is thrown to the ground of the private gym that Dilara *"borrowed from a friend"* for the occasion. In the evenings, Dilara drags Sarah, weak and bruised, round a circuit of her favourite bars in Istanbul, and in the mornings she brings a steaming mug of coffee to her room at sunrise before starting another gruelling round of training. Sarah is exhausted. She has muscles she never knew existed, and all of them ache. But after a week of practice she is pleased with her progress. She may never reach Dilara's level of effortless skill, but now at least she can hold her ground.

They sit on high stools at a rooftop bar in Beyoglu with panoramic views over the Golden Horn. The glistening furrows of the water reflect the sodium orange glow of the city at night and the twin turrets of the brightly lit mosques. A pair of men in tight black t-shirts are staring at them from across the bar, making lewd gestures with their beer bottles every time Sarah allows her eye to drift in their direction.

Dilara is oblivious to the unwanted attention. "Will you go back?" she asks, sipping a milky white cocktail known as a 'Corpse Reviver'.

"I think I'm ready."

Dilara laughs. "You're never ready, until you do it."

Sarah toys with the question she has not dared to broach all week. "Will you tell Michael I was here?"

Dilara tilts her head to one side, nodding to the beat of the dance track that pumps out of the DJ booth. "Not if you don't want me to. But be careful. If you want to tread on Michael's toes, be sure you know what you're doing. Are those creeps bothering you?" she asks, noticing Sarah's discomfort about the company.

"It's nothing; best to ignore them."

"And let them go and try and intimidate the next pair of pretty girls? Why not fight back?"

"I can't start a fight in a crowded bar," Sarah protests.

"They started it. What they are doing is a step away from assault. Why not retaliate? Remember the move we practised to disarm someone with a broken bottle? This would be a perfect moment to try it out." Dilara's warm eyes stoke Sarah's courage. "Training is nothing without practice."

Sarah looks back to the pair of dark-browed chasers. One

61

of them mimes the act of fellatio with his beer bottle, his eyes sucking straight at Sarah. His friend grinds and snorts in encouragement.

She stalks across the crowded bar, adding a little Dilara-style sashay to her walk and watching the temperature rise in the pair of creeps as they think their attack has paid off.

"Can I have that bottle?" she asks, deadpan.

The fellating creep offers her the bottle of beer, neck tilted towards her lips.

She grabs his arm and twists it behind his back, setting her hip forward to capitalise on her strength while he is unprepared.

He tries to struggle out of her hold, to grab at her hair with his free hand, but she thumps her fist straight down onto his elbow. He recoils with a yelp of pain as she forces his trembling arm into a shoulder lock. He folds to the floor to escape the excruciating pressure on his joints and Sarah jumps on his back, knocking him off-balance and leaving him sprawled across the glitter-shot floor tiles. She grabs the bottle of beer from his grasping fingers and flings it in a well-aimed arc towards the bin behind the bar. The stunned barman stares at her, a cloth in one hand, a glass in the other frozen mid-polish.

The shuddering creep on the floor is helped to his feet by his friend who looks ripe to wreak revenge but is silenced by Dilara's round of applause.

Sarah returns calmly to their side of the bar and knocks back half of her cocktail.

"You've worked hard," Dilara says with evident pride in her pupil. "He'll think twice before leering at the next girl now." She raises her glass to Sarah in a toast.

"Thank you," Sarah says. "For everything."

Dilara rolls back her powerful shoulders. "It was fun. And if you're going back to Sierra Leone, be sure to try the lobster. It's to die for."

"You've been to Sierra Leone?"

"I've been to most places. The family business has many

interests. Manufacturing, mining, construction—my father set up the monster that we all now try to tame. You know, Sarah, in this game, when you ask for something, you need to offer something in return."

Of course she knows there would be a favour asked in return. But what does she have to offer someone like Dilara? "If there's anything I can do for—"

"Not now." Dilara squeezes Sarah's aching hand. "But I will not forget. One day I will come to you."

CHAPTER 12

Sarah flies from Istanbul to Brussels and straight on to Freetown. She tries calling Elias—to apologise for running away, to reassure him that she's ready to return, to hear the sound of his voice. But every time she tries his phone is off and her texts go unanswered. As she boards the flight to Freetown, her phone finally announces the longed-for message,

Elias: *'I knew you'd come back. Fixer will meet you at the airport with chopper tickets.'*

Sarah rereads the message, trying to hear in it his disarmingly deep monotone. She pictures his laughing eyes, his broad inviting smile, his playful winks that always make her giggle—but still it sounds disappointingly factual. And chopper tickets? Sarah can't help but feel a little disappointed that she's been deemed ready for the flying death-trap this time round. And no kiss.

*

The moment she steps off the plane in Freetown, the wall of hot humid air strikes her once again with its full-on assault to her senses. But this time she is prepared. There is something already familiar in the damp bloom, a puzzle piece sliding into place, something regained that had been forgotten.

Elias's fixer is waiting in the arrival hall—heavy brow and heavier overbite, wearing a greasy canvas shirt in moss green. He greets Sarah with a gruff nod and hands her a soggy envelope with her name on it, leaving her to struggle with a bag weighed down with books. No pink hearts.

"*Tenki*," Sarah smiles.

The Fixer stares at her, waiting.

"Oh, here." She hands over a folded bank note.

"Mm," he raises his chin, takes the note and leaves.

*

No one is waiting for her at the helipad, so Sarah flings her bag into the back of one of the idling taxis.

"You came back, Miss Sarah!" a bright pair of eyes meet hers in the rear-view mirror. Sarah recognises the tight curl of the eyelashes and the collection of talismans hanging from the mirror. "Ibrahim!" Her body floods with relief at seeing a friendly face.

"Elias told me you were gone?"

"I just needed to work through some things. Did you know I was coming?"

"Not tonight. But I always meet the helicopters from international flights. You never know when you'll meet a big tipper."

"I'll try not to disappoint."

They bump their way up the hill to the hotel that Elias recommended—not as picturesque as Pietro's but comfortable enough. Sarah takes Ibrahim's number as she hands over a generous tip. "I'll call you next time I need a bone shake."

The hotel has touches that speak of a grander time, now long forgotten: a large grandfather clock, its pendulum frozen and hands perpetually stuck at two o'clock; the lobby clad in dark wooden panelling riven with worm trails; a ceiling fan in pale raffia marred by a deep purple stain. Sarah lets herself into her room, a single bed with no mosquito net and the same red tiles on the floor as Pietro's. She throws down the threadbare white towel to cover the ground and keep the tiles from slithering in her sleep.

*

The next morning at breakfast, Sarah fills her plate with a stack of pineapple and papaya, three boiled eggs and four pieces of buttered toast.

"Do save some for the rest of us, won't you." A loud voice with a British accent, boarding-school posh. "You look like you haven't eaten in a week. I'd recommend the scrambled eggs. They are a startling colour but taste rather good."

Sarah looks up, annoyed to have been interrupted at breakfast. Her uninvited companion is tall, young and handsome in a way that grates. His delicate bone-china features are all a little too sharp, nose a little too thin, cheek bones a little too angular. They give a shrewish look to what would otherwise have been a beautiful face with its porcelain skin and watery blue eyes. He wears a crisp white shirt with expensive cufflinks.

"I'm sorry," Sarah says, ladling on a spoonful of scrambled eggs. "Do I know you?"

"I'm Chris. Sorry, you must be new. It's such a small world out here you begin to treat every sympathetic face as an old friend. Do forgive my appalling manners. Would you mind if I shared your table? It seems to be the only one clear."

Sarah glances round the restaurant to check. He does have a point. Reluctantly, she removes her bag to make room for Chris and begins eating while finding her page in the *Journal of Microbial Ecology*.

She needed a cover that would explain her presence in Sierra Leone, and preferably one that could take her to the more remote parts of the country without raising too many eyebrows. She settled on a PhD in biochemistry, specialising in leaf decay. Suitably obscure, full access to the jungle and unlikely to prompt too many curious questions. Always liking to do things properly, her luggage is full of the textbooks she is ploughing through to bolster her cover.

"Looks like a jolly read over breakfast," Chris chips in.

"It's work."

"Is it now?" Chris plucks the magazine out of Sarah's hand. "And do you really understand what this means?" He puts on a mock-serious voice and reads aloud, "'Fungi are able to produce a wide range of extracellular enzymes. This special ability allows them to attack efficiently the recalcitrant lignocellulose matrix that is undecomposable in other organisms.' It might as well be Greek."

"It's not supposed to be popular fiction," Sarah swipes the magazine out of his hand. "This one is actually quite accessible."

"So this is work, is it?" Chris grins at her as he pops in another forkful of bright yellow egg. His grin is wide and eager, like a schoolboy asking his parents for money.

"Well, study. Sadly no one pays me for it. But hopefully one day." Sarah is not in the mood to be dragged into a conversation about leaf mould over breakfast, but Chris seems unwilling to take the hint.

"I love staying here," he says. "You really do meet all sorts. It's usually mining types, consultants working for the European Union, mercenaries and the odd shifty type who could only be from a foreign intelligence agency. But you must be the first 'microbist' I've met."

"I'm a biochemist actually," Sarah says, defending her imaginary self.

"Of course you are. Don't mind me, I'm clueless about the sciences. I studied History, Politics, and History of Politics at A-Level, essentially so I could do the same thing three times and never had to go near a science lab or a quadratic equation ever again in my life."

"Uh-huh." Sarah moves on to attack her pile of fruit. The pineapple is piercingly sweet, but the papaya has the faint taste of talcum powder and alcohol. She eats it all the same.

"Why Sierra Leone of all places?" Chris asks, leaning back in his chair and stretching his long legs towards Sarah.

"I'm interested in the tropical forest. So little work has been done here, I like the idea of being able to look at something that no one else has studied before."

"And why not somewhere like Gabon? Primary rainforest in a nice stable autocracy? Surely that's an easier place to work for a…" He catches himself. "Well… for anyone, really."

"I like a challenge," Sarah says, immediately regretting the form of words that could be read as a flirtation. "Science isn't supposed to be easy," she adds. "What about you? Why are you here?" She isn't particularly interested in who Chris is, or what particular part of the white-saviour story he belongs to, but she knows that most people like nothing more than to talk about themselves. The best way to move a conversation away from where prying words might pick holes in her cover is to feign interest.

"Foreign Office," Chris says drily. "London desk, but they send me out from time to time to check the staff in the High Commission haven't gone native."

Chris is most definitely not her type—too fair, too blonde, too full of himself with that unearned cockiness of an over-privileged upbringing. And yet there is something; in spite of herself, Sarah finds him somehow intriguing. Something in the ruler-straight bearing, the confidence to approach a stranger and dive straight in as an old friend, the perfect fit of his well-made clothes. She tries to focus her attention on the purple tinge of his eyelids instead of his porcelain skin.

"Where are you going leaf digging?" he asks.

"Koidu. I have some contacts up there who are going to help with logistics."

"Do you need a lift?"

Sarah drops her journal. "Are you going?"

"As it happens, I am. I can't promise you a chopper, but you can have a seat in an air-conditioned High Commission vehicle. It's a hell of a lot more comfortable than the public bus."

Sarah agrees, wondering whether she would be able to stand

Chris's incessant chatter all the way up country. For the moment, it is the best option she has.

CHAPTER 13

The driver from the High Commission handles the brand-new Land Cruiser in complete silence. The ride is so smooth, even over the roughened laterite, that Sarah feels disorientated, her brain missing the jerks and bumps that her eyes tell her to expect. The strange detachment between vehicle and road, combined with the new car leather smell, soon make her queasy. She opens her window a crack to counter the icy blast of the air conditioning and tries to sleep. Chris keeps up his stream of questions and expat gossip even after she has closed her eyes, but eventually he gives up.

The heat in Koidu is shocking after the artificial chill of the car. Sarah seeks shelter under a tired-looking beach umbrella protecting a stall selling loaves of white bread.

"Welcome to Salone, beautiful Nightjar." Elias's arms wrap around her waist. "Fantastic to see you. I didn't think you'd make it so soon."

"Hello! I don't think we've met." Chris bounds out of the car and offers a hand to Elias to introduce himself.

"Chris," Elias repeats the name as if trying to give it more gravitas. He shoots him a dismissive look, his alpha male status clearly not threatened by the arrival of this skinny pretty boy.

Chris is undeterred. "I'm with the High Commission. If I had to guess, I'd say you're in mining." Chris smiles like a puppet with his strings pulled too tight.

"You don't have to guess, you could just ask," Elias says.

"Chris very kindly gave me a lift," Sarah jumps in.

"The High Commission has a project—"

"Very kind of you, thanks." Elias cuts him off, picking up Sarah's bag and throwing it into the back of his pickup truck. "What have you got in here? It weighs a tonne."

"Books."

"Shall we?" Elias holds open the door of the cab for her to get in.

"Thanks for the lift," Sarah says to Chris, embarrassed by Elias's rudeness but still glad of the excuse for a swift escape.

"Any time," Chris replies with a bow. "I'm at your service."

*

"Who was that clown?" Elias asks as they drive off.

"He seems pretty harmless," Sarah says.

"I didn't like the look of him. Way too slick. Who on earth comes up to Koidu in a formal dress shirt?"

"He was good for a ride." Sarah wishes she could erase all thoughts of Chris from Elias's mind. She is flattered by this display of jealousy, but she prefers the affectionate tone in which he greeted her, to this sniping.

"I'm sorry," he takes her hand and places it on his leg, laying his own hand gently on top. "I wanted it all to be better this time."

"Don't worry," Sarah squeezes his thigh. "It will. I know what I'm getting into this time. And I'm taking my malaria tablets like a good girl."

They drive for a moment in silence.

"How was London?" Elias asks.

Sarah doesn't know why she didn't tell Elias where she had been. He assumed she'd been to visit a friend in London. She didn't set him right. Her last time in Istanbul was a delicious weekend just the two of them. She doesn't want to tell him she went back without him.

"And why did you come back?" Elias asks, his voice bearing

71

no trace of accusation.

"For your smiling eyes," Sarah replies.

"Really?" Elias gives an exaggerated crinkly-eyed grin.

"And for Skarparov. He has to be made to pay."

"Well I'm glad to see you fired up. I've got some business to do this afternoon, and it's not for the faint-hearted."

*

They drive out of town, following a narrow rutted track deeper and deeper into the bush. At the centre of a small unnamed village, Elias stops the car under the shade of an enormous mango tree. The fruit hangs ripe from the branches and strikes the roof of the cab. The mud and thatch huts of the village seem deserted, but the quietness rankles. In the eery silence, Sarah feels sure they are being watched.

Elias grabs his battered yellow canvas satchel that goes everywhere with him. Looking at Sarah, a shadow of concern crosses his face. "Do you want to stay in the car? I shouldn't be long, but it might not be all that pretty."

"No, I'm coming. It can't be worse than last time," she says with forced cheerfulness, knowing full well that it could.

Inside the hut, a group of young men sit on the floor. The air is ripe with unwashed bodies, testosterone-laced sweat and a smell like wet cement. They all wear baggy combat trousers, grubby faded t-shirts and carry Kalashnikovs slung over their shoulders. As much as their presence intimidates—the blank eyed stares from blood-shot eyes, the prominent muscles on their arms, their casually-held weapons—there is something about them that Sarah finds almost pitiable. They look like bored teenagers at a youth club: lost, clueless and waiting for someone to tell them what to do.

They stare at Sarah with undisguised fascination but say nothing. Elias pulls out a wooden chair for Sarah, then sits down next to the men on the floor.

"Mr Khalil said he'll pay a fixed price," Elias begins, "but he said no to a percentage of the operations."

"That wasn't our offer," one of the boys says, sucking his teeth.

"It wasn't, but you'd be smart to take it. It's fixed and guaranteed income. You know what you'll get each month, and it will come on time with no need to wait for the monthly books."

The boy scratches under his arm and looks to the others. They are clearly happy for him to do all the talking. "And what about the gas?"

"I'm sure he'll agree to the gas," Elias says.

"You didn't ask him?"

"Not yet, but I'll make sure he understands what is expected of him. In return for these payments, you will guarantee full safety of Mr Khalil's operations. And you need to provide the locations of your camps in this area so that we can make sure you also get left alone." Elias unfolds a large map from his satchel, the yellowed paper wearing thin along the creases. He spreads it out in front of them and starts asking questions about their camps—who, how many, how far?

The rebel leader looks blankly at the map. The visual representation of the land clearly means nothing to him, but he describes their locations using his own points of reference—twenty minutes walk through the second track to the right, off the main road after the tall palm tree where the white ibis like to roost at night.

Elias notes down everything in his book, drawing rough sketches on the map based on his description.

Watching him write, the spokesman for the group grows nervous. "What you need the paper for?" he asks, stabbing at the map with the nose of his gun.

"Don't worry, it's just for me. The concession area covers this whole map, and there are plans for more mines. But we want to be sure to stay out of your way." He folds the map back into his bag. "I'll tell Mr Khalil you have a deal?"

"With the gas," the young man looks suspicious.

"With the gas," Elias nods.

*

"Who is Mr Khalil, and why has he got you doing his dirty work?" Sarah asks as soon as they are back in the car.

"He's one of the Lebanese mine operators that operate in Skarparov's concession. They've had increasing trouble with the rebels pushing into the mines – mostly drunk, high or looking for food. But as you can imagine, it puts the heebeegeebies up them."

"So you're sent out to negotiate the blood money?"

"They listen to me. They have an innate distrust of the Lebanese, but somehow if it comes from me they take it. And anything I can convince them to take, less than what Mr Khalil offers, I get to keep." Elias grins.

Sarah is quiet for the rest of the journey. There is something about seeing Elias elbow-deep in the negotiations, representing parties that really have nothing to do with him, that feels like a growing pressure squeezing her oesophagus. She knows that she needs him deep on the inside with Skarparov to help to bring him in. But seeing how much he enjoys his role as Kingmaker makes her wonder whether he is actually called to a different purpose.

Elias seems happy with the silence. The sun is over the horizon and the purple light of dusk has grown suddenly flat. Elias pushes the car at growling speed to make the distance before the full fall of night.

"Where to now?" Sarah asks, searching for something familiar in the landscape but finding only vague shapes beyond the headlights' cone of white.

"We're going home," Elias says, his eyes fixed on the road to read the bumps before hitting them.

"Home?"

"Well, home for now. I've been staying in an abandoned

tourist camp. I've no idea when anyone would have thought this was the place to invest, but it's hard to imagine what life would have been like here before the war. Freetown used to be known as the Athens of West Africa. They even had double-decker buses."

Sarah finds it hard to picture in a city that no longer even has a functioning set of traffic lights.

"It was probably abandoned in quite a hurry because most of the infrastructure is still here," Elias continues. "I've had to hook up my own generator and it took quite a bit of work to get the water system functional again. The forest has taken over most of it. But then, that's part of the charm." He pulls off the track and under a wooden archway now burnt black. "Here we are: home sweet home."

Through the soupy darkness, Sarah sees the shadow of low-lying thatched huts. Most of the windows are broken and only one hut has a full roof intact. The jungle is swiftly taking over the abandoned camp, moss and mildew grow up the once white walls and climbers crawl out of collapsed thatch. "Allow me to show you around," Elias grins.

*

They settle down to dinner at a vast table shaped like a surfboard, made from a coarse mosaic of broken tiles and fragments of glass and mirror.

Even after sunset, the heat is oppressive; the air heavy and tropical, teeming with life and decay.

"Apologies for the food," Elias says, fetching plates from the makeshift kitchen. "I had grand plans of getting in a proper meal for you and even a bottle of wine. But supplies had been pretty low on the ground this week. And I've not been back to Freetown since you left. So I'm afraid it's beer and tinned spaghetti. But I can promise you the very best of company."

"Sounds perfect," Sarah says, lighting a pair of citronella candles between them. "There. If you squint, it's a candlelit dinner for two. So tell me, what have you got on Skarparov?"

"He's in this as deeply as it comes," Elias says.

"What does he get from the rebels in return for the weapons?"

"Undisturbed access to the diamond areas, and no one asking too many questions about what he does with the product."

"Have you ever heard any mention of uranium?"

"Here in Sierra Leone? I don't think so. Why?"

"I heard rumours that there had been a find. It wouldn't surprise me if Skarparov was involved."

"That might explain the influx of odd visitors coming to Koidu recently."

"What sort of odd?"

"Could be a meeting of the disunited nations—Libyans, Iranians, Pakistanis, Russians, Chinese. I've met all kinds of people, but they never have a clear story of what they're up to other than research."

"Hanging about Skarparov?"

"No, just in town. The late-night bars are full of unlikely faces. I imagine Skarparov is keeping well out of it. He's got enough on his plate keeping his current patron happy. The more you feed the snake the more his appetite grows. Foday Sankoh wants a helicopter next."

"But that's another violation of UN sanctions. Surely then we could turn Skarparov into the UN? Or Interpol?"

"There's nothing on him. Nothing official, nothing in writing. It would be my word along with the testimony of a bunch of rebels. Don't underestimate him, Sarah. He's been in this game a hell of a lot longer than you."

Sarah doesn't answer.

"If you're so obsessed with getting him, why don't you just take him out?" Elias asks, cracking open a second bottle of beer, using the empty bottle as an opener. "Or just tell the CIA—they'd kill him."

"That isn't justice. I need to do this properly."

"So it's personal?"

"In a way. Did you see this?" She unfolds the news article from her bag.

Elias reads, stifling a laugh. "Wow, someone really wants to drop you in the shit."

"It's not funny. Ibragimov is dead. Unless I can prove that Skarparov was behind that attack, it's going to look like Ibragimov planned it with my help."

"He's dead? I thought the Americans had him?"

"So did I."

"Anyway, that's just dodgy journalism. Surely the British government would back you up if anyone bothers to investigate?"

Sarah doesn't want to tell him that the only person who knew what she was really doing there might may have been behind the leak. "Okay, but think of what Skarparov was willing to do in Tbilisi. What he's doing here. Think of what will happen to all that Russian kit—every body that will end up a discarded piece of meat thanks to his munificence. Could we get him to put his name on the helicopter deal? Then we'd have something, wouldn't we? Could you arrange it?"

Elias takes a deep swig of beer. "I've told you before: Skarparov isn't the problem here."

"What?"

"Ending this war is the problem. You have to be an opportunist and use whatever advantages that gives."

"If you follow that logic, you'd let everyone get away with everything."

"Skarparov himself might have entirely selfish motives for being here. But my working for him gives me access."

"Yes, to all his papers and operations."

"I meant to rebels. Their camps, their organisational structure. I probably know more about how they work here than anyone. And it's all here," he fishes his moleskin notebook out of his trusty yellow satchel. "Ready to hand over to the good guys."

"You're not telling me that's really why you're doing all this? You're really going to stop the war? Are you sure you're not just an adventure junky who's enjoying playing kingpin in the jungle?" Sarah regrets the dig the moment the words leave her mouth. Her clumsy criticism pricks a hole in his joy—his face darkens, his ebullient presence retreats.

Abruptly he returns to the kitchen. Without him near, a fear creeps into Sarah alone at the oversized table. The darkness around her is all-encompassing, impenetrable and full of strange noises. Even the fragments of glass pressed into the mosaic on the table look jagged and sharp, reflecting the light from the hurricane lamps at unnatural angles.

Elias slams another two beers on the table. "It's good to know what you really think. Yes, I enjoy it and, as it turns out, I'm pretty good at this. But don't for a moment think I ever forget its horror." He lights a cigarette, blowing smoke towards the hanging lamp. "I came out here for you."

"I didn't mean to sound ungrateful. I'm sorry, I wasn't thinking." She reaches across to take his hand. "Tell me about your book: who are the good guys in this mess?"

Elias pauses, as if weighing up whether she genuinely wants to hear.

"Chief Norman," he mumbles. "He's the leader of the Civil Defence Forces and the Kamajors. They're a scary-looking bunch and claim their magic powers can repel bullets. But since the professional mercenaries were chucked out, they're the most effective force left. Chief Norman has brought them on side for the government. If we could get them to be supported in the way that Skarparov and many others like him are supporting the rebels, I'm sure we could turn things around." He speaks with passion, but with none of his earlier warmth.

"But surely getting rid of Skarparov is a step in the right direction?"

"I knew you wouldn't let that drop."

"He should be brought to the International Criminal Court for what he's doing here."

"If that's what you want, you'd need to go to the Russians.

They are the only ones who could provide evidence of the weapons transfer. And I don't see why they'd want to help."

"There must be some evidence. Can't you look? Agree to do the helicopter deal and see what else it gives you access to."

"I'll keep my eyes open. But you should think about whether that is really what you want."

*

They lie side by side on the foam mattress. The humidity hangs like a weight leaving Sarah's mind blowsy and full. It is too hot for physical contact, her skin too clammy to be touched. Heat and sweat radiate from Elias, even a hand's distance away. Never before has she lain so close to his lean and taut body, so close to the magical touch of his skin, without intertwining their limbs in a jigsaw puzzle embrace.

And yet it is not just the heat keeping them apart. The air is filled with two minds brewing, creating a physical space between them. She knows there is an element of her hunt for Skarparov that borders on the obsessive. He is an unfinished puzzle; he humiliated her, and he has never been made to pay. All thoughts of him explode in her head, taking up too much space, growing and multiplying like a tropical creeper, swamping all perspective.

Does Elias really understand, or is he starting to think she is delusional? He came here for her, but that isn't why he stayed. She bolted when all had cut too close to the darkness. But he remained. He continued his work with Skarparov. What is driving him to sell his soul to the very man she is trying to destroy? Is he serious in thinking his efforts could stop this hell of a war that has rumbled on for over a decade, or is he just having too much fun?

The night is stiflingly still. Sweat, rich with the smell of stale beer, runs in rivulets into the squeaky foam mattress. No trace of breeze to bring relief. Sarah lies awake facing the prospect of a long and sleepless night. Until suddenly the noises stop.

The constant hum of the insects cuts off. The night birds cease their eery call and the rustle of the leaves falls still. The night is suspended, as if the world outside is holding its breath. A baby preparing to wail, eyes squeezed shut.

In one snap the air is alive, pounding, teaming, cold and brand new. The noises come from all around like a roar—the pounding on the roof, the splattering and quaking of the leaves, the drops bouncing off the pounded earth floor outside. A tropical rainstorm envelopes the camp and in an instant, the heaviness of the day is gone.

Elias sits bolt upright, a broad grin spreading across his freckled cheeks. The light has returned to his troubled eyes. Sarah takes his hand and leads him outside to feel the cool water on their skin. They strip off their clothes to surrender more of their bodies to the cold caress of the rain. Sarah reaches to touch Elias's shoulder, he pulls her towards him, their skin cool and slippery and finally able to breathe. Slowly they dance to the rhythm of the rain, naked feet splattering on mud, fat rain drops hammering on the crown of their heads. Water splashes off their eyelashes, tasting sweet and new in their mouths. They dance and laugh, their bodies find each other hungrily and blindly until the distance between them washes away.

CHAPTER 14

The next few days are spent in the bliss of a tropical honeymoon: always too hot, always sweating, but in the complete abandoned bliss of being together, alone, in a forgotten corner of the world. Being with Elias, whether relaxing in the hammock or paddling the canoe to watch hippos, recharges her soul. She even manages not to ruin the mood too often by mentioning Skarparov, but her mind is busy assessing the board, playing through possible approaches and trying to second-guess his response.

She feels too in the dark. Too far removed from her opponent to be able to read him. She hasn't seen him in the flesh since he beat her at chess in Tbilisi. But so much has happened since then. She needs to see him again, to read his mood up close and sniff out what other distractions are playing in his mind that she might be able to use.

"George is heading back to Freetown tomorrow in the chopper," Elias says, draining the juice from the last tin of peaches. "He said he'd save us a spot if we needed a lift."

"I was thinking," Sarah spears a glistening yellow half-moon. "I want to meet Skarparov. Do you think it would be mad to let him know I'm here?"

Elias shrugs. "He let you tail him around the Caucasus, didn't he?"

"But that was different; he didn't know who I was then. And I hadn't yet ruined his plans to assassinate two presidents."

"He must have known from the day you turned up asking

questions about his Foundation that you were from MI6."

"Are you saying I'm no good at staying in cover?"

"I'm saying he knows far more than you give him credit for. In fact he probably knows you're here already. You might as well be polite and say hello. There's a big reception at the High Commission tomorrow for some made-up holiday—Europe Day or something. It's not really my scene, but Skarparov should be there. You can go and schmooze with the Freetown elite while I stock up on some more tinned spaghetti."

"Perfect. But there's something I want to do before we go."

*

Stepping across the Chief's threshold, Sarah braces herself on the doorframe, not trusting her legs to hold her. She shakes hands with the Chief and greets Fattmatu with a hug, feeling all the while that her body is not under her control, that the shaking might return at any moment. She sits on the sagging bench, averting her eyes from the spot where she watched Fattmatu begging for mercy, too scared herself to act. She notices the stains in the wooden coffee table which the rebels doused with kerosene. The Chief and his daughter sit opposite, clearly wary of this foreign stranger and no doubt reliving the same memories.

"I just wanted to say how sorry I am for what happened," Sarah says, her voice shaking and a sourness of tears filming her eyes.

"It was not your fault." The Chief speaks brusquely, scarcely able to look at her.

"But I'm sorry if anything about our presence made things worse for you. I am so sorry for what happened to you, Fattmatu; that I couldn't help."

"There is nothing anyone can do to stop them. They are animals made hungry by our fear," the Chief says.

"Is there anything I can do for *you*?" Sarah draws her chair closer to Fattmatu who is staring at the floor, not meeting Sarah's eye and allowing her father to answer on her behalf. But it is really to Fattmatu that Sarah wants to speak. "I am going back to Freetown now, but we will be back soon. Is there anything I can bring you? Do you need medicines? Or do you have a favourite food that is not available here?"

Fattmatu looks embarrassed and studies her feet.

"Can I bring you some hair oil? A comb? Some cloth?" Sarah wishes she could get closer inside the head of this damaged girl to guess what would make her happy. She is under no illusions that she can really help her, or can do anything to erase what was done. But she hopes to find a small gesture that would make her smile. Anything to bring back the open, curious grin that greeted them at their last visit.

"Foday Sankoh," the Chief intones, spitting out the syllables as if they contained a deadly venom. "He hides away in his luxury villa in Freetown while his army of the forgotten and the abused are free to wreak havoc over the innocent of this country. You want to help?" He fixes Sarah with his bloodshot eyes, a vein pulsing on the side of his temple. "You can bring me the head of the snake."

CHAPTER 15

The British High Commissioner's residence is named after the spot where the Magna Carta was signed. There is not much else to link the 1960s building at the top of the Freetown's fanciest hill to a meadow in rural Surrey, but the architects obviously dreamed big.

Sarah is glad to have arrived by foot, walking down from her hotel along the broken edges of the tarmac road. The entrance is in chaos as drivers and diplomats negotiate the temporary crash barriers that prevent any vehicle from approaching the residence. Security this evening is clearly on high alert. She slips through the queue of white Land Cruisers and into the garden, wearing her black linen dress, slightly crumpled after a week stuffed in a holdall, her shoulders wrapped in a pale pink scarf, fastened with a large safety pin to approximate an elegant stole. But as she surveys the crowd she realises that elegance is not a high priority. Diplomatic 'smart casual' is a motley collection of boxy suits and chinos, brightened only by the occasional woman in brightly patterned local fabrics and a handful of military types in full uniform.

She stops a boy carrying a tray of gin and tonics. After a week of lukewarm beer, even the sound of the ice cubes clinking in the glass is mildly hypnotic. She wants something stiff to steady her nerves. The evening's goal is clear—an approach to Skarparov and a chance to root out as much as possible from the Freetown crowd about the uranium find. But a direct approach to Skarparov is a gamble. In Tbilisi he had only ever been charming to her—Elias was right. But at the time he thought she posed him no threat. Would he still be as welcoming now?

Sarah nods to Pietro, the Italian from the beach resort, wearing another loud Hawaiian shirt and talking to a man with spiky hair, flecked with grey. His face looks permanently cheerful and his large solid cheesehead and sturdy build could only be Dutch or Afrikaner. The High Commissioner is easy to spot as the only expat wearing a suit, albeit one that could only pass in the tropics. His thick grey hair needs to be regularly pushed away from his incongruous black eyebrows.

"Good evening, Your Excellency," Sarah says, offering her hand. "I bring greetings from Alistair MacLeod in Tbilisi."

"You know Alistair! God it is a small world, is he well? Still as colourful as ever?"

"Always entertaining."

"And what brings you to Freetown? You're not the new DFID girl?"

"No, not anymore." Sarah is sorry to no longer have the access and protection that came with pretending to work for the Department of International Development. But since she cut ties with Michael, all official links to government went with him. "I've taken a sabbatical to finish my PhD in biochemistry," she says. "I'm just here to do some field work."

"Well that's a first. We have all sorts passing through here, but mostly journalists, NGOs and miners." He looks at Sarah with a hint of suspicion. "You're not in the mining industry, are you? There has been a flurry of new arrivals recently."

"For the uranium?" Always worth putting out a line.

"How on earth do you know about that?" the High Commissioner asks. "It's supposed to be top secret. This is a hopeless town for gossip. Or are you here to look at the samples?"

"Yes," Sarah improvises. "I'm curious to see if the isotopes are visible in the leaf matter. You wouldn't happen to know who I could talk to about getting access to some of the samples, would you?"

The High Commissioner laughs as if she's just asked for tea with Her Majesty. "Not a chance, I'm afraid. The whole thing is shrouded in complete secrecy. We've all been asking for updates but whoever is behind the find is keeping their cards close to their chests. I'd have a word with those two over there," he points out a pair of grey men in dark suits huddled in the corner talking in stiff whispers. "They're sure to be after the same thing. But please don't go getting yourself into trouble, we're understaffed as it is without having to send out a consular team to rescue you from the forest floor." Sarah notices that his upper lip scarcely moves as he talks, paralysed by a lifetime of carrying on in the face of adversity.

"Funnily enough, I felt safer out in the bush than I do here in Freetown," Sarah says, thinking of her honeymoon escape.

"I'm afraid that is a false security. Although, yes, things are hotting up here now too." As if on cue an ear-shattering explosion erupts from behind the perimeter wall. The babble of conversation silences and Sarah feels the chill of fear passing through the crowd. All eyes turn to the High Commissioner who stands, head down, with a brick-like walkie-talkie pressed to his ear. Moments later he straightens up, waving his arms to reassure his guests—it was just a car backing into one of the temporary barriers. Nothing to worry about. The speed of his reaction and the jumpiness of his guests make clear that everyone is expecting more.

"You see?" he says to Sarah when the hubbub of conversation around them is at last restored. "Everyone's on edge. Especially those of us who were here last time the rebels arrived in Freetown… It breaks my heart that we have to watch on, powerless to help, drinking our gin and tonics, while the country slips back into chaos around us."

"I would have thought you were better placed than most to make a difference," Sarah prods.

"So would I. Sadly my London masters have decided to stop listening to their man in country. It honestly wouldn't take more than a few properly organised, well-equipped troops on the ground to bring this almighty suffering to an end. I'm sending a special report to London tomorrow to make the case. Perhaps this time they might read it."

An elegant Chinese lady interrupts the High Commissioner to present the congratulations of the Chinese Ambassador on this celebration of European cooperation. Sarah watches the interpreter work between the two representatives, whispering translations into the ear of the Ambassador with lips painted coral red like a fresh ripe persimmon. She is too striking to fade into the background of the conversation in her dress that looks painted with real camellias, her hair held in an elegant chignon above her neck with not a wisp out of place despite the heat. But her posture and body language give full reverence to her companion, whose words she renders in perfect English.

Behind her, Sarah can hear a conversation tip over from heated discussion to all-out shouting match. The primary offender seems to be a slippery-looking man with a Belgian flag on his lapel and round moon glasses smeared with fingerprints. The redness of his nose can only have been achieved through many years of functional alcoholism. He stands with his arms folded, legs wide apart looking down at the feisty woman shouting at his chest.

"Who are you to criticise the Kamajors?" she bellows, her voice resonant and deep, bolstered by the solid mass of her bosom resplendent in iridescent peacock green. Sarah half expects a bright tail feather to flick out as part of her display.

"I just said I thought they were part of the problem," the Belgian boozehound replies, looking amused by the vehemence of her response. "They have no organisation, no leadership, they are accountable to no one. Just look at them with their feathers and animal skins—how can you put the hopes of the country in the hands of a stone-age militia?"

"They are our heroes," the woman declares in a strong Sierra Leonean accent, poking her finger deep into the Belgian's chest.

"They are protecting their families, their homes, their country. What have you done to help?"

The Belgian laughs nervously and looks around for someone to extract him from her onslaught.

"You stand here talking, talking, like you know *all* there is to know, but they are the ones who do something about it." The fearsome woman draws herself up, pushes back her head dress that has slipped down in her outrage, and makes a loud tutting noise that comes from the roof of her mouth.

"The UN are here with one of the largest peacekeeping forces ever deployed," the Belgian says. "ECOMOG are here. Why do you need the magic witchdoctors?"

"The UN are here. ECOMOG is here. But show me what they have done to stop the war? They are just as incompetent as our own bureaucrats—fighting over the spoils of the customs department while blind to our future." The Belgian diplomat looks horrified. Sarah, however, is keen to hear more. She pushes herself forward, offering her hand to the woman, allowing the Belgian to slip away from the line of fire.

"Pleasure to meet you, I'm Sarah Black."

"Mammy Kamara," the lady nods neatly, a hint of misgiving in her eyes. She shakes Sarah's hand in a firm grip.

"I couldn't help but overhear you talking to that gentleman about the Kamajors," Sarah says.

"That man is no gentleman. Did you hear him? Talking like he knows all there is to know. Here? In my country? People like him make my blood boil."

"I think he'll think twice now before venturing any unfounded opinions," Sarah says with a smile.

"I wish you were right, my dear. But these men, they don't listen, you know? They nod and smile at the crazy African lady and then they carry on like you was never there."

"It can only be their loss."

A man in full Sierra Leonean military uniform stands next to Mammy Kamara, listening to their conversation and smiling at

Sarah with an unnerving familiarity. He is wearing camouflage print top to toe, heavy black boots and a maroon beret at a jaunty angle over one eye.

"Sarah, you're here but you never called?" he says with an unreadable stare.

"I…I didn't…" The uniform throws her. She hasn't met any soldiers, has she? And why *would* she have called him? Then she notices the tight curl of his eyelashes. "Ibrahim? Is that you under there?"

"Yes, ma'am." He clicks his heels together and salutes with a grin.

"Where did the uniform come from?"

"I'm in the army."

"I thought you were a taxi driver?"

"I have to make money somehow; the soldiers have not been paid beyond our rice ration for months."

"And you find the time to manage both?"

"I have to. Actually," he draws out every syllable of the word, "I'm a piano tuner, but as there are only two pianos in the whole of Freetown it's not a great money-maker. One of them is here in the High Commission, but I don't think His Excellency plays enough to make it go out of tune."

"Where did you learn to do that?"

"My father taught me. He worked at the school for the blind—they have the other one."

"Does your father still play?" Sarah asks.

"My father passed," he says with a quiet reverence, "but my mother always says he was the best player in all of Freetown."

"And your mother is always right," Mammy Kamara interrupts.

"This is your mother?" Sarah asks.

"Mammy Kamara is the head of the Market Women Trading Association," Ibrahim says proudly. "She and her women reign supreme at the Victoria Park Market. Between them, these ladies know everything about everything that goes on in Freetown."

"Do you know any of the Kamajor leaders? I've a friend who would love to meet them," Sarah asks, hoping this formidable woman might be a lead for Elias in his hunt for the good guys.

"We know everyone. Come to the market and talk to some of my ladies. We'll find you anyone you want to meet."

"I'd be delighted."

"Ibrahim," she pinches at Sarah's arm, "why you always find the little skinny ones. She no get body. We need to feed you up, you eat fufu?"

"Um," Sarah has seen the bags of pounded cassava roots with plantain for sale in trays at the side of the road, pounded and mixed to a starchy ball of dough.

"My mammy makes the best fufu in Freetown." Ibrahim places a protective arm around his mother's shoulders.

"Come and see us." Mammy Kamara pulls Sarah in for a tight embrace, patting affectionately at her shoulders. "You'll not leave Freetown with that skinny chicken body."

"I promise," Sarah says, released from the sturdy bosom.

The dig of two sharp fingers in either side of her waist makes her jump forwards. From the intimacy of the gesture, she feels sure it must be Elias, come after all to take advantage of the High Commission's hospitality. Her face falls when she sees Chris.

"Hello you," he says, schoolboy grin cranked up to show off his deep dimples. "I noticed your glass was empty and brought you a refill." He hands her another icy gin and tonic. "I'm on duty tonight, got to do my bit as a gracious host."

Sarah stares at him, the condensation from the glass dripping over her fingers. She is still in shock at his shameless invasion of her personal space but he continues, intimate as an old friend.

"How was your Koidu trip? I take it from the fact that you completely disappeared with that red-headed chap that you were having fun?"

"It was very productive."

"He works for Skarparov, doesn't he? What's he got to do with leaf litter?"

"He's an old friend, helping me with logistics."

"Have you met the man himself? Fascinating chap: such a broad range of interests and so very dedicated to this country." Chris's manner is so dry, it is hard to read whether he is taking the piss.

"Skarparov?" Sarah asks, doing her best to look clueless. This is not a conversation she expected to have with Chris.

"I think he's around somewhere," he says. "Here, let me introduce you."

Sarah's chest tightens. She takes a deep swig of her drink. She came tonight to approach Skarparov, but on her own terms. Not with Chris and his irritating familiarity on hand to watch.

Chris interrupts a conversation between a tall dark-haired man and shorter man in navy blazer with large gold buttons—Skarparov. His suspiciously coloured hair is swept back from his forehead to show the sharp point of a widow's peak and he stands with his paunch held high, arms slightly apart from his body. A stance that says, 'this is me, take what you will'.

"Hello, Viktor," Chris shakes his hand. His whole manner seems to shift as he makes his approach. Gone the schoolboy grin and eager-to-please bounce; in its place his body language switches to something far more suave, a polite but serious smile, one eye slightly closed in a look of cultivated modesty. He now looks the erudite diplomat rather than the curious puppy Sarah first met. She is surprised by his chameleonic transformation.

Skarparov greets him warmly. "Can I introduce a friend of mine?" Chris asks. "This is Sarah, she's a leaf expert."

"Sarah," Skarparov squeezes her hand, taking her in with an unflinching gaze. His opal eyes pop from deep pouches of skin that give him a disarmingly innocent look. But Sarah knows not to be fooled by the wide-eyed expression. This is a man capable of unscrupulous violence against anyone who stands in his way. He brings her knuckles to his lips for the swiftest of kisses before releasing his grip. "*Enchanté.*"

"It's a pleasure to meet you," Sarah plays along, mortified that she is now going to have to rely on Skarparov not to give her game away to Chris. She feels an unwanted flush of blood to her cheeks and ears.

"A leaf expert? How intriguing," he smiles. "That's a new one."

"The microbial communities in the leaf litter of Sierra Leone have been very poorly explored," Sarah says, embracing the full absurdity of her situation.

"Perhaps its's one for Sergio here. Can I present Sergio from the European Union Delegation?"

The tall, meticulous man nods at Sarah, offering a slender hand with long pale fingers. He wears bright yellow statement glasses that could only have belonged to a European technocrat.

"Congratulations," Sarah smiles, raising her glass.

"I'm sorry?" Sergio looks to Skarparov for clarification.

"On Europe Day; isn't that what we're celebrating?" Sarah asks.

"Of course, of course. Celebrating our cooperation," Sergio nods.

"Sergio," Skarparov says, "do you have room in the program for a project on leaf decay? I'm sure this young lady could do with some funding for her research." He puts his hand on Sarah's arm, his grip a little too tight. "She's terribly... persistent."

"Only if you will run it, Viktor." Sergio pats Skarparov on the back. "The man is a wonder," he says to Sarah. "The only projects that run well here, all go through him. He is the only one of our implementers who puts in the time and effort to really get things done. You should see what he's doing to the customs department."

"Really?" says Sarah, her turn to suppress a smile. How many favours was Skarparov buying for himself by throwing EU money at the customs department? "I'd love to hear about that."

"Come, Sarah, there is a fascinating plant over here that I want your opinion on. Excuse us, gentlemen." Skarparov takes Sarah's arm and walks her towards the edge of the garden. She sees Chris smirking as he watches them depart. Once out of earshot, Skarparov lets out a fat laugh. "Leaf expert?!" he asks. "How on earth did you dream up that one?"

"Saviour of the customs department? I bet you were pleased when you stitched that up."

"Ah but it's worth it just to hear dear Sergio fawning," he says gleefully.

Sarah feels once more the niggle of tropical creeper that is now firmly lodged in her brain. Has she got this all wrong? Is Elias right and this is just a mad personal vengeance mission and not a legitimate quest for justice? This man was willing to kill thousands in Tbilisi, to attack the leader of the free world and drag a country full of post-revolutionary optimism back into the dark. And now, his weapons bring fuel to this endless conflict. All so that he can make enormous profit from the diamonds. And yet here he is in the High Commissioner's garden being fussed over and feted by diplomats and even joking with Sarah as if they were old friends. Is she the only one outraged?

"So, here is Sarah come to work out what I'm up to?" he says, his face wide as a happy cat. "Am I right? Oh please tell me I am. I would be so disappointed if you have a bigger, badder target to chase now."

"You flatter yourself, Viktor. I'm here on holiday. And for the leaves of course," she sips her drink.

"And Elias?" he asks.

Sarah gives a non-committal nod. There is no point denying the connection, but she doesn't want to risk damaging Elias's position. "He can be very useful," she says with a suggestive smile.

"He is fast becoming my most useful employee. He can get things done in a way that everyone else seems to find impossible. And what about you?" He turns to face her, so close he is almost pinning her tropical shrubbery. "Why don't you also come to work for me? You're bright, you're persistent, you're clearly intrepid or you wouldn't consider this a holiday destination. I could always find work for someone of your calibre."

"You need help with the uranium deal?" Sarah asks boldly.

"Uranium deal?" Skarparov's eyebrows push up to a point in the centre of his forehead, his lips purse in a pout. "I have no idea what you're talking about."

"Of course you do. There's been a find in country, samples are changing hands. Are you trying to tell me you're really not involved?"

"I am a man of peace," Skarparov says, his head tilted to one side. "What interest would I have in uranium?"

"A man of peace?" Sarah laughs, thinking it another joke, but Skarparov's warmth falters.

"I'd like you to think about my offer, Sarah," he says. His eyes have lost their sweetness and his broad smile suddenly doesn't fit his face. "If you decide not to join me, I will have to assume you're against me. It's your choice. Elias can tell you, I'm very fair."

"Thank you," Sarah steps back towards the comfort of the crowd. "But I'm not in the jobs market at the moment."

"Oh? I heard through the grapevine that you and Michael broke up?"

"Who told you that?" Did Michael mentioned her during their chat in Amsterdam? Or is Dilara passing information both ways?

"A mutual friend," Skarparov says with a cryptic smile, his eyes drifting over Sarah's shoulder. He acknowledges someone behind her with a short nod and checks his watch. "Excuse me, Sarah. There's someone I need to see. Do think about my offer. And come and play a game of chess with me again one time."

Sarah watches him walk away. The combination of tropical heat and generously poured gin exaggerate the sudden swaying of the lawn beneath her. Her heart flicks unsteadily but her brain is sharp and alert, like the peak of a chemical high. She is not so I to be won over by Skarparov's slippery charm and miss the menace behind his elegant manners. But she enjoys the gambler's buzz to have taken a step forward. She has made her opening gambit, and is curious to see his next move.

Amid the crowd of sweating expats and suit-stiff locals she suddenly feels out of place—a late night reveller stumbling into the early morning commute. She needs a moment to collect herself before diving back into the crowd to seek out the potential uranium leads. Slipping through the classical pillars and into the marble entrance hall of the Residence, the cool air envelopes her like a cloak.

Photos of visiting dignitaries smile down from the walls of the guest bathroom next to a large letter from the Queen marking the opening of the residence. Sarah wonders what Her Majesty would make of being relegated to the toilets. She splashes cold water on her face, dries her hands with a pink fluffy towel hanging on a golden ring, and marvels at the freely flowing water spouting from the taps. Elias had made an effort to provide privacy for her in their make-shift bathroom arrangements in the jungle, but an extra shower curtain did not make the drop toilet any less primitive. By comparison, the black and white tiles, gleaming with fresh bleach, feel like the height of luxury. Sarah sits on the closed lid of the toilet, allowing the cool air and solvent smell to revive her stupefied brain.

She studies the black and white chessboard of the bathroom tiles, trying to pin down what pieces are still in play and how to line up her next move. It was a stroke of luck that the High Commissioner confirmed the uranium rumours. There must be other people here who would be more willing than him to spill what they know. If uranium really is the reason that this motley collection are pouring into Freetown, it would no doubt have sparked Skarparov's interest. And if Skarparov is involved, then perhaps Michael also wants in on the deal. Turning a blind eye to a conventional weapons transfer is one thing, but did his perfidy really stretch to allowing fuel for nuclear weapons to fall into the wrong hands? The tiles seem to swirl in the bleach-laced air. She has to find out what interest Michael has in Skarparov, and she's certain the uranium find is the missing link.

She leaves the bathroom in search of the dodgy-looking pair the High Commissioner pointed out, but is intercepted by a man in a loose-fitting black shirt and black trousers. He is not much taller than Sarah, but his solid figure and patrician bearing create the impression of stature. His thick grey hair grows high on his forehead and the white around his temples highlights his black brows. His wide cheeks and soft beard have a jovial teddy-bear charm, but for the pink scar that runs from his nose to his shiny cauliflower ear.

"Escaping the heat or come to poke around the Residence while no one is looking?" he asks, with a definite look of mischief. His words are carefully annunciated, with just a trace of Russian in the vowels.

"Looking for the ladies' room, and you?" she asks, matching his tone of familiarity.

"I thought I might try a little of both," he smiles. "In which closets do you think the High Commissioner keeps his skeletons? Should we try the bedrooms?"

"I've no idea." Sarah edges towards the doorway.

"Don't worry, I'm only teasing. I just needed a moment out of that never-ending heat. I don't know how anyone copes with it all day long. Can you imagine what it feels like for a boy who grew up in Siberia? The most we ever knew of summer was the snow melting and the mosquitoes. At least that's one thing that makes me feel at home." His gaze falls on Sarah's bare arms and the rash of angry red welts gained from a week in the jungle. "It seems you are very tasty. But you mustn't scratch them. Vodka on a piece of cotton wool will bring relief."

"I'll be sure to try it." Sarah continues to move towards the door, eager to escape his uncomfortable intimacy.

"It's good to finally meet you, Sarah," he smiles, holding out his hand.

How the hell does he know her name? "I'm sorry, do I know you?"

"No, not yet, but I believe you and I might be after the same thing."

"What's that?"

"What everyone scuffing their best shoes on the grass outside wants to get their hands on. The uranium."

Has this stranger been reading her thoughts in the bathroom?

"Do you know who's selling it?"

"If I knew that, I wouldn't be talking to you." He lifts one quizzical eyebrow. "I've heard that high-grade samples have already been handed out to potential buyers. But no one is talking about who. I wonder if perhaps the RUF are protecting them in the mining areas? I wouldn't put it past Foday Sankoh to have got in first. How else could they get away with all this secrecy?"

"And how are you planning to find out?"

"That's where I want your help. Well, actually the help of your friend in the jungle. He must have an idea what's going on."

Does he mean Elias? "I'll tell him you're interested," she says, careful not to confirm his name in case this mysterious rival is just fishing for information.

He hands her a business card. Thick white card, no logo and no name, just a local phone number in an elegant black font. "Call me if you ever want to swap war stories." As his smile widens, his double-lidded eyes narrow into creases. "I'm off to explore," he gives her a mischievous wink and strolls off towards the bedrooms.

"But I don't even know your name?" Sarah calls after him.

"Oh? I heard you were looking for me. Kuznetsov," he says, looking back over his shoulder, "Nikolay Kuznetsov."

He is gone before Sarah can respond.

This, finally, is Kuznetsov. The name that was whispered into her earhole by the foul breath of Ibragimov. From his CIA interrogation room, Ibragimov named Kuznetsov as the Russian KGB handler responsible for the weapons transfer to Skarparov as payment for the attack in Tbilisi. Kuznetsov is presumably here in Freetown looking for return on his investment. Could he really be the help she needs to bring down Skarparov? At least he wouldn't be fooled by the saviour of Freetown line. Or is he just the competition?

CHAPTER 16

Michael always arrives late to the weekly meeting of the 'cross-Whitehall crisis group'. He is only really interested in Sierra Leone, but they insist on working through the agenda in alphabetical order. There is no point in him sitting through sob stories from Burundi and Chad. He strides smartly through the door of the Locarno suite conference room in the Foreign and Commonwealth Office and pulls up a high-backed chair next to Beverley Moreton, the Africa Director. She welcomes him with her sweetest smile, rearranging her papers to give him more space at the table, but the twitch of her fingers towards her blue enamel hair slide gives away her irritation at his interruption.

Michael is old enough to remember these rooms as they had been: a warren of plasterboard hutches in forlorn shades of beige. But following a full restoration, the room is once more as imposing as its architects had intended. False ceilings have been knocked away, partition walls destroyed, post-war carpets ripped up and the coffered ceiling, with its Corinthian capitals and gilded beams, restored to its full grandeur. Plaques bearing national arms of faraway lands shine in pastel colours highlighted with gold leaf. The polished table reflects the light cast by the elaborate chandelier. Michael always enjoys the feeling of imperial significance that the room can not help but imbue.

Beverley introduces him as the Team Leader in the Security Coordination team. It is always a grey area how open he should be about his actual role. Everyone in this room will have full developed-vetting security clearance so there is no real need to hide behind his public-friendly title. But you never knew who might suddenly decide to be antagonistic. It is easier to stick with the description on his business card.

He surveys the room while the others chew through their discussion of Rwanda. The Treasury and Ministry of Defence representatives he knows from previous meetings; both can be relied on to trot out the pretentious pontifications of people who think they're important. The DFID woman looks unobtrusive—no one would listen to her anyway. Beverley, clearly enjoying the chance to finally sit at the head of the table, chairs the meeting with management-course magnanimity—allowing everyone to talk but never for too long, seeking consensus on all decisions and expertly kicking each can a little further along the road. Only the man from the Cabinet Office is new. He looks like the typical eccentric they wheel out when they don't feel the need to send anyone serious. He wears a green checked shirt with a silk cravat and his eyebrows are so bushy he must have combed them out on purpose. As Jeff Black smiles benignly at the group, Michael is struck by a flash of recognition. Have they met before? Michael's memory for faces is professionally strong but he does have a tendency to erase any not deemed worth remembering. Black: it is hardly an uncommon surname, but surely it couldn't be?

"Shall we move on to Sierra Leone?" Beverley asks, pushing the plate of selection box biscuits towards Michael. "I hope you've all seen the cable from the High Commissioner—I have to note before we start that we did not ask for this briefing. He has sent it on his own initiative, based on his assessment of the situation on the ground. The content of the telegram, if taken at face value, is somewhat alarming, I think you'll all agree. I thought it would merit a discussion with the broader group."

"I've seen it, but I couldn't bring myself to read to the end." David from the Treasury wears a pale pink shirt and an air of presupposed superiority. "Military intervention? He can't be serious. We're still completely at capacity in Kosovo and you could hardly call that a resounding success."

"I do think we should give this its due attention," Beverley says. "Can we look at some of the options that could be achieved through a very limited engagement?" She looks at her Ministry of Defence Colleague, a red-faced Scot who is helping himself to a custard cream.

"We can certainly run some scenarios for you," he says, brushing crumbs off his moustache. "I don't think there'd be much appetite for it from the troops. Another unprovoked intervention with high casualty risk? It's a much harder sell if we're not actually under attack. Where is it anyway?"

"The UK has a long and rich history with Sierra Leone." The woman from DFID can always be relied upon to steer the conversation away from dead soldiers.

"Did you know that the PM's father used to lecture at the university of Freetown?" Jeff sounds like the question-master in a pub quiz. Michael is pleased to see that he is mostly ignored.

"Has the High Commissioner given an estimate of British casualties?" Michael speaks bluntly, keen to get the dead soldiers back on the table and at the forefront of Beverley's mind. "And using what assumptions? In the current climate, I'm not sure how we'd sell heavy casualties to a public already tired of hearing of British sacrifice for a country they've never heard of."

"But if the intervention succeeds," Beverley draws herself up to face down Michael, "as the High Commissioner seems confident it would, then there would only be positive news to sell."

Here she comes, Michael thinks, as he turns to the rest of the table to bury Beverley's point. She needs to be a bit hot under the collar before I can turn her. "And what about the risk of mission creep, and follow up? Are we advocating a full hand-over to President Kabbah? He might look like the better man in that unholy alliance, but do we really think he's the one to run the country? And what if we're wrong?"

"It has been UK policy to support Kabbah—" Beverley now

sounds distinctly annoyed. Lecturing the Foreign Office on foreign policy is one of Michael's favourite tricks.

"It's one thing to offer soft support," Michael says, addressing his MOD colleague. "It's quite another to go in all guns blazing. In our assessment, his support base is even weaker than your worst-case scenarios." Another favourite—we know something you don't know, but it's much too secret to share. "The High Commissioner massively underestimates the risk of British casualties in any military intervention. You can't rule out torture, abuse; this is a bunch of stone-age savages we're talking about here." Below the belt but worth it to watch the DFID woman bristle.

"And so they should be little match for a properly trained and organised fighting force," Beverley says.

"And I rather think the reports of the current threat level in Freetown are exaggerated. My colleague was at the residence last night quaffing gin and tonic to celebrate Europe Day or some such nonsense. It hardly sounds like the end of days."

"I'm sorry," Jeff removed his glasses and sets them down on the table. He stared at Michael with a look of distaste. "Are you seriously saying that it's both too dangerous to intervene and not dangerous enough?"

"Yes," says Michael with condescending firmness. "That is exactly the case." There we have it, all angles covered. Beverley can now pick from any of the spurious claims he has made, and take her own evidence-based decision. One final ploy. "The other option is that we move fast, a quick and dirty operation, keep numbers low to offer deniability. Focus principally on evacuation of UK nationals." Michael rolls out the option that would prove most disastrous for Skarparov. It is always the clincher. He isn't sure if it is just him, if something in his manner makes people desperate to do differently from what he recommends. Or is it just basic human psychology—draw people to one option by suggesting the opposite? Either way it works, almost without fail. Especially in ambitious women.

"I think it's clear that these options need further assessment," Beverley says. "Given the potential risks, we shouldn't be hasty in our decisions. I don't think we need to be too solutions-focused at this stage. Perhaps our MOD colleagues could come back to us with a few more detailed scenarios for next time we meet?" She looks to the Scot who nods and makes a note on his pad. "Shall we move on to Somalia?"

Michael excuses himself before the end, careful to maintain his poker face until he is out of the building, but he grins as he strides back across Westminster bridge. Perhaps it was too easy, but it was fun, nonetheless.

CHAPTER 17

Sarah and Elias meet George, the Koidu pilot, at his favourite bar to discuss helicopters. A small sign outside announces the China-Sierra Leone Friendship house. Nothing about the unremarkable grey building suggests that the Chinese invest much in their side of the friendship.

They sit at a small table by the bar, huddled in the corner of the open courtyard that makes up one side of the building. The other half houses a cluster of small dark rooms. An anonymous space that might host language conversation classes, or support groups that have been turfed out of the church hall. Even with no roof, the air feels obstructed and still. A rusty fan, whirling and clattering overhead, brings only the occasional stir to the unrelenting heat. Sarah tries to ignore the sweat running down every part of her body—slithering down her shins, down the centre of her chest onto her stomach, and pooling in the small of her back.

Two television sets showing a European football match balance precariously on a stack of blue plastic crates, their wires looped out the back through the open window to the generator behind. The football fans sit on rows of wooden chairs, oddly silent when the game is on, their rowdiness only raised by the frequent losses in power. Each time the screens flicker into darkness, the frustrated fans run around turning off lights to relieve the wavering generator.

By the time George arrives, they are on their second cold beer—the football fans have not yet come for the fridge, but

Sarah suspects it won't be long. The bottles leave puddles of condensation soaking the paper mats on the table. George looks even broader in a close-fitting t-shirt than he did in his flight suit. His curly hair is pushed back out of his eyes by his gold-rimmed sunglasses, and he knocks back a bottle of beer before even sitting down.

He introduces Kobus, a double-muscled Afrikaner, who came to Sierra Leone with Executive Outcomes, the South African mercenaries who had been the only force able to take on the rebels. Their presence and fighting ability had secured the diamond areas for much of the war, but they were forced to withdraw as a condition for the latest farce of a peace accord. Kobus, like many of his colleagues, stayed on doing private security work for the mine owners.

"And what makes you stay in a place like this?" Sarah asks. Kobus's smile marks him out as one of life's optimists, and his heavy work boots with cargo shorts suggest he's not afraid to get things done. Sarah is intrigued what brings anyone who has the choice into sitting behind a machine gun in a muddy mining pit.

"The luxury of the lifestyle," he laughs, running his hands through his spiky hair. "It's a good question: why do any of us stay? I don't know, there is something special here. I can't put my finger on it but every time I think I can't stand this hellhole any longer, something brings me back."

"A fat pay check?" George asks, pronouncing 'chehk' to rhyme with Kobus's 'behk'.

"Yah, of course the money's good, and not a lot of ways to spend it. But there are plenty of places in the world where you can earn big." His consonants have a machine gun rhythm. "I like the rawness here. You get people as they really are, there's no learnt civility to hide things." He turns his head to Sarah. "But what about you? George told me you're into leaves?"

"I like the solitude of the forest floor," Sarah says, hoping to breathe life into her sham persona to match Kobus's openness.

"The feeling that you are part of an enormous interconnected system that we know so little about."

Elias buries his head in his beer.

"I often feel that way out in the bush," Kobus says. "Like we are only very small, you know? And there aren't even any big animals here. Where I grew up, you know you're only top of the food chain with a gun in your hand." Sarah knew there would be a philosopher in there if you scratched deep enough.

"So," Kobus says, turning to Elias to talk business. "George said you wanted some logistics help?"

Sarah sets her beer down heavily on the table. "To cut a long story short, we want a helicopter."

Kobus shoots George a quizzical look and turns back to Sarah. "Who for?"

"Probably best if you don't ask."

Kobus nods, the cheerful smile draining from his face. "So you want a supplier who is dodgy enough to sell a helicopter to an unknown buyer in Sierra Leone?"

"Yes," Sarah says confidently. "But straight enough to insist on proper documentation. George thought you might be able to help."

Kobus turns to George. "Is this some kind of a wind up?" he asks with an awkward laugh.

George shrugs. "Don't ask me. She's in charge."

"Don't worry." Sarah tries to sound reassuring. "The helicopter itself doesn't even need to be delivered. It's the paper trail I'm interested in. What do you think?"

Kobus drains his whiskey and crunches on the ice cubes. "There's a guy who used to supply Executive Outcomes kit as well," he says, placing an unusual emphasis on the 'as'. "He's suffered since they were chucked out, so he'll be hungry, isn't it?" He pauses, eyeing Sarah up, trying to work out what he is dealing with. "You must be careful. I don't want my name anywhere near this."

"Don't worry," Elias cuts in. "I'll make the contact. I won't

106

even mention you if you'd prefer."

The football crowd erupts once again. Sarah expects a goal celebration, but the screens are both blank. She can smell the frustration threatening to spill over into unrest. "Excuse me a moment." She notices a welder fixing a section of fence outside, filling the air with the whine of machinery and smell of melting paint. She slips outside, offers a freshly opened beer to the workman, and invites him to come and watch the game. As soon as his welding machine is off, the generator hums louder and the screens pop back to life. Sarah's intervention passes unnoticed by the newly jubilant crowd.

"Any idea what kind of chopper he's looking for?" Kobus asks.

"That's where George comes in," Sarah says. "What do you think, George?"

"Depends what you want it for—people or kit?"

"Attack." Sarah says without pause.

"I'll bet they want an Apache. But there's no point having new kit in a place like this. It'll perish in no time. A Mi-24's what you want: 'the crocodile'," George says with a toothy grin before checking himself. "But I can't think of many people in Freetown I'd want to have in charge of one of those."

"We'll have one of those, please," Sarah says, undaunted by George's warning. There is something fun in ordering a warlord's weaponry, knowing it would bring about his downfall.

Elias returns from the bar with another round of drinks. He smiles at Sarah. "I knew you'd enjoy this."

"Are you guys sure you know what you're doing?" Kobus lights a cigarette and sits back, looking down his nose at Sarah.

"Don't worry, we know what we're dealing with. And we'll be sure not to bring you into it."

Kobus pauses, wiping a thick thumb down the side of his sun-scorched nose, building up for something he has to get off his chest. "You know what they called it last time the rebels made it into Freetown?" he begins, speaking softly, his small eyes focused straight on Sarah. "Operation No Living Thing. The RUF killed indiscriminately, they killed gleefully, they killed those who tried to escape and those who stayed to fight. They chopped off hands and genitals and heads. Can you imagine? They burnt people alive. They attacked the doctors trying to help, they raped old women and children. You can't imagine because the horror was more than any human can comprehend. They are devils and the devils are still here."

Sarah nods. What is there to say: 'I know'? She knows nothing of the real horrors of this war.

"You seem like a nice girl," he wipes away the sweat from his forehead with a square of paper napkin. "I don't know what your helicopter has to do with leaves, but if you're a friend of George then that's good enough for me. But I hope you know the risk you're running. If you make man the king of the jungle by putting a gun in his hand, what can you do to the devil by giving him a gunship?"

Sarah is sobered by Kobus's speech. But far from putting her off the idea, it only leaves her more fired up. Skarparov, if given the time, will no doubt deliver an attack helicopter into the hands of Foday Sankoh and his crazed bunch of rebels. "Look, I'm sorry we can't explain fully," she says. "But rest assured. It's exactly to stop the flow of weapons into rebel hands that we need to set up this deal."

Kobus taps his empty whisky glass on the table. "*Sho*, I'll get you the name. And I need another one of these—anyone else?"

Elias flashes Sarah a lopsided smile and squeezes her knee under the table. They have their next move.

With the football finished, the bar is soon packed. A ten-piece band jostles amongst the crowd to set up their instruments under the shelter of the overhanging roof. The air is so full of moisture you could wring it and even the fall of darkness has done nothing to lessen the grinding heat. With a squeal of feedback from the amplifier, the band starts up, playing a stomach-shaking up-tempo beat—reggae meets afrobeat with the infectiousness of a cheesy pop song.

Sarah can't sit still, and it is too noisy to talk. "Let's dance." She grabs Elias's hand and beckons to Kobus and George to join them. George raises his beer bottle towards her and settles back into his seat, but Elias and Kobus follow her onto the courtyard dancefloor.

Sarah knows she can be awkward. She has a tendency to think too much in social situations, to focus on positions and possibilities rather than being in the moment or remembering to be normal. She is always happier in the company of a trusted ally than with a big group. But all of that disappears when she dances. If the beat is good, she's off; no matter where she is or who's watching. In the crowded dancefloor of the China Friendship House, she finds her perfect spot.

Sweaty bodies pack into the central area. Men and women, young and old, dressed to the nines or wearing very little at all, pile onto the dancefloor. Kobus grins at her, his red face gleaming, his solid work boots firmly planted on the floor, both meaty fists pumping towards the sky. Elias takes her hand and spins her into the crowd. Other than their barefoot shuffle in the rain, they have never properly danced together, and she is delighted to see his unshakable confidence extends to the dancefloor.

He swings her round in something approaching a '60s swing dance, flinging her out into the crowd, drawing her back before dropping her down over his arm.

With a crack loud enough to make the ground quake, the pressure in the air finally breaks. From nowhere, a torrential tropical downpour pummels the open courtyard, rain hitting the ground in high splashes, thrumming on their heads, plastering hair to scalps, rinsing out the sweat-drenched clothing, running down faces and dripping down the back of necks. The band grins at the crowd from their tiny strip of shelter under the overhang, but the dancefloor remains packed. The volume is turned up to compete with the noise of the water hammering the metal roof. Sarah and Elias loop their arms around each other's waists. Elias reaches down to wipe away the stream of water running down

Sarah's forehead and kisses her, his lips tasting of sweat and heat and the soft sweetness of the rain. "Come on. I want to take this dance somewhere more private."

"Not yet; it's finally cooled down." She kisses him again. "One more song?"

"Okay, but I'm going to check on George. I'll leave you with Kobus." He tilts his head towards where the South African is enjoying his own private rave, face to the heavens, fists pumping skywards, eyes tightly shut.

Sarah feels a hand on the small of her back. She makes to grab it before snatching her hand away. It isn't Elias. It's Chris again, in another uninvited invasion of her personal space.

"I didn't have you down as a wild dancer." Chris lowers his lips directly over her ear.

Sarah shrugs, pretending she can't hear him over the noise of the music and backing away from his grasp. The dancefloor is so packed there isn't space to escape and he follows her, grinding his narrow hips in her direction with an unmistakably suggestive smile. He runs his hands through his pale blond hair and flicks the water from his fingers into her eyes. What is he doing? Surely he saw her dancing with Elias?

"How was your chat with Skarparov?" he asks, bending in close again. "You certainly hit it off like old friends."

Sarah waves at her ears to show she can't hear.

"Sorry, it was mean of me to throw you in like that. But you should have seen the look on your face as you stood there, talking leaves, hoping he wouldn't give you away." Sarah retreats but not quickly enough to miss the next bit. "I had fun describing it to Michael."

"What?!"

He turns away with a wink, his eyes focused behind her.

Elias is there, chest thrust forward, glaring at Chris. He sweeps his arm around Sarah's waist and pulls her towards him. "Come on, let's get out of here. The atmosphere seems to have gone a little sour." He shoots a savage look at Chris and leads Sarah towards the exit. Sarah wants to go back, to question Chris, but she doesn't want to provoke Elias any further.

Elias's serious stare lifts outside as they pick their way through the carpark extension of the dancefloor. He squeezes Sarah's hand with a lighter touch. "Come on, I'd like to pick up where we left off."

Sarah smiles but her stomach is in knots. What the hell does Chris have to do with Michael?

CHAPTER 18

The next day, Elias raps on Sarah's hotel door.

"I've got a surprise for you." He bursts through the door, almost bouncing with excitement.

"What is it?"

"It's big, blue and you'll have to come outside to see it."

"You brought me the sky?"

"I wish. These are for you." He fishes in his yellow satchel and throws her a bunch of keys. In front of the hotel, under the shade of a bright orange jacaranda, is a very ancient but very beautiful Land Rover. A short wheel-base Series III from the 1970s in pale powder blue, a hood-mounted spare tyre making it look ready for anything and wing mirrors like curled eyelashes on either side of the bonnet.

"This is for me?!" Sarah can scarcely contain her astonishment.

"Of course. Have you ever driven one before?"

"Are you kidding?" Sarah askes. "I was practically born in one of these. My father is an obsessive and has owned dozens over the years. I learnt to drive in one in the fields behind my house when I was twelve."

"Twelve?"

"It was private land, and I was just tall enough to see over the bonnet sitting on a cushion."

"So you know what to do with the red and yellow levers?" Elias asks. "Perfect, then you can teach me. I'm ashamed to say I've only ever driven Toyotas before, but I think this might be the start of a new love affair."

"Hop in and let's take her for a spin." Sarah climbs into the driver's seat, marvelling at her new toy. The interior, clearly untouched since the '70s, must have been top of the range at the time. The seats are pale tan leather—stained dark brown by decades of sweat and dust, but in better shape than the leather finish of the dashboard that hangs in tatters. The metal pedals are so basic that the clutch looks more like a crowbar than a car part. It is perfect.

"I thought you were going to teach me to drive," Elias says.

"I will, but you've got to let me get to know her first. Does she have a name?"

"The guy I bought her off just called her 'Landy', but I think we can do better than that."

"Let's see what's she's like." Sarah starts the engine. "Look at that: first time!"

They drive the hill road out of Freetown, only really passable in a 4x4. The road is steep and rutted and when the rain comes it washes entire sections of the laterite down the hill. The remaining steps, rivulets and washouts are perfect Land Rover terrain. Sarah turns off the main road and follows an even smaller rocky track.

"Where are you going?" Elias asks.

"I'm trying to find somewhere we can get stuck," Sarah says with a grin. "Nothing to learn if it's easy."

Elias leans his arm out of the open window. "By the way, you were right about that uranium."

"I know."

"How do you know? It's supposed to be top secret."

"The High Commissioner told me."

"Apparently they've found traces of ore in the north of Kono district, near Koidu and the diamond mines. The samples have been tested at the Rössing mine in Namibia and seem to indicate a high-grade deposit."

"How can they tell?" Sarah asks.

"Concentrations of the ore and which grade of isotope it is. Anyway, by all accounts it's pretty juicy cheddar."

"How do they make decaffeinated tea?"

"What has that got to do with uranium?"

"Nothing. As far as I know. I just wanted to test whether there was any subject that you didn't know about. Okay, I think this is a good spot. Want a go? Be careful with my baby."

"You only met her half an hour ago."

"Love is a powerful thing."

Sarah climbs over Elias's lap to make space for him to take the wheel. "Okay, first we're going to cross that ditch." Sarah points to a section of laterite at the side of the road that has been washed out, forming a gulley about a foot deep and two feet wide.

"Do I get to use the coloured levers?" Elias asks.

"I would," Sarah says. "Better to have it in low gears before you get stuck. Put your foot on the clutch and pull the red nob back towards you. It sometimes needs a little lift to get it in."

The red handle moves into position with a satisfying clunk.

"All right, over we go."

Elias steers the car towards the rut, face on.

"Stop." Sarah taps her hand on the dashboard. "If you go over like that, you'll be well and truly stuck. It's all about the angle of approach. Back up and try again."

Elias remakes the approach, carefully dropping one wheel at a time into the ditch and climbing effortlessly out the other side.

"Easy," Sarah grins. "Up there next." She points to a steep embankment at the side of the road. "This time you do want to tackle it head on. Otherwise we'll flip. Worst that can happen is that we'll slip back down the way we came."

Elias approaches the hill, and the little Land Rover climbs straight up, engine growling.

"Who's behind the uranium find and why is it all such a secret?" she asks.

"That's the weird thing. No one seems quite sure. Apparently it's someone involved in the mines here who first made the discovery and there may be a foreign partner involved. So now the Russians, Iranians and Libyans are all courting the government for access to the rights, and everyone has feelers out to try and get the best offer."

"How do you know all this?"

"Kobus. He works in security in the biggest mine, so has access to all the diamond field gossip. They're all in the bar every evening working through the imported booze and spreading their closely kept secrets."

"That way." Sarah points out a small track leading into the bush.

"Where does it go?"

"I don't know; that's why I want to try it. What about Skarparov—surely he's going to want to get involved in this somehow?"

"He's definitely interested. My guess is that he's trying to set himself up as the middleman—playing on his success with the diamonds. Introduce the parties, take a big cut, wash his hands of the result."

"Any evidence?"

"Not yet. But I'm working on it."

They leave the car at the end of the track and bash a path through the green, coming out to a sweeping view over the city and to the sea beyond.

"Land Rovers always know how to pick the best spots," Sarah says.

"I think its driver probably helps. By the way," Elias says, sitting down on a piece of red rock, "do you know a 'Michael'?"

Michael is the last person she wants reminding of. She is still rattled by Chris's cryptic comment and now here he is again, butting into her romantic drive. How does he manage to follow her even when he's on another continent? "Why do you ask?"

"Skarparov mentioned him. He was telling me about meeting you at the High Commission, said he couldn't work out if Michael had sent you to check up on him."

"He's my ex-boss," Sarah says.

"So he's legitimate MI6?" Elias sounds surprised. "From the way Skarparov was talking about him, he sounded dodgy. I heard rumours that one of the reasons the Lome Peace Accord was such a poor deal was because of suspect lobbying on the Americans. Skarparov seemed to think it was Michael taking significant kickbacks for helping skew the result."

Sarah is quiet. "Sadly, that wouldn't surprise me all that much."

"But it makes me feel better about him paying for this car."

"What?" Sarah asks.

"How else do you think I could afford to put you up in the swankiest hotel in Freetown and buy you the finest vehicle on the planet?"

"I had been meaning to ask."

"The suitcase of cash Ibragimov gave you in Baku? Presumably more of Michael's kickbacks? I've been using it to keep you in the lifestyle to which you are accustomed."

Sarah laughs, and once she starts, she can't stop. Michael, who haunts her, who refused to help her and is probably supporting Skarparov in his dodgy uranium deal, is also funding her solo mission, her boyfriend and her new car. Life is indeed very juicy.

"I've got one more surprise for you." Elias's voice grows serious. "After what you said before, I thought you should have this."

He reaches into the back of the car for his trusty yellow satchel and hands her a classic silver revolver in a dark leather holster and a packet of cartridges.

Sarah removes the gun from the holster and weighs it in her hand, opening it up and spinning the cylinder.

"You got me a girly gun!"

"What? It's a good-looking piece of kit. Here, let me show you how to use it."

Sarah slides three of the cartridges into the cylinder, then clicks it back into the frame. She turns to face a tree behind them, drawing in Dilara's magic spot, and fires. Bam! Bam! Bam!

116

Each bullet enters a whirled knot in the tree's bark.

"Okay," Sarah grins at Elias. "I'm ready to be taught now."

He stares at her, open-mouthed. "Where the hell did you learn how to shoot like that?"

"I've got some useful friends. Not bad, even with a girly gun."

Elias is quiet on the drive back into town. It is clearly an adjustment for him to surrender control. Sarah raves about the car and tells him stories of the previous Land Rovers she has known, the best places she's been stuck and the most ingenious ways in which the cars were fixed up.

"Dichloromethane," Elias says during a pause in her anecdotes.

"What's that?"

"It's what they use to make decaffeinated tea. It's a solvent that dissolves caffeine but doesn't impact the rest of the leaf."

"I thought you didn't know?"

"I never like to show off," he says, raising an eyebrow.

Sarah laughs. "You'd better watch it now; I'm armed and extremely dangerous."

CHAPTER 19

Sarah arrives at the High Commission to meet Chris in her new prize possession. She picked up his message at reception when she returned from her drive with Elias, but waited a couple of days before calling him back. Partly because she is wary—his revelation that he knows Michael throws everything he told her into doubt. He is clearly not just an ex-pat from the High Commission—over-friendly and over-pleased with himself but otherwise harmless—and he obviously knows more than he is letting on. But her delay is also to wait until Elias returns to Koidu. Sarah tried to assuage his jealousy, but Elias's antipathy towards Chris is visceral. He would go nuts if he knew she is meeting him, but she needs to know what links Chris to Michael.

Chris climbs into the Land Rover and casts a critical eye over the fraying upholstery and open footwells.

"Are you sure you don't want to take my car?" he asks. "It's a long way to push if this breaks down."

"It won't," Sarah says. "And if it does, that's half the fun. You are welcome to take yours if you need the sealed bubble of air-conditioning. I'm driving this beauty."

"Suit yourself." He folds his long legs into the car. He is wearing a pale blue shirt with sleeves rolled up to the elbow to show his firm biceps and baby smooth skin, a pair of chinos and a pristine pair of two-toned brogues with a bright red sole. Sarah is tempted to stall the car just to see whether he'd be up for getting his shoes dirty.

The security guard at the gate salutes Sarah as she hands back her visitor pass. He taps the Land Rover on the bonnet. "Fine vehicle, fine vehicle."

"See?" Sarah says. "Where are we going?"

"Pietro's. You know it?"

"Of course, everyone does."

"I was going to take you to the Mossad place—they have their own beach bar and dive shop. It's been here for years. God only knows what operational use it still sees, but that doesn't stop them from running it meticulously."

"Sounds fascinating."

"It is worth a visit, but they don't serve lobster."

*

The beachside bar at Pietro's could be a picture postcard of tropical paradise, looking out over soft bars of white sand emerging from the lagoon that protects the pristine beach from the rougher waves of the Atlantic, the sweep of the water gently lapping against the rough-built stone breaker. Chris heads straight for the same table where Sarah sat with Elias, but it feels too weird. Just being here with Chris feels like a betrayal, even if she knows it shouldn't. The restaurant is mostly empty—a pair who look like international consultants at one table, and a group of dusty mercenaries at another. Tucked in a corner near the kitchen, Sarah recognises the Chinese interpreter from the High Commission, looking poised and thoughtful over a pristine paperback. She steers them towards a table near the beach under the covered roof.

Chris gives a friendly wave to Pietro, who is ankle-deep in sand, throwing a chewed-up frisbee for his dog. Pietro waves back, but his face shows no recognition. Sarah keeps her head down. The last thing she needs is for word to get back to Elias that she is having lunch with a mystery blond.

"So, are you going to tell me who you really are?" she asks Chris as soon as the waiter is out of earshot, taking a sip from a tall bottle of coke.

"I thought it was time to put my cards on the table and perhaps encourage you to do the same." He sharpens the arch of his eyebrows and waits for her reaction.

She gives none.

"Okay, I'll start," he says. "I'm not on the West Africa desk of the Foreign Office. I work for Michael."

"Yes, I'd worked that bit out." Sarah leans back in her chair and folds her arms across her chest. Looking at him now, she wonders why she didn't realise this the moment he interrupted her breakfast. He has Michael's same attitude of smug self-interest, although without Michael's measured elegance. "Well, I'm happy to say that I don't".

"No, I know. But what I want to understand," he twirls a blue paper napkin around his finger, "is why not?"

"Why not? Because Michael used me as cannon-fodder. Because he sent me to draw out a contact that he undoubtedly thought was a trap, and when I did manage to uncover the real plot, he disappeared. Why would I stay?"

"By all accounts you were a complete natural. And what seems to have caused you such offence is just Michael's way—he likes to keep his distance, to be sure that his new recruits are up to the task."

"Chuck them in the deep end to see if they can swim?"

"There's always a support system in place. You just didn't need it."

"Is that what he tells you? I don't think he would have cared less if I came back alive or dead."

"I can assure you that is not true. When you disappeared, he was extremely concerned. Which I have to say surprised me, as it's rare to see any emotion on Michael."

Sarah always imagined Michael worked alone. She has never come across any colleagues or allies, unless you count Dilara. There is something strangely normalising about him having an employee, perhaps even a team of people. But the idea of

Michael discussing her kidnapping with Chris makes her bristle. The balance of information is too skewed, and she doesn't trust Chris not to use it to his advantage. "Well, he has a funny way of showing his concern," she says.

"And then look what you achieved! Thrown in the deep end as you say, and pretty green around the ears, let's be honest. And it still came down to you to thwart that attack in Tbilisi. I don't think Michael has ever had such a good first operation. Well, since my first outing of course." The boast is delivered tongue loosely in cheek. He plays a fine line between full-on arrogance and laughing at himself. In the right eyes, Sarah can see how this might be attractive. But not in hers.

"So I'm a natural—doesn't mean I have a dark enough heart to work for Michael."

"I think you've got him all wrong."

"What about the article in the press? Was that him?"

"Oh, you saw that, did you? I thought it was rather funny, but Michael seemed quite cross."

"Why? Because they got my name wrong? Are you really trying to talk me into coming back?"

"I'd be disappointed if you weren't a bit tempted."

A plume of black smoke rises out of the bush on the opposite side of the small bay—a forest fire or a deliberate burning of the scrub and grass? The sharp smell of charcoal and ash is tempered by the distance, but still it sours the atmosphere of tropical paradise.

"Okay, so what can you tell me about the uranium?" Sarah asks.

"What uranium would that be?" he says, eyes teasing.

"You know exactly what I'm talking about." Her bluff can only take her so far, but it is worth pushing to see what he might give away.

"Suppose for a moment that I did." He runs the edge of his thumb along his cheekbone. "Why would I tell you?"

"Because you know how this works. You want something, so

121

you need to give me something in return."

He keeps his eyes on her while tapping a plastic pot of toothpicks against the table. Sarah can tell he is enjoying himself. It doesn't surprise her he is the sort of male aroused by women being difficult. "Well," he says slowly, licking his lips. "I can tell you it's not the Libyans or the Russians who are going to win the bidding game, despite their strong suits."

"Then who is going to win?"

"Chen Xiaochang."

"Who the hell is Chen Xiaochang?"

"I think I've told you enough already. You haven't even agreed to my proposition yet, or have you?" he dips his blond lashes.

"I'm not coming back, if that's what you mean?"

"Just think about it. You clearly have a strong sense of natural justice. But how can you possibly go about setting the world to rights without a larger framework in which to operate? You can get on your high horse about your one particular small-fry baddy, but what difference does he make in wider world? With us, you get a seat at a much larger table—think of the impact you could have at a higher level."

"You've lost me."

"Come on, Sarah. You're not really here for leaves, are you? You couldn't let Skarparov go, so you're sniffing around to see what else you can get him with. Please tell me you don't think you can take down Skarparov on your own?"

"I'm not alone."

"What, because that oversized Dutchman is pretending to help you? Did you know that Elias had a fling with Skarparov's daughter in Tbilisi? The pretty one, not the one who looks like a horse."

Sarah feels her blood rise but does not respond.

"I wonder if that might be why Skarparov is so nice to him— courting a potential son-in-law? What makes you think he's loyal to you but not to Skarparov?"

"I know he's trustworthy," Sarah says, striking the table a

little too hard. "He's there now helping me set up the very sting that could nail Skarparov. Why would he take that risk if he wasn't onside?" Her eagerness to defend Elias sends the words flying out of her mouth, but as soon as they are out, she wishes she could claw them back. Chris has no need to know about the helicopter deal. He offered a pawn, and she swooped on it without stopping to look at what lay behind.

Pietro comes over to the table. He pours some more water from the condensation-soaked bottle and stares curiously at Chris.

"Now I know who you are. You're the gin and tonic boy from the ambassador's party! How are you doing? How is the food?" he looks down at the table and sees that it was still empty. "Johnny!" he shouts towards the kitchen. "Table sixteen, bring the food for the gin and tonic boy, he makes them nice and strong."

Chris gives Pietro his broadest smile, but it looks a little strained. "How's the prospecting going Pietro? Did you know, Sarah, that Pietro found the biggest iron ore deposit in the country?"

"Funnily enough I did." Sarah smiles. "And diamonds too."

"Oh, it has been too long ago," Pietro trills with mock-modesty. "Now I just dig sandcastles for Zingo to destroy. And I never got a cent for all my trouble! How is the 'igh Commissioner?" he asks Chris. "Tell him to come again for lobster soon, I will make him one special."

"Very good," Chris says.

A loud squeal erupts, and a wave of sand sprays from underneath a nearby table. A dark fawn-coloured piglet with a black spot up its side flies out and trots down the beach with Pietro's mutt in hot pursuit. "*Zingo! Vieni qua!*" Pietro hollers. "I'm sorry." He nods to Sarah and sets off across the sand, chasing the dog chasing the pig.

Sarah is grateful for the interruption. Pietro has, for the moment at least, released her from talking about Elias. She has no convincing answer to Chris's question—how does she know she can trust Elias? She knows only that her heart wants to follow wherever he goes, that the world seems more juicy when he is in it, and that, for all her doubts about him in Tbilisi, he stayed at her side. But she does not want to share any of this with Chris, knowing how flimsy it would feel under his pointed examination.

"What is Michael doing with Skarparov?" she asks, hoping Chris would have forgotten what they were talking about.

"Nothing, as far as I'm aware."

"So why didn't he hand him over to the CIA? Why let him go free?"

"It's not really our business, is it? That's for the Americans to sort out. He's no longer a threat to us, so we might as well let him be."

"What are you doing here, then?"

"Me?" He gives a shrug. "This and that. A bit of good old-fashioned intel gathering when I can, serving drinks at the High Commission when I must."

"It's funny," Sarah says. "Because from the way you keep popping up, I wondered whether you might have been sent here for me."

"You? Don't flatter yourself, darling." He leans forward, ruler straight back angled across the table towards her. "But of course I would consider it a great honour if you decided to come back to us. You might think you can be a solo operator, but you're too new in this game. You still have too much to learn. Just imagine what we could achieve if we joined forces. Your fire with my know-how? We'd be unstoppable." He rolls out the last word.

Is he serious? She would laugh, but that would only encourage him. He is entertaining, and oddly, somehow charming despite all his efforts to the contrary. Flirting with him, if that is what she is doing, feels like brushing towards a snake in the grass. You don't quite know what you are dealing with, you knew you definitely shouldn't, but there is something irresistibly inevitable about it. A danger that makes you lean in and poke it with a stick.

CHAPTER 20

After three messages left on his answer machine and one left with Angus, her daydreaming younger brother, Sarah finally reaches her father. She had forgotten he was back at work and would be in the office at the times she tried to call. It is only supposed to be a part-time advisory role, but she knows that her father will soon make himself indispensable.

"How are you getting on back in the office?" she asks.

"It's great fun. I don't think I'd realised how much I missed it. And I've managed to get up quite a few people's noses already so I must be doing something right. How are you getting on with…" His pause is hard to read. Is he protecting her confidentiality, or struggling to name what his impulsive daughter is doing in a war zone? "With what you're getting on with?"

"I think I'm making progress."

"At least you're safe from journalists there," her father says after waiting for her to elaborate. "I've had the Daily Mail on the phone three times wanting comment on that stringer's story."

"I hope you told them where to stick it."

"In politer terms, yes. But what is the situation like there at the moment? From some of the reports we've been getting, it's hard to judge what's really going on. Is it all-out hellish rebel war zone, or cosy expats quaffing gin and tonics in the luxury of a manicured garden?"

"Mad as it sounds, it's both those things. At least it is for the cosy expats, anyway. For those outside the high-security perimeter walls there isn't much let-up from the former."

"Oh. Disappointing."

"Why?"

"I thought it was a ridiculous thing to say. It's no fun if it turns out to be true."

"Who have you been talking to?" It is still new to Sarah that her father's world extends beyond his living room. When she was young, she took little interest in his work, and he, being the consummate civil servant, never brought it home. After her mother died, he was pushed into early retirement and seemed remarkably happy with his books, his chess and his roses. But Sarah is not surprised that he had been hankering for more.

"There was a chap at a recent cross-Whitehall briefing who seemed intent on painting a nonsensical picture of what is going on over there. One of your old lot, pushy and rather pleased with himself."

"Seems to be a common hazard. He wasn't called Michael by any chance?"

"You know, I think he was. Or that's the name they all give under cover. MI6—Mike for short. I've met dozens of them."

"Silver hair, immaculate, insufferable?"

"That would be him."

"What was this Michael saying?" Could her Michael really have been in a meeting room discussing Sierra Leone with her father without realising who he was? She lays a hand across the knot of tense muscle forming in the back of her neck.

"He was arguing against the High Commissioner's calls for military engagement, doing his best to discredit the Foreign Office on all their recommendations."

Her neck clenches tighter. "And did he mention uranium?" Sarah hopes the encrypted phone line is really as secure as it claims to be.

"In Sierra Leone?

"Apparently there's been a find, but no one seems to know much about it."

"Last thing they need. Odd that no one in Whitehall has

mentioned it. Shall I raise it at the next meeting?"

"No, not yet." It would be naïve to imagine that Michael wouldn't work out who her father was, but she doesn't want it to look like she is briefing him. "Oh and I've got a Land Rover."

"Have you now? A Defender?"

"No. It's a Series III."

"What year?"

"I'm not sure. It doesn't have any paperwork. Probably late '70s."

"Oh good. Funnily enough I feel better about you being out there, knowing you've got a Landy to look after you. It might be a rough road, but it should always get you where you're going. Have you worked out where you're going yet?"

Sarah laughs. "I'm not leaving here until I'm finished, if that's what you mean."

"Not literally. I meant have you at least got a handle on your opponent?"

Sarah wishes she could answer with greater confidence. Her conversation with Chris has planted another creeper of doubt in her mind—is she mad to be taking on Skarparov on her own? "I finally met him face to face again this week."

"I'm happy to hear you're still standing."

"And I know him, I know how he plays. I've beaten him before so I can do it again."

"But are you sure you understand what he wants?"

"Of course—personal enrichment and maximum destruction in his wake."

"You know as well as I do that people are rarely that straightforward. I'd wager that almost no one is all bad."

"Don't you start. He's been feeding people the line that he's the saviour of Freetown. Meanwhile he's keeping Foday Sankoh and the rebels in weapons and ammunition. It's madness. I don't get why I'm the only one who sees it as it is."

Sarah's father pauses, defusing her growing outrage. When finally he answers his voice is low, gently admonishing. "When you are a hammer, everything looks like a nail."

"I'm not a—"

"You know what I mean. Don't forget to think through all your pieces. No one piece alone can win. It's only when you get them working together that they have power."

Sarah knows he's right. Skarparov is a player of the King's Indian, he's a master of distraction and letting his opponent think they have the upper hand before launching the attack. It might look clear-cut, but has she really taken the time to study his position?

Sarah wishes she could have this conversation over a cup of tea, or watching the squirrels at their constant circus outside her father's kitchen window. He is always better in person. His kernels of philosophy can be teased out, allowed to mellow and blossom before Sarah needs to scoop them up in her careless hand. Over the phone she feels that each statement requires an answer, an immediate response, crushing a bud that might have borne fruit if given more time.

"I don't suppose there's much point in telling you to look after yourself, is there?" he says. "But do at least take your malaria tablets. And don't forget to give the Land Rover a regular top up of oil. Those old engines can drink it by the litre."

"I will, thanks Dad."

CHAPTER 21

Sarah thrashes through the murky water in a rapid front crawl, enjoying the small subversive thrill from ignoring all advice not to swim at Lumley Beach. With no proper sewage and heavy rain that sends torrents of water sluicing down from the hills, most of the city's refuse ends up in the sea. But in the sweaty heat of the day, even the lukewarm water is too inviting to miss, and she has not yet come across anything too disgusting blocking the path of her practiced stroke.

The exercise also provides the necessary distraction. Elias is up in Koidu, and today he will introduce Skarparov to Kobus's contact to discuss the helicopter. Sarah wanted to go along, but Elias insisted she stay in Freetown until she heard from him. Cut off and frustrated, she feels like a bit-part in her own mission. She knows Elias is right—Skarparov is bound to be suspicious of the deal if she turns up. But even so, she envies Elias his role at the centre of the action, while she stays stuck in Freetown. And though she knows her staying away only makes Elias safer, the distance and difficult communications magnify her misgivings.

She swims to the point where she no longer trusts her strength against the unpredictable currents beneath the waves. Turning back towards the dark patch on the white sand where she left her clothes, she plunges under the water to break through the surf. She emerges salt-splashed and soaking, enjoying the cool of the water on her semi-naked skin, until she realises she is being watched. A familiar figure stands on the sand next to her clothes, waiting for her return. But what on earth could she be doing here?

"Dilara?" Sarah says, summoning as much composure as her state of undress allows.

Dilara throws Sarah her towel. "I thought that was you," she says, holding up a manicured hand to shield her eyes from the lowering sun. "I like your suit." She nods at Sarah's bright blue bikini. "The colour suits your skin."

"Thank you," Sarah says, wrapping herself in her towel. "What are you doing here?"

"Looking for you," Dilara smiles. "My father sent me to check on some of our contractors working in the mines and I thought I'd come and see how you're getting on." She wears her luxurious hair in a loose plait down her back, cropped trousers over ankle-twistingly high wedged sandals, her generous make-up melting in the tropical heat.

"Did Michael send you?" Sarah asks, rummaging in her shoe for her car keys.

"I'm not his spy if that's what you think." Dilara touches her finger to Sarah's chin. "I wanted to see you."

"Well, here I am." Sarah wonders how she can get back into her clothes under Dilara's attentive gaze.

"And I still have that favour to call in."

Sarah is strangely relieved that Dilara's interest is transactional. "What can I do for you?"

"Let me buy you a drink first. I'm guessing you don't have your wallet hidden in there somewhere." She nods at Sarah's towel.

They take a seat at a bamboo shack that serves as a beachside bar. Sarah ducks into the toilets to get dressed while Dilara instructs the goggle-eyed bar man on how to make her favourite drink.

Sarah joins her at the bar, conscious of her salty damp hair and sticky skin, as Dilara slides her a glass of brackish-looking liquid. "It's Freetown's first Dou Dou shot," she announces. "He may not have had all the right ingredients, but let's try." She knocks back the shot with a big feline wink at the barman. "It's good," she purrs.

"What was your favour?" Sarah asks, knocking back the strange cloudy glass of salt-laced vodka that reminded her a little too much of refuse-rich seawater.

"I want to talk to the people behind the uranium find. I figured you might know who they are."

Sarah nearly spits out her salt water. "You're after the uranium? Have you asked Michael?"

"I prefer not to discuss business with Michael," Dilara says dismissively, unworking her thick braid.

"He didn't tell you, did he?"

Dilara's laugh is deep as a double bass. "I knew you were good. Two more please." She slides the glasses towards the barman.

"Why do you want to meet them?" Sarah asks.

"I want to make them an offer."

"You're in the uranium market now?"

"No. Construction—my family company. We want the civil engineering contracts for the mine. Few companies have what it takes to operate somewhere like this. We do, and we can do it well."

Dilara never ceases to surprise. "I'd love to help," Sarah says, knocking back the second shot. "But it's all too delicate at the moment. Can you wait until things are a little clearer?"

"You don't know either!"

Sarah laughs and signals to the bar man for two more. "How about we strike a deal? If I find out who is behind it, I tell you. But if you find it first, you tell me?"

"I can drink to that." Dilara raises her shot glass, her little finger lifted in a perfect curl.

Sarah chinks her glass and gulps down another mouthful of briny spirits. "What's in this, anyway?"

"It's supposed to be vodka with tabasco, lemon juice and an olive. But he didn't have any of that, so I told him to improvise."

Sarah pushes away the last of the murky water.

132

"That car outside—it's yours?" Dilara asks.

"How did you know?"

"It suits you. Will you give me a lift back to Hastings? I need to get out before dark."

*

Hastings is home to a tiny airstrip with a single short runway—the only patch of land on the peninsula, flat enough to land a plane on, but not long enough for a commercial airport. A tarmac road leads around the coast, but far more fun is the muddy track that climbs up and over the crown of the peninsula, passable only in a 4x4 or on foot. The dry season is ending, and the first rains have begun to lash the sun-scorched earth, cracked and uneven after six months of drought. The rain has dug out deep ruts and uneven rivulets in the steep slope. The Land Rover is in its element. Sarah feels a twitch of pride being able to show off her driving skills to Dilara, feeling for the first time competent in her presence.

"What's her name?" Dilara asks, gripping the dashboard as they navigate a particularly deep wash-out.

"I'm not sure yet," Sarah says. "I like Tonkolili, it's a district in the north of the country. I like the way it rolls off the tongue."

"It's a bit rough? She's a princess!"

"Princess Tonkolili?"

Dilara strokes her hand over the open window frame. "We'll see."

Not far from the airstrip, an extraordinary building towers over the road. A futuristic creation in glass and steel, still half-finished but already enormously out-of-scale with the low-level buildings that surround it. A forest of funnels and cones in green-blue glass with metal cladding covering all the external surfaces to assure complete privacy from the outside. Two turrets top the structure like watchtowers, wrought in silver and glass. The entire compound is ringed by a high perimeter wall crowned

133

with thick snakes of razor wire.

"What the hell is that? It looks like Dr Evil's lair," Sarah says.

"You haven't been up here before?" Dilara asks. "I thought you'd have been invited. It's Skarparov's place."

"Skarparov lives there?" Sarah asks, open-mouthed. "Could he do any more to make himself look like an arch-villain? I wonder what the neighbours think."

"It's a landmark, no? One of our contractors is helping with the construction, but apparently Skarparov insisted on them using local labour wherever they could. He says people like it. It puts Hastings on the map."

"It looks like the physical embodiment of ill-gotten gains."

"Money is money. And there is not much of it in this country. If someone comes and wants to spend it here, and employ local workmen, why would anyone want to stop him?"

Skarparov, the hero of Sierra Leone again. Sarah is astounded by how many people believe his spin. But perhaps they have little choice.

She drops Dilara at the airstrip where her private plane is waiting. The shiny red Beechcraft with its elongated nose and gleaming chrome propellor tips could not have looked more out of place on the deserted airstrip, rich with moss. Sarah wonders how many times she'll have to stop and refuel to cover the distance in the aviation equivalent of a girly gun. But before she can ask, Dilara kisses her on both cheeks, squeezing her in for an affectionate embrace and climbs into the plane. Sarah watches her take off, shielding her eyes from the sun now hovering at the horizon.

Back in Princess Tonkolili, she navigates the busy streets of Hastings following the slogans on the back of the poda-podas and shared taxis—the *'Big Boss Man'* takes her back to the main road, sticking close behind *'No Thing is Permanent'* helps her negotiate a street market that spilled out on the road and *'Marvellous'* swinging to a sudden stop at the side of the road makes sure she doesn't miss her turning to the mountain road.

Everything looks hyper-real in the golden evening light. She taps out an upbeat rhythm on the steering wheel, the fire in her stomach fuelled not just by the after glow of Dilara's Dou Dou's. She is revelling in the sense of freedom that comes from being alone in an unknown corner of the world, with a car that could take you anywhere. Until the oil light on the dashboard flashes red.

That is not a good sign.

The light flickers off and she pushes the car up the hill, trying to pick the gentlest angles of the steep slope to avoid strain. A sharp brake to avoid a pothole and the oil light flashes again. She should stop the car as soon as possible, but then what? On a completely deserted strip of road with no houses nearby, let alone other cars, the chances of someone arriving to help are small.

She pushes on, watching the temperature gauge on the dashboard creep up until the car shudders and a loud thumping starts up under the gearbox. Oh, come on Tonks—this is most certainly not princess behaviour—you can't give up now.

But Princess Tonkolili has other ideas. With a final shudder from the gear stick and another loud bang, she stops. Sarah turns off the engine and takes a deep breath. No reason to panic. This isn't the first time a Land Rover has given up on her at an inconvenient moment. There are always options. She goes to open the bonnet, but it won't move. Peering under the catch at the front, she tries to wiggle her fingers in, but the mechanism that holds the bonnet down is completely jammed. She tries pressing, jiggling, a few applications of brute force, but nothing moves an inch. She has got this far without even looking under the hood—her father would be horrified. But if she can't get the bonnet open, there isn't much she can do alone on a muddy hillside with no proper tools or kit.

The sun has long disappeared behind the hills, leaving only a dim glow around a bruise of clouds.

She tries to stay calm and think through her options.

Reluctantly she calls Elias—not wanting to admit she has already broken her new toy—but his number is not in service. She tries Ibrahim: he lives in Hastings and even if he isn't home, he should know someone who could help. His number rings out with a loud beep. Now what?

She slumps back against the bonnet, the radiator grill scalding her back. There is nothing for it, it is embarrassing and awkward but at least she is sure he'll come. She'll have to call Chris.

*

To his credit, he comes straightaway and even brings a proper tow rope, though he can't resist a bit of teasing. "Did you even open the bonnet and have a look?"

"Yes, I tried, but I can't get it open: it's jammed shut."

"It's not just too heavy for you with the tyre mount?" It's a genuine question, but it makes Sarah want to smack him. She tries not to smirk, watching him struggle unsuccessfully with the locked catch.

"Poor old thing," he says with more sympathy than sarcasm. "We'll get her back to the mechanics at the High Commission. They'll have her set to right in no time."

"What brought you all the way out here?" he asks as they secure the tow rope to the Land Rover.

"I was giving a friend a lift."

"And he couldn't help you out in return?"

"She's gone."

Chris raises an eyebrow. "I'm flattered that you called. And I'm glad I got here in time." He looks to the purple-stained sky. "It's a dangerous place here, Sarah. I know you enjoy striking out on your own, but some things are just more stupid than brave."

She stares out of the window, not in the mood for advice from Chris, but also slightly haunted by what might have happened if he hadn't come for her. She knows she was lucky.

"Sorry, I didn't mean to lecture. I just wanted to say don't be afraid to call. It's no shame to ask for help from time to time." He gives a reassuring smile as he climbs into the air-conditioned bubble of his Land Cruiser. For the first time since Sarah met him, he seems genuine, his many faces finally put aside.

Sarah sets her powerless princess in neutral. The symbolism of the moment is grim—sitting at the wheel of Elias's beautiful car, unable to do anything more than steer and brake, while relying on the uninspired engineering of Chris's boring box to get her home. They roll the car into the mechanics' shed at the High Commission, greeted by looks of commiseration and sympathy from the guards. The head mechanic looks delighted with the job. "I know this car. It used to belong to a friend of mine twenty years ago! He never looked after it. I can't believe it's still on the road. Don't worry," he says, placing a reassuring hand on Sarah's shoulder, "we'll get it running again soon."

CHAPTER 22

Sarah meets Elias at the helipad. On the phone, he had sounded like a stranger. She couldn't tell if he was just exhausted or pissed off. Could he already have heard about her meeting with Chris?

His tall, red-headed figure climbing out of George's chopper is unmistakable, but his face is unrecognisable. His eyes are small and shot with red, a deep crease digs between his brows and his chin juts forward in a way that Sarah has never seen before. She goes to put her arms around his neck and pull him in for a kiss, but he pushes her away. "Don't."

Still smarting from the rejection, Sarah goes to negotiate with one of the local taxi drivers.

"Where's the Land Rover?" he asks, looking at her with disbelief, as if she's deliberately forgotten to bring it.

"It broke down last night. It's being fixed up."

"What did you do to it?"

"Nothing, I've just been driving it. It gave up on the hill coming up from Hastings, but I couldn't open the hood and see what was wrong."

"You've been driving it around all week, but you haven't even looked under the hood to check the oil or fluid levels? I thought you were supposed to know what you were doing."

"I know, I should have checked. But I was too excited with my new toy."

He ignores her attempt to be light.

"Where are we going?" she asks, waiting to instruct the taxi driver.

"Fuck, I don't know, just drive."

*

They pull up at one of the bars that line the long flat strip of Lumley Beach—single storey, blue and yellow paint up the walls, rumpled sheets of dark green corrugated iron on the roof and a couple of skinny palm trees for shade. A placid girl behind the bar stares contentedly into the middle distance until Elias slaps the bar to get her attention. He orders two whiskey and cokes and a beer for Sarah. He downs his first drink without a word and starts on the second.

"What happened? How was the meeting?" Sarah wants to unlock whatever has caused Elias to shut down. His body language seethes and roils, his normally twinkling eyes are narrow and hard, and he can scarcely look at her.

"The meeting never happened," he says, draining his glass and waving it at the waitress for more. "Someone knew we were coming. It was a set-up."

"What do you mean?"

"I mean, Sarah," he says, using her name like a weapon, "that there was no meeting. I picked up Kobus's buddy and we were on our way to meet Skarparov when the car was ambushed."

"What? By who?" Sarah's mind goes immediately to the rebels Elias had been negotiating with in the bush, with their languid drug-addled stares and weapons worn like jewellery.

"A group of soldiers—Nigerian, I think—all skin-tight vests and flashy gold-tint sunglasses, waving their guns around and high as kites. They pulled us out of the car, had us lie down in the mud while they rifled through everything we had on us."

Sarah feels sick, picturing Fattmatu in the hands of the rebels and reliving her own powerless response. "What did they want?"

"Damned if I know. Money? Ammo? The chance to smack someone over the back of the head with a rifle butt?"

Sarah shudders. "Were either of you hurt?"

"Not too badly, more humiliation than torture, kicking dust in our faces, pulling off our clothes… But it was enough."

"How did you get away?" Sarah can taste fear in her own throat. She can smell the red grit of the road and the rubber of the hot tyres.

"They got bored, grabbed our bags and ran off."

"Thank God you weren't hurt. How was Kobus's contact?"

"Terrified and shell-shocked. I don't think we'll see him again."

Elias downs his third drink and lights a cigarette, sucking on it with such strength it is down to the filter in a few short puffs. He stares stubbornly at the sea to avoid having to look at Sarah.

"It must have been awful. But you're here, you're unharmed." She reaches for his hand. "It could have been worse."

"It's fucking terrible," he snaps, brushing her hand away.

"Please, don't take it out on me."

He looks at her, twisting his mouth to bite on the inside of his lips. "You really don't get it, do you?" His voice is slurred and loose. "They *knew* we were coming. Who did you tell about the meeting?"

"I didn't tell anyone. I never discussed it other than with George and Kobus, but they would never—"

"Who did you fucking tell?" Elias thumps his hand on the table making the glasses shake. "You could have had us killed."

Sarah is torn between trying to appease his terrifying anger and standing up to defend herself. "I promise you this was nothing to do with me. I've been waiting for you here. Who would I have spoken to?"

"Where's that snivelling little rat? I bet it was him."

"Who?"

"Your friend, the creepy blond who seems to be all over you every time I turn my back."

"Chris? He had nothing to do with it."

"So you're sticking up for him now? How do you know it

wasn't him?"

Sarah falls silent. How does she tell Elias that she had been with Chris without provoking his anger even further? And not just once, but twice? If the source of all this rage is that he already knows, she might make it worse by not admitting to it.

"I'm sure it wasn't him," she says, ripping off a piece of the red paper tablecloth and rolling it between her fingers. But she isn't sure. She had let slip to Chris that Elias was setting up a sting. Could Chris have betrayed him to Skarparov? She squeezes the roll of red paper into a hard little lump and digs it up underneath her fingernail.

"I wouldn't trust him as far as I could throw him, and I'd like to have a good go at chucking his smug face into the sea."

"I can see why you wouldn't trust him. But I don't think it can have been him." She takes a deep breath before looking into Elias's damaged eyes. "I was with him yesterday."

Elias flies up, almost kicking over the table. Sarah shrinks back as he slams his knuckles into the wooden post holding up the roof. The girl at the bar breaks out of her reverie to stare at them, her eyes quick with fear.

"Elias, calm down. It's not how it looks. He was just helping me out when I got stuck."

Elias turns to leave. Sarah realises it is the first time she has ever seen him without his yellow canvas satchel slung over his shoulder.

"Wait, Elias."

"Not now. I just can't."

Sarah stands to face him; she can't let him run away in this state. She has to try and bring him back. "Why are you so angry? Nothing happened. You got roughed up but you're here and you're safe. I promise you have nothing to be jealous about with Chris, he's not half the man you are."

"They took my bag, Sarah."

"I'm sorry."

"No, you still don't get this. They took my *bag*. I was carrying all the documents I've lifted from Skarparov's office over the last couple of weeks, they were all in my bag which I made sure never left my side. Now they have it."

An iron ring tightens around Sarah's chest. Please God don't let this be as bad as it looks. "But what are a bunch of Nigerian soldiers going to care about some papers in a satchel? Surely they'll only be looking for money?"

"Unless your friend told them what to look for."

"He's not my friend; stop making this into something it isn't."

Elias chucks some notes on the bar towards the terrified girl and storms out the door.

"I'm on your side," Sarah calls after him.

He spins round in the doorway and towers over her. "Are you, Sarah? Are you really? Because, you know, I've been wondering what the hell you've got me into here. And for what? Your affection when it suits you? How many others have you got doing your dirty work?"

"Elias, please—"

"I'm out. I've had enough of this place. I need to get out of here before this fucking mess blows up in my face. Here, you can have this, I've got no use for it now." He pulls his black leather notebook from his back pocket and throws it to her. It contains all his meticulously gathered data about the rebels' camps and movements and carefully illustrated maps.

"You can't really mean that you're leaving for good?"

"I'm done here." He storms out of the bar and takes off down the beach.

Sarah chases after him, having to run to catch up with his long-legged stride. "But we can still get him. Before he has the chance—"

"You can go to him yourself. He asked me to bring you to him. I guess my job is done."

Sarah stops dead in the sand. "He asked you *what*?"

"He wanted you on his side. He thought he could turn you. I think he was only humouring my presence because I could bring you in."

"Why the hell did you never tell me this before?"

"Because I knew you'd react like this."

"Like what?"

"Like you've got another crazed bee in your bonnet, obsessed that you're right and blind to everything else. Why don't you just take off the fucking bonnet?"

Sarah tries to laugh but Elias is still fuming.

"Look," he says with a trace of regret. "I thought it offered you some protection. So long as he thought you were a potential recruit, you were safe from him. But I think this has blown it for the both of us. Sorry." He turns away from her. "I can't."

"Elias! Please wait—you don't have to go."

He doesn't respond or even look back.

"Elias, please. I love you." The words tumble out before Sarah can catch them. The smallest of phrases, the lightest of words, but still something that has never been said.

He looks back over his shoulder, his eyes small and cruel. "Don't bother."

CHAPTER 23

Alec from the MOD has been talking for too long already. It is unusual for him to take up this much time. He normally looks more interested in the biscuits than the meeting's content. But today he is more wary.

"There's no doubt that the RUF is heavily rearming. The peace accord with its provisions for disarmament is clearly not worth the paper it was written on." His heavy Glaswegian accent gives a gravitas to his pronouncements that forces the others to listen. Are the reports getting worse, or is this just the first time he's read them? Michael is worried Alec's performance might prove too convincing.

"I do think it's time to reassess our position here," Alec finishes, looking to Beverley for confirmation.

Beverley straightens the brooch pinned to her pale pink cardigan and pauses, allowing Alec's words to lose some of their force before replying. "I think we need to put these reports in context. We have been receiving news of this variety for some time now. It shouldn't be a surprise to anyone that the rebels have access to arms. As far as I know, they never committed to the disarmament process in any real way. But is anything really new here? No one is pretending the situation is good, but has there been any substantial change that would merit a shift in our position?"

"With all due respect, Beverley, I think it's quite plain from the latest telex reports, things are worse now than ever. The rebels are closing in on key bridgeheads around the entrance to

Freetown, clearing the way for a march on an unprotected city."

"After the last time, we all swore it would never happen again," the young woman from DFID cuts in. She tucks her ruler-straight brown hair behind her ears, the tips of which are glowing red. This is the first time Michael has ever seen her speak up against Beverley's direction. He can almost smell her fear as she waits for Beverley's response.

Beverley turns back to Alec. "But is that really the situation we're facing? Do you see a risk of another full attack on Freetown?"

"I haven't got a crystal ball, but I'd say if the UN and ECOMOG are requesting back-up then we'd do well to listen to them. Another group of UN peacekeepers, Kenyans this time, have just been captured by the rebels. They're clearly up to the wall." He sits back, lifting his collar away from the shaving rash on his neck.

David from the Treasury sits down his coffee cup with unnecessary force. He isn't one for details, but when he does speak, he wants to be sure they are all listening. "Before we get too carried away," he begins, running a hand through his full hair, "can I please remind you of all the existing troop commitments. They're already complaining about shoddy kit. We can't magic money out of nowhere to fund another intervention." Michael nods in quiet agreement.

Jeff Black from the cabinet office takes off his reading glasses and pinches the bridge of his nose. "It's not mentioned in any of these reports," he says, "but I was wondering if anyone had heard anything about a uranium find in Sierra Leone?" he looks around the table before settling his stare on Michael.

Michael holds his eye. There isn't much resemblance, but the turn of the jaw and determined stare are enough to confirm his suspicions. This doddery-looking chap is indeed Sarah's father. He must be being briefed by his daughter, but what the hell is he doing throwing it in here? It must be a family trait—sticking their noses in where it doesn't belong.

Beverley rifles through her papers and looks to Michael for

145

support.

"Uranium in Sierra Leone? It seems unlikely." Michael stares at Jeff. "Where did you get that from?"

"Just a rumour I picked up from an old friend," Jeff says, undaunted by Michael's stare. "But if the regime there is really on the brink of absolute collapse, it would seem important to know if it's real."

Michael gives Beverley a wry smile. "I would be very careful believing anything passed on by untested sources. Surely, if it was true, the big mining companies would be sniffing around? Anyway, can't someone just ask the government? Isn't this the sort of thing the High Commissioner should know about? Has he reported anything on the find?"

Beverley turns over her briefing papers again, shaking her head. "I'll be sure to ask the High Commissioner to follow up. Right, Somalia?"

"But aren't we going to do anything about these reports?" Alec asks, his tone exasperated. "There are a number of Brits out there we're responsible to get out if Freetown does fall, not to count the other nationalities who'd expect our help. Surely we need some sort of plan?"

"I'll raise it with the High Commissioner." Beverley gives a decisive nod to Alec to indicate that she is ready to move on.

"And are you confident in his assessment?" Michael asks, never one to miss the chance to cast doubt on the opinions of others.

"I'll go out there myself if I have to. Nothing like a first-hand assessment. And I'm due a trip that way. Right, we do need to move on, who's read the latest cable from Mogadishu?"

Michael closes the lid on his fountain pen with a satisfying click. Another successful conclusion, and he scarcely had to open his mouth. Beverley's instinct to put off making any decisions serves him perfectly. But he would have to put pressure on Chris to hurry up. Sarah's meddling is trouble enough without her feeding unnecessary information to her father. It is time to bring her home.

CHAPTER 24

Sarah lets Elias leave the beach without chasing after him. She is too hurt to keep fighting, when everything she says only makes him more upset. Once the fury has abated, she will try again to persuade him she had nothing to do with his setup.

But the next day she can't find him. His phone is switched off or rings through with no answer. She sends dozens of text messages but hears nothing back. She tracks down George the chopper pilot—Elias normally crashes at his place when he is in Freetown with nowhere to stay, and after the ambush he might be one of the few people in whom Elias could confide. But George hasn't heard from him since he dropped him off at the helipad. She tries calling Kobus, but he is up in Koidu in the mines and out of reception. She even tries combing all the beach bars along the Lumley strip, right down to the seedier joints at the end, where bored-looking hookers swivel on bar stools, waiting for a deep-pocketed customer. No one has heard from him.

Hot, tired and despondent, she hails a taxi back to her hotel. She can't let him leave like this. Surely he wasn't serious about leaving the country because of this one incident? She remembers how she felt after witnessing the attack at the Chief's house, desperate for escape; but she had thought Elias was made of sterner stuff. Even if he is set on leaving, she can't let him go on this sour note. It makes her heart ache to think that he blames her for what happened, and her soul droop to think that he questions her loyalty.

There *is* a strange frisson with Chris. He intrigues her and attracts her in a way she finds difficult to explain. Particularly as she doesn't even like him. But that is all—a chemical reaction, a pheromone sniff, a primeval piece of mating ritual. She would never act on it. She has to reassure Elias that his jealousy is unfounded. But if she can't find him, how can she possibly convince him to stay?

*

Another day passes with no news, and Sarah grows desperate. She sits on the terrace behind the hotel restaurant where the phone reception is strongest and orders another black coffee. She can't face another sympathetic look from the girl at reception as she tells her, again, that she has no messages. Without Elias, her very presence in Freetown seems absurd. Should she just cut her losses and join Elias on the first flight out of here? Could she admit defeat and let Skarparov get away again? As an option, it offers only the illusion of escape. A return to London would mean a return to the circling journalists looking to connect her to corruption in the Caucasus. And how could she give up before getting to the bottom of Michael's involvement with Skarparov?

Her father is right. She has been too blinkered to take time to properly assess the board, to understand her opponent and think through her options. She has relied too heavily on Elias to do her dirty work, without thinking through the other pieces she has in play.

She lines up the salt and pepper shakers on the table like a pair of opposing pawns, and mentally fills in the gaps. The helicopter deal is dead. Skarparov won't trust Elias, and he certainly won't trust her, even if it's true that he wants to recruit her. What other pieces could be called into play. Chris? He knows as well as she does which crimes Skarparov has to answer for, and surely he hasn't been swayed by the 'Hero of Sierra Leone' spin. But Chris is condescending of Sarah's outrage, writing it off as a personal revenge mission and Skarparov just a small-fry villain. Besides, she can't bring herself to turn to him for help.

What weaknesses does Skarparov have in his position that she can exploit? She pushes forward the ashtray to join the imaginary ranks. Kuznetsov, the Russian agent she met at the High Commission. The Russians have even more reason than her to want to get Skarparov—they delivered their shipment of weapons as payment for an attack in Georgia that never happened. But is the enemy of my enemy really my friend? Can she honestly see herself cosying up to the KGB just to get even with Skarparov?

She keeps playing through her strategy book, looking for what might work on a player of Skarparov's calibre. If not Kuznetsov, is there another unexpected alliance she could form? She advances the bowl holding sachets of brown sugar. Dilara? She always seemed keen to help, and they are linked in their hunt for the uranium. But could Sarah really count on her to be on her side? Surely she is too close to Michael to ever be a true ally.

What are Skarparov's weaknesses? Greed, vanity, over-confidence? Which of these can she exploit to tempt him to make an attack that leaves him weaker? What does he want more than anything? The access to the diamond licences granted by Foday Sankoh is already a considerable prize. But one already won. Sarah has no doubt that his sights will be set on the next source of dirty cash and connections. He will be after the same thing that everyone in Freetown wants—the uranium.

She just needs to get there first.

She has already asked everyone she can think of, but still hasn't been able to track down who first approached the government with the find. Either no one knows, or no one dares say—either way, Sarah has to dig deeper.

The only facts she has are that the samples came from the area near Koidu and the diamond mines—deep in the rebels' stronghold—and were tested at the Rössing mine in Namibia.

Sarah stares again at her makeshift board, searching for what she might be missing. But for now it's clear.

If no one here is willing to talk, she will have to go there.

*

Landing in Windhoek, the capital of Namibia, after a twenty-two-hour journey, Sarah feels flung forward in time. The buildings are shiny and new, the roads look like a film set with a glossy topcoat of tarmac and bright white markings. Sarah marvels as a man on a bicycle wearing a helmet stops at a red light. She can scarcely imagine a set of circumstances more alien to Sierra Leone. But she still feels coated in the tropical blight—her clothing and hair smell stale and damp. The unmistakable sourness of mould seems to follow her around. The exhaustion of two overnight flights, snatching sleep on metal chairs in airport lounges, weighs heavily on her soul and she is tempted to sneak off to one of Windhoek's luxury hotels to sleep in a clean bed and soak in a clean tub. But there is no time for that.

The car rental salesman tries to fob her off with one of his fleet of shiny white Land Cruisers, but Sarah is having none of it. She sets off on the three-hour journey to the Rössing Mine in a Land Rover Defender—not about to let one breakdown shake the loyalty of a lifetime. The boost to her bank balance from her time working for Michael is now almost entirely depleted—she might as well enjoy what remains.

The landscape is invigorating to her weary soul. A palette of dazzling blues, yellows and greens turning to peach and apricot dunes as the savannah gives way to desert. Each time her eyes adjust to the majesty of the landscape, the crest of a hill reveals another heart-stopping vista. Something in the quality of the light makes everything look more alive—the shadows darker, the contrasts sharper. Even the soft-hued colours of the desert are more arresting than anything she has ever seen. She drinks in the dry air with great gulps, shaking off the tropical stupor and feeling optimistic for the first time in days.

As she approaches the mine, the flat desert landscape bubbles and roils; craters and hills in pale moon-rock grey sprout from the ground as if the surface has blistered in the unrelenting sun. The mine itself suddenly introduces man-made lines to the fluid formations, with terraces sinking down like amphitheatre steps to an artificial riverbed below, its yellow dusty banks churned up by truck tyres. The Rössing mine—one of the largest uranium mines in the world and operational for over twenty-five years—is a sight to behold.

Mr H Bok, the technician she spoke to on the phone, meets her at the entrance in full protective gear, thick black gloves, a mask and safety glasses that obscure most of his face. His name is neatly stencilled on the front of his hard hat.

"Sarah? You are our leaf friend from Sierra Leone?" he greets her with a broad smile, stripping off some of his protective gear to shake her hand and reveal a surprisingly young-looking face, pale brown skin and wide round eyes. Sarah sticks with her cover story—she is studying for her PhD in leaf decay and wants to find out more about the analysis that was done on the Sierra Leone samples. "Great to have you here." His open face is eager and open but there is a trace of calculated curiosity in his eyes. Is he trying to weigh up how she could be useful to him?

"Thank you for seeing me at such short notice. I've redirected some of my research since I arrived in Sierra Leone. There is so much excitement about the uranium discovery, I wanted to build it into my work."

"How does uranium fit with leaf decay?" Bok looks sceptical.

"I want to see if there are any plants that could be used as markers for uranium ore. But I need to understand a bit more about the composition of the samples and what other minerals are coming up alongside the ore." She hopes it sounds plausible enough.

"I've done all the sampling work myself," he says with evident pride. "I can get you the full breakdown. It's a wonderful story there, don't you think? Of all the times and all the places to come up a with a find like this. I've got a friend who's working out there, but he's learnt that I don't really want to hear his stories. It's all too sad, you know? You've got to hope a find like this might be able to finally do them some good. Luck can't always run bad." Bok speaks with the verbose patter of one who spent too long alone in the desert. As soon as there is someone else to listen, it all has to come out.

"Is the find significant?"

"If the samples they've sent us are representative of the whole deposit, and if it's a sizeable unconformity-type deposit, then yes, those guys up there in the middle of their civil war are sitting on some serious cheese."

"I don't know if that's a blessing or a curse," she says.

"Here, come and have a look." He bounds through the laboratory filled with gleaming machines, sleek metal tables and benches, testing equipment, cups, jars and vats of materials in every stage of analysis. It all feels clinical and clean, cold and precise after the muddle-through atmosphere of Freetown.

"It's quite an operation you have here," Sarah says, running her eye over the banks of equipment and top-of-the-range computers.

"We have a lot to process just here at the mine. Then it's not uncommon for us to get requests like this one from our friends in Sierra Leone. There aren't many labs in Africa that can do what we can. And people trust our results." He gives a satisfied smile.

"It must be difficult even getting things in and out of Freetown. How have you been sending things over?"

"DHL can do some great things, even in a warzone."

Sarah throws in a line. "Can I help carry anything back for you? I've got plenty of space in my luggage allowance. It's probably quicker and definitely cheaper."

"Yeah, logistics is a bit of a nightmare, but I'm good for now thanks."

No bite.

She casts again. "Have you been working with the guys in Kono, or the team based in Freetown?"

"I just know them as the Kono Uranium Company, but I guess they could be based somewhere else."

"And can you show me the results on the cores?" She might as well try to get something out of her visit, even if it is beyond her understanding of chemistry and geology.

"Of course, I can print it all off for you." He opens a file on a sleek black computer and sends the document to print. He flicks through the print outs before proudly handing her the data. A series of chemical compounds with respective weights and percentages that looks like code.

"The Kono uranium definitely has a unique signature—as you can see it's pretty rich in magnesium and calcites which makes it different from what we have here, but the isotopes are good."

Sarah runs her eye down the figures and nods knowingly. She recognises some names of the elements, but otherwise it is pretty meaningless. And there is no detail of the Kono Uranium Company—no name, no contact details, nothing that advances her position.

"These are fascinating." She ups her enthusiasm staring at the disappointing list. "I can't wait to compare this to some of my preliminary study results. Do you have a contact name for someone there I can talk to, to follow up? I think they might want to see some of my data when it comes to selecting the license areas."

Bok looks at her curiously, as if weighing up whether she is asking for more than he should give. There must be confidentiality issues at play, but surely he can overlook them for a harmless leaf specialist. "Yes, yes, I guess I can find that for you," he says at last. "Hold on, let me dig into the paperwork."

Finally, a lead.

He pulls out the bottom drawer of a sturdy filing cabinet and rifles through the files. "Here you go, this is the contact they gave us." As he looks down at the paper, his face falls in what might be relief. "Shame, I guess this isn't going to be much use for you." The paperwork is addressed simply to the Kono Uranium Company at a PO Box address in Freetown.

"That's it? No more details on the DHL receipts?" Sarah tries to swallow down the plummeting weight in her chest.

Bok taps his forehead with his finger. "You're after a job, eh? That's why you're so keen to meet this bunch. If you ask me, it's not the people that found the stuff you should be chasing. It's the guys who come in to buy the concession. They'll bring a whole team of geologists and prospectors and probably their own lab guys too. Who knows, they may look to hire a leaf specialist? A buddy of mine works for a company in Kazakhstan—he told me they hired two-hundred-and-fifty people overnight when the find was confirmed. And I can't imagine there are that many people queuing up to work in Sierra Leone."

Sarah gives a weak smile. Bok's endless chatter on all topics except what she wants to know is starting to grate.

"You know, I think you should come and work down here." Bok continues in his jovial manner. "It's a far nicer place if you ask me, and we've got some world-leading research going on. A nice young scientist like yourself would always be made most welcome."

Sarah gives a non-committal nod.

"I spend most of my time at the moment in research and development," he says. "We're trying to simplify the yellow-cake production using anthracite and gypsum to make the process less dangerous for those working on it. It's exciting times. And plenty of field trips up to the Skeleton Coast where they get the anthracite. Have you been up there yet? The landscape will blow your mind."

"I only arrived in Namibia this morning."

"Well, let me arrange your trip. You've got a good car?"

"I've rented a Land Rover, but—"

"Then you're all set. It's like nowhere else on Earth. I did an

155

amazing trip there once with a good buddy of mine. We were camping near the coast and kept hearing all these strange sounds. You know the dunes up there make noise like they're alive—they roar and grumble in the wind as loud as a low-flying plane. So you get kind of used to the noise, but this was different, you know? Like a pot coming to the boil."

Sarah is wondering how this story is going to entice her to go camping with him, but lets him continue.

"We went down to the beach, and there was a huge beached whale. Massive dead body, all puffed up and swollen. The noise was coming from the whale. It was the weirdest thing. It looked like it was moving. Then, as we were watching it, it suddenly blew. BAM! The thing went up like it was packed with TNT."

"It exploded?" Sarah says.

"Yup, it can happen when it's really ripe. You get a build-up of methane inside the carcass, and eventually something has to give. So there we were, watching this great beast on the beach, and suddenly it's spewing guts and intestines and blood and all this crap all over the sand. And man, the smell, you wouldn't believe it. *Eish—so vrot!* I thought I was going to smell rotten whale's belly for the rest of my life."

"I can imagine," Sarah stands to leave.

"Anyway, it's pretty rare, so I don't think you need to worry about it. What do you say? I can set up a trip at the weekend if you're keen. Where else can you watch elephants sliding down sand dunes? You might even get a lion!"

"I'm going to have to come back another time. I've got work to finish in Sierra Leone." Sarah can scarcely contain her frustration at another dead end, and is in no mood for Bok's incessant chatter. "And there aren't enough leaves for me in the desert," she adds, trying to resurrect Bok's crestfallen smile.

She takes the paperwork and a copy of the PO Box address—it might be possible to charm the post office into letting her know who holds that number. Bok keeps up his churn of stories until they are back at her car.

"Think about it, won't you?" he says as she makes ready to leave.

"Hmmm?"

"The camping trip. Now's not really the best time of year but if you come back in a couple of months..."

She starts the engine and drives off.

CHAPTER 25

Michael finds Sir Thomas Graham MP by the fire in White's, enjoying his second pot of tea. His afternoon tea habits were easy to predict. Michael hopes his opposition to anything that might smell of interventionism would prove just as reliable.

"Sir Thomas, may I join you? Michael Smith from the Foreign Office." He offers his hand as he slips into a red leather armchair opposite the Scottish Labour Party Member for Abercorn.

"Only if you'll call me Tam. Sir Thomas was my father." He speaks in a soft Scottish accent, looking up at Michael through thick, black-framed glasses that cast shadows over sceptical eyes.

"Tam. Of course."

Michael settles back in his chair and waits. Conversations are always smoother when the other party feels themselves to be the instigator. His eye roams the room, scanning the faces of the other men present, carrying out a final check that there was no one here he knew. Even for Michael, this place always feels unsubtle in its celebration of testosterone. The low lighting of the lamps on the marble sideboards almost seems angled to highlight the tight white breeches of the military portraits.

"Which bit of the Foreign Office are you from?" Tam asks, having slurped down his second cup.

"African desk. Sierra Leone."

"Are you now? Would you happen to know what's going to be in the statement of the Foreign Secretary to the House next week? There are rumours around that he's going to ask for a commitment of UK troops."

Michael makes a show of discomfort, knotting his brow as a conflicted civil servant might. "It does look likely. The circumstances are increasingly grave, but opinions on the appropriate course of action still vary right up to the top."

"So not everyone's behind the intervention?"

"Certainly not." Michael glances around the room and leans in, lowering his tone for effect. "I'm in no position to speak against the final decision of the Foreign Secretary, but I can't help but see it as a risk we can't afford to take."

"How so?"

"Another group of UN troops was recently kidnapped, taking the total to over five hundred. What assurances do we have that British troops won't go the same way?"

"It's refreshing to hear such honesty from one of your lot."

"To me it feels like a slippery slope," Michael continues furtively. "Who's to say the British forces won't be drawn into fighting for the government in their never-ending civil war?"

"Indeed." Tam nods as he spreads jam on a scone. Weighty jowls slump over the rim of his collar, pulling down his cheeks into a look of permanent disgruntlement. He resettles himself on his chair, creaking the buttoned leather. "The Secretary of State for Defence made a statement only a few weeks ago that the British forces are already significantly overstretched. And yet we seem to be considering an open-ended commitment to help."

"Quite so." Michael nods.

"I have a mind to put these very questions to the Foreign Secretary in the House. These are answers that need to be given."

"And I assure you there are many in the department would support your intervention." Michael says with a deferential nod.

"Yet again, here I am cast as Cassandra. You remember Cassandra?"

"Warning the Trojans of impending doom when no one listened? Of course. But she was proved right in the end."

"And so she was." Tam waggles a thick-knuckled finger towards Michael. "Someone has to be the one to ask the difficult questions, and it often falls to those of us cursed with the gift of foresight."

Michael gives an understanding nod. No need to push any harder on this open door.

CHAPTER 26

Sarah thumps back onto the tarmac in Lungi with a heavy heart. Her trip to Namibia was a waste of time, and she has still heard nothing from Elias. The journey and time spent in travellers' limbo left her soul lost halfway up the continent. Her natural optimism feels stifled and her brain too congested with worry to think.

She picks up her car from the High Commission garage, happily without having to make a show of gratitude to Chris, and goes in search of Mammy Kamara. If it is true what Ibrahim said about her market women knowing all there is to know in Freetown, perhaps they might know who is behind the mystery Kono Uranium Company. And a link to the Kamajors could be just the peace offering she needs for when Elias does finally reappear. More good guys to take on Foday Sankoh's snakes.

*

The stalls of Victoria Market overflow with silver cooking pots in bright tie-died buckets; rolls of linoleum balanced on yellow jerry cans; small pale cucumbers, long brown yams, gnarled carrots and mismatched tomatoes filling rusty wheelbarrows. Vendors walk the market balancing trays on their heads, selling everything from freshly shelled peanuts to cassette tapes. One small boy balances a basket of melons on his head, while using his hands to roll an old tyre along the dusty tarmac.

Mammy Kamara was easy to track down—everyone knew

her. Sarah finds her sitting on a deckchair, holding court amongst the tightly packed stalls. She hoists up her brightly coloured skirt when she sees Sarah and struggles to her feet.

"I know you, you're Ibrahim's girl from the High Commission." As she greets Sarah, she drops her smile and a flash of concern passes through her normally mischievous eyes. She shakes her head as if to flick away whatever unwanted premonition she detected in Sarah's face and squeezes her hand tighter. "Why you no come to see me before?"

"Sorry, Mammy. I've been away."

"But now you want something?"

"I do, in fact." Sarah is a little abashed at being so transparent.

"I can tell; you have that look about you. You're not just here to chat. There is no force equal to that of a determined woman." She hoots with laughter. "What can I do for you?"

"I've got a PO Box address for a company. I want to find out who they are. Any ideas?"

"I know just the woman for you. Eh-eh!" she calls to a girl with a tray of peppers on her head and shouts instructions in a stream of Krio too rapid for Sarah to follow. The girl bolts off through the market, managing not to spill a single pepper as she runs. "She de come, she de come," Mammy Kamara nods, pulling out an upturned tub for Sarah to sit on.

Sarah's mobile rings. Putting a finger in one ear to block out the noises of the market, she picks up.

"Is that Sarah Black?" a stiff and formal voice, echoing from many miles away. "This is Benjamin Griffiths, the British High Commissioner. I believe we met at my Residence on Europe Day." Sarah's stomach clenches and her heart pushes high in her chest, as if her body knows what is coming before her mind does.

"There's been an accident," he says in practised professional tones. "One of the Lungi helicopters has gone up in flames just before take-off. The firefighters' response was …" he cuts off, clearly lost for words. "All those aboard have been declared dead." The words come like the slow toll of a bell.

Sarah feels the ground beneath her pitch and sway. She stays silent, not wanting to ask the inevitable question.

"There was a Dutch national on the flight manifest—an Elias van Heemskerck. I believe you knew him?"

Sarah hears nothing more. She drops the phone and falls to her knees, beating her fists into the pounded mud. A cry—part-growl, part-roar—wretches from her throat in tremulous convulsions, as if her body is trying to expel a poison. She beats her head against the ground, kneading the skin of her forehead into the bitter dust.

A firm hand finds her shoulder. Mammy Kamara prises her off the ground, forcing her jack-knifed body to straighten, and drapes her over a staunch shoulder. Nothing feels real. Sarah's legs shake as they grope for level ground.

It can't be true. There must have been a mistake—an exaggeration, a rumour run wild. How could a whole helicopter full of people have been burned alive without even taking off? It is a story to test her, a terribly misjudged practical joke. Sarah clings to every possibility, no matter how unlikely. She has to see it for herself.

"Sarah, child, sit down. What is it?" Mammy Kamara has her by the shoulders, trying to lower her into the deck chair.

"I have to get to the helipad," Sarah says, struggling out of Mammy Kamara's grip and trying to remember from which of the identical alleys she came. Mammy Kamara takes control. "You need a taxi?" she asks.

"I left my car near the British Council," Sarah murmurs, her voice sounding alien in her ears. Mammy Kamara sets off through the crowd, one arm around Sarah's waist and one out in front to guide their way through the crowds. The Friday morning market has spread considerably; new stalls have been set up, piles of goods spread across the road or stacked up next to parked cars in the side street. When they turn into British Council Road, Sarah can see her car, but it is now in the middle of a recently erected extension of the market. In both directions, stalls and umbrellas, trestle tables and tubs block her exit.

Panic rides up her chest, her breath is laboured and shallow. "I've got to get out of here." Her voice comes as little more than a moan.

"No palaver, Sarah. I'll get you out. This your car?" Mammy Kamara points to Sarah's Land Rover. "Okay, you drive. Follow me."

Sarah climbs into the car, her body flooded with adrenaline. She doesn't trust her disordered mind and shaky muscles to operate a tonne of steel, but she has no choice. She starts the engine, staring at the steering wheel as it dips in and out of focus. Mammy Kamara shouts instructions to the stallholders blocking the road to move on, helping to shuffle their goods to the side to let Sarah through. Sarah creeps the car forward behind the formidable woman, using the space before the mass of people moves in to fill the vacuum.

Mammy Kamara whistles to a small boy with a wheelbarrow. He jumps to attention as soon as he sees her and runs ahead of Sarah's car, clearing a path with his wheelbarrow. Sarah crawls on behind him, aware, even through her stupor, of the disaster that would ensue if she clips one of the passing bodies while edging her Land Rover through a wheelbarrow-sized gap. But she has no choice. Finally, the crowds thin and she comes out on the main road. She tries to give money to the boy with the wheelbarrow to thank him, but he simply salutes her and dives off before she can hand over the notes.

Mammy Kamara, with considerable effort, climbs into the passenger seat of the car.

"My god, how do you do this without a ladder?"

"Thank you for your help," Sarah says. "I'll be okay from here."

"Nonsense you are okay. You are not going anywhere by yourself. I am coming with you."

"But your market stall—"

"Just drive."

There is no force equal to that of a determined woman.

Sarah is not ready to share her grief with a stranger, but grateful nonetheless for Mammy Kamara's presence. With no idea of what she will find at the helipad, or how she will respond, she might need someone to pick up the pieces. She drives as if wearing blinkers, head down over the wheel, focused purely on moving forward.

They smell the wreckage before they see it. A sickening thick stench of burning metal, plastic and petrol flames. And something more—the smell of a stock pot left to burn dry, bitter blackened bones. Sarah stops the car to dry wretch out of the window, bracing herself against the hard metal edge of the door frame. A black plume of smoke rises from the wreckage, still smouldering on the tarmac. What is left of the helicopter looks like a crisp packet that has been thrown in the fire—shrunken and twisted, black and charred and almost nothing left of its original form.

The approach road is closed off, and men in army uniform are trying to move away the growing crowd of onlookers who have gathered to gawp at the disaster. Sarah abandons her car at the barrier and pushes nearer. She doesn't know why, but she needs to see proof Elias is there. She has looked and looked for him for the last week, searching for his broad shoulders, his distinctive red hair, his twinkling eyes and broad grin. She has listened for the sound of his voice, his deep, unreadable monotone, and his quick laugh. Now she looks for him still, not knowing what she might see.

Face on to the heat of the smouldering wreckage, the spark that was lit inside her by the High Commissioner's call finally takes flame. A ravenous punch rips through her, tearing her open from the inside; a grief too brutish to bear. Her eyes rush with tears as she collapses into Mammy Kamara's waiting arms to sob until she can barely breathe.

CHAPTER 27

The next few hours leave no coherent traces on Sarah's memory. A man in army uniform tries to talk to her, her phone rings, more men and young boys push her into the crowds. Sarah moves as if underwater, not fully inhabiting her body. She takes in nothing that is said and registers nothing that happens around her. She floats like a piece of wreckage at sea: defunct, weathered beyond recognition, and left to the mercy of the waves to be thrown up and sucked back under. Her brain can register only one thing—Elias is gone.

She tries to anchor herself in happier times, forcing her mind back to their blissful week spent alone in the forest. But it will not stay put. For all that she tries to hold on to the electric touch of his skin, his inviting eyes tipped with lashes of pure white, to the way he could turn the most mundane of moments into an adventure, she cannot stop her mind from slipping back to the look on his face as he left. His beautiful features lost in anger, jealousy, betrayal and trust undone.

Dear God, not Elias. Let none of this be true, she begs to any deity who might listen. Let this be a dream, her brain's response to her endless longing for his return, a filling in of the wound he left in her soul. Let her awake in a feverish sweat to be chilled by the horror of her subconscious, before rolling back into a sweeter sleep. But Sarah awakes on a makeshift bed in Mammy Kamara's house and knows that nothing will ever be the same again.

*

Mammy Kamara clucks over her, producing dish after dish to tempt her into eating something, telling her stories from the women in the market, keeping up her sing-song patter that allows Sarah simply to be present, to sit without the need to listen or respond.

Sarah only stares in silence.

The ring of her phone sends her heart soaring and her hands scrambling through her bag—her hunger to hear from Elias overrules what she knows. But it can't be him, it will never again be him. She silences the ringing and flings the handset to the floor.

Mammy Kamara rubs her palm rhythmically over Sarah's shoulder blades, making a noise between shushing and song. "Don't fight it, Sarah," she whispers. "Let it come. It needs to come; it is bigger than you. Ibrahim had a brother, he was..." Her words break off, but her strong hand keeps up its careful movements across Sarah's back, tethering her against the wave of vertigo that threatens to sweep her away.

Sarah notices music playing—she thinks at first the piano must be in the room. The notes feel so close and intimate. She recognises the melody—*Chopin's Nocturne, Op 9, No.2*. Her mother used to play it every time she felt on edge to calm herself with the rhythmic waltz. But this is played much slower, the left hand drawn out and sombre, the drama of the melody more melancholy than playful. It is like listening with fresh ears to a long-known truth.

She opens her eyes to see Ibrahim sat at an ancient Casio keyboard. His eyes remain closed as he moves his fingers expertly over the keys. Having grown used to his incarnation as a taxi driver, Sarah has forgotten he introduced himself as a piano tuner. She listens in silence, feeling her soul soothed by the music, an offering of solace to her shattered world. As if sensing her watching him, he turns around. Though his hands no longer move on the keys, the music continues uninterrupted.

167

"Sorry, please don't stop," she says. "Was that you playing?"

"No." Ibrahim's face looks ashen and sombre, his body shrunken—even his eyelashes seem to have lost their tight curl. "It's a recording of my father. I used to try and imitate it. But then my keyboard got fried by a power surge. So now I just pretend."

"Can't you fix it?" Sarah asks.

"Here?" Ibrahim looks as if to check she is serious. "No."

The music continues around them, only a faint crackle and hiss of static to give away its secret.

Ibrahim stares at Sarah as if unsure of the words. "Sarah," he says at last. "There's something you need to see. Do you think you can face the drive back into town?"

*

They drive in Ibrahim's taxi, scarcely speaking as he pushes through the traffic on the main road. Sarah does not ask where they are going; it doesn't matter now, nothing does.

"You won't want to see this," Ibrahim says as they approach the helipad, "but you have to." The crowds have moved on, and even the army has left. Only a makeshift rope and a log lying across the tarmac guard the wreckage. Ibrahim pushes the log away with his tyres to approach the landing pad.

"What happens now?" Sarah asks, staring at the abandoned burial chamber. "Will they open it up? Will they remove the bodies? Will there be a formal identification?" She has no idea what would normally happen, let alone when something like this happens in a country with no basic infrastructure. She expects to see emergency vehicles: ambulances, fire, police and forensics. But there is nothing. There is no one to send. Only the blackened carcass alone on the tarmac, like the remains of a funeral pyre.

"It's more serious now than it first looked," Ibrahim says. "The choppers operating this route are all ancient and maintenance is non-existent. There have been fires before and no one is ever that surprised. But it looks like this one wasn't an accident."

"What?"

"The thrust of the explosion didn't originate from the fuel tank, and if you look under here," he ducks down next to the black and twisted hulk of the helicopter and points at something on the underside. "Down there, you can just see traces of wire and a piece of casing. Looks like a rushed job, probably not long before take-off."

"But who would want to blow up a civilian passenger helicopter? Was there anyone of interest on board?" Sarah's brain is slowly coming back to life—latching on to a purpose, a problem to be solved, the spectre of someone that could be blamed for this senseless loss of life.

"The embassies are still combing the lists. There was a junior official from the Ministry of Justice, a professor from the university, a couple of fly-in fly-out mining contractors, an elderly lady taking her first ever flight to visit family in London, a Belgian policeman who had been here as part of a UN training team. And Elias. No obvious target, just your average group of people heading to the airport."

"No one has claimed it?" Sarah asks.

"Not yet. It could be Foday Sankoh, another element in his reign of terror, a reminder to all that he still has control over life and death, despite his foray into government. But normally his attacks are well-publicised. He understands the power of communication only too well. It's unlike him to remain silent."

"How many people know this wasn't an accident?"

"So far not many—the army, police and embassies. But it won't take long before it's common knowledge. There's a theory that it might have been a rival logistics company. There used to be another group running the airport transfer, but they got banned for a poor safety record."

"Seriously?" Sarah asks, "There aren't easier ways of attacking a professional rival than killing a chopper full of passengers?"

"Maybe it was supposed to go off before anyone boarded?"

"I doubt it," Sarah says. She stares at the mangled wreckage and feels her blood boil. Could Skarparov already have discovered Elias's betrayal, and have exacted his punishment? The innocuous passenger list, the timing so soon after Elias lost his bag. Skarparov is one of the few to have both the means and the motive. And he has killed before to eliminate inconvenient risks.

But if so, he has enacted the most catastrophic of moves. He has at once changed the rules of the game and revealed his hand. He leaves Sarah no choice but to retaliate, but what response would he expect her to make?

CHAPTER 28

Sarah picks up Kuznetsov at the top of Spur Road. The Russian intelligence agent is waiting by the side of the road, dressed in an open-necked white shirt and the same dark linen trousers he was wearing to poke around the High Commissioner's residence. He sticks out as a foreigner, and an elegantly dressed one at that, and yet he looks strangely at home standing in the dust under the billboard that advertises the *Mammy for All dem Supermarkets*, undisturbed by the heat or the sun or the smell of ripening rubbish.

He did not sound surprised when Sarah called. He simply asked her to pick him up at this unusual landmark, and to be sure to bring her Land Rover. She did not even bother to ask how he knew what car she drove.

"And where is this secret destination?" Sarah asks as Kuznetsov settles in beside her, touching the dashboard with a quiet reverence, running his fingers along the leather fittings. "We're going to look at the chimps." He gives her a broad and enigmatic smile, his eyes folding into double-lidded creases.

"The chimps?" Sarah wonders if she has misunderstood his accented English.

"Yes, a birthday treat."

"It's your birthday?"

"Oh, Sarah, that is disappointing. I thought you would have done your homework. But yes, today is my birthday. And to celebrate, I'd like to indulge in a little nostalgia. You take the Hill Road." He points to the rough mountain road that leads over towards Hastings.

"I don't need to do my homework on you," Sarah says. "I know who you are. You're FSB. You were the case officer responsible for transferring the weapons and ammunition to Skarparov, which is now being dolloped around by the rebels."

Kuznetsov gives a throaty laugh. "You didn't bring me a present then?"

"Nothing wrapped up, no. Anyway, how was I supposed to do my homework on you? Look you up on Russian Spies dot com?"

"You could have asked Michael."

Sarah swerves to avoid a steep sided pothole. "Of course you know Michael."

"Michael and I have both been in this game a long time. When we started, we were on opposite sides. He was the big enemy. Or maybe that was us? But now, everything is different. I wouldn't say we are friends, but sometimes we can work together. To be honest, with Michael, it was always like that. He is a pragmatist, like me. Politics never got in the way of a job that needed to be done. Up there." He points towards a small turning off the road, little more than a muddy track that rises at a hair-raisingly steep angle up the side of the mountain.

Sarah engages the low gears and approaches the slope with enough speed to kickstart the climb. This would not be the time to get stuck. She can hardly call Chris for help when she is on her way to visit chimps with the enemy.

To her relief, they tip over the top and into a small clearing where three fenced enclosures stand hemmed in by dense forest. Each enclosure, kitted out with ropes, platforms and tree stumps, is home to a group of chimpanzees.

Two of the larger chimps approach the fence, hooting and thumping their hands into the walls of the cage and calling in a noise that sounds part show of aggression, part cackle of laughter.

"Hello Bruno, hello Little Man," Kuznetsov greets the animals affectionately and puts his hand up to caress them through the bars.

"You know their names?"

"I come here as often as I can."

"What is this place?"

"It's a chimpanzee sanctuary. They take in animals that have been rescued but can't be released into the wild. Some of them were taken away from their mothers as babies to be sold, others lived as pets in marble palaces until they grew too old and their owners chucked them out."

"I thought you said we were going for some nostalgia?"

"Why do you think I come here so often?"

"They remind you of your colleagues?"

He gives another chunky laugh. "They remind me of Chocco, my chimp. He was confiscated from a political prisoner; someone brought him in when he was still very tiny. He lived in the office for a while, people fed him the worst leftovers from the office canteen—the poor brute lived off grey cabbage for months. But he still grew and was soon too big to handle. After he attacked the tea lady—she said it was attempted murder. I think he was just bored—I took him home. Have you ever known a chimp?"

"I can't say that I have."

"They are wonderful pets. So full of personality, crazy and funny and boisterous, and nothing was ever boring so long as Chocco was there. I miss him." He traces his finger along the wire of the fence, his eyes far away.

"Aren't chimps the only animal other than humans that kill each other?" Sarah asks.

"Hardly. But they are the only primates that regularly gang up on their neighbour." He gives Sarah a long and thoughtful look. "It doesn't always end well."

One of the smaller chimps saunters towards them, banging a metal can against the railings and baring its teeth in a fearsome grin.

"The way they move, it's so powerful, don't you think?" Kuznetsov asks, offering his palm up to the new arrival.

173

"They've certainly got swagger." Sarah thinks this one looks like a shaven-headed lout spilling out of the pub at closing time. She looks forward to telling Elias about this surreal outing, certain he'd enjoy hearing that Kuznetsov has a soft spot for chimps. But then she remembers.

"I've been wondering how long it would take before you called." Kuznetsov interrupts her reverie.

"Tell me about Michael," Sarah says. It seems ridiculous to quiz a KGB rival about her former boss, but something about Kuznetsov tells her he would be willing to talk.

"Michael? That's not what I was expecting. What do you want to know?"

"Who is he?"

"He's a slippery fish. But under the armour he has grown for himself. I think there lies a good man." He looks at Sarah from the corner of his eye. "My favourite time, we were in Iceland for the Reykjavík Summit—you remember it?"

"I heard about it. But I don't think I was more than five at the time."

"Oh my days, so young. So young. Well, we had Reagan and Gorbachev—The General Secretary of the Communist Party of the Soviet Union, as he was then—holed up in a house in Reykjavik. No one had any confidence they were even going to talk to each other, let alone make agreements on nuclear weapons. They told us this house was the biggest place in Reykjavik, the only one suitable to host such important delegations. They also told us it was haunted."

"Full on rattling chains and visions on the staircase?"

"They weren't specific, but it was clearly something everyone believed. You get the feeling the spirits are very close to our world in Iceland." He gives an unreadable smile. Does he take this seriously? It is impossible to tell. "The atmosphere was jumpy, and with those two sides in close proximity, everyone was spooked at the best of times. So Michael, he realises this is something we can use."

"He wanted to spook the spooks? Sounds like Michael."

"These meetings are all about egos, big ones, and no one wants to give an inch. In the daytime, with the sunlight, everyone is posturing and hiding behind their delegations and we're getting nowhere. We needed to find a time to get rid of the hangers on and strip away the bravado. The first night, I was trying to sleep and there was a quiet knock at my door. Michael is there, in his dressing gown, and he beckons for me to follow. He led me up a ladder to the attic and into the space above the principal bedrooms. Then he started prowling back and forth, making noises." Kuznetsov begins imitating Michael's prowl, pacing next to the enclosure, stooping his powerful shoulders and drawing inquisitive looks from the chimps. "Some scratching, a few low moans, a quiet but mournful howl." One of the bigger animals joins Kuznetsov in his hooting call.

"Michael was howling?"

"Brilliant, no?" Kuznetsov's dark eyes light up at the memory.

"But why?"

"He kept it up long enough that neither of the great leaders could get a wink of sleep. And they both ended up in the kitchen, in the small hours of the morning—the fortieth President of the United States of America and the General Secretary of the Communist Party, sitting around the kitchen table with cups of cocoa, and talking, perhaps for the first time, as two men, in their dressing gowns pretending not to be scared. And it worked! Without that summit, well, we wouldn't be where we are today."

"How long did Michael manage to keep it up?"

"Three nights! I was so exhausted by the end I could scarcely stay awake for the last day, but Michael always looked fresh the next morning and convincing in his claims that he hadn't heard a thing."

Sarah can picture the scene: Michael happily breaking all the rules, but in a way that he determined was right, without a ruffle to his polished exterior.

"Now tell me, Sarah," Kuznetsov says, running his fingers

through his thick grey hair. "You didn't bring me here to talk about Michael, did you?"

A tall chimp with a wizened beard and deeply hooded eyes saunters over towards Kuznetsov, brandishing a half-demolished piece of watermelon. Sarah thought for a moment he is going to throw it at them, but he holds it towards Kuznetsov in offering.

"I don't work for Michael anymore," she says.

"So I heard. You know, if you are after a new boss, I'm very happy to talk. I know who you are—you were the one who blocked the attack in Tbilisi." He keeps his eyes on the chimp, who is forcing pieces of mushy watermelon through the bars.

Sarah holds her breath. This is the boldest part of her gamble and the element she agonised over for longest the night before. She has to hope that Kuznetsov didn't take her interference in Tbilisi as a personal attack. She remains silent and waits for Kuznetsov to continue.

"My superiors were pretty furious, but frankly I was happy you did."

Sarah releases her breath.

"This kind of rivalry is petty," he continues. "It demeans us. The West are not the enemy anymore and treating Georgia's President like the big bad wolf only plays into his hand."

"I'm flattered, but I'm not looking for a new boss." She looks directly at him. "I want Skarparov."

"Skarparov?" he gives a sharp laugh through his nose. "You haven't given that one up?"

"No."

"And you do know that your friend Michael is a friend of Skarparov?"

Sarah bites down on the inside of her lip, but says nothing.

"O-kay… Now I see what we are working with." He nods his head as if lining up his thoughts. "Yes, this is interesting. Can I ask why you are still determined to get him?"

"He's an evil man—motivated purely by profit and willing to jeopardise the future of this country and the lives of thousands for the next dirty way of making money. Sometimes I think I am the only one who sees it, but I know he needs to be stopped." Sarah knows she's losing her cool. But it is impossible to think about Skarparov without wanting to sacrifice him to a pack of angry chimps.

"And it doesn't have anything to do with him killing your lover?"

A wave of grief washes up from the pit of her stomach, flooding her chest and prickling her eyelids.

"Tell me," Kuznetsov said. "How did you think you were going to get him? Why come to me? Why not just take him out? No one would investigate too closely here. He has power but few friends."

"Because that would make me no better than him. I want him brought to justice. I want him to be made to pay long and publicly and painfully for what he's done."

"You do know that is not really our style?" Kuznetsov says, a quizzical look in his furrowed brow. "We can help you with the dark way if you don't want the dirty hands?"

"Why haven't you taken him out yet?" Sarah asks. "What do you want from him? Surely he's in your debt, having failed to keep up his end of the Tbilisi deal?"

Kuznetsov laughs, but the knot to his brow grows deeper. "Believe me, there are many within the FSB who want his head on a plate. And they probably wouldn't bother with the plate. But I think he's more useful for us scared."

"Useful how?"

"He's a powerful man here. And very well connected."

"Do you have the proof of the weapons transfers?" Sarah asks. "You must have the serial numbers, the paperwork and documentation? If that can be traced to weapons here in rebel hands, then we've got him. It will be enough to send him to the International Criminal Court."

Kuznetsov pauses, tapping his thumbnail against the galvanised steel of the enclosure wall. The chimps, who were playing with him, back off, as if instinct tells them what is in his thoughts.

"It's possible to get these things," he says after a lengthy pause. "But someone will get it in the neck. I'll need to make sure it isn't me." He looks tired, and suddenly much older.

"It's him I want to punish," Sarah says. "I don't want to bring anyone down with him."

"Don't worry." He takes Sarah's hand and gives it a gentle squeeze.

Sarah is surprised by the intimacy of the gesture, but lets him hold her fingers.

"I'll get what you need," he nods. "Give me some time."

"I can make it so that we both win."

"You know how this works, Sarah? I help you out, there needs to be something you do for me in return."

"I know how this works," she nods. She hopes that getting Skarparov is enough of a shared incentive that she would not be too heavily in his debt. But pushing him to do things in her way would not come cheap. "How can I help you?"

"As I'm sure you've guessed, I'm not only here for Skarparov. My superiors want what everyone in Freetown wants: the uranium. They want to know who's selling it, who's buying it, and if it's any good. You wouldn't happen to have any leads that might help us?"

Sarah is struck by the absurdity of her position. Is she really considering sharing secrets with a chimp-loving FSB officer? Is it treason if they are both after the same thing? Sarah's previously precarious position is suddenly looking less fragile. Knowing what an opponent really wants is the best way to understand how to play them. "It's a fascinating story," she says trying to mimic his sideways glance. "I'm certainly interested to find out more."

"I think we can work together." Kuznetsov fixes her with a dark-eyed stare. "I'm going back to Moscow tomorrow. I'll see what I can do help. You'll hear from me when I'm back."

"I'll keep rooting around for the cheese."

"After the helicopter, Skarparov will be waiting for your response. If I was you, I'd lie low until you are ready to bite back."

CHAPTER 29

Sarah has a week to wait for Kuznetsov to return. She follows his advice, laying low and staying away from any occasion where she might run into Skarparov until she has the ammunition she needs to make her attack. She has plenty of time to consider whether what she is doing is utter madness. But ends up no closer to an answer.

She tries a few more leads to tease out information from the Uranium company's PO Box address, but each one leads in a dead end. She wants to try again with the High Commissioner but can't risk running into Chris while preparing for a collaboration with the enemy.

She's short on cash. With most of the money she saved from Tbilisi wiped out by her Namibia trip, and without Elias's access to Michael's ill-gotten gains, she is forced to leave the relative luxury of the hotel on the hill and move into a shabby guesthouse close to the centre of town. Perhaps it is just the new location—out of the rarefied air of the expat enclave and into the hot and gritty life of the city. Perhaps it is just the yawning chasm created by Elias's absence. But something about Freetown feels more hostile; a wound reopened. The city rattles like a simmering pot.

She seeks comfort and company in Ibrahim and Mammy Kamara, spending days and evenings in their small house in Hastings, finally feeling well enough to eat the steaming plates of food pressed on her by her generous host. The pair of them with their gentle teasing, maternal bickering and their stories of Freetown before the war help make Sarah smile, but their house is so infused with memories of losing Elias that she can never stay for long. At least her charmless hotel room has nothing to remind her of him.

Returning to the hotel one evening, she picks up Kuznetsov's message. It does not even surprise her he found her here. Of course he had. His message is brief—he is back in Freetown and has what she needs. She should come to the Cotton Tree the following morning at 9am.

*

The founding fathers of Freetown first laid claim to the city under the branches of the Cotton Tree. Its towering buttress roots billow at the centre of a busy roundabout, while its crowning branches maintain their majesty, even hemmed in on all sides by traffic and buildings. Sarah waits for Kuznetsov on the black and white stone benches that circle the mighty trunk, listening to the soft squeak and ruffle as hundreds of fruit bats above her head twitch and jostle for space.

A group of soldiers pulls up opposite her. Four men in uniform pile out of the pickup and approach a young boy sitting on the steps of a building, apparently minding his own business. They are heavily armed, their faces hidden behind low-brimmed hats and sunglasses. Their uniforms bear no insignia, no badges and nothing to show if they are Sierra Leone army or rebels or ECOMOG. Whoever they are, they spark terror in the young boy who scrambles to his feet and runs. Their leader chases after him, dragging him into the road. The boy, wearing only trousers that hang from bony hips, gabbles. His words tumble out with increasing urgency: his name, his job, the street where he lives. He calls to the people in the surrounding street to back him up, to come to his aid; but no one comes. The uniformed men, deaf to his protests, march him back to their pickup.

The boy screams for help, grabbing at a woman sitting nearby, begging her to tell them who he is. "I live here, this woman she

181

know me. I done never go with the rebels, she know me."

The woman pulls away, keeping a tight lid on her silence. A mother takes hold of her child's hand and crosses to the opposite side of the road.

"I done never," the boy cries as he is kicked into the back of the truck.

The four men climb in after him, two of them holding him as he flails and screams for help. "I live here." He beats his bare heels into the metal bed of the truck until his words are cut by a gun smashed into the back of his skull. Sarah watches in horror. Who are these men? Who is the boy and what is he supposed to have done? Why will no one help? Life on the street continues as before, with no one other than Sarah seeming shaken by the incident.

Kuznetsov appears from the direction taken by the truck.

"Did you see that?" Sarah asks.

"See what?"

"A young boy was just forced into the back of a pickup, smacked on the head with a gun, and no one moved. No one even raised their voice to help. They just carried on as if nothing had happened."

"No one wants to be next," he says with a shrug, unmoved by the boy's fate

"Next for what? What had he done?"

"What does anyone do to deserve what they get? I would have thought you'd been here long enough to toughen up by now."

She swallows back the bitter lump rising in her throat. This is not the time to show weakness.

He takes her arm and walks her down Siaka Stevens Street. The main drag of central Freetown, where old colonial buildings with criss-crossed balconies crowd in with newer buildings in dirty cream, their blackened windows framed by curls of barbed wire. The road is gridlocked with slow-moving taxis, pop music blaring from their windows, punctuated by the honking of motorised scooters speeding between the cars. People pack the pavements—a woman in a blue boubou walks slowly in front of them, the strap of her bag biting into her fleshy shoulder; a boy wearing a red basketball vest weaves by balancing a tray of yellow mangoes on his head. The street smells like hot rubbish ripening in the sun, mixed with freshly cooked meat from the charcoal braziers smoking on the roadside. Sarah is glad not to be alone, still shaken by what she witnessed and the weighty impassivity of the on-lookers. She too had borne witness but done nothing. Would anyone come to her aid if she is attacked? The presence of Kuznetsov gives her some reassurance, but it is a strange comfort. He frees her from the hassle you come to expect as a girl walking alone, but is he really on her side?

"So, I have what you need." He taps a document bag slung across his shoulder.

"You have it here?"

"Everything you need to start your ball rolling."

"And you won't be in danger from your superiors for sharing this with me?"

"If I've played this well, two guys will get it in the neck—Ruslan Boshirov and Alexander Petrov."

Sarah stands back to allow a boy with a wheelbarrow to pass, trying to manoeuvre twenty kilos of onions along the busy street.

"Who are they? Will they be punished?" she asks.

"More likely executed. We like to keep things simple. Hold on, I think this is the street we need." He consults a scrap of paper from his pocket and looks up at the sign. "Yes, it's this way."

"I didn't want anyone to get executed," Sarah says, trying to read through his brusque tone whether he is joking. It seems best to assume he is not. "I just wanted information on Skarparov."

"I told you it would not be straightforward. But don't worry about these guys. They're assholes."

"You're saying they deserve it?"

"I'm saying, by your philosophy, they are bad men. Very bad

men. And they've done some nasty things. So yes, they deserve it. This is the place."

They arrive at a workshop that looks like a mechanic's garage. A darkened room packed floor to ceiling with spare parts, old electrical items being cannibalised for re-use, industrial-sized sacks of flour stacked up like sandbags, towers of square cut foam and a small forest of broken fans. At the front of the shop, an East Asian man sits on the floor underneath a red and white umbrella, behind a table displaying creations of carved vegetables—perfect pink chess pieces carved from the flesh of tomatoes, sovereign coins made from carrots and lifelike animal carvings in cabbage.

"Where are we?" Sarah asks, nodding a greeting to the silent man and kneeling down to inspect his extraordinary work.

"Ahmad's place. He's a fix-it man—he'll fix your car, change your dollars into stacks of leones, value your diamond and track down just about anything you need—for a price." He nods to the vegetable carver. "Boss man is here?"

The artist nods and scuttles away to the back of the shop. The workshop itself is lit by neon strip lights dangling from the ceiling on loose wires, casting a dull glow through the anarchic space.

A broad-set Sierra Leonean emerges from a door at the back and peers at Sarah and Kuznetsov over the top of a pair of reading glasses, dwarfed by his round face. "Yes?" he says, ignoring Sarah and speaking directly to Kuznetsov.

"We spoke on the phone. You said you could get me some penicillin."

"You're the chimp guy?"

"I'm a friend of the sanctuary," Kuznetsov nods.

"Wait a minute, I'll see what we got." He limps back towards the room at the back of the shop.

"You're the chimp guy?" Sarah asks with a raised eyebrow.

"Clara is sick. Some sort of respiratory disease. They wanted to put her down but agreed for me to try this first."

Ahmad shuffles back with two dog-eared packets bearing pharmaceutical company logos.

Kuznetsov removes a brick of notes from a black plastic bag.

"You got dollars?" Ahmad asks.

"No," Kuznetsov says. "Where did you get this from?"

"I never tell." Ahmad smiles like a wide-mouthed frog.

Kuznetsov hands over the cash and pockets the medicines. Ahmad weighs the wad of cash in his hand and disappears back to the depths of the workshop. Kuznetsov turns to Sarah, who is examining a perfect miniature ceremonial mask carved out of a turnip. "Are you sure you want this?" he asks.

Sarah sets down the mask. "Do I want to bring down Skarparov? Of course I do."

"Yes, that I know. But are you sure this is the way?" He takes her arm once again and walks her towards the colonial-era stone steps, glistening with moss and weeds that leads down to a landing stage on the water. "Think about it. What if we tried to work Skarparov for our ends? We have in our hands a bigger threat than even his Michael gives him cover for. What if we could influence where he lays his support?"

"You mean have him give his weapons and ammunition to Chief Hinga Norman's civil defence force instead of to the rebels?"

"For example…"

Sarah does not respond. She is not prepared for a lesson in philosophy and morality from an agent of Russian Intelligence. "But then don't we run the risk of getting ourselves in as deeply as him?" she says.

"Of course we do. That is the beauty of this game. Look, if we try to do things your way, the good principled way, there is a strong risk that he gets off anyway. It could take months, if not years, to come to court, during which time he can continue pretty much unhindered. Then, even if you get him in a courtroom, your case is only as good as a set of KGB documents. It might surprise you to hear it, but that kind of evidence rarely stands up

185

in court. No official would back you up. And two assholes get it in the neck." He pauses. "Or we try to use him. It's up to you."

Sarah feels trapped. At no point did she think that teaming up with the Russians was going to be easy, but she did not foresee the layers of grey they would force her to choose between. "What makes you think he will be so easily controlled? Even if we have this evidence on him, what if he just rats us out to your superiors or to Michael?"

"Skarparov is an old hand in the game. He will want no one to know that he has been compromised. He'll try to line up his pieces to meet our requests, while still pretending to be in charge."

"But I don't want him to stay in control. I want everything he has built to come crashing down on his head."

"Keep your eyes on the big picture, Sarah. And don't be blinded by your grief. In the grand scheme of things, what good is one dead rat? Another bigger, meaner one will just come along to take his place. If what you hate is what he stands for, then your fight is with the system that supports him. The war gives protection to a queue of Skarparovs with a nose for making dirty money. You chop off the head of the snake, a nastier one grows in its place."

"Do you really think we could turn him?"

"Turn him, no. You will not bring Skarparov over to the side of the light—not by threatening him, not by coercion, not by making the moral case. An old rat will always stink. He's too cunning, it's too deeply engrained. But what if we could have that cunning on our side? What if his ability to thrive in the shadows, to make the deals that no one else wants to touch, could be used to make the deals we want?"

Sarah is wary. Is Kuznetsov really driven by an urge for the greater good? Or is he taking Elias's line knowing that she'll listen? If knowing what your opponent wants strengthens your position, then Sarah's determination to destroy Skarparov makes her an easy piece to manipulate. "Is this about Skarparov, or the uranium?"

"Can't it be both?" Kuznetsov asks with a half-smile.

Small wooden boats bob on the water, their fragile holds rocked by the choppy movement of the waves. Women on the wharf hawk their buckets of sun-dried fish. "You make it sound easy," she says, certain that it will be nothing of the kind.

"So you are willing to give it a try?"

"I think we should talk to him. Present what we have and give him the option to save his skin."

Kuznetsov nods. He walks her back towards the Cotton Tree, a new lightness in his step.

CHAPTER 30

Heavy layers of security protect Skarparov's futuristic home, separating it from the simple, single-storey buildings that surround its perimeter wall. A spiked barrier rises across the road as Sarah turns into the driveway and two guards approach from behind a panel of bullet-proof glass. Behind the guard booth, a machine gun mounted on top of a camouflage vehicle points straight at them.

The guards treat them with suspicion, checking their names against their IDs before recording them in their book. They note the number plate of the car but insist that Sarah leaves it outside. She looks to Kuznetsov for reassurance as they leave the Land Rover parked at the side of the road in front of the compound. Is this a precautionary measure for all visitors, or is Skarparov already suspicious? He sounded surprisingly pleased to hear from her when she called to set up the meeting. She didn't mention that she would be bringing company.

"Don't worry," Kuznetsov says. "We're just here to talk."

Sarah slings her handbag over her shoulder. What does one bring for a meeting like this? She has her phone, a camera, and the classic revolver Elias gave her. She has always kept it with her, never really thinking she might need it. This time, it is loaded.

A guard inspects Kuznetsov's bag, showing little interest in the incriminating documents. Another sweeps a metal detector across his body. Kuznetsov does not flinch as he raises his shirt, revealing a pistol in a black leather holster concealed under the waistband of his trousers. The guard whips his own gun towards

Kuznetsov's face.

"Let's not get excited," he says, maintaining his calm and deliberate demeanour. "You can look after this for me while we're inside." He slips the gun out of the holster and hands it to the guard.

They nod for Sarah to approach. She holds her arms out, but as the guards come close they freeze, like dogs given a silent shock.

"There's no need. Sarah is an old friend." Framed by the oversized entrance, Skarparov looks surprisingly small. He strolls towards them, his white shirt unbuttoned slightly too far, revealing a large gold eagle nestled into the greying hair of his walnut-tanned chest. The guards shrink back as the boss approaches. Skarparov takes Sarah's hand and draws it to his lips, placing a dry kiss on her knuckles. His skin smells like burnt resin, bitter frankincense with a trace of parma violet.

"Sarah," he greets her as a long-lost friend, his voice affectionate, laying a cold palm into the small of her back to draw her in. "You certainly have an unusual taste in friends." He shoots a hostile look at Kuznetsov, who answers with a gentle nod. "I can't imagine what you and Nikolay find to talk about."

From the guard's booth, a concrete drive leads to a walkway of metal and frosted glass. The green shiny platform hovers over a pool of water that snakes around the house. Sarah wonders how quickly the drawbridge could be secured if the castle comes under attack. Inside, the ceilings are dizzyingly high. The whole central keep seems to be one huge cylindrical room, sparsely furnished with low sofas in white leather and a vast coffee table made from the cross-section of a giant tree, buffed and polished, sanded and lacquered until it looks like plastic. The metal cladding on the building bends the dying afternoon light—casting shadows etched at harsh angles, bending and folding over every surface.

Sarah's eyes are drawn to the paintings. Large canvasses line the circular walls, all of them portraits: some imitating classical masters, some more modern, some hyper-real like photographs.

The subject of each canvas is Skarparov himself—either alone or flanked by his two young daughters. One girl is dark with a cold and haughty face, one blonde with a mischievous look in her eyes. Remembering Chris's taunt about Elias, Sarah bunches her fingers into tight fists to resist the urge to scratch out the mischievous eyes in the exact shade of opal green as her father's.

Skarparov notices her looking and laughs. "What do you think of my glory wall?" he asks. "A friend of mine in China makes them for pennies. You send him any photo and tell him the style and within weeks you have the painting. Here, this is my favourite. The 'Rembrandt'." He points out a canvas in an elaborate gilt frame. The dark background, the curls of soft white hair and the indistinct folds of a cap lit from above in dazzling white light are perfect replicas of the Dutch master. But the features of the sitter, his walnut skin toned down to porcelain whiteness, are Skarparov's. He stares down at Sarah with the agitating call of a Rembrandt self-portrait—the same defiant pose, the same unflinching gaze. The arrogance is grotesque.

Sarah knew facing Elias's killer would be difficult. She was expecting the hot rush of blood that takes control of her face and ears, that twists and trembles her lips and runs a film over her eyes. But she is not prepared for having to face him from every angle at once.

"Please sit down." The real Skarparov, looking unnaturally healthy and high-coloured next to his portraits, leads them towards a U-shape arrangement of white sofas. Kuznetsov is staring out of the window at the back, where the moat culminates in a large, shallow pool of grey slate. Something the colour of the water pushes a large, round nose against the glass.

"Viktor, you don't seriously have a pygmy hippo in your pool?" Kuznetsov asks.

"Frida? I'm just looking after her for a friend. London Zoo wanted a female to make a breeding pair."

"London Zoo asked you to poach them a hippo?" Sarah asks.

"Not directly. But poor Thug does need a mate," Skarparov

says.

"There is really nothing you won't do for money, is there?" Kuznetsov says.

"Money? Do you have me pinned so low? I'm helping a friend. There aren't many people who you can ask to look after a pygmy hippo. I offered to help. What do you want, Nikolay?"

"We want to make you a proposal." Kuznetsov removes the papers from his bag and spreads them out on the over-sized coffee table. "Go on, have a look."

Skarparov unfolds a pair of golden reading glasses from his top pocket and examines the papers. Slowly his face changes, his smile loses its easy charm.

"We have enough evidence here to send you to the International Criminal Court for war crimes," Kuznetsov says. "We have evidence of the current location of some of this kit, in the hands of Foday Sankoh's rebels, and we have evidence that some of it was used in the most recent attack on Freetown."

Solemnly Skarparov removes his glasses and looks at Kuznetsov. "Is this a joke?" he asks, with a side glance at Sarah. "You sold me these weapons?"

"But you never paid for them," Kuznetsov replies.

"I kept up my end of the deal."

"We paid for results."

Skarparov's jaw tightens, and his eyes narrow. Sarah has never known him to look so serious. "You came to my home to threaten me? You're trying to frame me after all I've done for this country? I should get the Nobel Fucking Peace Prize for the investment that I bring in."

Sarah suppresses a laugh. Is his ego really so monstrous?

"We want to make you an offer," Kuznetsov continues calmly. "A suggestion, if you like, for how you can better use your considerable talents. If you agree to withdraw your support from Foday Sankoh, and start genuinely doing the good work of which you boast, we would be happy to keep this to ourselves."

"Sarah," Skarparov turns to her, attempting to reignite the

charm, but the effort is too obvious. "How did you get yourself mixed up in this? I thought you were worth more than a piece of dirty KGB blackmail."

"It was my idea," she says, facing him square on. "I went to Nikolay. This is my way to make sure that you don't escape, as you did in Tbilisi."

"Why not come to me directly? We're old friends, are we not?"

Sarah gapes in stunned silence.

"How about we ask this scumbag to leave, and you and I can talk about this like adults?"

Sarah feels her hands begin to shake. "I'd prefer if he stays." Her voice quavers in time with her thundering pulse.

"Suit yourself. But tell me, you've had plenty of chances to turn me in. But you didn't. Come on, Sarah, admit it, you were curious. You enjoyed our little game in the Caucasus, and you wanted to play another round."

"No, I just wanted to do this properly."

"And coming to my house with the KGB feels proper to you?"

"What about Elias? Was it you?" she asks, her heart beating directly in her throat, the words thrumming in her mouth.

"Elias was disloyal. And I can't stand disloyalty. Besides, he had already brought me what I wanted." He gives her a sickening smile.

"You killed him, and everyone else on that helicopter, because he damaged your trust?"

He looks confused, surprised by the force of her reaction. "He knew the risk he was taking," he says with a shrug. "And you did too. Or you would have come to me directly instead of using him to do your dirty work."

His words strike Sarah like a blunt instrument. Does he think that she deliberately put Elias in danger? "And what about everyone else who died alongside him? Burnt alive inside a metal can while the fire engine looked on helpless with no access to water?"

"Helicopters are risky." Skarparov flashes his puckish smile. Sarah has seen it before, perhaps even been charmed by it. But now she wants to hurl the half-tonne table at it. She smacks him across the face so hard her hand smarts and a red outline of her palm blushes across his leathery cheek. Skarparov looks more amused than hurt by Sarah's attack, giving further fire to her rage.

Kuznetsov puts his arm around Sarah to draw her away. "Sarah, calm down. This cannot be personal," he whispers urgently in her ear.

Skarparov removes a white linen handkerchief from his trouser pocket and dabs at his scarlet cheek. He nods towards the documents on the table. "So, this is what you have? And you know that I only need one copy of those and I can produce an 'original' that will make yours look like fakes? Tell me, Nikolay, you stole these papers, didn't you? What will happen when your superiors realise they're missing? Why did you do it? You fell for this girl, too?" He raises his chin towards Sarah with a look of proprietary disappointment. "I like her. She reminds me of my daughters, and she plays an excellent game of chess. I was even hoping to offer her a job, but it seems you got your stinking hands on her first."

"I don't work for either of you," Sarah shouts. How has it come to this? How has she ended up the plaything for two corrupt old sinners to fight over?

"But I bet your loyalty doesn't go that far either, does it?" Skarparov continues, the same nauseating smile laughing at the world and everyone in it. "I am about to seal the deal on a major uranium find for an international investor. Would I be right in thinking that a piece of that pie might make you change your mind about our little friend here?"

Kuznetsov snorts. "You really think you control that deal? Surely you know that the Russian government will do whatever it takes to ensure they end up with the resources. You're about to be out-manoeuvred there, my friend, and then you have nothing to offer me. You have two options—you cooperate with us, or you get indicted for war crimes. You choose."

A bite of doubt pinches around Skarparov's mouth. He reaches slowly behind his back as if to tuck his shirt into his trousers. With one swift movement he has a gun pointed directly at Kuznetsov's head. "I'll tell you how this goes," he says, his voice chillingly calm. "I kill you, and then this all goes away."

Sarah has no time to process what is happening, no time to check on Kuznetsov's response. She cannot look away from Skarparov's cold opal eyes narrowed on the sight of the gun. It is no bluff.

Magnified by the cage of glass and steel, the shot is amazingly loud, but true—the bullet hits directly between the eyes and he falls straight backwards, hitting the side of his head on the mammoth tree trunk table.

Sarah is shaking, both hands still clasped tightly around the grip, her arms wilting downwards, shocked by the strength of the recoil. She looks to Kuznetsov, his face ashen but opening into a broad smile.

"You're a hell of a shot," he says. "I thought you wanted to do this the clean way?" His shoulders shudder—is it laughter or shock?

"He was going to kill you."

"So you chose me over him?"

"Don't get sentimental. He was asking for it. Are you sure he's dead?" Sarah stares down at Skarparov's body lying prone on the floor. A large red stain blooms across the white deep-pile carpet.

"Sarah? His brains are all over the couch. I think we can say he's dead."

Sarah looks at the dirty pink smear spreading down the creamy leather, the agglutinated mass of pulverised organ dripping off the cushion.

"What now?"

"You could have saved me a lot of trouble if this was what you wanted to do." A gentle chuckle softens his words.

"This is not the way it was supposed to go," she says. "Okay, you have to help me now. And please stop laughing."

"Your first time?" Kuznetsov asks.

"Yes," Sarah mumbles.

"Don't worry, the first one is always the worst. You'll get used to it."

"I don't intend to make a habit of it."

"No one ever does." He shrugs.

"We need to work out what to do with this body."

"Why not just walk out?"

"My very distinctive car has been parked outside all evening and we signed our names in the guards' book as we came in."

"You used your real name?" Kuznetsov rolls his eyes. "There won't be many who'll miss him."

"Are you kidding? Skarparov, the nation's hero? We need to make it look like a suicide."

"What? He killed himself with both of us here?"

"No, we came, we threatened him with the documents, then we left. He shot himself rather than face the consequences. It's a good narrative, no?" Sarah is already trying to convince herself that this is what happened. "We leave the documents on the table—if they do get picked up by the investigating authorities, so much the better."

"What are the Sierra Leonean police going to do with documents in Cyrillic?"

"Hopefully not link them to me," Sarah says, stifling the panic clawing at her chest. "Okay, help me here." She picks up Skarparov's gun from where it fell, careful not to leave any prints, and places it back in Skarparov's hands. The clammy touch of his skin makes her gag as she curls his fleshy fingers around the grip. His face is taking on the pale and sickly hue of his 'Rembrandt'. "Does that look about right?" she asks.

"Get more prints on the documents too; you never know."

She dabs Skarparov's limp hand on the papers. His arm is heavy, like a hefty leg of mutton. "Sorry, Viktor," Sarah says, trying to avoid looking at the red third eye that has appeared between his trademark eyebrows, forever raised in hurt surprise.

"Okay, now we have to get out of here before anyone comes," Kuznetsov says, shouldering his bag. He turns towards the heavy steel doors. "Sarah, hurry."

Sarah takes a last look at Skarparov's death mask. "I bet you didn't see that coming."

Before Kuznetsov reached the door, it opens and one of the guards enters, brandishing his gun. "What was the noise?" has asks, pointing the gun at Kuznetsov, his bottom lip thrust forward in an aggressive leer. "Where the boss?"

"He's not here," Sarah steps forward, trying to block his view of Skarparov's corpse on the rug. But it is hopeless. He lurches towards her; his gun is almost buried in her abdomen when he sees the dark red stain on the white carpet and Skarparov's body. "You killed him?" he wheels round to face Kuznetsov.

"It isn't what it looks like," Sarah says. "It was an accident."

"You killed him!" the guard shouts again, fear rising in his voice.

"No, look—" Sarah starts.

The guard makes a grab for his walkie-talkie. "You will pay for…"

He can't finish his sentence. Kuznetsov stabs a three-inch blade into his neck and holds him, pinned like a butterfly to a plate, as the guard shocks and convulses, his mouth foaming and fluid dripping from his no longer menacing lower lip. The guard's face grimaces and gurns before finally growing still.

Kuznetsov calmly drags the body towards the centre of the room and piles him on top of Skarparov.

"Great. Now we have two bodies to get rid of," Sarah says.

"Did you have a better idea?" Kuznetsov asks. "He was seconds away from summoning the other guard." He bends down to wipe the blade on the guard's shirt and slips it back into the holder in the back of his sock. "I always like to be prepared." He smiles at Sarah. "It's lucky the forensics capabilities in this country are non-existent. This is a mess." He extracts the guard's walkie-talkie from his holster and sets it on the table. "So Skarparov killed his guard and then killed himself."

"But they know the guard came in before we left. It needs to look like an accident." Sarah's brain races as she scans the room.

"How can you accidentally stab yourself in the neck?"

"You can't. We need to make it look like he died some other way. Do you think between us we could carry him outside?"

"Of course."

"Okay. Take his shoulders, we need to get him into the pool."

Kuznetsov picks up the torso of the dead guard, propping him against an already red stained cushion to soak up the blood, while Sarah lifts his feet. The boots alone must weigh several kilos, and Sarah can do little more than steer them in the right direction. Luckily Kuznetsov is strong. They carry the body to the glass doors at the back of the house.

"And now what? It's hardly going to look like he drowned if he's got a hole in his neck."

"That's where Frida will help," Sarah says. The watchful eyes of the pygmy hippo hover just above the level of the water, her nostrils snorting at the surface.

"You want to feed him to the hippo?" Kuznetsov asks, as if talking to a child with a runaway imagination. "Sarah, my dear, hippos are herbivores."

"Most of the time, yes. But they've been known to feed on dead meat if they're hungry enough. Some even eat their own dead. And I'm guessing this one is pretty hungry. I don't see much grass in that pool. Anyway, she doesn't need to eat him. Just take a few exploratory nibbles."

Kuznetsov lowers the body into the water with a loud plop. The lifeless form sinks to the bottom, face down, palms floating towards the surface as if swimming an underwater butterfly stroke. Frida waddles over to take a closer look at her new pool-mate.

"How do you know all this?"

"Pygmy hippos are unique to this region—I did my homework. Didn't you?"

"I'm more a primate man. Okay, we really need to leave now."

"No, wait, they need to hear the gun after we leave."

"Sarah, give it up. The testimony of one guard on the timing of events will not take this off your conscience. We'll walk out together, we stay calm, we get as far as away as we can before they find him."

Sarah looks at Skarparov's defunct body sprawled across the floor. Kuznetsov is right, this is mess enough. She grabs his hand, and they walk back across the drawbridge towards the guards' booth, looking as much as possible as two blackmailers who could definitely not be murderers. The one remaining guard at the desk is shouting into his walkie-talkie, "Hello? You read me? Hello?" He bashes the unit into the desk and presses all the buttons before trying again to get a response.

He blocks their exit. "What happened in there? We heard a big bang."

"Inside the house?" Sarah asks. "We didn't hear anything."

Kuznetsov scans the fence. "Have you checked the perimeter? Maybe the compound is under attack? Give me back my gun."

The guard tries again to get a response from the walkie-talkie. He removes Kuznetsov's gun from the desk drawer. "Where's the other guard?" he asks, swinging the gun by the trigger guard. "He came inside to check everything was okay, but he never came out."

"He went out the back. Hurry. If there's trouble here, we want to get back to the city before it gets dark." Kuznetsov casts a worried glance at the gathering dark clouds soaking up the last of the evening light.

"Why you want to get out of here so quickly?" the guard points the gun at Kuznetsov. Kuznetsov moves with such speed, Sarah misses how he disables the guard and turns the gun back on him. Only the guard's crumpled position and protective hand over his crotch gives away where Kuznetsov struck. Kuznetsov fires twice in quick succession. The guard slumps to the floor.

"What did you do that for?" Sarah cries, staring at another corpse at her feet. "I thought we were walking out of here calmly?"

"Just tidying up," Kuznetsov says, replacing his gun in its holster. "Now we don't need to worry about timing."

Sarah finds the entrance log in which the guards noted their details and rips out the incriminating pages and a handful more for good measure. "And we were never here. Are there any more guards?"

"I'm not staying around to find out."

They run out the front gate and almost collide with a woman carrying a mop and two buckets heading towards the house. Kuznetsov reaches for his gun, but Sarah pushes him into the Land Rover.

"What the hell are you doing?" she shouts. "You can't shoot the cleaning lady? She wasn't even there."

"She's just about to go in and find Skarparov's brains on the couch. And she saw us come out."

"So? That's no reason to kill her. Someone's got to find him."

"I just thought it would be good to have more time."

"You're trigger-happy." Sarah throws the car into gear.

"You started it," Kuznetsov says with a grin.

They tear off up the unmade road, back over the mountain. Away from the built-up areas, the darkness falls like a weight. As they reach the section where the car gave up on her last time, Sarah tries to calm her ragged breath, her foot firm on the accelerator. Her stomach feels bloodless, her heart races and a cold sweat pricks through her shirt. *Come on Princess, this is the time to show what you are made of.* As they fly over a bump, the red oil light flashes on. Sarah swallows down the sick taste in her throat and focusses on the road, maintaining speed and picking out the best path through the washouts and bumps. It just needs one final push. She hunches over the steering wheel, the back of her neck like a knotted rope, her knee locked on the accelerator pedal. Kuznetsov speaks, but she doesn't hear. She sees only the road and the flickering red on the dashboard.

A shout rises behind them. It is too dark to see if they are being followed. The road is sucked into blackness beyond the faint red of their back lights. Have back-up guards arrived? Did the cleaning lady raise the alarm? The car keeps its steady grind up the steep slope and finally, as it comes over the top of the hill, the roar of the engine lulls and they pick up speed as Sarah works it into third and then fourth gear. She taps the dashboard appreciatively. "Well done, Princess. Now get us home."

CHAPTER 31

Sarah drives Kuznetsov home to a top-floor apartment in a house off Spur Road, hired presumably by the Russian Government. She drops him off, pulling inside the walls of the compound to turn the car under the curious gaze of the night guard, who nods at Sarah approvingly.

Kuznetsov watches her manoeuvre around the tight courtyard. "Would you like to come in for a drink?" he asks.

"Just a quick one." Sarah cuts the engine. She can already hear her better judgement clearing its throat, but she isn't ready to be alone.

Kuznetsov lets them in, opening three separate doors with keys held on a massive bunch clipped to his belt with a chain. Once inside the darkened hallway, Sarah immediately questions her judgement. Which part of this is a good idea? Kuznetsov is the enemy, or at least a rival. The only task that links them is now very much completed. She knows next to nothing about him and has no one to call if she needs help. But as he flicks on the lamps, revealing his extraordinary bachelor palace, she has to laugh.

"Welcome to my humble abode. What do you think?" Mirrored ceilings reflect the enormous shiny surface of the glass dining table, replicating an image of the room to infinity. "Classy, no? The landlord is Lebanese. You should see how many mirrors he's stuffed into the bedroom." He pauses. "Don't worry. I'm sure you can imagine the look. Gin and tonic?"

"Please." Sarah sinks into a plush velvet armchair, exhausted.

When she closes her eyes, the whole room spins, and her trembling limbs feel numb with cold.

"Here, I made it strong, it looks like you need it." Kuznetsov hands her a large tumbler filled with ice and plenty of lemon. The alcohol smell brings her back to her parents' glass decanter, brought out for her mother's bridge four, strong enough to swoon. She knocks back half the drink in one go. It does little to help her spinning head but does settle the shaking.

"Well, normally this is when we debrief on the mission." Kuznetsov sits down on a footstool opposite Sarah, his manner relaxed, he's been here hundreds of times before. And yet there is something about him that seems nervous, eager to please. "You know, comment on what went well, what less well, and agree on next steps? But, er," he gives a gentle laugh, "I'm not sure what to say."

"Am I supposed to be debriefing with the enemy?"

"Are you supposed to be doing anything with the enemy?"

Sarah gulps back the rest of her drink. "Do you have any more of these? Mine seems to have evaporated."

"Of course. I can't live in an apartment with mirrored ceilings and not have a well-stocked drinks fridge. Same again?"

With Kuznetsov in the kitchen, Sarah takes the chance to nose around the living room. The fully furnished flat contains no single personal detail. Mirrors and beads, candles and mother-of-pearl on every surface, but nothing that might have been chosen by the inhabitant. Not a book, a magazine or a piece of paper dropped on arrival. It could have been put together for a photo shoot. Sarah spots a frame on the mantelpiece above the fake fireplace—who has a fireplace in Freetown? To her surprise the frame holds a black-and-white shot of a young couple strolling hand in hand along the beach. But on closer inspection it's clearly the stock photo that came with the frame. Kuznetsov's presence is nowhere to be seen.

He comes back to find her inspecting the picture.

"Funny, isn't it? But you know, you get used to it. Living

with other people's things. Nothing that makes you feel at home. Those two are now almost like friends—I've seen them in the last few houses I've been assigned. FSB decorators must have got a job lot. I call them Ruslan and Lyudmila."

"Pushkin would be proud."

Kuznetsov sinks into an armchair and crunches on an ice cube. "How old are you, Sarah?" he asks.

"Twenty-four. How old are you?"

"Twenty-four," he says, a smile spreading across his face. "My wife was twenty-four when I met her."

"You didn't answer my question."

"I am fifty-seven. I have two children who are older than you and I no longer have a wife."

"Sorry to hear that."

"No need. She's happy."

"And you?"

"What is it they say? I'm married to the job."

"A happy marriage?"

Kuznetsov snorts into his tumbler. "That's not the first word I'd use. But they've treated me well. It's all I know." He gazes at Sarah, his pupils unnaturally wide. Is it the atmospheric lighting or has the drink gone to his head as quickly as it has to Sarah's? "You know the most important thing in this world is that you have at least one person you can trust. I know they always say trust no one, and they're right, but if you're in it for the long haul—and let's be honest, we all are—there needs to be one person on your side. Do you have that person, Sarah?"

"I had Elias..."

"What about Michael?"

"I don't work for him anymore. I quit."

Kuznetsov gives a deep belly laugh. "You quit? Is that what you think? So what were you doing putting a bullet through poor Viktor's head?"

Sarah pulls her knees up under her, wedging herself deeper into the pale blue velvet. There is a dream-like quality to her memories from what happened—the Rembrandts, the pygmy hippo, the blood-spattered cushions—surely none of that is real? It is a fevered dream, fuelled by malaria drugs and a wish for revenge. It can't have played out that way, not really. She rubs deep into her eye sockets. Her nails look blue and, despite the clammy, sticky sheen, her skin feels cold to the touch. "That was nothing to do with my job."

Kuznetsov tilts his head to the side. "It was personal?"

"No," Sarah says quickly. "Maybe yes," she adds. "It wasn't how I wanted it to end. I don't even remember deciding to shoot him. He had his gun raised at you. Next thing, he was dead."

"But you brought the gun with you?"

"I brought it for defence, I never thought I'd use it to kill anyone."

Kuznetsov reaches behind him to turn on the stereo, filling the room with the piano introduction to Miles Davis' *Kind of Blue*. It reminds Sarah of late nights in a university dormitory, a soundtrack to stretched-out conversations setting the world to rights.

"I was very grateful for your defence," he says in a soft voice, choosing his words with care.

"Are we even?" Sarah asks.

"Even?"

"You did me a favour, I did one for you."

"I think that leaves me more in your debt now. I certainly won't forget this evening. And neither will you. You always remember your first. Gradually the names and faces of the others blur, the exact number becomes shaky, but the first stays with you."

"Who was yours?"

"Igor Vasiliev."

"Business or pleasure?"

"You really need to ask? What do you think I am? Four years into the job. I think the powers that be thought it was time I got my hands dirty. Igor was leaving his apartment. I was waiting in a cafe next door. I finished my coffee too early but knew I couldn't stomach another. So I sat, staring at the dark ring at the bottom of my empty cup, clattering the spoon into the dish, trying to look inconspicuous until he came out. Sometimes the bottom of a coffee cup, the ones with the centre slightly raised, can still bring it all back."

Miles Davis's saxophone soars in the background. Kuznetsov drums his fingers in time to the bass guitar. "The funny thing with men," he says. "After they kill someone, they get an unbelievable urge to have sex. I've often wondered if it was the same for women." He raises an eyebrow in question

"You're asking if I want to have sex?"

"Don't worry, it doesn't have to be with me if that's what's putting you off. I'm just curious, does it work in the same way? After Igor, I found myself the first *shtuka* I could lay my hands on and fucked her brains out."

Sarah laughs. If this is supposed to be a chat-up line, it is a little too Russian for her taste. But there is something in what he said. She does want sex. Is it just a yearning for the touch of a warm and vital human body? Or for something deeper— procreation to cancel out destruction? It feels more raw than that, less sensuous, less romantic, just the urge to rut.

"I do want sex," Sarah says. "But the person I want to have sex with is dead."

"Skarparov?" Kuznetsov's face blanches.

"No! Oh God no! I meant Elias. But I think you might have killed the mood."

"Sorry." He holds his hands up in innocence. "I make no assumptions. I don't know your history."

Sarah raises an eyebrow. "Of course you do."

Kuznetsov laughs.

"I still don't understand how Skarparov could possibly think I would want to work for him," she says.

"The mistake that you both made was in thinking that you understood each other."

"I do understand him…" Sarah's voice dies before she finishes the sentence.

"So you knew he was using Elias as a sacrificial pawn?"

"I—" Again, Sarah's words fail her.

"He probably thought he had the whole game sewn up move by move. He was using Elias to get to you. And of course it helped to have someone disposable to do his dirty work—that was his style, no?"

Sarah remembers Irakli, Skarparov's right hand man in the Caucasus whose corpse had been fished out of the Tbilisi river. How had she missed the parallels?

"After Elias's disloyalty became too obvious, he had to get him out of the way. But he didn't need him anymore anyway—he could come directly to you."

"But how could he think—"

"His fundamental miscalculation was in thinking that your relationship with Elias was a functional as his. He totally misread his opponent. He must have thought you were just as scheming and transactional as him."

Sarah huffs out her nostrils—part sigh, part bitter laugh. "He couldn't have been more wrong."

Kuznetsov's voice softens. "I imagine Skarparov forgot that people can be motivated by love." He gives a small chuckle, not much more than an exhale of air, that builds and builds until his whole body is shaking.

"What's so funny?" Sarah asks.

Kuznetsov composes himself and wipes his eyes. "Sorry. It's not really funny. Skarparov was a Grand Master in this game. What he set up in Tbilisi was a masterstroke. Even with you sticking your oar in, he still came out on top. So how do you beat someone at the top of their game? We were always trying to out-play him. Trying to pitch grand-master against grand-master. You come in, a total novice, and pull such a completely unexpected move, you throw the whole strategy out the window." He is shaking with laughter again. "You beat him because you fell in love."

"I beat him because I shot him in the head," Sarah says, sending Kuznetsov into another fit of laughter. "You know," Sarah says, "I've been wondering, the story you told me about Reykjavik—what made you decide to do what you did?"

"It seemed like the best way to get something out of the meeting," Kuznetsov shrugs.

"But why bother? Why not let it be another dead-end summit if the presidents couldn't be relied upon to sort it out themselves? Was it really to save the world and help bring the cold war to a close? Or was it just the chance to pull on the biggest strings, to manipulate the two most powerful people in the world at that time?"

Kuznetsov swirls the ice-cubes around his empty glass. "Even if I knew the answer to that, I'm not sure I'd tell you. Can't it be both?" He takes Sarah's glass, allowing his fingers to brush against hers. "Let me get you another drink."

"Not just yet, I think those have gone straight to my head." She stands up, giggling at the slow-motion sway of the carpet following her up. "I think the floor might be drunk," she says, trying to steady her balance.

"That happens sometimes," Kuznetsov holds out a hand to steady her. "Perhaps the FSB got a job-lot of sozzled carpets too?"

Sarah weighs up what she is going to do about his hand that is still gently curved around her waist. The voice of better judgement is now clamouring to be heard, hollering over the swell of the saxophone, ordering her to go straight home. But she isn't in the mood to listen.

He drapes his other arm over her shoulder and draws her in. His cologne reminds her of the sea, fresh and clean smelling above the animal scent of his sweat. He gazes at her, pupils still dizzyingly wide, face set in a gentle smile. She can feel his body roused by her touch, his hands reaching out to gently trace the line of her shoulders. She feels caught in a fast-flowing stream, a flood of chemicals and impulses pushing her to surrender to his touch, the draw and inexorable lure of a warm human body. At least in the meeting of this need there is no risk of confusion—no risk it could be repeated.

Sarah kisses his thick lips, moving her hands over his back taut and firm under her fingertips. Is this a betrayal to Elias? Is this a betrayal to herself? It feels perfectly meaningless, a secret known only to a professional keeper of secrets. He kisses her tenderly, the smell of his breath unfamiliar and strange. Elias always tasted sweet, like a late summer apricot. But Kuznetsov tastes like the bitter tannins from a strong pot of tea. In place of attraction she feels only need—to mate, to be held by a warm-blooded male, to be wanted.

He draws back and looks at her, a look of surprised delight on his face. "Thank you for saving my life," he whispers in her ear.

"It wasn't for you. It was for him."

"It's all the same to me."

"Is this how all your debriefs end?"

"No. Luckily. Imagine the emotional exhaustion."

"So now I'm emotionally exhausting?"

"No." He presses his thumb to her cheekbone. "I know this is nothing. It's me because I'm here. It's uncomplicated. Tomorrow nothing ever happened. If that's what you want?"

Sarah smiles at his efforts to put her at ease. "Tomorrow, nothing ever happened."

CHAPTER 32

A loud bang startles her awake. Sparse moments have passed since she pressed her throbbing head against the pillow, but the pale light creeping through the cracks of the blind suggests early morning. Her fuddled brain scans the room, searching for an anchor. To her relief, she sees her sweat-stained clothes strewn around the floor of her dingy hotel room and her stack of books on the side table. She has no recollection of leaving Kuznetsov's place, but thank God she did. Another bang, sharper than the first.

"Sarah? Are you there? Sarah, you need to come now." An urgent whisper from outside her door.

It takes a moment for Sarah to place it. The two syllables of her name made to rhyme. "Ibrahim?" She pulls the sheet around her chest.

"You need to come out to Hastings. We have to leave now."

"Hastings? Is it your mother? Is she okay?"

"My mother's fine. You have a plane to catch."

"What?" Sarah swivels up to sitting and sticks her feet out the side of the bed, waiting for the ground to stop swaying before standing. In her haste, she dresses in the clothes from the night before, still chilled with damp and pungent with gin-laced sweat. Leaving the chain in place, she opens the door, peering through the crack at Ibrahim's curly-lashed eyes.

"What the hell are you doing here?" Sarah asks.

"You need to come. I'll explain in the car. Are you ready?"

"For what? What do I need?"

"Nothing. I think. Just come."

She scoops up her bag—it still contains Elias's gun, now missing one bullet. She shoves in the collection of 'valuables' on her night table, grabs her passport from the flimsy safe and pockets her hotel door key. She follows Ibrahim into the darkened hallway, glimpsing herself in the greasy mirror opposite the stairwell. She looks shocking—her hair clings to her scalp and falls matted and tangled at the tips. Her skin is pale and sweat-stained with purple circles under her eyes, as thick as bruises.

She follows Ibrahim down the stairs, wiping at the make-up smudged down her cheek, and out to where his taxi is waiting. Instead of taking the main road out of town, Ibrahim heads up the hill towards the bumpy shortcut.

"Are you sure your car can take this road?" Sarah asks.

"I've done it before. Going this direction you have gravity on your side for the worst bits. Besides, it's quicker."

"Why the great hurry? And what did you mean about me having a plane to catch?"

"Someone's waiting for you at the airstrip. She didn't tell me her name. But she pays well." He flashes his broad smile, the first reassuring sign since he hammered at her door.

"I don't like the sound of this. Did she say why she wants me? Did she tell you anything at all about where she was from?" Hastings is home to the tiny strip of runway where she left Dilara after her last visit. It is where Ibrahim lives with his mother. But it is also where Skarparov lives; or where he lived until yesterday. Sarah feels her insides pulsate. She trusts Ibrahim. He wouldn't knowingly take her into danger—would he? Has he sold her out to a high-paying stranger? Is someone after her already for what she did to Skarparov?

"How did this woman find you?" Sarah asks.

"She asked for a driver, and someone fetched me."

"And she told you where to find me?"

"No." Ibrahim looks a little sheepish. "She paid me extra for that."

"Stop the car; I'm getting out." Sarah makes a grab for the door handle.

"No." A note of panic creeps into Ibrahim's voice. "Don't worry, you'll be fine," he says as he pushes the car a little faster.

*

Sarah recognises the plane on the runway—overextended nose, black and red stripes down the side, and swooped wheel covers that brings to mind a dog in high heels. Dilara stands next to the plane in her red leather aviator's suit.

Sarah is swept in for a triple kiss, her face lost in the perfumed tendrils of Dilara's windswept hair.

"Sorry to get you out of bed. You look like you didn't sleep?"

"I probably feel about as good as I look."

"Climb in. We can get going straight away. There's not too much other traffic around here." She laughs her deep purring laugh, waving towards the deserted airstrip.

"Thank you, Ibrahim." Dilara presses a chunky curl of notes into Ibrahim's hand and kisses him on the cheek. Sarah never realised skin so dark could blush, but watching Ibrahim stagger backwards out of Dilara's embrace it is clearly possible. "Miss Sarah, everything is okay?"

"It's okay, thanks Ibrahim, I know Dilara."

"Dil-a-ra, Dil-a-ra" he walks off, rolling her name around his mouth.

"What are you doing here?" Sarah asks once he was out of earshot.

"Michael wants to see you."

"Michael? What the hell does he want?"

"He asked me to bring you."

"And if I refuse?"

"Please don't." Something hardens in Dilara's silky demeanour. The slightest hint of an edge beneath the glossy leather. She takes Sarah's arm in a firm grip. "You'll be fine. He just has some things

211

to discuss."

They climb into the tiny plane, Dilara sliding her long legs into the pilot's seat. A large leather holdall occupies the co-pilot's chair so Sarah sinks into the baggy leather of an armchair in the back. The chair scoops her back to a forty-five-degree angle. She half expects a seatbelt to pop out and grab her.

Dilara looks back at her like an owner leaving a puppy in a shelter. "You should sleep," she says gently. "You don't want to go into this feeling weak."

"Go into what?"

"You'll see when we get there."

CHAPTER 33

Sarah sleeps through most of the flight; a deep, groggy sleep fuelled by a hangover of adrenaline and gin. Images of the day before gallop through her dreams like a drunken carousel. Each new spectre of regret—the gaping hole in Skarparov's head, the foaming bottom lip of the guard, the scratch of Kuznetsov's beard—swoops in to elbow the last out the way. She awakes, stretching out the cricked muscles in her neck.

Dilara smiles back at her from the cockpit. "Buckle up, we're coming down."

The landscape outside is featureless and grey. No sign of an airport, no visible runway or landing strip, no guiding lights or flapping windsock. Just a solitary figure in a pale grey suit, one arm raised to shield his face from the dust thrown up by the plane, alone in the contour-less desert. The erect bearing, the drama of the set-up, the apparent ease in his hostile surroundings: it can only be Michael. The little plane bounces down on the stony ground just beyond where he is standing.

He watches them climb out, his face immobile. Trained by many years of control, the muscles in Michael's face are sculpted into a mask of careful disdain. Even his rare smiles look learnt. There is nothing fluid to his face, nothing loose; from the set of his jaw to the slight drop of his eyebrows, he is conscious master of every muscle.

He nods to Dilara, who discreetly wanders off into the desert emptiness.

"Sarah." His voice is low, carefully regulated.

Sarah feels hauled up in front of the headmaster. What the hell does he want with her, and why bring her here to tell her?

"Beautiful, isn't it?" His guarded blue eyes scan the featureless wasteland.

"Here?" She follows his stare. Not even the shadows of the small sharp stones give relief from the barren expanse of sandy grey monochrome. There are no plants, no signs of life, human or otherwise, not a weed, not even a stoical blade of grass to break the grey.

"There's something uniquely calming about the desert. Especially when it's so… exposed. I could stay here all day." His tone suddenly changes. Whimsy shut down. "Except I can't. And neither can you. We'll need to be out of here soon, preferably within the hour, to avoid being exposed to dangerous levels of radiation."

"Where are we?"

"Algeria. The site of the French nuclear testing in the 1960s. They named the bombs after the colours of the French flag and a rather unlikely-looking desert rat that hops on long legs. Cute, no? The desert lit up with seventy kilotons of plutonium and the ground burnt liquid white. And now, nearly half a century later, it's still contaminated. The kangaroo rat left behind its leopard dark spots and a legacy of uncontained radiation that threatens any living creature." Michael speaks as if describing the features of a suburban high street. "Of course, this site was chosen because there wasn't much here before. A few passing herders, nomads who knew no better, but no fixed people, no buildings, nothing man-made to destroy. Funny thing is," his face shows no trace of mirth, "this is exactly how it might look if you started with Manhattan, or Paris. London razed to the desert. The power of a nuclear weapon in the wrong hands could reduce any of these great cities, these pinnacles of human endeavour and achievement, to this." He addresses the bleak solitude, not once turning to look at Sarah, confident that she would follow his every word. He begins a slow walk away from the plane.

Sarah follows him, reluctantly leaving the relative safety of the plane. "Why are we here, if it's still contaminated?" she asks, wondering, not for the first time, how much of Michael's carefully cultivated persona is grounded in reality. Did he start with a caricature of himself—magnifying the eccentricities for dramatic effect? Or is the total act a fabrication, like a suit of armour put on only for battle?

"I have other business in the region. But I thought it might help you understand the magnitude of the risk."

Other business in the region? Where has Michael even come from? And how? There is no sign of another plane or vehicle. Just Michael, not even breaking a sweat under the blazing sun.

"This is the devastation caused by a test from one of our so-called responsible allies." He sweeps an arm across the barren moonscape. "Now imagine this power in the hands of a despot with scant regard for international law?" He finally looks Sarah in the eye. "I took a chance on you, and this is how you repay me?"

"What are you talking about?"

"Skarparov. You killed him."

How the hell does he know that? The body can scarcely be cold. She decides not to confess immediately. "He's dead?"

"Yes, of course he is. You put a bullet through his head."

"Did I? How do you know?"

"Don't try to smart your way out of this. It's irrelevant how I know, but it's crystal clear that you have made a cock-up of quite epic proportions."

As the sun rises higher in the sky, the force of its rays becomes crueller. Sarah has no hat, no sunglasses, nothing to shield her pale skin from the strength of its bite. She squints her eyes into the distance, trying to comprehend the shimmering structure that rises out of the whiteness ahead of them. Where is Michael taking her?

"Wait, how did I cock up? Last I checked, you are the one who took advantage of me? You used me to suit your ends. You sent me off to carry out your dirty work so that if it all blew up, it would be in my face and not yours. All I'm doing is finishing off the job you set me."

"No, you're not. You're on some petty vengeance mission. Your boyfriend got killed and now you've got no fucking clue what you're doing."

Boyfriend. Sarah has never liked the word; it is reductive, infantilising and wholly unsuited to describe a relationship between adults. But wielded by Michael, it makes her skin crawl.

"This is not just personal," she says. "Yes, Skarparov killed someone I loved, but he also killed everyone else on that helicopter. Innocent people. And he's facilitating the never-ending brutality of the civil war. Are you seriously trying to tell me you're mourning his death?"

"I never said I liked him. But I needed him."

The shape in the distance solidifies into a small enclosure—a white fence draped with desiccated palm fronds and a string of flags in childish colours bleached by the force of the sun. Inside the fence rise swoops of cement shaped like the tails of an aircraft, painted with the Algerian flag. The brightness of the white memorial stones under the desert sun sting her eyes. The shapes seem to dance and shift under her efforts to bring them into focus. They make her want to look away, to escape this exposure of sun and dust and thirst. Perhaps that is the point—to create a memorial so blindingly bright it hurts to look upon. A small snatch of the force of the bomb. Michael does not even shade his eyes.

"What did you need him for—another of your corrupt deals?" Sarah asks. "How much was he paying you to fight his corner?"

"You have no idea what you're talking about."

"Don't I? I think the situation is pretty clear. You're pissed off because your little cash cow has gone to the slaughter."

Michael's disciplined calm trembles. "Do you have any idea what you've done?"

His words echo off the bare white walls, carrying with them her creeping thirst, the prickling heat on her unprotected skin and engulfing her in the full magnitude of her act. She killed someone. She pulled the trigger to end a human life. Her actions have irredeemably wiped out all future possibilities. A human life lost. Deleted. In all that happened since, she has scarcely stopped to consider this truth. What she did could never be undone. That she is a murderer will never be erased from her story.

"I killed him," she says quietly. "But only in defence. Are you telling me you've never taken a life?"

"Of course I have. More than I care to remember. But that's not my point. You didn't just kill anyone. You killed Skarparov, the key player in an operation I have been working on for years."

Her eyes search for Dilara's plane—her anchor and means of escape—now a small dot shimmering in the haze. "What operation? The plot in Tbilisi?"

"No, of course not. That was small fry. There he showed himself to be a serious enough player for me to use. But I've been trying to reel in a far greater catch and a far greater threat."

"Are you going to tell me who?" Sarah's head is pounding and white spots dance in front of her eyes. Surely staying out here much longer is madness.

"A Chinese businessman—Chen Xiaochang—attracted our attention for consistently being in the wrong place at the wrong time. His connections to known criminals were staggering, but we had nothing on him. Recently he has been putting out feelers for uranium. We don't know for sure who he's buying for, but the North Koreans are the most likely customer. I've been watching him for years, but he's almost impossible to follow. His print is so fluid, for a long time I wasn't sure he actually existed. Skarparov was going to be the man to lead us directly to him, to establish the relationship and to set up a trail that could be followed all the way to the buyer." Michael's top lip pinches upwards in the beginnings of a sneer. He speaks slowly, labouring his words. "We finally had a way in."

Sarah bites her thumb. "Can't you just move on to the next guy who pops up to replace Skarparov? Freetown is crawling with people trying to secure that uranium find. The snake will grow another head."

"Do you know how difficult it is to set up a relationship like that, while maintaining your own invisibility? Getting all relevant partners biting at once is as rare as catching a blue marlin, and just as difficult to prevent the prey from slipping the hook. Skarparov was unique because he needed me. I can hardly sidle up to the Russian government and ask for a favour, can I? Now, thanks to your heroics, we're back to square one. Chen Xiaochang will vanish back off our radars and we'll know nothing about it until the North Koreans launch a fully armed nuclear weapon."

Sarah is silenced. From the moment she set after Skarparov, she had been confident that she was on the side of the angels. She was told repeatedly that it was too complicated, that he was a good guy really, that his good work made up for his willingness to sacrifice the future of a country for personal gain—but she saw through it. She had clarity where everyone else was dazzled by his spin. Her horizons were satisfyingly black and white—she was not drawn into the murky moral equivalence that blinds people to right and wrong. Her goal was crystal clear, and she knew that stopping Skarparov was the right and proper thing to do, the choice of good over evil. Fewer people would suffer if he was stopped, of that she had been certain.

But she had also been wrong. Only now, when it is too late to reverse what has been done, does she see how blinkered she has been. She stares at the scene of devastation around her, the featureless wasteland stripped of life. Is Michael right that the loss of Skarparov makes another nuclear strike more likely? If Sierra Leonean uranium ends up in a nuclear weapon used against a civilian target, would the blood of millions be on her hands? She feels as if someone has scooped out her flesh like rotten fruit. Her knees give a putrefied shake.

"I killed for this," she murmurs, her voice half-raised in question.

"No, you killed in self-defence," Michael offers the first note of sympathy, reining back his attack. To Sarah's relief, he begins walking back towards the airstrip.

"It wasn't self-defence. Skarparov would not kill me. I shot him to protect Kuznetsov." Her voice sounds hollow in her ear.

"Nikolay Kuznetsov?" Michael looks as if he's just bitten into an unripe banana. "What had he done to earn your protection? Chris told me he suspected you'd been cosying up to the enemy, but I didn't believe him."

The smell of Kuznetsov's cologne returns to Sarah, the warmth of his body too close against her skin. What had she done? "He told me he was a friend of yours."

"A friend? We might have shared the respect of a long-term rival, perhaps. He's the only person I've ever met who is as good at this game as I am. But I have no doubt he'd chuck me under a bus if the need arose." Michael's lips twitch. "What were you doing going to Skarparov with him, anyway?"

"It's a long story. He was helping me."

"My God, Sarah." He turns away, closing his eyes.

"Just don't, okay. You don't have to say anything more. It's clear. I've cocked this up. A cock-up of history-altering magnitude. You don't need to rub it in."

"There's no need to blow things out of proportion. It's always important to keep perspective."

"Perspective? You are the one who brought me to a nuclear waste ground to drive home your point."

"It was a convenient mid-way meeting point."

"Most people would have picked up the phone."

"I wanted to see you, Sarah. To talk this through face to face. I knew you'd never come if I asked. But I apologise for the excess of drama." He drops his chin towards his chest. "I may have misread your motives."

"Misread how?"

They pass a low wall, painted a watery peach to blend into the stony landscape. It bears a large black and white skull, hand painted with rudimentary, almost cartoonish features, stuck in a frozen grimace. Thank God they are nearly back at the plane. The small traces of human hand are more macabre than the devastating lifelessness of the terrain.

"I thought you might have sabotaged my mission on purpose," Michael says. Sarah can almost hear a note of apology in his voice.

"On purpose? You thought I sabotaged a counter-proliferation operation on purpose?"

"I thought you did it to spite me."

"Does your self-importance know no bounds? Is that really what you think of me? I didn't even know you were involved with Skarparov."

"Really?" he raises a well-groomed eyebrow. "I find that hard to believe."

"I was suspicious, but I had no idea what for. I thought you were using him to line your pockets. But that was no reason to kill him."

"Well, you were wrong. Part of my role is fund-raising. I don't enjoy it, but it is a necessary evil. If I want to operate fully off-the-books, my unit has to be self-funding. If we have a budget line, we also have oversight and I'd rather not have auditors poking around our work. But I wasn't taking money from Skarparov, if anything he was going to prove quite an expensive project."

"You fund your work on behalf of the British Government by extorting money?" Sarah is gob smacked.

"Never extorting; no, that would be illegal. Most of my funds come from diverting the ill-gotten gains of those we bring down. It all goes back into the pot to help us with the next target."

"Robin Hood of the shadows. By the way, how did you find out so quickly?"

"Chris had an agent on the inside, in Skarparov's house. She called it in."

"The cleaning lady?"

"She said she'd seen a blonde girl running out with an old man."

"Kuznetsov could have killed him?"

"Nikolay would never have made such a mess."

Sarah nods in reluctant agreement.

"I'm sorry to have brought you into this," he says. "And I'm sorry it's ended this way. I had always hoped things might be different, that you might come back to us. Chris seemed to think it was in the bag."

"What about that news story? The cock-and-bull piece with the pictures from Baku?"

"That was unfortunate. But luckily it wasn't too widely spread. And the name was wrong. We'd have been able to bury it."

"Was it you?"

"Why would I leak something like that?"

"To shut me down?"

Michael shakes his head. "I require a high level of trust from those around me. In fact, from those who report directly to me, I need complete and unquestioning loyalty. I always sensed you didn't fully trust me, but I hadn't realised your opinion of me was so low."

Sarah has nothing to say in response. He is right; she did suspect the worst of him. In every way.

"But now you need to walk away," he continues, "and stop playing at being a secret agent."

"And do what?" Sarah blurts out. She had always intended to cut all ties with Michael after he refused to help her with Skarparov. But now that it is clear how closely entwined their paths have always been; now that she understands the scale and complexity of the battles he is fighting; now that she realises how utterly scuppered her chances are of ever being trusted by him again, she wants nothing more than to join forces.

"Go home, Sarah. See your father. Call your friends. Get yourself out of this hellhole, you have nothing left to do."

It is the obvious answer. There is nothing left for her now. She should go. Nothing holds her to this continent anymore, and it has brought her nothing but tragedy. It is the easiest path to choose to run back to the safety of home. Flee, deny, pretend she never had the misfortune to step onto that luckless soil. It is the obvious answer, but Sarah cannot do it.

She's sat at the board of a totally different game. She knows nothing about who her opponent is, what weaknesses they may have to exploit. Her own position looks uncomfortably weak, and she has no idea which pieces she has available to call on. All that she knows is that she has to try. And she has to win.

"What if I help you?" she asks, digging her hands into her jeans pockets and taking a few steps ahead so that Michael is forced to look at her.

"I think you've been enough help already."

"No I mean it. What if I help you set up the uranium deal? I am still deniable; you could remain invisible. But if it works, you have your route back in."

Michael does not answer.

"I know the ground," she continues, now walking backwards to stay facing him while maintaining their progress towards the safety of the plane. "I know some of the people involved. I can be your new middleman to lead them to your buyer. I can be the new head of the snake?"

"Sarah, forgive my bluntness, but everything you have touched since you arrived in Sierra Leone has ended in shit. What makes you think this will be any different?"

"That's exactly why I have to do this. It is too easy to give up. To walk away because it's difficult. Because people die. Because bad things happen. I can't bring Skarparov back to life, but I could help make sure that my mistake doesn't have greater ramifications. Will you let me try?"

"I don't need your help, Sarah."

"But I'm close to uncovering the source of the uranium. I'm your best bet. Besides, what other options do you have?"

"Chris is there."

"And what progress has he made? I've got a lead from the Rössing mine which I'm sure will lead me to the source. Surely two of us is better than one?"

Michael squints towards the bright sun. "It's not a good idea—"

"It doesn't have to be."

"Arguing with you is giving me a headache."

"That's just the radioactive poison." Sarah grins.

They have reached the plane. Sarah can see Dilara hanging back, just out of earshot. In her large sunhat and oversized sunglasses she looks as if she's been for a stroll along the riviera. At Michael's nod, she saunters back towards them, climbing into the plane and starting up the engines.

"If I send you back in, you're working for me." His hand reaches for his hair before snapping back to his side. "Which means you follow my instructions—is that clear?"

"It would be quite a novelty to be guided in what to do for a change."

Michael ignores her dig. "And you report directly to Chris. He is in charge."

"Chris? He's going to nanny me?"

"No. Chris, an experienced field officer is going to be there to keep you under control. He will be your connection back to me." Michael pauses, running his thumb across the shiny surfaces of his fingernails. "And I advise you to stay away from Nikolay Kuznetsov."

"What if the Russians are first in to the find?"

"Then you find another way in."

"Fine." Sarah is not too disappointed with the excuse to stay away from Kuznetsov.

"I can't believe I'm agreeing to this," Michael says, pressing his lips into a weak smile.

"What have you got to lose?"

"Everything."

CHAPTER 34

An arrival can be telling. The immediate, visceral reaction to returning to a place can uncover secrets hidden from your conscious mind. Somewhere that you thought was new and alien can feel reassuringly homely on return—its strangeness and rough edges now become familiar and real. Somewhere you once felt quite happy can seem shapeless and flat when seen with fresh eyes. The first thought, the chemical reaction of the body to the smell as the door of the plane opens, can reveal more than a month of soul-searching.

Sarah had been nervous about a return to Freetown. Michael was right. Everything she touched had turned sour. Her lover was killed. She took a life in her search for revenge. She left behind a deeply awkward departure from her FSB counterpart. And the never-ending brutality of the war leaves little space for optimism. But curiously, as Dilara's plane touches down on the short runway at Hastings, she is excited to be back. She has a purpose now, a place in the bigger picture. And very little left to lose.

"Are you sure you want to stay? You can come on with me if you prefer?" Dilara says, looking sceptically at Sarah's growing grin.

"No. I have things to finish here."

"For Michael?" Dilara asks.

"And for me."

"It's always better that way." The same closed look crosses Dilara's beautiful features. Sarah can tell there is something she wants to say. "What happened between you and Michael?" she asks gently.

"My father is a very wealthy man," Dilara replies, opening the door of the plane. "And with that wealth comes influence. When I was young—very young, still a child, and very foolish—I was targeted by a foreign agent who wanted dirt on my father. I met a man, he was older, alluring, exotic in ways I had never imagined, and he told me he was in love with me. What did I know of love? I was very privileged, but my childhood was also very sheltered. I had no idea about the world. He persuaded me to… he took advantage of my naivety. He compromised me, and then he threatened to go public."

"Was it Michael?" Sarah asks, horrified.

"No. God no. Michael was the one who ended it. I don't know how he did it, but Michael called this man off. He buried it. He made it all go away before my family ever found out. You asked me before why I would help you. I owe Michael my life, my reputation. Everything I have, I owe to him. And he never lets me forget it."

Sarah is stunned. She knew Michael and Dilara's relationship was deep and trusting, but she did not know it would be such a complex web of personal indebtedness.

"Michael and I work well together," Dilara says, picking up her tone. "We have fun together. I have repaid his favour many times over. He has given me many more. But he thrives on control. Don't let him have that over you, Sarah."

Sarah nods, unable to find the words to thank Dilara for her trust, to acknowledge the warning. She squeezes Dilara's hand, causing a gentle blush to steal across her broad cheekbones.

"Any news for me on the uranium deal?" Dilara asks, swiftly moving back to business.

"I'm working on it. I think I'm getting closer to the source of the find, but can you put out feelers for potential buyers? Get your ear to the ground, find out who might be interested—especially the Chinese."

"The Chinese?" Dilara raises an eyebrow.

"Play it cool," Sarah says, wondering if such a thing was possible for Dilara. "Try to be discreet, but encouraging if necessary. And if you hear anything come straight to me."

"I don't want to ruin my suspension on this runway too often."

"There is also the phone?"

"But that's not half so fun." Dilara blows Sarah a kiss as she turns the plane back down the landing strip cracked with tall grass.

CHAPTER 35

To Sarah's surprise, Chris is still waiting for her outside the EU commission two hours after she went inside. He'd found her in her grotty hotel the morning after Dilara dropped her back, eager to get going on their hunt for the uranium. And to show her he was in charge.

She decided the best start to their working relationship was to make him wait, guarding her car, while she banged her head against a few more bureaucratic brick walls.

She climbs back into her Land Rover, sweat pooling in the hollows under her ears and hair sticking to the back of her neck. She has spent the best part of her time in the Commission ignored in the waiting room, slowly sticking to a leather-look seat until finally the deputy commissioner agreed to see her.

"So?" Chris asks.

"You were right. It was a total waste of time. There will be no follow up on forensics from the crash site. No investigation team is coming. They won't give me any information about Elias's next of kin—to be honest, I wasn't convinced they even had it. Apparently they don't have the resources to do more. And an additional intervention would have to be pushed by a member state."

"And the Netherlands have made no request?" Chris asks.

"No." She beats her wrist into the plastic of the steering wheel.

Chris lets out a slow sigh. He sits in quiet stillness, allowing her to rant.

"I can't understand why they wouldn't take this more

seriously. Twenty people died in that helicopter, twenty people burnt alive…"

"Look around you, Sarah," Chris says. "This is a warzone. People die here every day. They die pointless, gruesome, violent deaths. They are all owed a proper investigation, follow-up, justice, closure for grieving relatives. But no one will get it."

She resents Chris's boldness, his lack of scruple to speak so candidly to her grief. But she knows he is right. Elias's death turned her world upside down. It seems impossible that someone so vibrant and passionate for life could be snuffed out in one preventable tragedy. But his death is one of many everyday tragedies in this country. And the world has closed its ears to the cries of thousands. Sarah slumps her forehead into the steering wheel and bites her bottom lip until it hurts.

"Come on," Chris says. "There's work to do and uranium to find. Let's go to the High Commission. There must be someone unscrupulous in the diplomatic circle who knows more than they are supposed to tell."

"I think we'd be wasting our time here. The samples came from Koidu. The only way we're going to get our hands on the prize is heading East."

"Koidu? Right in the rebel-held diamond-rich heartland? Are you sure you want to go back there?"

Sarah pushes away memories of the jungle honeymoon with Elias and the attack on the chief's daughter. "Of course. Besides, if no one can tell us where the uranium is coming from, we could go and dig a sample out the rock ourselves?" Even if the memories are painful and raw, it would also give her the chance to get back to Elias's camp to follow up on any further intel he may have left behind.

"You know that might not be such a bad idea? If only to see who comes sniffing around to try and stop us. We'll need to secure access to one of the mine sites. Do you have any contacts up there?"

"We could try Kobus?"

"Who's he?"

"South African, works in security in one of the mines."

"Shall I arrange a High Commission vehicle to drive us up?"

"No need. I've got a better idea."

*

George meets them at the helicopter pad. He puts his arms around Sarah and pulls her into his barrel chest for a breath-constricting hug. "I'm so sorry, Sarah. It still gets me every day," he says, squeezing her so tight she is unable to answer. "You'd better take this for the flight." He hands her an enormous sick bag.

"Thanks." She presses at her eye-sockets with the heel of her hand. "I'll be fine. I never get travel sick."

"Believe me, you'll need it." George loads her and Chris with the rest of the cargo in the back of the helicopter.

She has every confidence in George. He maintains his chopper with the love and dedication of a classic car enthusiast and would certainly have carried out more thorough pre-flight checks than the surly Ukrainian crew of the airport ferry service. She knows it is statistically safer than the roads. But George was right. From the moment the engines start up, the noise is not just loud—it is as if her head has been buried inside the engine itself. Deep surging vibrations rampage through every soft fibre of her body. Her undulating vision fixes on Chris, strapped to the opposite wall in Elias's seat. The stale sweat smell of the shoulder harness sends her intestines into revolt. The rest of the flight is spent emptying the contents of her stomach into the copious sick bag.

George offers her a bottle of water on landing and another hug. "Told you it would be rough, but you made it. Next time will be better."

"Did you manage to get hold of Kobus?" Sarah asks weakly, chugging back most of the water in one go.

"Yeah, he's waiting for you at the mine. But take care." He

shoots Chris an uncertain look. "It's getting rough out there. I'm going back tonight if you need out."

They find Kobus at the top of an escarpment, looking down at a scraped and raw riverbed. Young men in filthy shorts, naked from the waist up, carry vast sacks of gravel on their heads, silty water the colour of milky tea left to curdle drips down their wiry chests.

Kobus looks like an Afrikaner hunter posing with a trophy in the Kalahari—khaki shirt with multiple pockets, filthy baseball cap, baggy shorts with walkie talkie strapped to the belt, heavy workman's boots, a pair of binoculars and a Vektor R4 assault rifle slung over his shoulder. He greets Sarah with a kiss on the cheek and a bear hug. Sarah pushes back her memories of the last time –he saw him - dancing with Elias at the China Friendship House bar.

"Have you met Chris from the High Commission?" she says. "He's helping facilitate some of my research work."

Kobus gives Chris a sceptical look and throws him a hard hat with some force directly in his stomach. Chris catches it with ease, unfazed by the hostile delivery.

A long line of workers in sun-bleached shorts and vests stand knee-deep in the muddy water. Backs bowed, faces down, shaking wide pancake trays under the watchful eye of an overseer stroking his gun in the shade of a rainbow umbrella. Swinging from his left hand is a loop of rubber, like a vehicle fan belt with a knot in one end that twitches and flicks. She hadn't been expecting the Rössing mine but still, the reality of mining for alluvial diamonds is shockingly basic. One of the world's most precious substances, the sparkle that promises commitment and eternal love, scrabbled out of the earth by barefoot boys in the crosshairs.

"It's really that simple," Sarah says, watching the closest workers poke and prod at the silt in their trays with pale-tipped fingers swollen by the water.

"That's it," Kobus says. "Well, here anyway. Other places have industrial production but no one's going to make that kind of investment in a place like this. What did you want to come out here for anyway?"

"I've heard rumours of uranium," Sarah says.

"First helicopters, now uranium? Interesting research you do, Sarah."

Sarah acknowledges the dig with a smile but stays in character, sensing a change in Kobus's easy manner. "I'd like to get a feel for where the deposit might be to take some samples from the leaf matter."

"You and everyone else. And what's that guy doing here?" He nods at Chris, who has wandered off towards the pit to take a closer look. Sarah thinks she can see him picking up some soil and running it through his fingers. Scrabbling for his own uranium sample or hoping to get lucky with a diamond?

"City boy in the mud?" she laughs. She does not want Kobus to think that she and Chris are in any way romantically involved. Somehow, even the conjecture in someone else's mind feels like a betrayal to Elias. Although it might be easier to let him think they are in a relationship than to have him guess at what really brings them together. "The High Commission is supporting some of my research," she says. The lie sounds weak.

"Well, I think you're crazy coming out here at the moment looking at leaves. You know there's a war on?"

"That's partly what makes it interesting to study—no one else is doing it."

"And for a very good reason. It's heating up again, you know? I'd get back to Freetown if I were you." He watches Chris clawing in the earth again and goes to pull him back. "I'll get in trouble if you two get in the way." His joking tone isn't reflected in his narrow eyes. "Let's get a drink."

Plumes of thick black smoke rise up from the forest around them and new noises join the grind of the machinery and slap of trays in the water. Kobus watches the black plumes and rubs the back of his wide neck as he hurries Sarah and Chris onto his quad.

"What's that?" Sarah asks, picking up on Kobus's unease.

"Probably just scrub clearing. Somewhere always seems to be on fire," he says with a weak laugh.

"You must need nerves of steel working security here," Sarah says, taking in the high double fences with foot-high coils of barbed wire, the watchtowers positioned at each corner of the compound, the security lights fed by whirring generators strung up along the fence.

Kobus's walkie-talkie crackles into life, but it is impossible to catch what is being said. He keeps his eyes on the growing towers of smoke. "I never know if all that is to keep the rebels out or keep the workers in."

The bar, the site office, and the sizeable canteen all could have arrived as flat-pack—and been folded down with a flick of a screwdriver. Kobus orders three beers from the glassy-eyed bar man who sets them down on foam mats advertising a local beer that has long-ceased production.

Sarah unsticks her shoes from the floor and climbs onto a bar stool. "You must have heard of these uranium finds. Surely everyone up here knows where the samples are coming from?" She takes a swig of lukewarm beer.

"Yah, funny story, right?" Kobus says, switching his gaze from Sarah to Chris and blinking in quick succession. "One day the entire town is buzzing about the fortune to be made in uranium, next thing you know it's all gone quiet. I guess they figured it's harder work to get at than these shiny fellers."

"But you must know where the samples were taken from? This is a tiny town—surely outsiders and foreigners coming in doesn't go unnoticed?"

Kobus snorts into his beer. "Look, it wasn't here if that's what you're digging for. Probably one of those smaller Lebanese-run outfits, you know, Chinese investors taking a punt. It was probably them." Kobus focusses on peeling the label off his beer bottle with a long thumbnail.

"Y'alright Kobus? Surprised to see you're still here?" The new arrival is a deeply tanned expat with a long curly mullet, the likes of which Sarah has never seen in real life—thick bouncy waves down the back, slicked in close to the scalp with a smear of gel. "You got company, mate? 'Scuse his manners, I'm Matt," the mullet says, stretching out his Australian vowels. He reached across to shake Sarah's hand, transferring an economy-sized packet of toilet paper across his heavy beer belly to his other arm.

"You brought your girlfriend to the bar, I see," Kobus says, nodding at the voluminous packet of loo-roll that Matt balances affectionately on his knee as he lowers his sizeable backside into a white plastic garden chair at a nearby table.

"I tell you, I'm not letting this out of my sight now. Second packet this big I hand carried all the way from Oz. First lot filched right out of my room. Can you believe it?"

"Can't you use newsprint like the rest of us?"

"You Africans might think it's okay to wipe your arse with a picture of the Queen, but me? Nah. I'm bringing my two-ply quilted with me and I'm not sharing."

"Matt, you great charmer. There are ladies present."

"What? I bet even the pommies wipe their arse. Don't worry, Sarah love. If you need to go, you can take a piece of my date roll."

The canteen is filling up with local workers, hunched over their trays is as they had been over their sieves in the riverbed. It isn't formally marked but it is clear to Sarah that the bar is for white expat staff only. At least for lunchtime drinking.

"If you ask me," Kobus says, thrusting a meaty hand coated with thick golden hair into one of his shorts' many pockets. "I think someone got a bit carried away with a Geiger counter and started putting the word around there were mountains of the yellow stuff all ready to be dug up. There's radioactivity everywhere. I bet if you point one of those things into chef's groundnut stew it would go bananas."

"I heard there were confirmed samples," Sarah said. "Surely it can't have been just talk?"

"Really? I didn't hear about that."

"That's what they say, is it?" Matt butts in from the next table. "Well, I say never trust a white African, isn't that right Kobus?"

"Sorry, Sarah, I can only apologise for our convict friend here. Security jobs and mine sites the world over aren't known for the delicacy of their company. But diamond mine security in a warzone turns up some pretty special types." Kobus drains the last of his beer and stands up. "Is there anything else you guys want to see while you're here?" He looks at his watch. "I've got to be back on shift any minute."

"No. Thanks. But if you do hear any more about the uranium, give me a call. Someone must know where those samples came from."

"Yeah, will do." Kobus escorts them back to the gate and leaves them with a hurried goodbye.

"Did you get anything useful scrabbling about in the mud?" Sarah asks Chris.

"Not much more than dirty fingers. Seemed a bit odd, your friend, no?"

"Yeah, he was a lot less helpful than I was hoping. I guess it's not the sort of job where you can spend too much time entertaining tourists."

Matt's spectacular mullet appears through the gate. He nods to Sarah and Chris. "By the way, you know your friend in there is full of shit?" he says.

"What?" Sarah asks, steeling herself for another round of ill-taste expat ribbing.

"That claptrap he was telling you about uranium. There have been loads of oddballs sniffing around. Just yesterday there was a pair of Middle Eastern guys skulking around, asking questions. I swear I saw them talking to Kobus in the bar."

"And they were talking about uranium?"

"Damned if I know. But what else would bring a pair like that out here?"

"Any idea where we can track these guys down?" Chris asks.

"Don't look at me, mate. You might get lucky hanging around the Chinese bar in town? But I wouldn't bother if I were you. Guys in the comms office are going mental. Word is the rebels are moving in. I'm getting out of here while I still can."

"Cheers, mate," Chris says in a distinctly Aussie twang, as Matt flings his economy pack of toilet paper into the front seat of his car and tears off.

"What do you reckon?" he asks. "Any better ideas or do we set up shop in the Chinese grog shop and hope for the best?"

"You go on ahead," Sarah says. "There's somewhere I want to go first."

"No way am I leaving you alone out here."

"I won't be long."

"But how will you get back into town?" They had borrowed a battered pickup truck from a contact of George's to get to the mine. Chris is clearly not about to let Sarah take it.

"I'll get a taxi."

"Sarah, are you mad? I'm coming with you."

She gives a reluctant nod. "Fine. But I'm driving."

*

Sarah isn't sure she'll be able to find Elias's jungle camp. During the time she spent there with Elias, they hardly left. Luckily there aren't many roads on which to get lost and a tall termite mound with a distinctive shape reminds her when to turn off the bumpy laterite. But after the familiar driveway, nothing is recognisable. Only slowly does her brain make sense of the destruction that meets them at the end of the rutted track. The decaying huts have been burned to the ground. All thatch, wood and most of the walls are destroyed, leaving only blackened concrete pads where the huts once stood and the soot-covered water tank that never worked. Rebels passing through, or Skarparov's mob come to finish their job? The acrid smell of ash and smoke still linger in the humid air, bringing burning tears to Sarah's eyes and a wave of nausea to her stomach.

The destruction is complete, nothing remains beyond the blistered black scars. She had hoped to find some memento of Elias—another notebook he left behind, further information on the locations and strengths of the rebel forces, something personal that she could keep, knowing that he had held it in his hands. But all traces of him are gone.

She walks through the charred remains of the place that Elias made his own, clumps of ash crumbling under her feet, remembering their romantic dinners by citronella candlelight, their happy hours swinging in the makeshift hammock. Her eyes stop on a flicker of brightness on the ground where the smashed shards of mirror that once adorned the mosaic table now lie dug into the mud and ash. A square tile in bright scarab blue lies almost untouched amongst the dirt. She brushes it off and slips it into her pocket, hoping perhaps the amulet would bring her luck. Nothing else in this broken place gives rise for hope.

"Where are we?" Chris asks, picking through the debris.

"Nowhere," Sarah says, her voice strained. "I was looking for something. But I realise now it's gone." The devastation of Elias's jungle camp revives the truth that her unconscious brain has been denying. Nothing she can do will bring him back. Nothing remains of his vital being. Her memories of him are all she has left. But there is something she can do to honour those memories. Sarah sees an opening on the board that she had previously missed. An arrangement of pieces that could be used, a new strategy to test. She cannot bring Elias back, but she can finish what he started.

Chris remains silent, kicking a pile of ash. "So, what are we doing here?" he asks with only a muted hint of his usual irreverence.

"Strengthening resolve," Sarah says, pushing back the caustic tears that threaten to overflow. "Come on, we're wasting time."

CHAPTER 36

As they pull into town, the air feels charged, the atmosphere soured, the everyday bustle of the streets has evaporated. They stop at the market to return the keys to the borrowed truck. Its previously packed alleys are now deserted, the stalls have been emptied of produce, metal shutters clamped down in front of every shop. All around them people are vanishing, disappearing into shadows, retreating to a safer place.

"I don't like this," Chris says as they head for the Chinese bar on foot. "We shouldn't be here."

Sarah regrets surrendering the vehicle. When filled with noise and people, Koidu town centre had not felt like a threatening place. But now in the eery quiet she feels dangerously exposed to every hostile look, every unknown face and the danger all around that cannot be seen.

On the main street, a crowd has gathered outside one of the Lebanese-run shops. At first, Sarah is reassured—they are no longer the only ones out on the street. But then she sees the body. Face down in the mud lies a man, arms spreadeagled in surrender, face pooled in blood. A strange smell fills Sarah's nostrils—stale sweat, fear, something organic, something dead. A woman in an emerald dress bends over the body, howling uncontrollably. As they draw closer, it becomes clear that the crowd Sarah had taken for concerned onlookers is busy looting the dead man's shop—carrying out armfuls of boxes and crates and piling their loot in the back of a blue pickup truck. Sarah wants to run in, to stop them, to draw attention to the callous horror of their actions but what can she do against a crowd?

A white UNAMSIL vehicle drives by, windows up. Sarah runs onto the road to flag it down, blocking its path with her body. "Stop! A man here needs help." The vehicle swerves to avoid her and keeps on driving. She hammers on the side panel of car as it slips past. "You're supposed to be here to keep the peace. A man is hurt, his shop is being looted, you need to do something about it," she yells, catching the eye of the man in the passenger seat. His haunted eyes look away as they drive on.

"What the hell was that?" she shouts at the back of the retreating car, ignoring the hostile eyes that are settling on her like flies.

Chris pulls her out of the road. "We need to get out of here, and you need to stop drawing attention to yourself."

"But no one is doing anything to help."

"That's because they're all scared. It might be time you were too."

Sarah wipes the sweat from her forehead with a dust-smeared hand. "But what about the uranium?"

"That'll have to wait."

"But I promised Michael—"

"And I promised Michael I'd look after you."

The looters' blue pickup truck barrels past, loaded with booty and empty gas bottles. A handwritten sign on its roof announces, *'Oh Yes! No condition is permanent'*. Following the pickup, a dusty white Land Cruiser screeches to a halt behind Sarah and Chris. Kobus flings open the passenger door, his face red and sweaty, the golden hair on his double-muscled forearms slicked to the skin.

"Get in, quick!" he orders, shoving a khaki bag off the front bench to make room for them both. "What are you still doing here? And what were you thinking walking in town alone? You need to get out now."

"Why?" Sarah asks, bracing herself against the dashboard as Kobus tears off at speed.

"The rebels arrived at the mine just after you left. All the ex-pat staff have fled. Everyone else has slunk off into the bush. I spoke to George a few minutes ago—he said he'd wait. But if they come for the airport, he won't be able to hang around."

"I thought the mines were safe," Sarah says, trying not to catch Kobus's fear.

"Nothing's safe anymore. We'll head back to Freetown, but I don't fancy our chances there either at the moment. Shit."

A burning tyre blocks the road, belching thick smoke into the air. A group of rebels holds a man at gunpoint, one slapping his sobbing face with the back of a hand, while the rest unload the recently plundered loot from the back of his blue pickup truck. Oh yes, Sarah thinks, no condition is permanent.

She looks for a way past the checkpoint and the rebels with guns positioned either side of the burning tyre.

Kobus spins the car around in a handbrake turn, sending dust flying and adding to the smell of burning rubber. "There's another way to the airport, round the back," he says. "But you better buckle up, it's going to be rough."

They speed back through the centre of town—the crowd of looters outside the shop has dispersed, replaced by another crowd of well-armed rebels kicking the bloody corpse into the wide storm drain, shrieking and calling to each other as if it was a game of football. Kobus picks up speed as they fly past.

"If we can't make the airport, couldn't we drive back to Freetown?" Chris asks, looking pale.

"That would take us back towards the mining areas—it'd be crazy. And we'd never make it before dark." After the last cluster of buildings, he swings them off the road and through the low green grass. "You can get to the airport this way in the dry season." He blinks rapidly as he pushes the car on towards the bush.

As the vegetation grows thicker, the track becomes harder to spot, and Kobus is forced to slow the pace. With lowered momentum, Sarah feels the tyres struggling to gain traction over the increasingly water-logged ground.

As the airstrip comes into view ahead of them, the car grinds to a halt in a slick of mud. Kobus engages the four-wheel drive and edges the car back and forth, trying to rock it out of the ditch. But the spinning wheels only dig a deeper trench in the mud.

"Time to get out and push?" Chris suggests, rolling up his double-cuffed sleeves.

"Time to make a run for it." Kobus nods towards the airstrip where they can see the rotor blades of George's helicopter beginning to spin.

"But what about your car?" Sarah asks.

"It belongs to the mine. I think the mine owner has probably had a bad enough day as it is without worrying about a stuck vehicle."

They jump out the door, landing ankle high in warm, oozing mud. The car has broken through the top layer, exposing pockets of rapidly decaying organic matter buried below the surface. The stench of rotten leaves and advanced decomposition released into the air through pockets of noxious gas is atrocious. They heave on the rotten air as they struggle to run through the mud in time to catch George's helicopter. Sarah covers her mouth and nose with her hand, trying to mask the rancid smell, but it makes little difference. Kobus shouts expletives while waving desperately to George. Sarah is fast, but Chris's long legs give him the advantage. Seeing her fall behind, he reaches back and offers a hand, dragging her in his sprint away from the thick and foul air and towards a break in the perimeter fence.

George jumps out to open the back. "Where did you guys come from? I was about to give up on you." He slams the doors behind them and checks the controls.

"We took a shortcut," Sarah says.

"Felt like a bit of exercise," Kobus puffs out next to her.

George shakes his curly mop and restarts the engines. Sarah has never been so glad to leave solid ground.

"*Eish!*" Kobus shouts as they lurch up into the air, unlacing his enormous work boots and holding them up at arm's length. "*Sho!* The smell of that mud, *sies man*. These boots are going to stink for weeks."

Chris has kicked off his shoes and is unrolling his long socks. "I think this lot is headed straight for the bin."

"I don't want to know what was buried in that mud to release a stink like that," Kobus says, wiping his thick hands down the front of his shorts. "We'll all be barking the dog on this flight. It was like an explosion of rotten whale's belly."

"Exploding whale belly?" Sarah asks, surprised at his choice of analogy.

"Yah, I was once up close to one when it went off. BAM! The thing went up like it was packed with TNT. And the smell, shame, it was like burying your head in that mud. *So vrot!*"

Sarah is struck with a powerful sensation of deja-vu. She has heard this story before. Even the language is almost word for word the same as Bok's story at the Rössing mine. "Was that in Namibia?" she asks.

"Yah! Skeleton coast. How did you know?"

"Good guess. I've heard of that happening there. How amazing you were there."

"Man, I wasn't happy about it at the time, I can tell you. But it made a good story."

Kobus must have been Bok's camping buddy. They must have dined out on this story so many times they even told it in the same way. Kobus keeps talking, building up his account, adding colour and sound effects, goaded on by Chris who wants to hear the full gory details of what the inside of an exploded whale really looks like. But Sarah is no longer listening—her mind is busy connecting the dots.

CHAPTER 37

The helicopter landing pad in Freetown is busier than Sarah has ever seen it—the car park is packed with white UN vehicles and a pair of UN choppers stand ready for take-off. Peacekeepers in blue berets ferry kit and equipment back and forth, supported by Sierra Leonean army troops. There is a sense of urgency that makes Sarah's skin tingle, especially against the backdrop of dark smoke rising from the forest around the city.

"I'm not sticking around here any longer than I have to," Kobus announces as they leave the chopper. "I'm off to lie low at Pietro's—they've left him alone this far. It should be a pretty safe spot. You guys want to join? Pietro and I are old buddies, I can make sure he gives you the best lobster at mate's rates?"

"Thanks," Sarah says, relieved that Kobus has recovered some of the easy friendliness of their previous meetings. "But I'd rather get home and change out of these clothes." She lifts a mud-encrusted ankle. The draw of holing up at Pietro's corner of paradise is tempting, but it is yet another place that reminds her of Elias.

"Each to their own," Kobus shrugs. "But be careful on the roads, yah?" He nods to the commotion at the helipad. "Something tells me it's going to get hairy out there. You must get where you're going quickly and stay there."

*

Outside the helicopter pad, the city is quiet. The streets are empty, the normal hustle and bustle around the sea front gone.

Sarah drives Chris back to the High Commission in silence, her mind piecing together the puzzle thrown out by Kobus's story. Kobus and Pietro are old friends—both arrived here as young men seeking their fortune, but both endlessly passed over by opportunities to cash in on their experience. Pietro nursing the resentment grown from years of never having profited from his geological insights, Kobus surrounded by untold wealth but only ever in the pay of a middleman. What if they cooked this up together? An old friend working at the Rössing mine's laboratory providing just the right level of incontrovertible proof to keep anyone from asking the obvious questions. Is the truth of their uranium wild goose chase that there is actually nothing to find?

"What if it's all a hoax?" she says to Chris, still feeling her way to an answer.

Chris sucks in his cheeks. "What if what's all a hoax?"

"The uranium. What if it's a story dreamt up to bring in unscrupulous investors?"

"Impossible. There are far too many people involved who would have found out. You think Skarparov would have been happy to sell Chen Xiaochang some yellowcake that didn't exist?"

"What if he didn't know it didn't exist?"

"That's up there with the stupidest thing you've asked all week." Chris leans across the car to check the rear-view mirror. "If you ask me, the Russians hold the key to this. I wouldn't put it past your friend Kuznetsov to have set up that 'misunderstanding' with Skarparov to clear the way for a new buyer. Trust me. They'll know who's behind it, and if we follow them, we'll know too."

Typical Chris, so certain of his own version of events. He isn't even curious what made her suggest it. But the more Sarah thinks about it, the more it makes sense. No wonder Kobus was so keen to get them out of Koidu—he must have thought they were on to him.

This changes everything. It also finally gives her an advantage.

The question now is how she can benefit from busting their set up. How can she get them to cooperate with her to help rescue Michael's deal? How can she play this out to suit her preferred endgame?

She wonders whether she should return to Kuznetsov with her suspicion. Is he any more likely to listen to her than Chris? He could well have already worked it out himself. She doesn't even know if he is still in Freetown. Despite the awkwardness of their last meeting, she hopes he has not been reassigned now that Skarparov is no longer a target. An FSB agent in your debt could be a useful asset.

"Where's all the smoke coming from?" she asks. "Do they do grass clearing this close to the city?"

"Perhaps," Chris replies curtly, staring straight ahead.

"What else would it be?" It is unlike Chris not to jump at the chance to tell her something he thinks she doesn't know.

"As the rebels pass through a village," he speaks mechanically, eyes focused on the road ahead. "Having taken what and who they want, they set it on fire, torching the main buildings and burning people alive."

Sarah wishes she hadn't asked.

"Looks like they're making another push on Freetown," Chris says through clenched jaws.

As they approach the end of Lumley Beach Road, where the road turns away from the coast and up towards the diplomatic hill and the High Commission, the road is blocked by a group of children who have positioned a heavy two-wheeled cart laden with scrap metal across both lanes.

"There's a shortcut that way, we can cut across the creek from the opposite direction." Chris instructs, his voice growing in urgency.

Sarah turns off, following Chris's shortcut, and joins the road further up. But trying to turn back towards the High Commission they are blocked. A wide creek, swollen with recent rains and floating with rubbish, is passable only by a narrow bridge. But the bridge is shut off. Dark towers of dense black smoke frame the road from a stack of lorry tyres rung around a metal post, smouldering with low flames and filling the air with the smell of burning rubber. A pair of oil drums lie across the road, watched over by a group of men with guns. Their pose is pure theatre, pumped up muscles, blood-shot wavering eyes, guns held like beach towels—casually slung over an arm or dangling from a wrist. But the drama is designed to impart maximum terror. These are no children looking to empty your wallet, these are killers.

"Turn the car around," Chris instructs. "You saw what Kobus did in Koidu. We'll find another way around."

"Where?" Sarah asks. "This is the only bridge. Any higher up and we'll be back in the bush and the road was blocked the other way. We need to get home." She rolls the car up to the roadblock.

A group of young men circle the car, leering in the windows, their lustful stares dripping down Sarah like sweat. One of the boys wears sunglasses straight out of Top Gun, another has a white curly Marilyn Monroe wig, but the effect is all the more menacing for its absurdity. They look unhinged, unpredictable and brushing at the border between reality and madness. Two more point guns straight at them, faces impossibly blank. Sarah sees a shiny mass glistening in the creek beneath the bridge. A body lies face up in the garbage-strewn riverbed, floating on a sea of plastic bags, discarded newspaper and empty bottles. His limbs lie hidden under the sheets of his slimy bed. Clothes drenched in sweat, in blood and in the runoff from the refuse, his skin shining like a freshly dug up earthworm. A co-conspirator fallen out of favour, or the last person to try to pass the roadblock?

Sarah locks her door and keeps her window shut. One boy tugs at the door handle, tapping on the window with his gun. An animal tooth hangs round his neck on a black leather cord, and his army beret sticks straight up from his head like a diadem.

"Eh-Oh," he calls out in the sing-song slur of a football

hooligan at closing time. "Open for me." Another whooping shout, like a tropical bird, accompanies the rhythmical tapping at the window—the same pitch as the animal in the chief's house who attacked Fattmatu. The same incongruous call, the same dead eyes that look as if they are playing a game. But this time Sarah is not just the onlooker. Only the window separates her from his madness.

She meets the eyes of the rebel, unblinking. She meets his cruel, stupid smile, determined to hold her nerve. Slowly she leans forward and feels with her right hand in the cubby box between the two front seats. Chris freezes, his hands gripping the door and his chest bowed forward over his knees, braced for impact. Without looking down, Sarah raises her gun and points it directly at the rebel. She rests her thumb on the hammer, ready to pull it back. The rebel laughs, his pale pink tongue flicking between the gap in his front teeth. "Look at this white gal," he shouts, gesturing to his back-up to come closer. "She want to kill me," he laughs again, a terrifying high-pitched squeal.

"What are you doing?" Chris chokes out from the passenger seat.

"I'm getting us out of here," Sarah replies, her gun held high, her eyes still on the rebel. With the gun in her left hand, Sarah puts the car into first and starts inching forward.

"This is not the time to take risks," Chris says.

The lead rebel leans his face right up to the glass of her window. "No, no, whitegal," he calls. "I no done ask you to leave." He laughs again, teeth bared and nostrils widely flared.

Sarah pulls the car into second gear, drops the gun on her lap and flings her door open as hard as she can, clouting the rebel in the face. She stamps on the accelerator, the door held open as a cattle prod, ploughing the others out of the way. The Land Rover clatters and lets out a terrible squealing crunch as she forces it on and into the oil-drum barrier, nudging it forward like a steamroller in front of them, sending the rebels scattering to the edges of the road. One jumps sideways over the bridge into the slimy rubbish pit to escape. "Sorry, Princess," Sarah whispers to the car. "We'll fix that later. Just get us out of here." Once they gain momentum, she grabs her gun again and drives on, door open, one hand on the steering wheel, the other pointing the gun out the window.

Only once she reaches third gear and a steady speed away from the roadblock does she risk a glimpse in the rear-view mirror. The rebels wave their guns, threatening to shoot but clearly wary of wasting precious ammunition. She can't see the one she smacked with the door—hopefully, he's still reeling from the impact. She presses on, driving like a maniac, weaving around children and potholes and sending stray dogs barking into the patches of weeds at the edge of the tarmac road. Next time she looks back, the group has turned their attention to harassing the next group of women and young children who want to cross the bridge.

"How does this continue to happen?" Sarah screams into the steering wheel. "A country ruled by these maniacs, broken down by the blood-thirsty mob. How has the world let this go on for ten years? This must stop."

Chris sits mutely at her side. His mouth drops open, but he makes no sound.

"It must stop," she says again, her voice faltering as the adrenaline ebbs away, leaving space for the magnitude of what has just happened to creep into her muscles and blood. Her limbs are cold and weak and by the time she pulls into the High Commission compound she is shaking and sweating from her eyelids to her toes.

*

The guards meet them with alarmed stares and hurries to pull shut the heavy black gate behind them, sliding the bolts firmly into place. "What are you doing out?" The head guard shakes his head. "A curfew has been in place for all staff since the morning.

There have been reports of rebel advances in the city. It's not safe out there."

"Thanks, Solomon," Chris says. "Don't worry, we're not going out again. Sarah, you'd better stay here for now."

Sarah is only too happy to agree. The security around the High Commission has always seemed over-the-top—a high perimeter wall topped with rolls of barbed wire, a constantly buzzing generator to power a battery of security lights, guards on the gate and in front of every building on the compound. Sarah thought it gave the wrong impression, a diplomatic mission that is securely sealed off from its host country. Now she is happy to be on the inside.

The High Commissioner appears from his residence. His face looks grey and drawn, his black eyebrows even more prominent against his ashen skin.

"Chris, I'm glad to see you back. They told me you were still out. You weren't anywhere near the beach road, I hope?" His tone is professionally concerned, but not warm.

"We were at the helicopter pad."

"Good Lord, we've had reports of shooting and burning around the creek. How on earth did you get through?"

"Sarah's nerves of steel," Chris admits with a begrudging smile.

The High Commissioner looks at Sarah, taking in her pale and sweating face, her weak arms still gripping tightly to the steering wheel of her ancient Land Rover. "Thank you, Sarah, for bringing him home safely." He gives her a nod of quiet, inexpressible emotion, the smallest quiver to the top lip and gentle narrowing of the eyes. Sarah realises she has not seen him since he broke the news to her of the helicopter disaster. She nods to acknowledge his silent condolences. "You will stay, I hope?" he says. "Come in to the Residence, I'll get them to bring tea. Or would you prefer something stronger?"

The High Commissioner presents Sarah with a tartan flannel dressing gown. "I'm afraid I don't have much else to offer you," he says. "I know I always feel rather chilled after a shake up. I thought this might help. And perhaps these might be more comfortable?" He offers her a thin pair of hotel bathroom slippers to replace her mud-caked shoes.

"Thank you." Sarah slips into the oversized dressing gown, laughing at her reflection in the mirrored hallway but grateful for his care. He leads her to the sitting room where a harassed-looking woman in a crumpled business suit, hair held back in a pink plastic clip, watches Sarah from one of the apricot-coloured sofas.

"Sarah, this is Beverley Moreton, Africa Director from the Foreign Office," the High Commissioner says.

"Hello Beverley," Sarah offers a hand, which Beverley shakes without getting up. Her pale blue eyes look watery and tired, and she has deep purple creases etched into her cheeks.

"Beverley's come out to assess the situation on the ground."

Sarah instinctively looks down at her mud splattered ankles.

Chris flops down onto the sofa next to Beverley. He looks a mess. His usually perfectly styled hair is sticking up in all directions, his tailored shirt clings to his chest, and his bare feet are still topped with a caking of putrid mud. Nonetheless, Beverley takes more notice of his entrance than she did of Sarah's and adjusts herself to make more space for him on the sofa.

"And what's your verdict so far?" he asks her. "Are we all getting out of here?"

"We have yet to reach our final decision," Beverley says, her voice clipped with the impersonal note of authority.

"But if the rebels are back in Freetown," Chris says, "surely it's madness to keep the full staff here. Will it be another evacuation to Guinea? I'm sure Benjamin can keep the show running with skeleton staff, even if he has to do it from a hotel room in Conakry."

"As I said, we will consider all the options." Her speech sounds practised, her pitch artificially modified to give her greater authority.

"Where have you been, for your assessment?" Sarah asks, "Are you focusing on the situation in Freetown, or will you travel up-country as well?"

"Well," Beverley, looking annoyed, reaches for her tea. Sarah notices the pale pearly pink lipstick mark on the rim of the white cup. "The cook here seems to have poisoned my deputy; he's not left his room since the day we arrived. And I'd rather not take the risk of malaria up-country."

"I'd recommend a quick drive down to Aberdeen if you want to see what things are like here," Sarah says. "Or the High Commissioner has a beach hut along the peninsula road; I'm sure he'd take you."

Beverley allows her eyes to settle on Sarah, making her silent assessment, but does not answer. "What did you say your name was?" she asks.

"Sarah Black."

"And you're part of the High Commission?"

"No," Sarah says. "I used to work for DFID, but we parted ways."

"Well, Sarah, thank you for your advice. I understand you and Chris had a bit of a hairy drive back from the helipad. But we have to weigh up the potential risks to expatriate staff of remaining in post against the risk of taking action too early. People look to us here as leaders. If we evacuate, it will look like we are turning our backs on the people of Sierra Leone. We may even exacerbate the security situation with our leaving. People feel reassured by our presence. They see our white Land Rovers driving around and feel safe because we are here."

"But that's not really enough, is it?" Sarah asks, emboldened by a swig of her stew-brewed tea.

"I'm sorry?"

"Giving people a false sense of security isn't really 'help', is it?" Sarah continues. "If we are the leaders you suggest, then why not do more? Why aren't we talking about military engagement rather than just evacuation?"

"But we are. UNAMSIL is now the largest UN peacekeeping force in existence."

"But are they really making any difference?" Sarah asks. "They look completely out of their depth to me."

"We will continue to give logistical and technical support for them to continue in their mandate," Beverley says, looking to the High Commissioner to shut her down.

"Beverley," his tone is conciliatory but firm. "You know as well as I do, UNAMSIL are on their knees. Another group of peacekeepers were captured last week, effectively donating a free cache of weapons and armoured vehicles to the rebels. I think Sarah is suggesting a bilateral UK military intervention."

"We already have two brigades in the Balkans, on top of commitments to Cyprus, the Falklands, and elsewhere. We are spread too thin as it is. Even if we had the troops to spare, there is absolutely no guarantee that they would succeed where the UN have failed." Beverley's pitch creeps higher as her annoyance grows.

Listening to a lecture on the situation on the ground from someone who has only just arrived, who has seen nothing, and who has consistently ignored the High Commissioner's advice, makes Sarah's blood boil. What is the point of coming all this way if you aren't interested in looking at anything, don't take the opportunity to talk to anyone, and are too scared to leave the residence? Why are the crucial decisions left in the hands of people like this who would rather hide behind due process and procedure than ever take decisive action? Sarah had been planning to give Elias's notebook about the rebel positions to Beverley, hoping she would pass it on to the appropriate person. But it is clear now that Beverley would do nothing with it. Sarah hopes her father would have a better idea of how to ensure Elias's painstakingly gathered intelligence makes it into the right hands.

Beverley clatters her cup to the table. Sarah has no idea how the High Commissioner can bear to host his guest with such calm. She would have turfed her out onto the street by now in the interests of fact-finding. But Benjamin's face shows only a trace of strain at the uncomfortable conversation as he pours himself another cup of tea.

"There may have been an escalation of petty violence, but there is nothing to suggest that the rebels are poised to take the city," Beverley continues.

"But how can you say that?" Sarah asks, open-mouthed. "Based on what? You haven't even left the compound?"

"With all due respect, Sarah, being roughed up at a roadblock does not make you a foreign policy expert."

Sarah bites down so hard on her tongue she can taste blood. Who does this woman think she is?

"If you'll excuse me," Beverley says addressing the High Commissioner, "I think I'd better check on my deputy, see if he needs anything."

"Of course," the High Commissioner says, standing to see her out. Once she left the room, he slumps back into his chair.

"You see what I'm up against?" he says to Sarah. "I don't believe she can have read a single page of the briefings I've prepared for her, but she is still firmly convinced she knows more about what's going on here than I do."

"I'd send her in a poda-poda up to Koidu and see how she changes her tune," Chris suggests.

"Your lot has hardly helped." The High Commissioner shoots him a look that borders on unfriendly. "I've heard from the desk officers in London that Beverley is getting most of her information from some chap in the Security Coordination team—that's a front for your lot, isn't it? What the hell are you feeding them that gives them such a different idea from what I see?"

Chris holds up his hands. "I assure you it's not coming from me. I'd like nothing more than to see what a properly organised army could do."

"If I ever find out who it is, I will give them more than a piece of my mind," the High Commissioner says, propping his feet up on a peach coloured pouffe.

"Surely there's more we can do? There must be someone in London who will listen," Sarah says.

"I've been putting the case for military intervention to Whitehall since I arrived. But my Foreign Office masters are notoriously risk averse, and the Ministry of Defence has no appetite for another foreign venture. I don't know who their sources are and why they won't listen to their man in country, but with respect, Sarah, what makes you think they will listen to you?"

Sarah is pretty sure she can guess who is briefing Beverley and it must stop. But what else can she do? She feels out of options. All potential lines of attack shut down, her most valuable pieces out of play. It is infuriating to feel so powerless, to have so little influence over decision makers who sit comfortably many thousand of miles away.

"Where is Foday Sankoh in all of this? Can't someone just hunt him down? Chop off his head?" Sarah asks.

"If only it was that easy," the High Commissioner says. "Mr Sankoh is living comfortably in his house in Freetown. He is refusing to meet the President or any UN or foreign officials. He demands cash to arrange the meetings and then doesn't show up. But I hardly think beheading the Vice-President is the answer to ending the violence."

"What right does he have to call himself the Vice-President?" Sarah asks. "He's done nothing to keep up his side of the bargain that bought him that position. The RUF haven't disarmed, they've just enriched themselves more readily from the diamonds."

The noise of raised voices followed by a loud shout comes from the corridor and one of local housekeepers comes running into the hallway from the bedroom wing, her face tight with undisguised fury.

"Oh dear," the High Commissioner says. "I'd better see that Sally is okay. That's the second run-in she's had with Beverley since this morning. Do excuse me."

Sarah and Chris are left alone. "I don't know about you, but I'm well ready for something stronger now. Do you want to stay here and raid the High Commissioner's whiskey cabinet to set you up for round two with Beverley, or would you rather come back to mine? As you know, I mix a wicked gin and tonic."

"I'm going back to my hotel."

"Sarah, that's madness. You have no idea what's going on out there."

"I'd rather know, than spend my time cowering in the residence. Beverley's already got that angle covered."

"Do you want to come with me tomorrow to talk to the Russians? I'm fairly certain we can squirrel out their middleman if we turn on the charm."

Sarah wonders if she should try again to explain her suspicions to Chris, but doubts he would take her seriously. Why not send him off on his wild goose chase to keep him off her back? The uranium is unlikely to fall into the wrong hands, especially if it doesn't actually exist. He would clearly love nothing more than to tell Michael he pulled off the job that had been given to Sarah. Why not give him time to let him try to work it out himself? Even out the playing field a bit. "I might leave that to you. You're charming enough without me. I want to go back to London."

"You're running away? I thought Michael gave you a job to do?"

"It's Michael, isn't it?"

"What is?"

"He's the one who's been briefing Beverley against the High Commissioner."

"I can't see why he would be doing that."

"In some misguided effort to maintain the status quo so as not to move the goalposts on the uranium deal."

"I hardly think he'd go that far."

"I need to talk to him. This has to stop."

"Can't you just pick up the phone?"

"Have you ever had a useful conversation with Michael over

the phone?"

"Well… there is that."

"And besides, I'd like to see my father."

Chris snorts. "I knew you'd never hack it staying out here solo, but I didn't think you'd be running home to Daddy."

"Watch it, Chris, or I'll deliver you back to the beach road."

CHAPTER 38

"Helloooooo?" Dilara's voice sounds like golden winter sunshine, even at the end of a static-filled phone line.

"Dilara, it's Sarah."

"Oh?" She sounds more surprised than put out. "Michael gave you this number?"

"Yes."

"That's good to hear. He must like you again. I knew he'd come round." Is there a note of disappointment in her voice? Sarah wonders whether Dilara perhaps enjoys playing the go-between.

"How are you getting on with your hunt for uranium buyers?" Sarah asks.

"These are maybe things best not discussed on the phone. Can you come and see me in Istanbul?"

"No. No time. If anyone's listening, they're in luck. Michael said this line was safe."

"Nothing is ever safe." She falls silent.

"I need to make contact with a particular Chinese buyer—Chen Xiaochang. Do you know him?"

"No way. I'm not getting back into that."

"What do you mean?"

"I had a not-very-subtle message from some Chinese businessman warning me off pursuing the uranium. It was pretty clear he was trying to shut me down."

"Was it Chen?"

"I don't know. Maybe. He had a picture of my favourite

niece; he even knew which school she went to."

Sarah swallows back a nasty taste in her mouth. "Surely that's a bluff? A nasty one, but they are just trying to scare you." She takes a deep breath. "If it was Chen, I want you to go back to him. You need to clarify that Skarparov's killer is now in charge and that the deal is unchanged. Then you tell them to contact me." Did she really just ask that?

"You are leading this now? What does Michael think?"

"You can ask him that yourself."

"And our little understanding about the civil contracts?"

"Still stands. If you bring me Chen Xiaochang, your company is first in line." Sarah feels a pinch of guilt, giving Dilara what she knows to be an empty promise. Reeling in Chen Xiaochang with some fake uranium is in itself far-fetched. Keeping up the hoax long enough to benefit a civil engineering company is never going to happen. But she needs Dilara's help.

"Make sure they understand they are not to trust or contact anyone else, otherwise the deal will be off." Kuznetsov may well reach the same conclusions, and she needs to reel this in herself.

"I like this new you, Sarah. But I liked the old you, too. Don't let her go too far away. I'll call you when I can. *Güle güle.*"

CHAPTER 39

Sarah reaches Lungi Airport in time for the last commercial flight to leave Freetown. News of the rebels' advance has spread, and most people are clearly not waiting around to follow the lead of the British High Commission. The flight is packed, and the sunburnt crew subdued and sober.

London feels like a foreign country. Everything brushed and sterile, seen to and finished. Blades of grass cut to equal length, roads uniformly covered with tarmac, safety barriers stand firm and rust free, traffic stops at traffic lights and follows predictable courses around roundabouts. The smallest features in the organisation of life that Sarah has always taken for granted are suddenly glaringly visible. She is both astonished at such careful precision in the every day, and a little sad that all of life's rough edges can be filed away.

She takes the train straight into Victoria and walks up past Buckingham Palace towards Whitehall, leaving her now somewhat dubious-smelling duffel bag in a left luggage locker at the station. The price of the locker is probably more than the value of any individual item in her bag, but she needs to dump it somewhere. She craves the anonymity she can only really feel in London—being able to walk down a crowded street, drawing no particular notice, a refreshing contrast after months of being a pale-skinned blonde in West Africa. And she can't blend in lugging a mouldy kit bag.

Walking through St James's Park to meet Michael reminds her of one of their first meetings when he briefed her on her mission in the Caucasus and sent her on the next flight to Tbilisi. The parallels are clear—the manicured paths, the slow-moving groups of tourists posing for photos with pelicans, the quiet grey of the sky overhead. But now all is different. Then, she was painfully naïve, allowing herself to be sucked in by Michael's exciting tales of intrigue and espionage. Walking through the park arm in arm, in awe of her new mentor despite the weight of her apprehensions, she was happy to be led by his tune. He held all the pieces and understood the rules. She simply moved as instructed. But now she is a player in her own right. She is coming on her own terms with information that she is sure he can not know. The board feels more evenly balanced. Neither side has a material advantage.

She stops to pick up a piece of litter from the ground, doubling back on herself to put it in a nearby bin and take in a full view of the pavement behind her. No one stops. She takes a path that leads into the gardens at enough of an angle to force an unexpected move if anyone was following her, but again no one reacts. She crosses the bridge over the lake, stopping for a moment to admire Michael's favourite view across the water to the rooftops of Whitehall with one final look for a trail, before walking up The Mall towards Trafalgar Square.

Michael is waiting on the steps to the National Portrait Gallery. Even a few minutes after their agreed meeting time, he gives the impression of having just arrived: a master of the ability to blend in, to look in place even when he isn't.

Michael nods a greeting. "Upstairs? I feel like the Victorians."

Sarah follows him up to the first floor and through the Statesman's gallery, strolling leisurely past grand portraits and white marble busts of Dukes and Earls.

"I'm assuming you have some news for me on that uranium," Michael says, his tones hushed to suit the lofty surroundings.

"I do," Sarah says, enjoying having the advantage and unable to resist drawing it out a little longer. The sound of Michael's heels resounds through the grand corridor.

"Who is it then? Skarparov seemed to think it was one of the smaller Lebanese outfits—did you work out which?"

"No." Sarah smiles.

"Then what are you doing here?" he asks with undisguised irritation.

"If I tell you, I want you to promise me something in return. You know how this works."

Michael gives a derisive laugh. "No, that is not how this works. You work for me, Sarah. You tell me what I need to know. What did you find?"

Sarah pauses to look at the portrait of Ad—lina Patti - the opera singer in white and pink lace was a breath of fresh air amongst the dour men in black frock coats. "There is no uranium, at least no more there than the low-level trace quantities you might find anywhere. It's a hoax."

"Nonsense. It can't be. The samples have been verified by the Rössing lab. It's a legitimate find."

"The lab technician at the Rössing mine is in on the hoax."

Michael allows a beat of silence.

Sarah is delighted.

"But Skarparov was on the verge of introducing the buyer. He must have had more proof."

"Or he was in a hurry? Perhaps you put too much pressure on him?" She turns to Michael, trying to channel Adelina's look of urbane wisdom.

"I don't believe this. Why would anyone set up a fake uranium find? Surely they would get found out before too long?"

"Eventually, yes. But not before they had taken their hefty share of the data room fees and any exploration deal. And then they could disappear."

Michael leads them through a doorway off the main gallery and into a room that celebrates Victorian Expansion and Empire. It comes as no surprise that this is his favourite spot.

"I assume you know this chap." Michael stops in front of a large canvas of a man in the dress uniform of the Royal Horse

Guards, lounging on a sofa, a cigarette artfully poised in his left hand. The composition of the painting sets the viewer's eye precisely at the level of the extraordinarily long scarlet stripe down his casually folded right leg.

"I don't," says Sarah. "But he looks like fun."

"Frederick Burnaby—you must have heard of him? Our most popular forefather, as it were. I don't think there's a man in the Service who didn't join this game hoping to end up a little like him. He was your classic swashbuckling spy: fantastically tall, fluent in several languages and an accomplished balloonist."

"How is your ballooning coming on?" Sarah asks, leaning closer into the painting to see how the artist achieved such a convincing shine on the Roman breastplate propped casually against the sofa.

"Rather poorly I'm afraid." Michael gives the hint of a smile, moving on to the next painting. "Who is it then?"

"Is this a test?"

"No. The hoaxers."

"An Italian geologist and a South African, ex-Executive Outcomes, currently working on security at a diamond mine. They've definitely got the lab technician at the Rössing mine on side, not sure who else is on with it. I suspect it's just the three of them."

"And presumably you have proof of this. They've admitted to the hoax."

Sarah pauses. This is the weakest point in her case. "Not proof exactly…"

Michael lets out an exasperated sigh.

"But it all adds up," she continues. "Since Skarparov died, the whole story has gone quiet. They're running scared now that they've realised what a murky world they're in."

"But you didn't put it to them?"

"Not yet, no."

"Why not?"

"Freetown is a small place. The moment they are rumbled,

the story would get out. And then you've lost your bait for Chen Xiaochang."

"If what you're saying is true, there never was any bait."

"You were fooled, weren't you? If it was real enough to spark his interest before, we might be able to keep it real enough to keep stringing him along. I like the look of this chap." Sarah stops in front of a portrait of Sir James Brooke—a portrait painted in the mid-nineteenth century, but something in his pose and demeanour looks distinctly modern. His left hand is folded on his hip, clutching a white handkerchief. He leans into his right arm with an expression that said he has much more interesting things to do than pose by a fake rock, but is too polite to tell the artist to get a move on.

"He would be your type. The Rajah of Sarawak."

"How did a dandyish English gentleman end up a Rajah?"

"He helped the Sultan of Brunei crush a rebellion. It helps to have friends in high places. And appearances can be deceiving." They move on to the next canvas. "If Chen Xiaochang is to stay interested, he'll need proof of the find."

"Which exists," Sarah says. "The samples that have clearly been cooked up at the Rössing mine have a unique Sierra Leonean signature. This was the beauty of their hoax. There is such a thing as Sierra Leonean uranium, it's just that it's been put together in Namibia. The deal will obviously never progress to production stage, but thanks to our Namibian friends, we've surely got enough to keep Mr Chen's interest?"

"Would these hoaxers play along?"

"They are way out of their depth and probably have no idea what a Pandora's box they've opened with their get-rich-quick scheme. But from what I can see, they are fundamentally good guys. I'm pretty sure they can be persuaded to help in the interests of international security. Especially if the alternative is for their plan to get publicly rumbled and they all lose their jobs."

"And you're sure no one else already knows about this? What does Chris think?"

"Chris is convinced the Russians are about to buy it."

Michael raises an eyebrow perfectly in line with his ruler-straight parting. "You didn't tell him your theory?"

"I tried. He didn't listen."

"Not entirely out of character. You need to follow this up, and quickly, before someone else comes to the same conclusion or this bunch of clowns give themselves away."

"First, you have to promise me something."

"I don't make that sort of promise."

"You've been briefing the Foreign Office and the Ministry of Defence against military intervention in Sierra Leone, haven't you?"

"Not exactly…"

"You've been lobbying Beverley Moreton against the High Commissioner's advice, to delay any decision on increasing British military presence."

"I've only been trying to ensure she takes into account all relevant angles. She will make her own decision in the end."

"Have you any idea what it's like out there? The fake peace of the Lomé Accord has fallen apart. The rebels are back in Freetown. It's entirely possible there will be a repeat of the carnage that erupted last time they were there. 'Operation no living thing' mean anything to you?"

"I've simply been playing for time, Sarah. Of course, you are right that we need to explore the opportunities to help when the time is right. But this war has been rumbling on for ten years, and for the four million or so people of Sierra Leone that is indeed a tragedy. But right now, reeling in Chen Xiaochang and preventing nuclear material ending up in the hands of a rogue state is a greater priority."

"It has to stop. If something can be done, it needs to be done now. We can still work on keeping Chen Xiaochang's interest, but the thin possibility of reeling in an international criminal with a fake find of uranium is not worth further risk to the lives of millions."

Michael stops and looks at Sarah with a small shake of the head. "God, I knew I should never work with an idealist," he mutters. "So what exactly are you proposing to do? How are you, with your wealth of experience, planning on stopping this war? Sadly, it's not quite as easy as in the good old days." He nods towards an enormous painting showing a haughty Queen Victoria presenting a bible to a black man in Sultan's robes, who bows before her on bended knee. The work was entitled 'The Secret of England's Greatness'.

"It's not our job to stop this war," she continues, keeping her voice measured and controlled. "But I want you to promise that you will stop your influence over the Foreign Office, immediately."

"They're perfectly capable of dragging their feet without me, you know."

"If I'm going to stay with you on this, if we're going to keep up the ruse for Chen Xiaochang, I have to know that you and I are on the same side."

"How are you planning to get back to Freetown? All commercial flights have stopped. Most people are trying to get out."

"I thought you might be able to wangle something. Can't you pull a string to get me on a UN flight?" It has not passed Sarah's notice how deftly Michael changed the subject.

Michael rubs the crease between his brows. "I'll see what I can do. It won't be easy, you're not even an official Service employee."

"I'm working for you on your dodgy arrangements. I'm sure you can work it out."

"Okay," Michael quickens his pace back through the central gallery towards the stairs. "Stand ready to go at any moment. I'll call you when it's sorted."

"Can you get me one of their blue passports while you're at it?"

"Don't push your luck."

CHAPTER 40

Sarah's father had offered to meet her at the airport to take her home first. But it feels easier to see him here, within his world of work. At home, ever since her mother's death, part of him has shrunk. His once powerful personality slips often into absent-mindedness. He embraces his eccentricities with too hearty a welcome, almost as a way of opting out of the responsibility of life. Although not yet sixty, Sarah worries he is cultivating the 'doddery old man' persona a little too readily. But the Cabinet Office have asked him back, even after they forced him into early retirement when he failed to come to 'professionally appropriate' terms with his grief. At work he is sure to retain more of his previous self; and that is who she needs now.

Her black linen dress still looks vaguely presentable after weeks in the tropics. Her unwashed hair is scraped back into a ballerina bun. There isn't much she can do about the fatigue written into her face, but she is sure the Travellers' Club has seen worse. Her sparring match with Michael left her energised and hungry. Hopefully, the club food isn't really as bad as its reputation suggests.

Her father pulls her in to a long hug, pressing her nose against the soft cotton of his shirt. Everything about him smells of home. He wraps his arms around her shoulders, tapping her gently as if to check she is real, before letting her duck out of his embrace. "Gosh, I'm glad you're here," he says, taking her arm and leading her up the grand central staircase. "I've got us a table in the Coffee Room."

"Do they do food? I'm starving."

"Yes, of course. Meals only. Coffee is served in the bar downstairs."

"Of course," Sarah nods. "It's a club that doesn't accept women. Why would any of their other rules make sense?"

"Nothing wrong with a bit of tradition for tradition's sake. I like that most men here choose their solitude rather than having it thrust upon them. Besides, I like being surrounded by those driven to find out what happens off the edge of the map." He nods at the portraits of intrepid explorers that adorn the walls. "And the armchairs will have soaked up so many tales of derring-do and adventure, I can sit here and read my paper and feel that some of it must surely rub off by association."

They take a seat at a table set for three, next to the long windows that frame the steely grey facades of Pall Mall. The spring sunshine reflects off three huge crystal chandeliers in the centre of the room, casting dancing flecks of light across the white tablecloth.

"Robert should be joining us a little later."

"Robert?"

"Brigadier Robert Knight, Chief of Joint Force Operations. He's the chap they've put in charge of assessing the situation in Freetown. An excellent pick—been there already several times, knows the score, and happens to be an old friend of mine. You wanted to know who to give your notebook to? He's your man."

"How do you know him?"

"Well," Sarah's father taps the side of his thumb against the tabletop but does not meet her eye. "I realise I've never really told you about Berlin."

"When were you in Berlin?"

"During the '80s, leading up to the fall of the wall, I had the oversight for a lot of HMG's operations in Berlin. At the time, West Berlin was still carved up between the allies and was the espionage capital of the world. We were all living in fear of the bomb and Berlin was the hottest seat in the Cold War. I was never based there, but spent quite a bit of time passing through, got to know most of our chaps there pretty well."

"How did I never know any of this?" Sarah realises she never thought to question what her father did for most of his career, but it still shocks her that he was present at such a seminal point in history and never mentioned it.

"You were only a child; you wouldn't have understood any of it. And besides, it wasn't the sort of work you took home."

"Did Mum know?"

"Enough. She knew that's where I was going. I even sneaked her out a furry Russian winter hat, complete with the Soviet sickle insignia. But obviously she didn't know the details."

Sarah pictures her mother. Always discreet, always calm. Sarah remembers her always fully wrapped up in one project or another: an artwork on the go, a volunteer position at the school that had got out of hand. But she was always available for her children and wanted to hear the smallest details of their lives. She used to pretend to spin the worries out of Sarah's mind like weft from a loom and wrap it on a shuttle that could be launched into space. It occurs to Sarah that she never asked her mother if she could return the favour. Beneath her smiling, calm exterior, did her mother harbour worries about an absent husband she kept stoically to herself?

"Brigadier Knight," her father continues, "was at that time the Major in charge of the Berlin Brigade. He and I had always got on well—seemed to see eye-to-eye on most things, which is pretty rare for military and civilian oversight. He's highly cerebral for an army type, always had something worthwhile to say. But also always happy to break the rules. When the wall finally fell, it caught our side napping. No one had any idea it was coming. You can imagine the chaos. Most people's primary concern was how to get themselves and their families out of there as quickly as possible, but Robert saw the opportunities in the chaos. I persuaded him to come with me straight to the Stasi offices—we secured a sizeable haul of files and documents before they could be burnt or destroyed. It felt like sheer madness at the time, and we both could have faced severe disciplinary action. But Robert had nerve by the bucketful and somehow always seemed to know what had to be done."

It is odd to picture her father as a young man running high-exposure missions into East Germany, putting himself at significant personal risk for the good of Queen and country, then returning to his quiet life in the Home Counties. Sarah was only a child, but would she have noticed anything unusual in him at the time? Did he come back pepped up with the same unstoppable excitement that she feels when she recognises an advantage in the game—the feeling that keeps her running back to Michael despite her better judgement? His face is now lit with an energy she has missed. They are clearly fond memories.

"And you've kept in touch all this time?" she asks.

"We try to meet up at least once a year when we can. Always come here. It's fun to reminisce." Sarah's father stopped a passing waiter. "Excuse me, I think we're ready to order."

"Shouldn't we wait for Robert?"

"No need. We always have the same thing. Most of the food here seems to be designed to give grown men a nostalgic taste of boarding school dinners, but the smoked trout is the best in London. Robert!" Sarah's father stands and waves across the room to a delicately built man with light, rimless glasses on his long aquiline nose. He has a soldier's bearing, despite his civilian clothes, and eyes that slope downwards at the edges, making him look pleasantly sceptical about the world.

"Jeff!" He calls back and walks briskly towards their table, stopping for a moment to cast his eye over the leather-bound books on the shelves around the fireplace, before greeting Sarah's father with a broad smile.

"This is my daughter, Sarah," Jeff says.

Robert squeezes Sarah's hand in a firm grip before sitting down.

"So, Dad tells me you'll be in charge of any military

engagement in Sierra Leone?"

He studies her while unfolding his napkin and swiftly swallowing half a glass of water. "That's right, although it's not clear yet what that might look like. Whitehall has been spectacularly slow on this one, even by their usual snail-like standards." He speaks at a rapid pace, his words carefully enunciated and precise. "Apologies Jeff." He adds, nodding to Sarah's father, seeming to remember belatedly that he is a member of the Whitehall gastropods.

"No need," he replies. "I quite agree. It's been just as excruciating to watch from the inside. The MOD and the FCO have been at loggerheads, and the MI6 boys seem intent on driving in the wedge between them."

"With any luck that might change now," Sarah says, half to herself.

Her father shoots her a quizzical look but lets it pass.

"And will you be given a mandate for bringing in a larger British military operation if needed?" Sarah asks. "I can't help but thinking that all it would take is one organised and disciplined group to take control of Freetown and the rebels would run."

"I'm afraid it might not be that straightforward," Robert says. "Our mission so far is only the logistical arrangements of an evacuation of UK staff. It's a long jump from that to a military operation. And, in any case, it won't be my decision to take. Sadly, it's our snail friends in London who'll make the final call."

"But it's got to be taken out of their hands!" Sarah bangs her fist on the table with greater force than she intended.

Robert laughs using only the left side of his face, the right side maintains its quizzical poise. "I quite agree, but that is the way it works. In a proper democracy you can't send out the military without the cover of the executive."

"But how can the powers-that-be in London make decisions, when they're not even listening to their people in country?" Sarah asks.

"And as far as I'm aware," he continues, brushing over her

question, "the prime reason for ruling out military intervention is that a request has not been received. Unilateral action, unbidden, with little international support is going to turn the stomach of most ministers."

Sarah is quiet. She looks from her father to the Brigadier. Is this it? Is this how it goes? You spend your younger years doing what you believe in so that you can sit in comfort beneath the elevated ceilings of a London dining room and wring your hands? "I suppose it happens to everyone," she mumbles.

"I'm sorry?" Robert asks, looking to her father to see if he is following.

"But it is disappointing nonetheless," Sarah continues, staring out the window at the imposing facades of the buildings opposite. "I suppose it's logical that even the rule-breakers end up toeing the line once they rise up the ranks. It couldn't really work any other way." She turns to face Robert straight on. "But my father knew a man once who took delight in knowing when to bend the rules. I rather thought he would be joining us at lunch."

"Sarah!" her father hisses, his cheeks growing red. "Robert, I apologise for Sarah's rudeness, she's come straight off a long flight."

"No." Brigadier Knight raises a hand towards Jeff but holds Sarah's eye. "No, don't apologise—she is right. I was busy spouting the sort of waffle that would have got right up my nose at her age and she called me out on it. You are right, Sarah. Sometimes decisions need to be taken out of the hands of the desk-bound career-focused mice. This may well be one of them."

"The problem with these so-called decision makers," her father says conspiratorially, "is that they are all, by nature, extraordinarily risk averse. With one eye firmly on their chances of advancement, a non-decision is always a more attractive option than one that might go wrong. The trick, I find, in playing for the outcome you want, is to make it easy. Give them the deniable option and they'll pounce on it."

Sarah is delighted to see that her father is just as keen as the Brigadier to show himself on the side of the good.

"But it's not that straightforward to launch a military action, you know." Brigadier Knight wavers. "Even if we could present it as a deniable option, we'd need preparation, kit, troops. And we know so little about the rebels' movements and capacity, we'd essentially be going in blind."

"Can I give you this?" Sarah slips Elias's battered notebook out of her bag and hands it to Robert. "It contains details of most of the rebels' camps around Koidu—their locations, leaders, quality of training, armaments and so on. If you do get the chance to send teams in, this is where I would start."

"Where on earth did you get this?" Robert asks, thumbing through the carefully notated pages.

"A concerned friend," Sarah replies.

"Is he a military man?" Robert asks, admiring a detailed hand-drawn map.

"I… er yes, perhaps." It takes Robert's question to make Sarah realise she never asked.

"This is extraordinary. How on earth did he get access to this level of detail? I bet even Foday Sankoh himself doesn't have such an accurate position of strengths and weaknesses of the disparate bands of thugs he is supposed to lead."

"He was good at making himself useful."

Robert looks up at Sarah, clocking her use of the past tense, and his look of concerned sympathy sets her off. She can feel her cheeks stain with dark red blotches and her eyes swim with tears.

"He paid dearly for this access." She just about manages to keep the wobble out of her voice but has to look away and stare steadily out of the window at the grey clouds to hold back the tears.

"I'm terribly sorry, Sarah. But you do realise what a game changer this is? With this intel, a targeted intervention might just be possible."

"So what's the trick in making a military intervention seem

like an easy non-decision?" Sarah asks her father. "Could you start by pushing for the evacuation mandate to be as broad as possible? If it covered all territory controlled by UNAMSIL and ECOMOG, that could be interpreted to cover the entire country—no one needs to know that they're actually helpless outside of Freetown."

"There's always the Friday Night Memo," her father says.

"The what?" Sarah asks.

"You send the memo informing the Prime Minister of action 'unless otherwise instructed' at nine o'clock on a Friday evening before a long weekend. Then you can take advantage of a freer mandate until Tuesday morning, giving the PM full deniability if necessary."

"And isn't his baby due any day now?" Sarah asks. "If you could slip it in near the birth, you'd be guaranteed a few days leeway."

"Good thinking. But it would require having the right people in place to play the full advantage." Her father slips his glasses down the reddish skin on his nose and looks at Robert over the top of the tortoiseshell frame. Robert gives a nod of comprehension.

"And are you heading back to Freetown, or will you be based in London now?" Robert asks.

"I'm going back as soon as possible. I've got some unfinished business to take care of." Sarah cannot risk any further delay. It is astonishing enough that Kobus and Pietro have kept the ruse going this long.

"Are you mad?" Her father cuts in. "Robert is being sent out to plan the logistics of an evacuation, and you're considering going back?"

"Not considering, just waiting for a flight to be sorted," Sarah says.

"Do you have daughters, Robert?" her father asks with an exaggerated sigh. "I do hope for your sake you don't, they are only ever causing grief."

"Do you need a lift?" Robert asks. "I've got a team going out the day after tomorrow. If you can get yourself to the Air Mounting Centre in South Cerney, I'm sure we can find a seat for you."

"That would be perfect." Sarah delights at the idea of flying in with the British Military—and telling Michael she no longer needs his help.

"Robert!" Jeff gives best 'disapproving father' look. "You can't be serious. You're supposed to be on my side."

"Sorry Jeff, Sarah's got work to do. Don't worry. I'll look out for her and make sure she keeps out the way of any trouble."

"Robert, you're a very capable man but I wouldn't make promises you can't keep."

CHAPTER 41

Arriving at the Air Mounting Service in South Cerney feels like landing on another planet. Everyone wears military uniform; even the check-in staff wear green camouflage fatigues, belts and berets. Sarah is dressed in plain dark clothes, her hair tied back in a neat low bun, hoping to blend in with the military types. But she might as well be wearing a cocktail dress. She stands by the entrance long enough to attract her share of curious stares, and is beginning to wonder exactly how she is going to blag her way onto a plane when Brigadier Knight appears. He marches over to Sarah, greets her with an energetic handshake and leads her directly to the front of the check-in queue, now a row of unguarded stares from curious to hostile.

"Didn't know we were taking tourists now, sir," says a jug-eared soldier waiting near the front of the queue.

"Watch the cheek, Sergeant," Robert replies, shooting a serious look at the speaker but maintaining his lop-sided smile. "Sarah's my guest. I expect you all to look after her."

Sarah checks in, leaves her black duffel bag among the pile of matching camouflage packs, and is ushered through to the waiting room where men sit slumped on sofas staring at a football match playing out above their heads. "I'll have to leave you here, I'm afraid," Robert says, kicking the shins of a nearby soldier who springs up to offer Sarah his seat. "I'm sure the boys will look after you. It might be a while to wait yet, nature of the game I'm afraid. See you over there."

Scanning the waiting room, Sarah realises they are indeed

all boys. There were a few females outside, long hair neatly held back in sensible styles, wide belts cinched in over camouflage overalls. But other than Sarah, the waiting room is exclusively male. Although completely surreal, she has to admit she is rather enjoying it. Admiring a man in uniform feels a ridiculous cliché, but clichés are born in truth. Being in a room filled with young, uniformed men in the peak of physical fitness gives Sarah a heightened awareness of her own warm bloodedness and makes her sit a little taller.

"I'm Mouse," the soldier who made space for her offers a hand. He is unusually small, not much taller than Sarah herself and looks like a child among some of his more strapping colleagues. Side on, his jaw almost tucks into his collar, but what he lacks in chin he more than makes up for in nose.

"Mouse?" Sarah asks.

"Yup. For these." He waggles his oversized ears without touching them.

"That's some trick."

"What did you do to deserve the VIP treatment?"

"Asked if I could hitch a lift," Sarah grins.

"Friend in high places, is it? It always comes down to who you know. My old man's a pig farmer in Dorset. Still haven't worked out how to use that to jump the queue." He smiles at Sarah, giving his ears another waggle.

"Is Mouse giving you his sob story already?" a large, blonde squaddie plants himself in front of Sarah. He looks pure Viking—biceps straining at the sleeves of his uniform, high angular cheekbones, wide jaw and pale blue eyes almost hidden in his cheeks. But his voice is soft and Lancastrian. "Pulling himself up by his bootstraps is his favourite line, but don't believe a word of it. I'm Malc, but most of the boys call me Magnet." Sarah assumes it was for his comic-book good looks. "Have a bit of a rep for attracting bullets," he grins sheepishly, and pulls up his t-shirt to reveal a set of unusual scars up the side of his toned torso.

"That's quite a collection." Sarah tries not to blush.

"I think that's why the others like having me along, say I'm their lucky charm."

"There's plenty of you to aim at," Mouse says. "Come on, I think they're loading the bus. Follow me," he says to Sarah. "I'll make sure you don't get lost."

*

After the short drive to Brize Norton, the coach drops them right at the steps of the aircraft—a C130 Hercules, a fat sausage of an aircraft with four propellers and a loading ramp at the back for vehicles and crates of kit. Sarah watches a pair of desert-coloured roofless Land Rovers being loaded on, kit bags and boxes strapped to the bonnet to maximise use of space. She marches with the others onto the plane, swinging her arm in time, and sits down next to Mouse, with Magnet the Viking on her other side.

"How did you get involved in Operation Blind, then?" Magnet asks as he loosens the seat belt to fit over his tree-trunk thighs.

"I just needed to get back to Sierra Leone."

"What the hell are you doing going back in? I thought the point of this was to get any sane people out of there?"

"Got some unfinished business." Sarah speaks in a nonchalant tone, as if flying into active warzones was an everyday occurrence for her, but part of her is questioning whether she is doing the right thing. She already had a lucky escape last time she was in Freetown. If the security situation has deteriorated sufficiently since then to send in these boys, what is she doing going back?

It is one thing brushing off her father's worries. It is his job to be over-protective of his only daughter. But the look on Magnet's face makes a trip into an active conflict zone feel less brave than foolhardy. Chris is still there. He could get the proof Michael needs from Pietro and Kobus and set up the next step of the deal with Chen Xiaochang. The thought of Chris's insufferable gloating if he was the one to bring back the prize to Michael is enough to reassure Sarah she is in the right place. Anyway, it is too late now to change her mind.

"Is Operation Blind the mission name?" she asks.

"That's what we're calling it. No one seems to have any idea what's going on. We only got our call up yesterday. Word is even the top don't know what's going on. It's a classic SNAFU."

"SNAFU?" Sarah asks.

"Yeah: Situation Normal, All Fucked Up," Magnet snorts. "So what's it like out there? Are we all going to get malaria? Don't even have any tablets."

"You probably will. Most people do. Feel like death for a bit, but you should be fine." Sarah adopts her best battle-weary tone.

"How d'you get sat next to the eye candy?" a man with a neck as wide as a bowling bowl asks as he shuffled by.

"I hear he's your lucky charm, as well as easy on the eye," Sarah lays a hand on Magnet's knee, to sniggers from Mouse. The bowling ball shakes his head and moves on down the aisle.

"I fuckin' hate the tropics," Mouse says. "Plays havoc with all my kit. None of my radios take kindly to getting wet. And then we're all stuffed."

"Mouse is a typical comms guy," Magnet says. "They always think it's all about them. As if the war gets won by clear radio signals."

"Don't underestimate us," Mouse says. "You know Foday Sankoh, the leader of the rebels, was a radio comms officer in the army before he started stuffing kids full of drugs and burning down villages? That's where he learnt the power of propaganda. Watch out or I might follow in his wake."

"You're such a swot, Mouse," Magnet says.

"Someone's got to be," Mouse says, unfazed by Magnet's teasing.

"At least you've got your kit. We've had no briefings, got no maps, no aerial photos. Rumour has it we haven't even been issued with proper ammo yet."

"That's probably for the best. You'll be less likely to kill yourselves when the SA80s get stuck," Mouse says.

"Our shit kit is no laughing matter."

"I like the look of your vehicles." Sarah points towards the back where the Land Rovers have been loaded into the massive cargo hold.

"The Pinkies? We'll never get a look in at using one of them," Magnet says. "Those are for the SAS boys only. We'll be walking if we're lucky."

"I've got a Land Rover you can use," Sarah says. "It's only a short wheel-base and can be temperamental."

"Can't they all," Mouse laughs.

"You're welcome to borrow it if it would help."

"Don't make promises you can't keep," Mouse says. "An extra vehicle and a sat phone could be enough to make sure we get back on this plane alive. But you'll never be able to get it where we're going."

The noise of the engines starting up kills the conversation, the sound rising in pitch as the propellers gather speed. Soon they are hurtling down the runway and en route to Dakar in Senegal and then on to Lungi, across the water from Freetown. As soon as the plane lifts off, Mouse and Magnet fall asleep—bolt upright, heads scarcely supported, jaws hanging slack. The ability to sleep, on command, anytime and anywhere, must be an essential skill for the job.

Sarah is soon surrounded by lolling heads and snores to rival the engine noise. Just as she thinks she is going to pass a long boring flight, a stockily built redhead from the row behind sidles over and strikes up a conversation from the aisle. In groups of two or three, all remaining soldiers from the group who aren't asleep come over and take their turn talking to the fascinating stowaway. Sarah feels half museum exhibit and half team mascot. She hears life stories, looks at family photos, is baffled by jargon, impressed by imaginative swearing, and tries to remember as many of the obscure nicknames as possible. If anyone asks what she is doing there, she tells them she is Foreign Office, and that is normally enough. But each of them tell her in no uncertain terms that a civilian return to Freetown is completely mad.

CHAPTER 42

Sarah flies across the water to Freetown in the Chinooks that are waiting at Lungi. The helicopters recently arrived from the UK, but as the RAF has no aeroplane large enough to fly them out, they have made the 3,000-mile journey on their own, stopping to refuel in almost every country they passed along the way. It gives Sarah confidence in the craft and their crews—if they made it here from the UK, they should be fine to cross the estuary to Freetown.

Chris is waiting at the helicopter pad, his face a mixture of wonder and scorn seeing Sarah pour out of the chopper with the rest of her new army friends. His polished appearance looks vain, his careful grooming more like preening, next to Sarah's travelling companions.

"That's quite a way to arrive. I thought you were supposed to be coming in with the UN?" he says, trying, as always, to identify Sarah's mistakes.

"This was quicker, and more fun."

"To be honest, I'm not sure why you bothered. Michael has filled me in on your theory. It's hardly going to need your unique skillset to get these clowns to do what we want them to."

"And leave you to cock it up? Never. Glad to see you've brought my car. I hope you've been looking after her. Are we going straight out to Pietro's?" Sarah slings her duffel bag in the back of her pale blue Land Rover and elbows Chris out of the way when he tries to return to the driver's seat.

"Are you mad? Or did your new action man friends not fill

you in? The RUF has arrived in Freetown. Most of the entrance roads are blocked and the peninsula road is out of bounds."

"But Pietro…" Sarah knows he has survived there through the last ten years of civil war and his business continued to run. But everyone's luck runs out, eventually.

"Pietro is safely installed in the Mammy Yoko Hotel. Don't worry. He and Kobus got out in time. I even offered them a lift," Chris says with a wink. "We'll meet them there."

The bar of the Mammy Yoko is packed. It looks as if all remaining ex-pats in Freetown and a good number of the Sierra Leoneans have decamped there, as the security situation deteriorated. The security of the hotel is good, the United Nations mission is headquartered upstairs and there is a helipad on the roof in case you needed to get out in a hurry. Sarah looks warily at the security guards on the door. Is it really safety in numbers? She is pretty sure if she were a rebel leader, this would be the first place she'd come. Imagine the morale boost to your side if you could take out all the top brass in one go.

All the diplomats who have not yet evacuated are installed in the lobby. Sarah waves to the High Commissioner, who is deep in conversation with the head of UNAMSIL, their brows tightly knit. The Chinese Ambassador is talking to the head of the European Delegation—both look hot and harassed. Only the Ambassador's elegant translator with her trademark coral lipstick looks unaffected by the hot, close air. She smiles at Sarah with a slight tilt of her head.

Kobus and Pietro are at the bar—their skin aglow with sweat and alcohol. Chris greets them both with a nod and gently suggests they take one of the quieter tables near the window. Kobus seems reluctant, stoically gripping his pint glass. There is probably a good reason why the most exposed tables are empty. Kobus greets Sarah with suspicion. He is no fool and Chris's manner is enough to let on that this is more than just a friendly catch-up over a few beers. Pietro is warmer, but distracted— hopping up and down to greet every newcomer to the bar. And there are many.

Sarah jumps straight in. "We want to talk to you about the uranium find."

Kobus throws a sideways glance at Pietro and touches his fingers to the gold chain around his neck.

"Ah, rumours, rumours," Pietro says jovially. "Everyone talks, but no one knows anything about it. This town is crazy for rumours, especially now we all have cabin fever." He gestures round at the crowded, sweaty bar.

"It was you, wasn't it?" Sarah maintains her composed smile.

Pietro throws a glance at Kobus. "Not this time I'm afraid," he says, clasping his hands. "The diamonds, yes, of course, that was me, the iron ore you all know I found it, but I've hung up my boots now, the uranium—"

"Bok gave the game away," Sarah says, looking from one to the other.

Kobus lowers his fist to the table with enough force to make the glasses rattle. "What did that idiot tell you?"

Sarah sits back. "Less than you just have."

Kobus closes his eyes. Sarah watches his blood pressure rise, his face and ears glowing in a ruddy flush.

"Come on, Kobus," she says. "It was a brilliant scam, but you might as well admit it. You know as well as I do, it's a lost cause."

"It didn't do anyone any harm. And we've dropped it now, anyway. Most of the buyers backed off after Skarparov died and we've let the trail go cold."

"That was wise. But we'd like your help in keeping one potential buyer interested."

"Wait a minute, who are you, anyway? Aren't you supposed to be some leaf scientist? And Chris is an embassy dork. Why do you both care about this?" Kobus asks.

"Chris and I both work for the British Government. We have reason to believe that one of your potential customers is searching the market for uranium on behalf of a buyer who wants it for the development of nuclear weapons."

Pietro looks sobered. "But this has nothing to do with us. You know this, we just cooked a few samples, we made no deals."

"Who did you think would be interested in buying uranium from a group so shady no one knew who they were?" Sarah asks.

Pietro holds up his hands. "But we stop now, it's over," he insists.

"For everyone else, yes. But we're asking you to help us keep the interest of one particular buyer open until we can find out more about him. Have you had any contact with a Chinese businessman called Chen Xiaochang?"

"We've met some Chinese," Kobus says. "Here and in Koidu, but I can't remember any names."

"You should be receiving a call soon from his representative. They will want to arrange data room fees for access to all the current findings."

"And what do we do then?"

"Exactly as you had planned. I assume you had thought this through? How else were you planning to make money out of it?"

"Of course we would help you, Sarah, if we could. But unfortunately it's impossible." Pietro wipes the sweat from his forehead with the relief of a gangster who's just spotted the getaway car.

"Why?"

"The Chinese will want to see new samples and the latest reports from the Rössing mine. But that's impossible. The shipment from Bok is stuck in Lungi. All the helicopters are down for servicing for the next couple of days. And once they start the evacuation there's no way a civilian will be allowed to make the return trip. We can't help you." He gives an exaggerated shrug.

"What if I pick it up from Lungi?" Sarah asks.

"You can't; it's impossible."

"Leave that part to me," Sarah says. "Would Bok's shipment be enough to keep an interested buyer on the hook?"

Kobus and Pietro exchange more nervous glances.

"And what if we want out now?" Kobus asks, blinking frantically.

"You don't really have that choice," Sarah says. "Not if you want us to keep this to ourselves."

"And if they pay? What happens to the money?" Pietro asks.

"If you pull this off and we get what we need from it, you can keep any profit you make. I suppose we can say you've earned it."

Pietro purses his lips and nods.

"How did you find him, anyway?" Kobus asks, his face still flushed with anger.

"I went to visit the lab, hoping to find out where these mystery samples were coming from."

"And did he really give the game away?"

"No, not really. It was just a hunch."

"I'm going to smack that *dopkaas* when I next see him. I knew he was getting too pleased with himself. All that clever isotope shit, it always smelt risky to me."

"His clever chemistry could be exactly what we need to reel in one of the biggest players in the proliferation of nuclear weapons," Chris says. "I wouldn't smack him just yet."

"*Oddio*," Pietro mutters, "what have you got us into?"

"Nothing that wasn't of your own making. We're just giving you the chance to turn your scam over to the greater good. And we'll offer you protection against Skarparov's killers," Sarah says.

"You know who it was?" Pietro asks, his voice hushed.

"We do," Sarah nods solemnly.

*

"Hey look, it's our very own stowaway." A heavy hand lands on Sarah's shoulder and she turns to see Mouse. "Should'a known we'd find you here," he says with a grin. A rowdy group of army boys are piling into the room and jostling with each other for the best spot at the bar.

"I thought you lot were supposed to be here saving the

country, not hanging out in bars," Sarah says. "That's what the High Commission staff are here for," she says with a nod at Chris.

"We are. We're off tomorrow, just got our order in. The rebels are headed for the airport. We're deploying as first line of defence. So tonight a pre-operational amount of booze will be consumed before our last night in a proper bed. Was that little beauty I saw in the car park yours—the blue Series III?"

"Yes, you still want it?" Sarah asks.

"Are you kidding? The boys would give an arm for an extra vehicle. They're dropping thirty of us in a village, thirty clicks from Lungi with one Pinzgauer. Not sure anyone has thought about how we get out in a hurry. An extra vehicle could be a lifesaver if the comms kit goes down. Shame it's stuck over here—the ferries are down."

"Can't you sling it under a Chinook?" Sarah asks.

"A civilian vehicle? Fat chance. It's the jungle trek for us. Wish us luck. Watch out," he nods towards the entrance. "The boss is here."

All the soldiers at the bar suddenly draw to attention. The raucous noise hushes as Brigadier Knight walks into the bar. He waves them down. "Don't mind me, boys, I know this is your last night. Sorry to cramp your style." Robert wears an unusually broad smile.

"Sarah." He kisses her on the cheek with an exuberance that takes her by surprise.

"You look like you've had good news," Sarah says.

"I think I might have just promised President Kabbah we'd end this war for him," he says, almost bouncing on his toes.

"So you've got the request you needed?" Sarah says.

"Looks like I do. And the best bit is that my Rules of Engagement haven't even been issued yet. It's highly unusual to be in a country without it, but it helps to put together a bit of a looser interpretation of what I'm here to do. And I've made a promise now."

"The easily deniable decision…" Sarah says. "And over the long weekend too. What a perfectly convenient coincidence."

"It does look like your father may have had a hand in this, and if so, he's played a blinder," Robert says, brim full with enthusiasm. "I hope you've got done whatever it was you came back to do because you're going to need to stay safe in the High Commission for the next couple of days until we evacuate."

Sarah looks down at the table.

"Come on, your father's held up his side of the deal. I better make sure to hold up mine."

Sarah nods vaguely.

"Do excuse me, I'm meeting the UN Commander here. Time to convince them to fight back."

Kobus and Pietro watch the Brigadier leave, their mouths hanging agape.

"You got some hotshot friends," Pietro says, nodding at Sarah.

Sarah gulps down the last of her beer and stands up. "Where do I find Bok's delivery?" She pulls out a stubby pencil from her bag and dries off a beer mat from the table. "Write down all the details and anything I'll need to get them to release it to me."

Pietro shrugs at Kobus and starts writing in beautiful sloping cursive on the beer mat.

"If I keep up my part of the agreement, you keep up yours. Do we have a deal?"

"I still think you'll never make it. But you can try." Pietro looks like he can't decide if he should be celebrating a lucky escape or drowning his sorrows. Kobus looks like he wishes they'd gone to a different bar.

"I'm going to leave you with Chris for now; he'll be your point of contact until I get back. Be nice to him, he's not as simple as he looks," she says with a grin. "Chris, do you have a satellite phone I can borrow?"

"Mine is in the car."

"Perfect—I'll bring it with me. Need to do my bit for the war effort."

"But where are you going?" Chris asks, standing up to follow her.

"To Lungi, of course," Sarah says.

"By land? But that's complete madness."

"We can't let Chen Xiaochang slip the hook because of a logistics difficulty. We need those samples, and preferably before the security situation gets any worse."

"Then I'm coming with you."

"No. You need to stay and babysit those two. Don't let them out of your sight. And don't let them screw this up."

*

Ibrahim takes some convincing to come with her, but Chris is right: it would be madness to go alone.

"Sarah, the RUF are approaching Lungi. You know there is only one road? To drive there you'd have to pass straight through the rebel-held areas."

"But a foreigner, in an old civilian vehicle? Surely that's not worth their while trying to attack. They'll be after the military targets now, not a white girl in an ancient Land Rover."

"We're not talking about an army. This is a bunch of drug-fuelled killers. They don't care if you're a civilian or not. They've maimed, raped and killed in every village they've taken—women, children, babies. I'm telling you, it's madness."

Mammy Kamara stands over them, her arms firmly folded over her chest. "If they really need you there, they can get you there themselves. I've seen all the helicopters coming and going—UN ones, big army ones."

"They're all down for servicing until the evacuation begins. Besides, it's not me they need," Sarah explains. "It's my car. There is thirty of them there in the direct path of the rebels, and if their comms go down, they're stranded."

"No way," Ibrahim says, shaking his head. "Forget it, Sarah."

"I thought you might back me up."

287

Ibrahim is quiet, his tightly curled eyelashes lowered. "If I say no, you're going anyway, aren't you?"

Sarah doesn't want to lie, but her mind is made up. They need to get to Bok's delivery before Chen loses interest. And if she can combine that with helping the army to face down the rebels, so much the better. It has to be better than sitting holed up in the High Commission compound waiting for something to happen.

Ibrahim breathes a heavy sigh. "I can't believe you're making me do this."

Mammy Kamara explodes in a local language Sarah doesn't understand. Judging by her tone, it is probably for the best.

"So you'll come?" Sarah asks, not daring to look up at Mammy Kamara's face.

"I'll come," he says, still shaking his head.

CHAPTER 43

The road to Lungi is rough going. It is so little used that almost nothing is ever done to maintain it; any effort would be futile against the onslaught of tropical rain on ancient laterite. It is just still early enough in the season to try. The heaviest rains have yet to fall. Later in the year it will become impassable as floods and temporary water channels take over the road surface. For now, there are many deep holes to straddle where the track is deeply riven by water flow, and complete sections where the surface has been entirely washed away; but it is passable, in a Land Rover at least. The engine is well oiled, and Sarah has stashed several extra cans in the boot just in case.

Their progress is painfully slow. It is less than forty kilometres as the crow flies between Freetown and the village on the Lungi side where Mouse told them they were headed. But the road has to cut deep inland to where the wide estuary of the Sierra Leone River becomes narrow enough to cross. It is close to one-hundred-and-fifty kilometres to drive, and Ibrahim guesses it will take them at least six hours, much of which will be spent outside the car filling in the deepest holes or laying down branches across the stickiest mud to avoid being sucked into a boggy blockade.

"Where did you learn to drive like this?" Ibrahim asks after they sail through a hairy stretch, the Land Rover picking its way elegantly over a staircase of rocks.

"My father always had Land Rovers. I learnt to drive in fields when I was a teenager. But in England you don't get much more than mud to contend with. This is a more advanced course," Sarah grins across at Ibrahim. "The car knows what to do."

The Land Rover handles beautifully, as Sarah knew it would. But the heat and the need for constant revs in low gears is taking its toll on the engine. By late morning, with the sun fully up out of the forest cover, it is feeling the heat. The engine light flashes on occasionally after the more difficult bits. Sarah knows she should stop, but what then? She tries to drive as gently as possible over the rare flat sections. "Come on Princess," she coaxes as the red light illuminated once more. "This is not the time to give up."

Ibrahim is following their route on a dog-eared paper map, produced by Shell in the 1980s to show the location of their filling stations. The red-and-yellow Shell branding and most of the filling stations are long gone, but it is still the best map available of the country. The solid red line on the map suggests a more optimistic interpretation of a road than what they find, but at least they knew where they are.

After they turn off the main road towards Port Loko, Ibrahim's mood noticeably tightens. Once over his disbelief at what they are doing, he started the day almost enjoying himself—pointing out wildlife tracks at the side of the road and optimistic that they were making good progress despite the frequent stops. But after the turning north—marked with a solid-looking yellow line on the map but scarcely more than a muddy track on the ground— he grows quiet and restless. Sarah can feel his nerves rise and fray as he squeezes his palms together between his knees.

The main road out of Freetown is risky, but nothing compared to this. The rebels prefer the quieter routes, swarming into the impassable anonymity of the forest for cover: harder to track and almost impossible to follow. Sarah and Ibrahim are now willingly putting themselves in rebel territory.

They stop to drink a bottle of coke each to replace some sugars lost from the endless sweating. Ibrahim takes a cigarette from his top pocket and offers one to Sarah. She doesn't normally smoke, but this feels like a moment to make an exception. The paper burns fast as she sucks the smoke deep into her lungs, her head spinning from the triple hit of nicotine, sugar, and caffeine. Her heartbeat quickens, her blood races through her veins, her fingers and toes tingle with anticipation and a cold emptiness pervades her stomach. She makes to climb back into the driver's seat, but Ibrahim stops her.

"You'll have to let me drive this bit. It's too dangerous."

"Why here?"

"We need to cross the river soon. It's almost certainly under rebel control. We'll be completely at their mercy."

Sarah climbs into the passenger seat in silence, unnerved by the new set to Ibrahim's jaw and his stony stare.

He strips off his t-shirt to reveal a sweat-stained, grimy vest underneath. He peels a grubby sticking plaster from his foot and sticks it to the centre of his forehead. He scoops up a handful of the red laterite dust from the surface of the track and smears it into his eyes, completing the effect with another rapidly smoked cigarette, the smoke blown straight up into his unblinking stare. He threw a bag in the back of the car before they left, notably large given how little time he had to pack. Sarah now understands its size as he pulls out a fifty-centimetre-long machete. He climbs behind the steering wheel, reclining the seat as far as it can go, then sets off. His hand dangles the machete loosely out of the window. "Let me do the talking," he says, his voice tense and mechanical, "and look scared."

"I don't think that should be too difficult."

When the crossing comes into sight, Sarah belatedly realises the full extent of the mad risk they are taking with this journey. She looks at Ibrahim, eyes fiery red, staring intently ahead, his face set in a scowl that she has never seen before but which he wears with unnerving conviction. She had imagined a bridge and thought that at the very worst, they could use the same tactic as last time—driving straight through the blockade, hoping for the best. But in place of a bridge there is a 'ferry'—a floating platform made of rough wooden planks, just long enough to balance a car. The platform is propelled across the river by a couple of young boys hauling on a metal cable. They are literally placing themselves into the hands of the rebels.

Ahead of the crossing a small boy stands in the road, his hair cropped close, his mouth squeezed into a practised pout, bowed forward under the weight of an AK-47. High above the neckline of his black vest, tight around his slender throat, he wears a floral necktie. It is widely cut, and the pastel colours remind Sarah of tie her father wore in his 1970s wedding photos—but there is nothing celebratory in the boy's fixed stare.

He points the gun at Ibrahim. "Usai yu de go?"

"Wi de go na Lungi," Ibrahim speaks without moving his face. He gives his machete a casual flick.

"Udat na di titi?" the boy asks, pointing his gun at Sarah.

"I na wit mi. Wi wan foh pas, orders kohmoht General Papa." At the mention of the nickname for Foday Sankoh, the rebel leader, the boy backs away.

A figure in a shiny cropped wig approaches the car with a wide-hipped swagger. At first, Sarah takes it for another piece of incongruous cross-dressing, designed to shock and unsettle; but as the figure comes close, she realises it is a woman. "Where you going?" the female rebel asks Ibrahim, leaning with interest through the open window to look at Sarah. She wears a faded Jim Morrison t-shirt, loose enough to give her an androgynous form. But her wide cheekbones and painted lips are distinctly female. Her top lip hangs slightly open, as if stuffed with something under the gums.

Sarah is completely stunned that a woman would join this group of senseless killers. What would have brought her to choose this life? Had she been abducted and forced to fight? Or did belonging to the rebels offer protection and safety from harm that you could otherwise never know? Sarah assumes that this woman must be here against her will. But as she looks from the woman's face—defiant, cruel and powerful—to the vacant stares of the men at the ferry, she realises she is wrong. There is no reason why a woman can't have chosen to join the rebels, just as so many men had. Cold-blooded killers come in many guises.

But the woman is humanised to Sarah because of her gender. A shared characteristic creates a connection, a point of comparison that makes her seem more real, more relatable than the men. But really, she is no different. All these fighters have made the transition—whether by force or by choice—into unthinkable brutality. Whipped up by Foday Sankoh and his band of RUF commanders, the impossible to even imagine has become the norm for thousands of men, women and children. Everyday people have become killers and are terrorising the population into joining them.

Ibrahim repeats what he told the boy—Sarah belongs to him, he is taking her to Lungi on orders that come directly from the boss, and they better let them pass quickly. The woman shows no signs of letting them through. Ibrahim grows impatient. He jumps out of the car and shouts in language Sarah can no longer follow. His rise in aggression is met in kind by the woman, who now has three men behind her wanting to get in on the fight. Sarah sinks down in her seat, scarcely able to watch. Ibrahim's act is so convincing she wonders how often he has had to pull a similar ruse to get away. The jut of his jaw, the simmering roil of his shoulders, the jerking spasms of his movements—he is somehow able to outdo the rebels in his show of unpredictable danger. She needs no effort to look terrified.

The woman leaves Ibrahim arguing with the men at the ferry and swaggers over to Sarah. "You want for go with dis man?" she asks, pointing at Ibrahim. "Why you no stay here with me? Ah de teach you how for fight," she grins, showing a row of yellowed teeth.

"Ah wan for go," Sarah mumbles, her voice little more than a rough whisper.

The rebel woman clicks her tongue against the roof of her mouth, keeping Sarah under her fiery gaze. Would she try to claim Ibrahim's prize by delivering Sarah herself? Sarah can read nothing in her swollen eyes. She looks down, as if to show submission to a wild animal. The woman reaches in through the open window and touches Sarah's skin, prodding at her arm before running her fingers up across her throat and along her jaw. She winds a lock of Sarah's hair around her finger, holding it up to examine it in the light. Sarah can feel her breath coming hot and fast, the woman's wrist in front of her mouth, then the hand yanks away with one violent swing and a red-hot finger of pain sears through Sarah's forehead. She claps her hands to her scalp, pushing her fingertips into the open wound to stem the pain. The rebel dangles a thick lock of Sarah's hair from her index finger and leers at her with a wide, syrupy smile. "Dis na for me," she waves the hair under Sarah's nose, then returns to Ibrahim and calls off her men.

Ibrahim looks with horror at the macabre memento and climbs into the car, slamming the door behind him. As his eyes fall to the red open wound on Sarah's forehead, the blood seems to drain from his face, but he says nothing. He rolls the car onto the floating platform and watches as the rebel boys heave on the thin cable to pull the ferry across to the opposite bank.

Once back on the road again, Ibrahim's rebel alter ego is cast off, but he seems changed by the experience. The light in his eyes has lost its vibrancy. His soul seems to sink into the ripped leather of the seat. "Are you okay?" he asks, looking again at Sarah's head.

"I'm fine." Sarah draws herself up, forcing her hands down into her lap and clenching her jaw against the stinging pain in her scalp. "It's just hair, could have been a lot worse."

"That's bad juju," he says, shaking his head.

"You were amazing, I can't believe you pulled that off. I was almost more frightened of you than of them."

Ibrahim does not reply. He barely speaks for the rest of the drive towards Lungi.

CHAPTER 44

"What the fuck are you doing here?" Mouse comes running over as they roll into the village after almost eight hours on the road, hot, sweaty and exhausted. Sarah cannot tell from his voice if he is impressed that she survived the trip or annoyed that he now has a pair of civilians to look after. Probably both.

"I've brought you the vehicle, as promised," Sarah says, giving Princess a tap on the bonnet. "And a satellite phone, courtesy of the High Commission."

"You've got to be fucking kidding me! You really meant it? But how are you going to get out of here?"

"One of you can drive us over to Lungi and come back with the car. We'll make our own way from there."

"Fucking A." He walks around the car, inspecting it from all angles. "She's an absolute beauty. But you know we can't promise to get her back to you in one piece?"

"It's okay," Sarah says. "She was a present from a friend. I'm just passing her on." There is no doubt in Sarah's mind that Elias would have wanted them to have her.

"You're a mad fucking cow coming out here at a time like this, but I'm bloody glad you did it. Just about doubles our chances of getting out of here alive. They've dumped us here with a couple of VHF radios and promise of a helicopter back-up if it gets hairy. But how exactly we're supposed to get the message across if the comms kit packs up, I don't know. You have no idea how valuable one of these is," he says, tapping the hard case of the satellite phone. He looks up at the sky where pink streaks are creeping across the forest line. "We can give you a lift back to Lungi, but there's no way we'll make it there and back tonight."

"It's not that far, is it?" Sarah says. Staying overnight in the jungle had not been part of her plans. She would rather spend the evening locating the customs officer Pietro had told her to contact about Bok's delivery. And preferably not in the line of the rebels' advance.

"It's not far, but you'd need a death wish to try it after dark. Someone can take you in the morning."

"Are you sure we can't make a dash for it?"

"Don't worry. You'll be fine here. We can't offer you much by way of luxury, but so far we've seen no action. Intel says they're coming and there's shedloads of them. But so far it's all eerily quiet. You should get a good night's sleep."

Sarah nods, not wanting to meet Ibrahim's disapproving eye.

Mouse studies the pair of them, stroking his receding chin. "The boys are getting bored with the waiting. Not what we're good at, really. Come and have a look round and I'll get a brew on."

The village is small, a few mud houses with thatched roofs set around a clearing of beaten red earth. The central house in the clearing, presumably the Chief's house, has a concrete porch stuck onto the mud brick construction to show his status. The house next door has been given over to the army—the single room turned into a makeshift kitchen with a hexi stove on the floor, jerrycans of water and some upturned blue plastic crates to serve as chairs. Grass mats are rolled up next to the wall—the 'dormitory' as Mouse calls it, for those lucky enough to bag a spot. The others take their chances with the rain in tents outside.

Ibrahim fetches his bag from the car and quickly changes from his rebel gear into his Sierra Leone army uniform. The same kit Sarah first saw him wearing at the reception at the High Commissioner's residence. The transformation is extraordinary and if it wasn't for the blood-shot eyes Sarah would not believe he could have put on such a terrifyingly convincing display.

Men wearing camouflage fatigues are keeping themselves busy in ways only those long used to waiting could do. Checking kit, rechecking kit, polishing, cleaning, checking the cleaning. Sarah recognises many of them from the flight over and waves in reply to their gob smacked greetings.

"What's the hitchhiker doing here?" a short man with stocky shoulders that swallow up the base of his neck asks Mouse, staring at Sarah with a trace of hostility.

"She's brought us her wheels," Mouse says. "Sarah, have you met M? No one knows what it stands for, but no one calls him anything else. If you take my advice, I wouldn't listen to a word he says. He's an incorrigible prankster and will take any chance he sees to set you up."

"The Landy's yours?" M asks in amazement.

"It's yours now," Sarah replies.

"Nice one." He nods to Sarah and throws a sceptical glance at Ibrahim. "And who's this? Our back-up?"

"Major Ibrahim Kamara," he offers his hand in a dignified greeting, not rising to the sneer in M's tone.

"Ibrahim came with me for the drive," Sarah says.

"But when I'm not escorting crazy English women through the jungle, I'm a Major in the army. Happy to help in any way I can."

"Yeah, nice one." M nods to Ibrahim, rubbing at his crotch. "Mouse, mate, have you got any more of that cream. My Gareth's playing up something chronic."

Mouse tries to steer him out the door, his cheeks colouring with a blush. "I'll get you some later." He raises his eyebrows towards Sarah. "Just looking after the visitors."

"Gareth?" Sarah asks.

"You really don't want to know. And luckily as a girl it's not something you need to worry about. Do you find this climate plays havoc with your skin? If we have to be out here much longer, we'll be more boil than bloke."

"No way! Sarah?" An oversized Viking ducks through the doorway of the hut. "Someone told me you were here. I knew you were nuts when I saw you getting on that plane." Magnet folds Sarah in an oversized hug.

"Good to know you're here," Sarah says with a grin. "Hope you've got your bullet magnet turned up. Should improve the chances for the rest of us if you're here to take the shot." Sarah is enjoying the banter—even if here in the jungle, her blood still pumping with the adrenaline of the drive, the joke feels a bit close to the bone. She understands now why the army are masters of dark humour—to be joking about grave danger gives an air of normality to where they are. It is easier to laugh at the risks than be forced to face them.

"I've volunteered to drive you back to Lungi tomorrow, so I get the first go in the new toy," Magnet says.

"Look after her, she's served me well."

Mouse takes them to admire his 'office'—the wooden shack that serves as a temporary comms room. "This is our nerve centre, the most important part of all our set-up," he says proudly.

"He would say that," Magnet adds under his breath. "If I had to save one thing it would be the ammo store, but Mouse would lay down his life for his beloved radios."

Mouse shows them his rather sorry looking collection of kit, to which he now adds the satellite phone in pride of place. A pair of VHF radios—long range for reporting back to Lungi and short range for communication within the camp. Both apparently suffering from water damage and playing up in the humid air. He shows off his parabolic microphone used for listening in to enemy chatter—it looks like something out of a kid's spy kit. A cone-shaped device with headphones and an attached microphone that you have to fling up over a tree to get the best reception. "You can laugh," Mouse says as he demonstrates his well-practised swing. "But it works. Foday Sankoh's boys use radio for most of their comms, and if the weather gods are on our side, we can listen in."

The sun has dropped beneath the trees. As the colours of the forest fade to grey in the last of the evening's light, the insects are called to action, striking up their syncopated song.

"Have you seen these?" Mouse picks up a piece of bamboo from the floor as they walk back towards the main hut. The bamboo is sharpened into a mean and ragged point. "We've had the local villagers making them for us, they've been brilliant."

"What's it for?" Sarah asks.

"Punji sticks," Mouse says, testing the spike against the palm of his hand. "The villagers have cleared huge sections of vegetation and prepared these little beauties to plant our own punji traps. We guide the rebels into these kill zones before they approach the village, then they get stuck on these sticks or in the holes filled with spikes so they can be shot down, or at least give our boys the chance to inflict as much damage as we can while they try to escape. Nice little trick taken from the villagers in Borneo."

Sarah isn't able to summon the same level of enthusiasm as Mouse for his improvised killing zones. For all the jokiness and the banter, this is not a boys' camping trip. These men are trained to fight to the death and have orders to do whatever it takes to stop the advance of the rebels. When they do arrive, much blood will spill.

Flickering light from the stove and a couple of hurricane lamps set to burn low at the corners of the room cast a low light inside the hut. Men are filing in and taking seats wherever they can. Sarah is treated to an upturned plastic crate, but most others squat on grass mats or on the bare beaten floor. The stultifying heat buzzes and shimmers like a physical presence in their midst.

A man with a completely shaven head, both ears swollen into misshapen souvenirs of a rugby-playing youth, is crouched over the stove stirring something in a massive pot and raking out coals under a makeshift grill. His face, hair, and clothes are drenched in sweat.

"What's for chop, Dingle?" Mouse asks, peering into the pot.

"Grass Cutter," Dingle says in a thick Yorkshire accent. "One of the villagers brought them in this afternoon, proud as punch as he handed them over, he were. Not sure how much meat will be left once we've got the fur and skin off, but it makes a change from peanuts."

"What's a Grass Cutter?" Mouse asks.

"It's a cane rat," Sarah answers in her most matter-of-fact tone, enjoying the disgust on Mouse's face. "You can buy them spit roasted at the side of the road. Tasty, really, for a rodent. Tastes a bit like chicken."

"You're cooking rat?" Mouse asks Dingle. "It's a good thing I'm bloody starving. How are the snails getting on?" he peers under one of the upturned crates, which are being used as cages for giant snails; their conical shells twice as long as a man's fists, their tentacles poking curiously through the holes in the plastic.

"Still testing for poison, but no one's reacted to handling them yet so we should be good to go soon."

"I've seen these for sale in Brixton market," Sarah says, admiring the size of the weird alien creature. "Buckets of them in with the fruit and vegetables."

"Good to know we won't be the first ones mad enough to try eating them," Mouse says. "Watch out, incoming basher." All the men quickly duck their heads as a walnut-sized beetle comes flying into the hut. Sarah, too slow to follow suit, squeezes her eyes shut as the huge bug cracks against her forehead and buzzes off to throw itself against the hurricane lamp. The men fall about laughing.

"You're one of us now," Magnet says through a snigger. "Don't know what the fuck they are or why they go for the head, but we've christened them Basher Beetles. We've all taken a hit."

"Any news from the chatter?" a stern-looking soldier say near the door asks Mouse. He is naked from the waist up but for a couple of belts of ammunition strung across his shoulders. Mouse introduced him earlier as 'Grimmy'—'as in the reaper', the best shot in the unit and wicked with the Gimpy—the

General Purpose Machine Gun or GPMG. His softly spoken voice is in surprising contrast to his rugged physique.

"Nothing new. Still gathering numbers, latest reports say there'll be about two thousand of them coming. But I reckon we should all get a good night's sleep tonight; it's been a quiet day on the radios."

"How do you know which way they'll be coming?" Sarah asks, amazed at how calmly they all sit here eating their rat, knowing that two thousand drug-fuelled rebels might attack at any moment.

"The road you two came on is the only passable route through to the airport," Mouse says. "All around is waterlogged swamp and dense jungle. You can't move that many men through that kind of terrain."

"But there's only thirty of you. How the hell do you expect to see them off?"

Magnet laughs. "That's our job. And besides, we only need to hold them back until the Paras get here. So long as Mouse can get word through to Lungi when it gets hairy, we'll have reinforcements on the way."

Sarah feels vaguely reassured to know that one of the most elite fighting forces in the world is ready to swoop in for back-up, but continues to hope she will be long gone before they do.

After dinner, the men file out, thanking Dingle for his culinary skill with the rat and preparing for another night trying to sleep while all is still quiet. Sarah notices that dozens of people have appeared in the village after nightfall—creeping in with the darkness to occupy whatever temporary accommodation they can find, or sleeping on mats on the ground in the village square. It might be on the rebels' direct route, but Sarah understands why people feel safer in proximity to the army; even with only thirty men. They are trained, equipped, and ready to fight back.

*

Sarah lies awake, listening to the noises of the forest. Mouse gave her his grass mat and his prime spot in the dormitory. Ibrahim disappeared after dinner. Sarah isn't sure if he was fed-up feeling like the odd-one-out amongst the in-jokes and banter of the British army or whether he just didn't want anyone to sacrifice their bed for him. She hopes he's found somewhere comfortable to sleep. She still feels guilty for having dragged him here against his will—when she burst into his house in Hastings, she had somehow failed to comprehend the impossible scale of the favour she was asking.

Through the walls of the hut you can hear a constant call from the jungle, as if the forest is declaring a warning—the shriek of insects, the cackle and swoop of birds, tremors in the earth and low rumbling growls that sound neither human nor animal. The wind moves through the trees as if the very foliage is ringing the alarm. Time and again, just as Sarah adjusts her brain to the constant rustling, chirruping and repetitive wails of the cicadas, all noises would stop. The buzz and hum of insects would vanish, leaving a thick, palpable silence, broken only by the thud of a falling nut.

She battles to stay awake, to stay alert to the unknown presences lurking beyond the tree cover, but the overwhelming tiredness from the heat, the journey and the intensity of the day finally win out, sending her into a tense and restless sleep.

CHAPTER 45

Movement, noise and the sour smell of adrenaline—everyone in the dormitory is on their feet. "Maximise! Maximise!" Shouts echo around the hut—the code word for rebel attack—and within seconds the men who were snoring in oblivion are piling out the door, fully armed and ready. Sarah looks at their sleep-weary faces in the light of the hurricane lamps, their waxy features set in expressions of strict determination. No one looks at her, no one catches her eye. They have a purpose, and she is now invisible. For all the camaraderie and welcome they showed her, they are now in the theatre for which they are trained; and she has no part to play.

The flickering lamp casts ghoulish shadows across the mud walls and thatch. She wants to follow, to see the threat with her own eyes, to help in some way and support their efforts rather than sitting here feeling useless. But to go outside now seems madness.

At first, it is impossibly quiet for a field of battle; but soon strange sounds ring through the forest—whoops and cries, growls and shrieks like an onslaught of wild animals. Noises made with throats and hands, tusk and bone, closing in. Have they surrounded the village before the watch sounded the alarm? A loud snap of branch underfoot is met by the first deafening call of gunfire.

Sarah knows that ammunition is tight. Without full orders to engage, the provision had been limited. The men are all under strict instruction to fire only on sight. The bullets ring out in staccato clusters—the rebels are here, close enough to see.

A low-pitched whistle soars overhead followed by an explosion that shakes the hut. Sarah's ears ring with the pounding crash, replayed as pain against her eardrums until it takes on the form of a high-pitched moan—a human cry. Somewhere in the village has been hit.

"Casualty!" The shout goes up from close by, but Sarah can't tell if it comes from village or the jungle.

M's thick neck pokes round the door. He shouts to Sarah, "Look lively, casualty incoming, we're going to need some space." Surely this is not one of his wind-ups? His dark humour can't be so macabre to joke at a time like this.

Four men burst into the hut, carrying a fifth between them, a limb each, struggling to move with the delicacy due a casualty. They place the injured man on the floor in the kitchen corner of the hut.

One of the porters meets Sarah's concerned stare—she recognises Magnet's uncommonly blonde head, but not the look in his eyes. Fear and shock suppressed by the need for action.

"Sarah, it's Mouse. Can you look after him? We've got to get back to our positions." He places a solid hand on his friend's shoulder and follows his comrades back out the door. Mouse lies between the blue plastic crates, the snails extending a curious tentacle, his face slicked with mud and sweat and his leg hanging at an excruciating angle. He lies terrifyingly still, his eyes shut. Even his oversized ears seem to droop at the side of his head. Sarah approaches his body, forcing herself not to look away. She places her fingertips gently on the leg, trying to feel where the bones lie beneath the fabric of the camouflage trousers. What does she do now? Her brain freezes in its desperate race for something helpful to do. Come on, pull yourself together, think. What would her brother do? He'd know exactly how best to use the minimal kit she has available. Flashes of her first aid training come back—check for signs of life—A, B, C. Tentatively, she sticks a finger into a section of exposed throat inside Mouse's collar.

"Fuck me, that hurts!" he hollers, to her considerable shock and relief.

"Sorry." She snatches away her fingers.

"No, not you. My leg." He attempts to raise his head to look at his twisted limb, but the pain is clearly too much. He collapses back to the beaten earth.

"Tell me what to do," Sarah instructs. "Do you want me to strap it? Can I get you something for the pain?"

"I need my fucking kit," Mouse groans. "What good am I to anyone here if I can't get the message through to headquarters that we need back-up?"

"Where is it? What can I fetch?" Sarah asks.

"It's stuck inside the comms hut that took the first direct hit. They must have been in the village doing their recces right under our noses. They knew exactly where to aim. The roof collapsed, right on my bloody leg and it trapped everything useful inside. Fuck!"

She grabs a water bottle and the first aid kit and places them near Mouse's head. "Can you sit up enough to help yourself to drugs, or do you need me to help?" She stands over him, hurriedly lacing her shoes and rolling down her sleeves.

"Where are you going?"

"To the comms hut, of course. I'm the smallest here. If there's any chance of getting back inside, it will be easiest for me to squeeze in."

"Sarah, that's nuts. There are two thousand blood-crazy rebels out there, and their kit is no laughing matter. That was an RPG that got my hut. This is no hand-to-hand fighting with machetes. Since they've been kidnapping the UN, they're properly armed."

But not all of that kit was pilfered from the UN. Skarparov brought in a good amount in his scruple-less deal with Foday Sankoh that gave him access to the best diamond areas. If Sarah had stopped him earlier, the weapons never would have left Russia. "I've got to try," she says, heading for the door before she has time to think better of it. "If there's no way to call for back-up, then we're all screwed. The numbers are too heavily on their side. Stay there."

Mouse laughs weakly. "I don't have much choice, you mad cow."

The darkness is shocking. The sticky air feels like a blanket pulled tight over her head. She holds out her hands, as if she could feel her way in the humidity towards the comms hut. Her fingers brush something slippery and warm—sweat-drenched human flesh. She pulls away in alarm, ready to run, but a heavy grip on her bicep drags her back. She has no breath in her body to scream.

"Sarah," the two syllables of her name pronounced to rhyme. "Where are you going? Get back inside, it's not safe," Ibrahim hisses while trying to push her back into the hut.

She struggles out of his grip. "I've got to get to the comms hut and see what I can recover. Mouse is injured."

Ibrahim's face inches from her own. The wide-stretched blood-red eyes would have been enough to make her retreat were it not for the familiarity of his curled lashes. He looks from her to the hut. "Then I'm coming with you for cover." He slips an AK-47 from his shoulder and nods in the direction they need to go.

"Where did you get that from?" Sarah whispers.

"I took it from one of the injured. Every bullet counts."

The rebels shoot up tracer rounds—blindingly bright and dangerously close. The snaky white trails trace an arc that encompasses almost half the village, a deadly firework display illuminating the trees in a ghostly snapshot before fading out. She can see the damaged wreckage where the comms hut had stood, but over two hundred metres of unprotected space lies between her and the hut.

Sarah drops to the floor and belly crawls forward, using her toes to propel herself while staying snake-flat to the ground. Every few strokes she stops to check on Ibrahim—following her at a distance but struggling to keep pace with the bulky gun. As the adrenaline floods her body, looking round the grim tableau of soldiers in position, listening to the explosive rat-a-tat of gunfire echoing in all directions and the animal cries and calls from the forest, she feels an overwhelming urge to giggle.

What the hell is funny about this? Objectively, she knows that she is utterly terrified; but her body's response to the weird exhilaration of finding herself in the line of fire seems to be to want to laugh. Is it a strange mode of protection—to make herself feel bulletproof and untouchable—or the ultimate peak of black humour?

The crawl is a move she has not done since she learned to walk. And yet it feels practised, elbows edging through the dirt, body surging forward on toes, chin raised just above the earth, lower back tense and taut. The surrounding smells are a glorious mess of jungle organic night-time decay, the iron-rich earth like a wet and rusty pipe, bodies and foreign unknown sweat, an ammonia-laced smoke hangs in the air—somewhere between urine and rotten fruit juice—and over it all the smell of burning. A rusty pipe comes readily to mind, conjured by the smell of the earth. But from where? Has she really licked the rusty bubbles on a piece of metal piping that she can now taste on her tongue? Why is she thinking about rusty piping? She's crawling through the mud under direct enemy fire and her mind keeps shooting off on weird tangents, working seven hundred times at its usual speed.

"Stop!" Ibrahim shouts from behind her. He is on his knees, gun aimed into the blackness surrounding them. What has he seen? Who or what does he have in his sights? He rattles out a few rounds toward the dark forest—Sarah can only see the flames jumping and stretching at the end of his gun, like alcohol sprayed through a Bunsen burner. "Go," he calls to her without moving his position.

Sarah edges closer to the hut, her eyes training to where Ibrahim pointed his gun. She can sense something or someone closing in—but who and what and where are they? In the darkest pitch of night she catches only momentary flashes of the scene around her, illuminated by tracer fire to pick out faces and forms. With each flash of white she scans the jungle line; but can only see the familiar shapes of the British soldiers—Grimmy the Sniper, still naked from the waist up but now rattling through his ammo belts, Magnet's big Viking profile squeezed up against the sight of his rifle, M's prankster face frozen in ghoulish black and white.

The enemy remains inescapably close, but invisible. With nothing to give life to their faceless threat, the danger feels somehow spectral. The spitting flashes of the AK-47s reflect sharp points of light—the reflection of an eye? The flash of teeth? Human or something else? The forest teems with evil spirits, the chatter of gunfire is met with fevered cries for blood.

The comms hut is now less than a hundred metres away, but the ground is completely exposed. Nothing between her and the line of invisible fire coming out of the jungle. She forces herself on, focusing on the hut, the ground, the terrain. 'Think of the pipe,' she tells herself. 'The tangy smell of the rust, the strangely fizzing taste, don't look up'. The world fades out of focus and for a stomach-churning moment she thinks she is going to pass out. Her vision blurs and she is struggling to make out what little she could see before. Fat, salty drops fall to the floor as she blinks and suddenly the world returns. Nothing is wrong with her vision—she was just blinded by sweat.

She pushes on.

*

"STOPPAGE!" She hears Grimmy's voice, ripe with frustration and anger. Sarah understands well enough what that means—Grimmy's SA80 has jammed. Dust or humidity or just poor design has failed him. "Get me one of those bastards' AKs!" he shouts to anyone who might hear. Ibrahim slips across the ground like a shadow towards Grimmy's dugout and hands him his weapon. He looks back at Sarah with a shrug, as if to say, 'You're on your own now'. Sarah nods. He did the right thing. She'll just have to hope Grimmy spots her if anyone is waiting at the ruin of the hut.

The explosion has half-buried the corrugated iron roof into the ground, making it impossible for one person to lift. Sarah tries from all angles but can get no purchase on the ripped metal and shattered wood. Pushing with all her weight, she manages to slide the roof back far enough to create a crawl space underneath, but even straining at full effort, the metal remains swallowed by the ground. The crawl space is her only hope.

Back down on her stomach, Sarah reaches first her hands into the hut, then her shoulders. With arms fully outstretched, there is just space for her to squeeze through, but she can't propel herself forward. She flips onto her back and shuffles in, using her feet. The gap is too tight and the rough metal tugs at her hair and skin and clothes as she pushes into the claustrophobic space.

Inside, the darkness is complete. Her probing hands meet metal, wood, and mud. This must be how it feels to be buried alive—heart thumping, sweat reeking of sour panic, engulfed by darkness, hemmed in on all sides and scarcely enough air to think.

She reaches out with blind fingers. The blockage above her head is wood, but it's lying at a different angle to the collapsed walls and the wood feels different, more polished. She punches the shiny surface with all her strength until the wood tears away with a shattering of splinters. She reaches through what must have been the desk Mouse borrowed for his kit—the MDF weakened by years of full humidity. Beyond it, she can feel the ridged black plastic of the satellite phone case and the radios.

The release is overwhelming. To have the kit in reach, apparently undamaged, fills her with crushing relief. As the euphoria spreads, her muscles droop and her head grows heavy. Like the end of a dream, part of her wants this to be it—to close her eyes and drift back into consciousness, knowing she has reached her goal.

But it is not enough.

She still has to get them back to Mouse. Pushing the mental button to fight back the overwhelming urge to stop, she pulls the kit towards her. The space is too tight to fit them through, but with a series of kicks and flicks, the sweat pouring down her face and neck, she manoeuvres the radios and the box towards the open triangle beyond her feet. She has to scrape her shoulders and back against the ruptured metal to escape without dropping the kit. She squeezes her eyes against the pain as the roof rips a wide hole through her shirt and skin and holds her breath until she is released from her tomb.

*

The return journey feels much slower—Sarah is tempted to take her chances and run, but she knows it is a pointless risk. The whole effort would be in vain if she gets herself blown up on the way back carrying the precious load. She keeps up the commando crawl, now one handed, with the satellite phone and radios clutched under her chest. Ibrahim crawls in behind her as they pass Grimmy's dugout, and takes the radios, freeing up a bit of movement. Grimmy gives them a silent nod and a thumbs up as they pass his dugout before fixing his gaze back on the jungle line.

Just over half-way back, another explosion rips the air. Sarah is swallowed by the noise, and a wave of pressure sends her rolling sideways. She focuses all her energy on keeping the plastic case firmly clenched against her chest as her body is thrown to the side, coming to a halt with a pain in her left thigh like a scorching knitting needle inserted deep into the flesh to fillet muscle from bone. Has she been shot? Where did the explosion hit? Her cry is more grunt than scream as she reaches down to her leg and finds one of the carved 'punji' sticks jammed into the flesh. With a shaking hand, she seizes the stick and pulls it out, the needle singeing her flesh as it tears its way to the surface. But she has no time for pain. She needs to move fast before one of the Brits mistakes her writhing body for one of the rebels in the punji pit and puts her out of her misery.

Sarah limps towards the hut where she left Mouse as an illume round goes up with the fizzing crack of someone flicking on the floodlights over a sports field. Sarah blinks her eyes against the blinding brightness and for the first time, the enemy becomes clear. No longer jungle spirits. The white light shows boys, children, lost young men with skin and hair thick with sweat and blood. Their faces, frozen in the glare, ruinously intent on killing.

The soldiers coordinated the timing of the illume with the movements of the rebels—flooding them with artificial dawn, just as they funnelled their approach towards the punji pits. They flank them on either side, leaving them with only two options— to advance through the pits or retreat to the jungle. With the enemy trapped, the hit rate for the scarce ammunition becomes almost guaranteed and the fast-paced clatter of automatic fire replaces the controlled bursts. Between the deafening cracks, Sarah hears screams and calls—human voices fractured with fear and the same haunting animal cries that marked the rebels' approach.

The illume round flickers out, and the gunfire dampens, leaving just the sound of tearing flesh and agonised cries as the injured and the dead are ripped free of the punji sticks. Shadowy figures, with carcasses slung across their shoulders like hunters bringing home their kill, slink back into the jungle, dripping shiny trails of blood.

The silence that follows is almost more ominous than the screaming, ripe with the threat of a renewed attack, a counter flank, a regrouping now that the punji field's location has been revealed. Sarah takes her chance to run, sat phone still clamped to her ribcage, ignoring the shooting pain that ignites her left thigh.

Mouse lies on the floor of the main hut, sweating and ghostly pale, but still conscious. She thrusts the equipment down next to him.

"Blimey! I didn't expect to see you back here. Especially not with that. How the hell did you get it?"

"There are some advantages to being small," Sarah says with a grin before collapsing onto one of the grass mats and allowing her eyes to close over the spinning ceiling. Exhaustion takes over and she slips unconscious.

*

She wakes to a noise that sounds like the earth cleaving, preparing to swallow her up. She jumps up, her heart pummelling in her throat as she casts around for shelter, convinced it is another attack. But the faces of the other soldiers who joined them in the hut after she passed out are jubilant. The earth-thumping shocks are apparently something to celebrate, and they all pile out of the hut to watch.

The sky glows with the pink light of dawn, bringing shapes and form back to the village. Just behind the huts, a Chinook is coming in to land, the downward force of the blades so strong it flattened trees and even ripped a piece of corrugated iron from one of the huts. The collective sigh is palpable—after a night of going it alone, the back-up is here.

The soldiers stand and watch. A few give welcoming whoops as they wait for the Paras to roll out the back—fresh eyes and legs, new kit, and substantially bumped up numbers. But the celebration soon sours when the rotors slow and only one man appears.

"You're having a laugh," M says as the new arrival comes over to present himself. "Where are the rest of you?"

"Still at Lungi," he says with a confidence that seems forced.

"I thought you were supposed to be the rapid response

team coming in for back-up? Did we not make it clear we were surrounded by two thousand rebels?"

"You did. But it sounded like you had it under control. I've just come for a recce and report back."

"Then get a fucking move on. We've got a wounded man and we're dangerously short on ammo. They'll be back again by dark—you better have sorted some back up before then." He looks at Sarah and seems to do a double take, as if with all the night's action he forgot she was there. "And you can take the hitchhiker back with you. Sarah," he offers her a gruff handshake, "you played a blinder with that comms kit, but it's time to leave us to finish the job. Look after Mouse, won't you?"

Sarah nods. She is still buzzing from the adrenaline flood of the night and sorry to leave the action—even if she has used up several lifetimes' worth of luck. She knows she is more likely to be a hindrance than a help if she stays on, but it still feels like leaving early from a party that has just taken off.

She and Ibrahim climb into the chopper next to Mouse, who is laid out on a makeshift stretcher, his leg bound roughly to a plank of wood and wave to the others as they take off. Sarah tries to lessen the limp from her own wounded leg. It hurts like hell, but it doesn't feel serious enough to waste the time of the army medics. And the pain helps mask the nagging thought that there is more that can be done. Last night was the first night the British army came under direct attack by the rebels, and they fared amazingly well. Mouse's mangled leg was the only serious injury sustained. But who knows how many times the rebels would try again? Can they keep them back just by better planning and training? The enemy is numberless; it swarms the jungle, adding in number with each attack. More men could always be found to put themselves up against the British firepower, even if it meant certain death.

As soon as they land in Lungi, they take Mouse to the medical team to have his leg cleaned up and set. Sarah takes her moment to seek out the airport customs official who unlocks a deserted office for her and tracks down the package from Bok, addressed to the Kono Uranium Company and the PO Box number she knows by heart. Pietro's signature on a beer mat is apparently proof enough to release the package. There are bigger things to worry about than mail theft. Sarah shakes the surprisingly small box wondering what might be inside. It had better be what Chen Xiaochang is looking for.

She returns to the medical hut in time to see Mouse hobbling out on crutches, determined to stop by his comms colleagues before going any further. They greet each other with a barrage of banter, ignoring his patched-up limb.

"What's the chatter after last night?" Mouse asks.

"Mate, it's like music to my ears," a tall Northerner named Noddy says, a pair of headphones still hung around his neck. "Sounds like they're retreating. I think it's safe to say they won't try that again in a hurry."

Ibrahim, who remained silent for most of the journey, breaks the mood. "But they will try again," he says, his voice stone cold and still. "You guys have homes to get back to, families to stay alive for. The boys in the bush have nothing. They have nothing to return to, no one who'll take them back. So long as they live, they'll keep trying. So long as the snake has a head, it can still bite."

Mouse and Noddy sit in awkward silence, but Sarah understands.

"Where is Foday Sankoh?" she asks.

"That's the funny thing," Noddy replies. "No one knows. He's been in hiding since a protest outside his house got nasty a few days ago. His men ended up mowing down some of the protesters and he fled. He's disappeared without trace."

Where would a rebel leader hide? Would his men protect him now that he is a wanted man? Which allies can you rely on to provide shelter and protection without the risk of discovery? One of Foday Sankoh's bush wives had her tongue cut out and hot oil poured into her ears. He is not a man who places his trust easily. Sarah studies her imaginary board and watches the pieces fall into place. She is sure she's right. What better guardian than an ally who can no longer talk, a trusted business partner who can no longer turn you in?

"Promise me you'll go easy on that leg, Mouse," Sarah says, her mind racing to the logistics of the fastest way to get back across the water. "Ibrahim? Are you coming with me back to Freetown?"

"Not this time, Sarah. I'm not leaving you English to fight our war. I'm going back. This is finally our chance." She thinks she might be forgiven for dragging him into the battle.

"Look after yourself," she says, offering an awkward hug.

"Don't tell Mammy," he says with a wink.

"You better come back alive, or she'll call for my blood."

"Where are you rushing off to now?" Mouse asks.

Sarah stuffs Bok's package into her bag. "I might just know where to find the head of the snake."

CHAPTER 46

Sarah is amazed when Iain, the owner of the speedboat, answers first time and even more surprised to hear that he is in Lungi and can take her straight over. Her plan had been to use her brownie points won with the car to blag her way onto an army chopper back to Freetown. But the only aircraft flying are all involved in operations on the Lungi side, and no one will return to Freetown for another couple of days. Elias left her Iain's number, but she's never needed his boat since their first night-time arrival in Freetown, pitching over the inky black water. That first journey, so full of excitement and anticipation, seems a lifetime ago, not a matter of months.

"Iain, you're a lifesaver," Sarah said as she hoists herself up out of the water and into the small speedboat. "Are you really going, anyway?"

"Yes, as it happens. There's a group of French fishermen stuck down the coast who seem to have belatedly realised there is a war going on and want help to get out."

"Tourists? Here now?" Sarah asks, astonished.

"Nothing gets between an angler and his fish."

"It's been a while," Sarah says, skirting carefully round the awkward truth that last time she saw Iain had been with Elias. Everything about the journey—the smell of the waves, the wade out through the warm saltwater lapping at rolled-up trousers, the outline of the headland and the lighthouse in t–e distance - reminds her of him.

"Yeah, I'm not over in Freetown so often now. Elias used to

drag me out, make me come to the band nights in the bars, a few ill-advised late nights at Paddy's." He tails off into silence, staring ahead at the horizon. Finally, he speaks again. "It's a shame he's gone."

Is this a peculiar reticence picked up in a British boarding school along with the accent? A shame? The weather turning might be a shame, a fishing trip interrupted might be a shame. Elias being burnt alive in a tin can is a fucking tragedy. She fixes her eyes on the landing beach—clutching on to the boat as it flies and thumps beneath her.

Sarah grabs a taxi from the beach, surprised to see more than one rolling along the flat stretch. The driver throws open the passenger door for her with a broad smile. From the back seat, Sarah takes the chance to inspect the wound to her leg. The thick red circle where she tore out the punji stick looks like a cartoon bullet hole. She can hear her brother's voice in her head telling her it will need some serious cleaning, but the bleeding has stopped and at least she can still walk. A car approaching from the opposite direction slows as it passes, horn honking and arms waving through open windows. The jubilant faces seem directed at Sarah.

"What was that?" she asks as the driver hammers out a series of honks in return.

"They think you are British."

"And so what if I am?"

"They want to congratulate you on giving the RUF a bloody nose in Lungi. People say the rebels are already on the run. Freetown is waking up. All week the streets have been empty. I stayed home. But today people are not afraid. Look, they come." He points to another passing car crammed full of passengers.

"But how on earth did you hear about that already? The operation only finished a few hours ago."

"Word travels fast on the bush telegraph," the driver smiles at her, turning up the tinny radio.

Skarparov's futuristic fortress on the hill is deserted. The gate is closed, but a gap where it meets the perimeter wall is just wide enough for Sarah to slip through. A macabre figure sits hunched inside the guard booth, but on closer inspection it turns out to be nothing more than a camouflage print canvas jacket slung over the back of the chair with a black beret propped above the collar. An empty pair of steel-toed army boots stand abandoned on the floor. Sarah picks up the jacket, disembodying the ghostly apparition, and slips it on. She stashes her bag with Bok's precious delivery inside the guard's booth, unsure what she might find inside.

She eyes the security camera. Is anyone watching? She expects one of Skarparov's henchmen to appear from behind the house, gun trained straight at her. But no one comes. The house has the neglected air of a place forgotten; a fortress sealed off from the outside world. Except, now that Sarah draws closer to the building, she can make out the faint whir of a generator. Surely no other house in the neighbourhood would have their own power supply?

She tries the door—locked tight, but always worth checking. You never know when luck might smile on you. She crosses back over the moat-like water feature and follows it round the side of the house. The water smells fetid, stagnant, and rich with decay. The pool where Frida the hippo was kept captive is now empty. Sarah wonders what has become of its inmate. And her lunch.

The glass windows are streaked with tracks of dust-filled rain. Sarah tries the handle of the back door, remembering its flimsy feel, but even with an extra hard shove it holds firm. She'll have to do it the messy way. She returns to the guard booth and comes back with one of the steel-toe boots. Carefully wrapping the army jacket in several layers around her arm, she smashes the boot, toe cap first, into the window near the door handle. Her thigh muscle throbs at the effort. The noise is loud enough to wake the whole of Hastings, but still no one comes. Sarah reaches through the shattered glass and opens the sliding door.

Inside, the house is dark. The shutters are closed, and the tinted windows let through very little of the early morning light. Like a nightmare hall of mirrors, Skarparov looks down at her from every angle on the wall, the same enigmatic smile both pale and perma-tanned, impressionistic and hyper-real, his opal-green eyes unmistakable. Sarah is glad Ibrahim stayed in Lungi—this place is full of bad 'juju'.

The sound of raised voices erupts from the corridor. Arming herself with a shard of broken glass wrapped in the canvas jacket, Sarah approaches the noise.

"Who's there?" she calls out, her voice echoing around the slate grey corridor. Nothing. Her feet seem stuck to the tiled floor, resisting her brain's instructions to move forward.

The door at the end of the corridor stands ajar. Hands trembling but determined, she pushes it open.

An enormous bed faces an oversized television screen from which loud voices of a Nigerian soap opera bicker and blare. Propped up on pillows like an invalid in his nightshirt, his face lit only from the glare of the television, is Foday Sankoh, the leader of the Revolutionary United Front, the formidable rebel leader and the most wanted man in Freetown.

He confronts Sarah with a look of utter disbelief. His beard is grey and unkempt, his hair grown into matted locks, but he maintains the scornful sneer of a man with limitless power. "Who the fok are you?" he asks, not moving from his position.

She clutches her makeshift weapon tightly in her fist. "I'm from the British Government; I've come to turn you in."

He begins to laugh. A snort, growing into a chuckle, rising up to a full lion-throat roar. "You?" he jabs a finger towards her. "You've come for me?"

She takes in the discarded bottles on the floor—beer and whiskey, all empty. There is no telling how long he's been holed up in here, but his stay has clearly been well lubricated. The

319

room smells like a neglected animal cage—rancid, sickly, stale sweat and alcohol.

"This is not the process of democracy." He speaks with strange unnatural pauses between his words, as if reciting lines. "Why you come to the premises of a man they call the peace-maker?"

"Peace-maker?" Sarah laughs at the absurdity of the title. "You and your rebels have led a systematic campaign of abduction, rape and murder. You are responsible for unimaginable atrocities. People call you many things, but I've never heard you called a peacemaker."

"Atrocities? How can you prove the RUF were responsible?" He turns his head to one side, a slight tilt of his neck to accentuate his sneer. "Everyone who took part in this war, they are responsible. Intervention forces, Kamajors, government soldiers," he spits out the names like insults. "They are responsible."

"You've had every chance to bring this to an end."

"What do you know? White gal from the British Big Brother? I have seen our people become slaves. They become beggars." He leaves his mouth hanging open between each sentence like a dog baring its teeth. "The war is a political struggle for what you call democracy. People shed their blood to bring change."

Never has an impersonal statement filled Sarah with such horror. Which people willingly shed their own blood for this madness? How can he shift his culpability onto his victims?

"I have a vision for the people of Sierra Leone," he continues, with one eye squinted towards her, a deep crease squeezed between his nose and forehead and his nostrils flared in disdain. "To make a revolution which is progress. Revolution is progress for people. Nothing else."

"And you honestly think you have brought progress to the people?" Sarah scans the bed, the bedside tables, searching for his weapon. Surely he wouldn't be here unarmed and alone? His guards forced him into hiding by opening fire on the crowd at his house—has he lost trust even in those who protect him? "This country is on its knees," she says. "People are crying out for peace, and you offer them nothing but blood."

"I am the peace-maker." He grins again, showing stained teeth. His grin hints at a once powerful charisma, the force of personality that dragged followers in his wake. But it is tired, its shine has tarnished. How many people still believe his words? "I signed the peace accord in Abidjan. I signed the peace accord in Lomé. Even if the president is a monkey, I would sign a peace accord with him, to give a peaceful atmosphere in this country." He sits up, both hands visible on the sweat-soaked bedsheets. No trace of self-consciousness, no embarrassment to be caught in such a compromised position. He speaks as if atop a throne rather than a soiled mattress.

"But what have you done to keep your side of the deal?" Sarah asks. "The RUF are still armed. I have seen their terror with my own eyes." She remembers the faceless spirits in the jungle, the blank but murderous expressions of the faces lit by the flares. The jungle army that terrorised a nation for over ten years marches to the beat of his drum.

"Yes, they still have their arms. But you British now are arming the government to cheat. They are always trying to blame the RUF, but it is you who feed the bloodshed. You who steal the natural resources. You who let the government enrich themselves while they grow fat. Look at me!" he taps his grizzled chest in its filthy white nightshirt, rattling a heavy gold bracelet on his wrist. "I am the poorest rebel leader in the world. My people call me their saviour, because I only give. I do not take."

"So, what are you doing hiding here in a dead man's house? A dead man whose dirty arms and weapons you took in return for resources that were not yours to give?"

"You are vanity," he hisses, shaking his head in disgust. "All men are vanity. Only God we can trust because he is the almighty God, our shepherd, the shepherd of the RUF."

Sarah tries no further to make her case. What is the point in arguing with a man so completely convinced of his own good that he is willing to invoke God's guidance over his bloodshed and slaughter? "You have two choices now," she says, keeping her voice slow and steady. "Either you stay here and I turn you over to the international forces. You will be tried for war crimes, and they will put away you for life. Or you leave here and take your chances with your people. If, as you say, you are their saviour, they will protect you."

Sarah makes a show of pulling out her mobile. She knows what she should do—whatever her questionable status in Michael's hierarchy, in this moment she represents the British government. She has a duty to turn him in. To report his position to the authorities so that he could be arrested. But watching the grizzled face of General Papa spout his revolutionary claptrap, Sarah wonders who would really be served by following the route to justice—the expense of an international criminal tribunal, the inevitable delay, the possibility of his being made a martyr. He would be called on to defend his crimes before the court, a mouthpiece given to his madness. His example twisted to serve as inspiration in place of deterrent. Is that the justice he deserves? Is that the justice owed to his victims?

He stands up and approaches Sarah. "I started this struggle," he hisses into her ear, "and I am going to end it."

Sarah holds her phone to her cheek, the shard of glass trembling inside the sleeve of her other hand. Does he have a concealed weapon? Would he attack her with his bare hands? He is old, but still powerful enough to crush her. Would a slash of glass hold him off? There are no acts too depraved for this monster.

She holds the phone out in front of her chest, arm rigid with fear, trying to summon up the power of everything it represents. "It is your choice," she says. "You leave here now. Or I turn you in."

"Little girl," he laughs as he comes closer. His body smells of ancient potatoes left to fester. "Little girl, you don't scare me." He snatches the mobile out of her hand and smashes it to the floor.

He is close enough to reach. Should she attack first? Would she kill another man in this house?

"I am here to bring peace to the people of Sierra Leone. My people will greet me as their saviour." His voice rises in defiance, in madness, in messianic blindness. "You know nothing of my people." Barefoot in his nightshirt he walks out the door, his palms turned out, his face aglow with sweat and righteousness. "I am their saviour."

Sarah watches him leave the house, his gait unsteady, but his head held high. She stands alone in Skarparov's deserted fortress. The remnants of her phone scattered across the floor. The glass still clutched in her hand.

It does not take long before the shouts rise over the perimeter wall. A single voice, quickly joined by more, raised to fever pitch. Above it all comes Foday Sankoh's cries, still defiant: "I come for peace. I come for peace."

Sarah creeps to the front gate. A crowd has gathered around his fallen frame, wild-eyed men ripping the dirtied clothes from his body. Women shriek and yell with an animal ferocity, making chopping motions with their hands—mirroring the favourite cruelty of the RUF. The mob grows in size and frenzy, welcoming their saviour to its embrace.

CHAPTER 47

Sarah stays in the house until the baying for blood is replaced by celebration. Between Skarparov's portraits, like death masks preserving his macabre smile, she watches the crowd grow as people came from all over Hastings, gathered to see if the news is true. She loses sight of Foday Sankoh until a battered body is slung onto a makeshift stretcher and bundled into an army jeep. As he is driven away, the crowd rejoices.

Sarah retrieves her bag and slips out of the gate to join the impromptu party that fills the street. An old man, his body warped with age and ill-health, taps out a rhythm on a wooden drum, joined by women singing and calling in unison. Everyone dances—hands and elbows raised, hips alive. A woman in a faded purple dress takes Sarah's hand and spins her into the whirl of bodies, clasping onto her fingers with a firm grip. Waving a gold pendant in the shape of a lion's head, a man in army uniform careers through the crowd in a lap of honour. "I am the scorpion," he declares to whoops of joy. "I captured the lion!" He spins the pendant, ripped from Foday Sankoh's body, in a circle over his head.

Another man barrels through the ululating masses, re-enacting the sorry figure of the rebel leader stumbling barefoot over the sharp stones, dragging a leg behind him in an exaggerated limp, as others pretend to beat him. The charade, like a life-size Punch and Judy show, is met with eruptions of laughter. Two men try to drum up support for a raid on Sankoh's house—certain they'll find his stash of diamonds. Others call for his blood—frustrated that the army arrived to remove his battered body before they finished him off. One sole voice urges caution to the crowd—warning of RUF retaliation. But it is soon drowned out by all those determined to celebrate the possibility of freedom. There is a chance now, however small, that peace may lie within their grasp; that a future is possible, free from the never-ending horror of war. And that hope is reason enough to celebrate.

Another strong hand grabs Sarah and pulls her into a tight embrace. Mammy Kamara has clearly dressed for the occasion. Her tightly fitted dress highlights the best of her ample proportions: a firm tuck at the waist, tulip sleeves with petals fanning to the elbows, a mermaid tail skirt and a wide-open neckline to set off her chunky gold necklaces. The fabric is a bold print of white and pink feathers, tessellated like the scales of a pangolin with a matching voluminous headdress, fastened like a chef's hat with swagger.

"Sarah!" she cries above the noise of the party. "What are you doing here? When did you get back? Where is Ibrahim?"

Sarah does not know which questions to answer. She hardly dares tell her she left Ibrahim to continue the fight in the bush and came back alone. Now is not the moment to sour the celebration with a mother's wrath. "I came back this morning. Ibrahim wanted to stay at Lungi," Sarah mumbles, not meeting Mammy Kamara's eye.

"You hear that!" Mammy Kamara calls out to the crowd. "My boy is in the fight! Foday Sankoh gone, my boy in the fight. Now we can win!" she shouts, visibly bolstered with pride. She takes hold of Sarah's hands and dances her around the crowd. "Now we can win," she calls again, wiping tears from her eyes. "Ibrahim will fight back the RUF. Now we can win."

*

When Sarah reaches her dingy hotel room, she is a 'dead man walking'—her skin welted with angry mosquito bites and smelling of adrenaline-tinged sweat mixed with digesting rat. She is ready for a trickle shower, some fresh clothes and several days' worth of sleep. She is not ready to find Kuznetsov. He sits on the sole armchair under the window, apparently engrossed in one of her books about leaves.

"What are you doing here?" she asks, her hand still holding the door.

Kuznetsov looks up and smiles. "I came to say goodbye. I hear all the Brits are being evacuated. I didn't want you to leave without the chance to say farewell."

"What are you doing in my hotel room?" Sarah asks, still in shock.

"Sorry, I didn't mean to impinge on your privacy. I thought this would be the best place to find you. But I realise how this might look."

"You can't just break into a girl's room."

"Apologies. We are trained to break in anywhere we please. Old habits die hard." he says with a shrug. "Are you really reading these?" He folds down a page of the book to mark his spot. "I thought the interest in leaves was just a front?"

"It is." Sarah pulls open the flimsy curtains to let the daylight into the shabby room, skirting between Kuznetsov's knees and the end of the bed. "But they're interesting. Have you ever heard of Astrogalus? It's used to improve the immune system, but it can also indicate the presence of uranium underground—at least it can in Colorado."

"And can it also tell you if the uranium does not exist?" Kuznetsov says with a knowing grin.

Sarah busies herself scooping up piles of clothes from the floor. She does not answer.

"Did you know, when I was a boy, I wanted to be an astronaut?" He swirls an empty glass ashtray over the surface of the table. "I forced myself to study science that meant nothing to me; I ran in the freezing cold every day. I wanted to do whatever it took to get to space. I gave up all the literature that I loved for books like this." He taps on the cover of the textbook. "In the end, I failed the selection because of poor eyesight. So I joined the *kontora* instead, like my parents always hoped that I would."

Sarah ceases her tidying and sits on the end of the bed.

"I often wonder how it might have been if I hadn't ruined my eyes with all these books." He speaks with a deep, creased-eyed smile and a touch of sadness. "Don't lose sight of your inner astronaut, Sarah. I can see a bright future for you in this business, if that is what you choose. But there are other ways to do this well—you don't have to become a battle-hardened old cynic like me. Or like Michael."

"You two are from another age. Things are different now."

"That's true. But also not."

"I don't ever want to be Michael. But I want access to Michael's world."

"And have you given yourself time to think about why?"

"Because there you have the chance to make a difference on a global scale. To influence the right and wrongs in the world at a level that most people never get near. Actions that change the course of history for millions, even if no one ever knows that they took place."

"It can be like that." Kuznetsov looks at Sarah, his head to one side. "But things are rarely so simple."

Sarah stacks piles of books and clothes into her duffel bag. "Perhaps not, but my inner astronaut likes to think they could be."

"Goodbye, Sarah." He stands and offers a swift kiss on the cheek. The marine scent of his cologne brings back awkward memories of their last encounter, but this time there is no chemical urge clamouring to be met. "We will meet again, no doubt."

*

Brigadier Knight waves to Sarah as she climbs out of the

Chinook, back at Lungi. Having safely deposited Bok's delivery with Pietro and Kobus, still sweating in the bar of the Mammy Yoko, she is finally ready to go.

Robert looks weary; his eyelids sag at the edges, and purple bags suggest he has also seen very little sleep. But he maintains the bounce in his step.

"Did you hear about the firefight last night?" he asks. "I heard a mad rumour you were there, but I told them that couldn't be the case as you were safely installed at the High Commission." He raises a disapproving eyebrow. "Anyway, I'm glad to see you coming off that chopper."

"Yes," Sarah smiles, "I've been in Freetown." Which isn't entirely untrue.

"Our boys put up a hell of a show—totally outnumbered but only one shattered leg to show for it. They'll think twice before trying that again. We should be able to get on with this evacuation now without fear of attack."

"And what next?" Sarah asks.

"Next we charge ahead. We still have forty hours until Downing Street has to respond, and I intend to use that time to full effect. With this invaluable source of intel," he taps Elias's notebook in his breast pocket, "we can move in with a big push, fronted by the Sierra Leone army and backed by British and UN troops, to seize control of as much rebel-held territory as possible. And hopefully secure the release of the Peacekeepers still being held hostage. And did you hear the best bit?" his face spreads into a broad grin. "Foday Sankoh was arrested in the early hours of the morning. We were called to pick him up after he had been treated to a well-deserved bout of mob justice. I have to say, there's a part of me that feels sorry we got there on time. I'm not normally one to wish anyone dead, but in his case I am prepared to make an exception. But what are the chances of that? Coming on the same night we finally show his boys a bit of firepower?"

"Really?" Sarah tries to suppress her own grin. "What a

perfectly convenient coincidence."

Robert pauses, surveying Sarah over his eagle nose as if reassessing all his previous impressions of her. "You know your father always talked about you as someone special. Even in the Berlin days, when you must have been still a young child, it was clear you ruled his heart."

Thoughts of her father bring a warmth to Sarah's chest and a filminess to her eyes.

Robert puts his hand on her shoulder. "We've another evacuation plane leaving this afternoon. I can get you on it if that's what you wish?"

She nods. "I'm ready to go home."

CHAPTER 48

"Do you think I could get away with this?" Jenny pulls a '60s mod dress in mustard yellow off the rack and holds it up against her for Sarah's inspection.

Sarah laughs. "If you were going to a fancy dress party as a bottle of Colman's."

"You're not being very helpful." Jenny continues rifling through the racks of Bethnal Green market. "I've got to find something to wear to this 'do' this evening. I need to look young and funky, but also sexy and alluring, professional, without being stuffy, and like someone you just couldn't help spilling your secrets to."

"How about this then?" Sarah holds up a micro-dress in magenta, psychedelic swirls.

"Somehow I don't get the feeling you're taking this seriously."

Sarah is delighted to be teased. Months have gone by since they last saw each other, the longest they have ever spent without each other since they met in their first year of university. The last time they were apart, while Jenny was travelling in South America and Sarah brushing up her French in Senegal, they kept up a sensational correspondence that chronicled every conquest and grappled with every philosophical dilemma they encountered in the absence of their wing-woman. But since Sarah started working for Michael, it became too difficult to lie about what she was doing to someone who knew her too well. It is easier to say nothing than to be forced to weave a carpet of lies and remember which threads she used. Since she has been in Sierra Leone, Jenny's emails have been left unanswered. Sarah was worried that her silence would have built a distance between them, that Jenny would be hurt by her so-called best friend's negligence. But if she was, she brushes over it bravely.

"You could dress in a paper bag and you'd still manage to pull off your brief," Sarah says.

"Well, help me find a 'to die for' paper bag then. There's only so long I can bear writing gossip about the London party scene. There are a pair of property developers coming tonight who I'm sure are a front for dodgy money. If I get a scoop like that, they've got to let me get my teeth into something more serious."

"I might have just the thing for you."

"Are you finally going to tell me what you were up to in Sierra Leone?"

"Eventually. But first I've got another story for you. Did you see this?" she passes Jenny a copy of the news story of Sarah White's involvement in the attack in Tbilisi.

Jenny's eyes pop as she examines the photo. "That's you!" her voice shoots up an octave. "But what the hell are you doing taking that briefcase?"

"It's a long story. And I can tell you most of it. If you promise me to sell your editor a story about Viktor Skarparov—the real mastermind behind the attack who was propping up Foday Sankoh in Sierra Leone. I want any trace of my involvement, or Sarah White's, erased from the public record."

"Are you sure about this?" Jenny's brow knots as she examines her friend. "It sounds like a great scoop, but..."

"I can give you all the details you want. I even have copies of the documents that link him to the transfer of weapons received from the KGB to Foday Sankoh."

"But why give it to me? Why not hand him in to the police?" Jenny pulls another dress off the rack and holds it up against herself.

"He's dead," Sarah says, shaking her head at the dress choice.

"Oh." Jenny hastily returns the dress to the rack. "Well, at least he won't be coming after me for revenge. Does anyone else know about the connection?"

"Not as far as I'm aware. It will be yours to reveal to the world. But you need to promise to keep me entirely out of it."

"Oh. I was hoping you'd be the poster girl for my scoop. Can I hint at my source?"

"Not a chance."

"And what do we do about Sarah White?"

"Just wipe her out."

*

"You're still here!" Sarah's father, still in his navy dressing gown, grabs her into a bear hug when she comes down to breakfast.

"Of course I am. I told you I'd stay a few days."

"Yes, but somehow I was worried you'd be charging off again."

"Not this time," Sarah says, switching on the kettle.

"It's wonderful to have you back." He radiates good cheer, which is unlike him first thing in the morning. But Sarah suspects it isn't just her return that has lifted his spirits. He seems brighter, more energised that she has seen him for years. "I told you Robert was the man for the job. I wish you'd been there to see me sock it to Beverley at the Tuesday morning meeting. She started off again, insisting on inaction—I don't think she'd read the updates from over the weekend. The look on her face when I told her it was too late and that Brigadier Knight had already secured Freetown and released the first batch of hostages. It was pure joy to see her so backfooted."

"I hope she was suitably contrite."

"Not really, but it was clear to all present that she'd mucked it up. I was thinking of starting work on the Airstream today—do you want to give me a hand?"

The ancient aluminium camping trailer has sat in the garden for the best part of a decade growing moss. Sarah's father bought it as scrap metal, dreaming of turning it into an adventurer's haven, but Sarah assumed he'd long since given up the idea.

"Are you sure? That's a heck of a lot to take on?"

"Exactly," her father says with a grin. "Blast! The milk's out. Can you run to the shop? I'm not quite eccentric enough yet to face the corner shop in my dressing gown."

*

Sarah pays for two pints of milk and swaps a few banal observations with the shopkeeper who she has known for as long as she can remember—the wind is picking up today, she learns, and the school children would be about a bit earlier. He throws her a bag of past-their-sell-by-date mini eggs, knowing they have always been her favourite. She opens the packet as she leaves the shop and crunches down on a handful of sugar shell, sinking her teeth into a solid mass of chocolate. She lets the door swing shut behind her with a jangle of bells.

A familiar figure waits on the pavement outside. Sarah has grown so used to seeing her, delicately poised in the background of Freetown's regular haunts, that she almost passes the Chinese Ambassador's elegant translator with no more than a nod of recognition. Until she remembers she is not in Freetown.

The translator steps in beside Sarah as they walk back towards her house.

Sarah rapidly swallows her mouthful of sticky chocolate.

"Good morning, Sarah," the translator says in her perfect, softly spoken English. She is an extraordinary sight in a small Hertfordshire village, not known for its diversity. But somehow, even in her bright coral-coloured lipstick, she manages to make herself look unobtrusive. "I'm sorry. I don't think we've ever properly met. But I know who you are. I work for the one you know as Chen Xiaochang."

Sarah hides her astonishment in a slight cough to clear her throat.

"Dilara told me I could find you here," Chen's representative says as they turn the corner past the church. Sarah chooses to walk in the opposite direction to her father's home. It is probably a futile precaution, but she does not want her father associated with her alter-ego as a uranium middleman.

"Delighted to make your acquaintance properly." Sarah nods.

"Mr Chen would like to meet you. The samples have been tested and the ten-million-dollar fee will be delivered to your courier in Freetown, as per the deal."

Sarah can't believe the package she casually picked up at a deserted customs office in Lungi and flung through the crowd as she danced in the streets of Hastings held the key to unlocking ten million dollars.

"Do you have the details for the wire transfer?"

"Of course. I'll confirm the account details later this morning," Sarah says. Pietro and Kobus are going to be paid handsomely for their creative efforts. She can think of worse people to receive a windfall from an international criminal. "And I'd be very happy to meet your boss whenever is convenient for him."

"He will come to London next week. I trust I can tell him you'll be there?"

"Of course," Sarah says, mirroring the translator's delicate manners. "It would be my pleasure."

*

Sarah meets Chris and Michael in the cafe of the crypt at St Martin's in the fields off Trafalgar Square. The self-service cafe is suitably busy and anonymous, and the bare brick vaulting and heavy stone slabs suit Michael's taste for the macabre. The two men are sitting close together when Sarah arrives, heads bowed in conversation, clearly a unit. Neither stands to greet her or moves a chair to allow her to join their group as an equal partner. Michael, at least, offers her a lop-sided smile. Chris scarcely looks up. She can sense in his body language that he is fuming.

"We were just discussing alternate routes to Chen Xiaochang

now that your plan to leave this to that pair of idiots in Freetown has fallen apart," Chris says.

"Oh? What part of it has fallen through?" Sarah asks.

"You vanished at the crucial moment to go God-knows-where, leaving Kobus to screw everything up. He fluffed the meeting with Chen's representatives and came away with no follow-up. I'm fairly certain he did it on purpose—he wants out. And with you here, what's stopping him from dropping us now?"

"The ten million dollars he is due to receive from Chen Xiaochang."

"Yeah right."

"It should be wired over by the end of the day."

"If you believe that, you'll believe anything," Chris replies. "And what with the military intervention, things are going to look very different in Sierra Leone soon."

"You say that as if it's a bad thing?" Sarah says.

"I wouldn't put it like that. But there are certain things you can only get away with under cover of societal breakdown. It would be naïve to pretend that our work there won't be very much more difficult now."

"Yours perhaps. But I'm pretty pleased with how all is looking. Chen Xiaochang has asked for a meeting."

The look on Chris's face is exactly as she'd hoped—undisguised, fuming envy. Michael, however, does not react. Is it possible that he already knew? He nods at Sarah, a touch of pride in his mercurial smile.

"Well done, Sarah," Michael says, draining the end of his coffee. "I'm pleased. Obviously you'll need to lead on this one for now. Chris and I will be here to back you up." A silencing look pre-empts any objection from Chris. "Are you sure you're ready for this? Going in deep cover to negotiate a uranium deal is a far cry from posing as a leaf specialist."

Sarah enjoys a last glance at Chris's crestfallen face. Ever since Chen Xiaochang's representative surprised her at the corner shop, she has felt charged with a new energy; her veins run with a potent cocktail of nerves and venom.

She is coiled, poised, ready to attack.

"I am ready," she says, "to draw this conspiracy of death out of the shadows, with the lure of a prize that doesn't exist."

She has become the head of the snake.

End

Historical Note

Although Sarah's involvement is pure fiction, the circumstances of the end of the war in Sierra Leone are based on historical fact. The British Brigadier (later Head of the Armed Forces General David Richards) who was sent in to organise the evacuation did arrive without clear terms of engagement and consciously used that freedom to escalate military intervention beyond the evacuation. The account of the firefight against the rebels draws heavily from the memoir of Steve Heaney MC, a member of the Pathfinder team that fought the rebels at Lungi Lol. The very same day as the battle at Lungi Lol, Foday Sankoh appeared from hiding and was attacked by the mob. But without Sarah, this must have been pure coincidence. All characters in the book are fictional other than Foday Sankoh. I have taken almost all of his words verbatim from interviews he gave. He was mad enough to let him speak for himself. An American businessman with interests in Sierra Leone started off a short-lived frenzy about a uranium find in Sierra Leone, but nothing has ever been proven.

Did You Enjoy This Book?

If so, you can make a HUGE difference.

For any author, the single most important way we have of getting our books noticed is a really simple one—and one which you can help with.

Yes, you.

Us indie authors and publishers don't have the financial muscle of the big guys to take out full-page ads in the newspaper or put posters on the subway.

But we do have something much more powerful and effective than that, and it's something that those big publishers would kill to get their hands on.

A committed and loyal bunch of readers.

Honest reviews of our books help bring them to the attention of other readers.

If you've enjoyed this book I would be really grateful if you could spend just a couple of minutes leaving a review (it can be as short as you like) on this book's page on your favourite store and website.

The King's Pawn

Book One in the Sarah Black Series

Sarah Black is the ultimate rookie. Young, naïve and inexperienced, she is thrown into a world where nothing is as it seems, and no one can be trusted. Unsupported and out of her depth, Sarah must learn the rules of the game to survive.

Fresh out of university, Sarah is drawn to the enigmatic Michael, a suave but elusive MI6 agent who draws her in to a world promising adventure and intrigue.

But she finds herself faced with much more than she expected.

When MI6 hear rumours of a potential attack on a new oil pipeline across the Caucasus, Sarah finds herself thrust into the middle of a web of deceit and intrigue.

Alone and without support in an unstable Eastern Europe, can Sarah solve the puzzle before it's too late?

Can she draw on all her ingenuity and courage to survive in a world where all is not what it seems, and no one can be trusted?

"If you're looking for the next Le Carré, Ludlum or Silva, then she has arrived and her name is Lucy Hooft, the refreshingly new female spy author. Steel yourself for her spectacular and much anticipated British spy series set in Eastern Europe that catapults you into a world of 21st Century intrigue, deception, and a perilous slalom of twists and turns you—I'll warn you now—might never recover from."

- Richard Lyntton, author of North Korea Deception and The Deception Series.

Acknowledgements

The Head of the Snake is a work of fiction, but I wanted to make the historical setting of the end of the civil war in Sierra Leone as true to life as possible. It is always difficult to present all sides of a complex conflict in a work of fiction, especially in a novel of this kind where the demands of plot and pace trump historical exposition. But I hope I have succeeded in giving an accurate impression of the time.

The spark of the idea came from reading Steve Heaney MC's explosive account of the Pathfinders confronting the rebels at Lungi Lol - *Operation Mayhem*. The army scenes draw heavily from his vivid descriptions of the first engagement between the rebels and British forces.

I was helped in my research by reading the reports of the Truth and Reconciliation Commission - the first-hand accounts of the victims and survivors are difficult and traumatic reading, but they are an important part of understanding the horrors of the conflict. For capturing the brutality of the time, I am grateful for Sorious Samura's documentary *Cry Freetown* and for the political context I was informed by *Taking Command* by General David Richards, *From SAS to Blood Diamond Wars* by Fred Marafono and extensive interviews given by Peter Penfold, the British High Commissioner at the time. Ismael Beah's memoir *A Long Way Gone* was an important first-hand account of the war and Aminatta Forna's *The Devil that Danced on the Water* paints a vivid picture of Sierra Leone in the run up to the conflict.

I spent time in Freetown working for the Department for

International Development but that was five years after the end of the conflict, by which point it was difficult to imagine the horrors that had taken place in the recent past. It was very important to me that the work was read by a Sierra Leonean who was there at the time to pick up on anything that I got wrong or misrepresented. I am extremely grateful to sensitivity reader Alusine 'Showers' Jalloh for his careful reading and generous feedback and I apologise for the Krio still not being as authentic as it could be. Any remaining mistakes are all mine. Thank you to all the people I met in Sierra Leone whose friendship and support helped make my time there so memorable.

I wrote this book many, many miles away from Freetown while living in Brisbane, Australia and a good deal of the first draft was written during National Novel Writing Month 'NaNoWriMo'. A big thank you to the Brisbane-based NaNoWriMo family who helped keep me going with enthusiasm, encouragement and writing sprints. Somehow just knowing that other people are engaged in the same form of madness as you make it easier to keep at it. And a very special thank you to Sunny Sanderson who helped look after my children so I could hit my writing targets and was - and continues to be - the most amazing source of support. She has celebrated every draft and milestone with more enthusiasm that I would ever allow myself and for that backing and her generous friendship I will always be grateful.

Thank you to Ian Walker who taught me to drive a Land Rover off-road in Sierra Leone and helped ignite my love affair with the world's finest vehicle.

Thank you to beta readers Orson Lit, Rose Rae and Adam Jackson for their generous and thoughtful feedback. To Daniel Aubrey who has been Sarah's cheerleader from the start and suggested some brilliant ways to fix the structural holes in the early drafts. And to the rest of the VWG - Virtual Writing Group @virtwriting - whose support has been invaluable throughout the journey of bringing Sarah into the hands of readers.

Thank you to my agent, Tom Cull, for his editorial guidance in making the plot much tighter and insisting I kept cutting. It is a much better book because of your input. Thank you to the team at Burning Chair for another fantastic publication process. I have enjoyed every aspect of working with you. Thank you to Burning Chair for the stunning cover - I did not think I could love a cover more than The King's Pawn, but this one has a Land Rover on it.

Thank you to friends and family for the fantastic support for Sarah's opening gambit.

To my children - the bringers of pure joy.

And, as always, to Daniel - the world's best collaborator, a source of endless inspiration and ideas, for being the 'head of plot', 'schemer in chief' and for not getting too upset about Elias.

About The Author

For as long as she can remember, Lucy has always been in love with books – stories of adventure, of weird and wonderful places, and seeing the world through someone else's eyes. She always dreamed of writing, but there were other things to do first.

She studied languages and philosophy at Oxford and joined the Foreign Office straight out of university in search of adventure and new people and places. She quickly moved across to the Department for International Development (DFID), where she spent time in Georgia, Armenia and Azerbaijan, China and Sierra Leone. She left Sierra Leone to join her now husband in Jordan, taking the long way there across the Sahara, Europe, the Balkans, Turkey and Syria in a much-beloved Land Rover. In Jordan, she worked for Her Majesty Queen Rania while spending much time bumping around the phenomenal Jordanian desert.

After Jordan, she spent several years in a jungle camp in Gabon surrounded by elephants and humpback whales, which is where the Sarah Black books began. They took life as a way to record all the best bits of people she had met and places she had been, with a plot to make them much more exciting. Lucy has always plausibly denied being a spy – but the books were written to show what that life might have been like.

She spent three years in Brisbane, Australia, and another two experiencing deep culture-shock in the Netherlands during the weirdness of the pandemic, and is now enjoying the freedom of living at the end of the world in Lüderitz, Namibia, crafting stories and making films about the adventure of growing giant kelp.

She also wastes a considerable amount of time on Twitter @ HooftLucy

About Burning Chair

Burning Chair is an independent publishing company based in the UK, but covering readers and authors around the globe. We are passionate about both writing and reading books and, at our core, we just want to get great books out to the world.

Our aim is to offer something exciting; something innovative; something that puts the author and their book first. From first class editing to cutting edge marketing and promotion, we provide the care and attention that makes sure every book fulfils its potential.

We are:
- Different
- Passionate
- Nimble and cutting edge
- Invested in our authors' success

If you're an author and would like to know more about our submissions requirements and receive our free guide to book publishing, visit:

www.burningchairpublishing.com

If you're a reader and are interested in hearing more about our books, being the first to hear about our new releases or great offers, or becoming a beta reader for us, again please visit:

www.burningchairpublishing.com

More From Burning Chair Publishing

Your next favourite new read is waiting for you…!

The King's Pawn, by Lucy Hooft

The Other Side of Trust, by Neil Robinson

The Brodick Cold War Series, by John Fullerton
    Spy Game
    Spy Dragon
    Burning Bridges, by Matthew Ross

Killer in the Crowd, by P N Johnson

Push Back, by James Marx

The Casebook of Johnson & Boswell, by Andrew Neil Macleod
    The Fall of the House of Thomas Weir
    The Stone of Destiny

By Richard Ayre:
    Shadow of the Knife
    Point of Contact
    A Life Eternal

The Curse of Becton Manor, by Patricia Ayling

Near Death, by Richard Wall

The Blue Bird series, by Trish Finnegan
Blue Bird
Blue Sky
Baby Blues

The Tom Novak series, by Neil Lancaster
Going Dark
Going Rogue
Going Back

Love Is Dead(ly), by Gene Kendall

The Infernal Aether series, by Peter Oxley
The Infernal Aether
A Christmas Aether
The Demon Inside
Beyond the Aether
The Old Lady of the Skies: 1: Plague

The Haven Chronicles, by Fi Phillips
Haven Wakes
Magic Bound

Beyond, by Georgia Springate

10:59, by N R Baker

The Wedding Speech Manual: The Complete Guide to Preparing, Writing and Performing Your Wedding Speech, by Peter Oxley

www.burningchairpublishing.com

The Head of the Snake

Ingram Content Group UK Ltd.
Milton Keynes UK
UKHW022004130423
420127UK00014B/1278